John Henry Newman, Thomas Aquinas

Catena Aurea

commentary on the four Gospels, collected out of the works of the Fathers - Vol. 3,

Part 2

John Henry Newman, Thomas Aquinas

Catena Aurea

commentary on the four Gospels, collected out of the works of the Fathers - Vol. 3, Part 2

ISBN/EAN: 9783337688820

Printed in Europe, USA, Canada, Australia, Japan

Cover: Foto ©Andreas Hilbeck / pixelio.de

More available books at **www.hansebooks.com**

Catena Aurea.

COMMENTARY

ON THE

FOUR GOSPELS,

COLLECTED OUT OF THE

WORKS OF THE FATHERS

BY

S. THOMAS AQUINAS.

VOL. III. PART II.

ST. LUKE.

OXFORD,

JOHN HENRY PARKER;

J. G. F. AND J. RIVINGTON, LONDON.

MDCCCXLIII.

ADVERTISEMENT.

THE following Compilation not being admissible into the Library of the Fathers from the date of some few of the authors introduced into it, the Editors of the latter work have been led to publish it in a separate form, being assured that those who have subscribed to their Translations of the entire Treatises of the ancient Catholic divines, will not feel less interest, or find less benefit, in the use of so very judicious and beautiful a selection from them. The Editors refer to the Preface for some account of the natural and characteristic excellences of the work, which will be found as useful in the private study of the Gospels, as it is well adapted for family reading, and full of thought for those who are engaged in religious instruction.

Oxford, May 6, 1841.

1. And it came to pass, that, as he was praying in a certain place, when he ceased, one of his disciples said unto him, Lord, teach us to pray, as John also taught his disciples.

2. And he said unto them, When ye pray, say, Our Father which art in heaven, Hallowed be thy name. Thy kingdom come. Thy will be done, as in heaven, so in earth.

3. Give us day by day our daily bread.

4. And forgive us our sins; for we also forgive every one that is indebted to us. And lead us not into temptation; but deliver us from evil.

BEDE; After the account of the sisters, who signified the two lives of the Church, our Lord is not without reason related to have both Himself prayed, and taught His disciples to pray, seeing that the prayer which He taught contains in itself the mystery of each life, and the perfection of the lives themselves is to be obtained not by our own strength, but by prayer. Hence it is said, *And it came to pass, that, as he was praying in a certain place.* CYRIL; Now whereas He possesses every good in abundance, why does He pray, since He is full, and has altogether need of nothing? To this we answer, that it befits Him, according to the manner of His dispensation in the flesh, to follow human observances at the time convenient for them. For if He eats and drinks, He rightly was used to pray, that He might teach us not to be lukewarm in this duty, but to be the more diligent and earnest in our prayers.

Tit. in Matt. TIT. BOST. The disciples having seen a new way of life, desire a new form of prayer, since there were several prayers to be found in the Old Testament. Hence it follows, *When he ceased, one of his disciples said to him, Lord, teach us to pray,* in order that we might not sin against God in asking for one thing instead of another, or by approaching God in prayer in a manner that we ought not.

ORIGEN; And that he might point out the kind of teaching, the disciple proceeds, *as John also taught his disciples.* Of whom in truth thou hast told us, that among them that are born of women there had arisen none greater than he. And because thou hast commanded us to seek things that are great and eternal, whence shall we arrive at the knowledge of these but from Thee, our God and Saviour?

Greg. Orat. Dom. Serm. 1. GREG. NYSS. He unfolds the teaching of prayer to His disciples, who wisely desire the knowledge of prayer, directing them how they ought to beseech God to hear them. BASIL; Basil. Const. Monast. cap. 1. There are two kinds of prayer, one composed of praise with humiliation, the other of petitions, and more subdued. Whenever then you pray, do not first break forth into petition; but if you condemn your inclination, supplicate God as if of necessity forced thereto. And when you begin to pray, forget all visible and invisible creatures, but commence with the praise of Him who created all things. Hence it is added, *And he says unto them, When you* Pseudo-Aug. App. Serm. 84. *pray, say, Our Father.* PSEUDO-AUG. The first word, how gracious is it? Thou durst not raise thy face to heaven, and suddenly thou receivest the grace of Christ. From an evil servant thou art made a good son. Boast not then of thy working, but of the grace of Christ; for therein is no arrogance, but faith. To proclaim what thou hast received is not pride, but devotion. Therefore raise thy eyes to thy Father, who begot thee by Baptism, redeemed thee by His Son. Say *Father* as a son, but claim no especial favour to thyself. Of Christ alone is He the especial Father, of us the common Father. For Christ alone He begot, but us he created. Matt. 6. 9. And therefore according to Matthew when it is said, *Our Father,* it is added, *which art in heaven,* that is, in those heavens of which it was said, *The heavens declare the* Ps.19,1. *glory of God.* Heaven is where sin has ceased, and where there is no sting of death. THEOPHYL. But He says not, *which art in heaven,* as though He were confined to that place, but to raise the hearer up to heaven, and draw him away from earthly things. GREG. NYSS. See how great a preparation Greg. thou needest, to be able to say boldly to God, O Father, for Orat. Dom. if thou hast thy eyes fixed on worldly things, or courtest the serm. 2. praise of men, or art a slave to thy passions, and utterest this prayer, I seem to hear God saying, ' Whereas thou that art of a corrupt life callest the Author of the incorruptible thy Father, thou pollutest with thy defiled lips an incorruptible name. For He who commanded thee to call Him Father, gave thee not leave to utter lies. But the highest of et serm. all good things is to glorify God's name in our lives. Hence 3. He adds, *Hallowed be thy name.* For who is there so debased, as when He sees the pure life of those who believe, does not glorify the name invoked in such a life. He then who says in his prayer, *Be thy name,* which I call upon, *hallowed in me,* prays this, " May I through Thy concurring aid be made just, abstaining from all evil." CHRYS. For as when a man gazes upon the beauty of the heavens, he says, *Glory be thee, O God;* so likewise when He beholds a man's virtuous actions, seeing that the virtue of man glorifies God much more than the heavens. PSEUDO-AUG. Or it is said, Pseudo-*Hallowed be thy name;* that is, let Thy holiness be known to all Aug. ubi sup. the world, and let it worthily praise Thee. *For praise becometh* Ps. 33. *the upright,* and therefore He bids them pray for the cleansing of the whole world. CYRIL; Since among those to whom the faith has not yet come, the name of God is still despised. But when the rays of truth shall have shined upon them, they Dan. 9, will confess the Holy of Holies. TIT. BOST. And because in the 24. Tit. name of Jesus is the glory of God the Father, the name of the ubi sup. Father will be hallowed whenever Christ shall be known.

ORIGEN; Or, because the name of God is given by idolaters, and those who are in error, to idols and creatures, it has not as yet been so made holy, as to be separated from those things from which it ought to be. He teaches us therefore to pray that the name of God may be appropriated to the only true God; to whom alone belongs what follows, *Thy king-*

dom come, to the end that may be put down all the rule, authority, and power, and kingdom of the world, together with sin which reigns in our mortal bodies. GREG. NYSS. We beseech also to be delivered by the Lord from corruption, to be taken out of death. Or, according to some, *Thy kingdom come*, that is, May Thy Holy Spirit come upon us to purify us.

Greg. ubi sup.

ubi sup.
Luke17,
21.

PSEUDO-AUG. For then cometh the kingdom of God, when we have obtained His grace. For He Himself says, *The kingdom of God is within you.* CYRIL; Or they who say this seem to wish to have the Saviour of all again illuminating the world. But He has commanded us to desire in prayer that truly awful time, in order that men might know that it behoves them to live not in sloth and backwardness, lest that time bring upon them the fiery punishment, but rather honestly and according to His will, that that time may weave crowns for them. Hence it follows, according to Matthew, [a] *Thy will be done, as in heaven, so in earth.* CHRYS. As if He says, Enable us, O Lord, to follow the heavenly life, that whatever Thou willest, we may will also. GREG NYSS. For since He says that the life of man after the resurrection will be like to that of Angels, it follows, that our life in this world should be so ordered with respect to that which we hope for hereafter, that living in the flesh we may not live according to the flesh. But hereby the true Physician of the souls destroys the nature of the disease, that those who have been seized with sickness, whereby they have departed from the Divine will, may forthwith be released from the disease by being joined to the Divine will. For the health of the soul is the due fulfilment of the will of God.

Greg. Orat. Dom. serm. 4.

AUG. It seems according to the Evangelist Matthew, that the Lord's prayer contains seven petitions, but Luke has comprehended it in five. Nor in truth does the one disagree from the other, but the latter has suggested by his brevity how those seven are to be understood. For the name of God is hallowed in the spirit, but the kingdom of God is about to come at the resurrection of the body. Luke then, shewing that the third petition is in a manner a repetition of

Aug. in Enchirid. c. 116.

[a] This verse is omitted in the following MSS. of St. Luke, B. L. 1, 22, 130, 346. in the Versions Arm. Vulg. Corb. For. Mm. Gat. and by Origen, Jerome, Aug. Bede, Scholz in loc.

the two former, wished to make it so understood by omitting it. He then added three others. And first, of daily bread, saying, *Give us day by day our daily bread.* PSEUDO-AUG. In the Greek the word is ἐπιούσιον, that is, *something added to the substance.* It is not that bread which goes into the body, but that bread of everlasting life, which supports the substance of our soul. But the Latins call this " daily" bread, which the Greeks call " coming to." If it is daily bread, why is it eaten a year old, as is the custom with the Greeks in the east? Take daily what profits thee for the day; so live that thou mayest daily be thought worthy to receive. The death of our Lord is signified thereby, and the remission of sins, and dost thou not daily partake of that bread of life? He who has a wound seeks to be cured ; the wound is that we are under sin, the cure is the heavenly and dreadful Sacrament. If thou receivest daily, daily does " To-day" come unto thee. Christ is to thee To-day ; Christ rises to thee daily. TIT. BOST. Or the bread of souls is the Divine power, bringing the everlasting life which is to come, as the bread which comes out of the earth preserves the temporal life. But by saying " daily," He signifies the Divine bread which comes and is to come, which we seek to be given to us daily, requiring a certain earnest and taste of it, seeing that the Spirit which dwells in us hath wrought a virtue surpassing all human virtues, as chastity, humility, and the rest.

CYRIL ; Now perhaps some think it unfit for saints to seek from God bodily goods, and for this reason assign to these words a spiritual sense. But granting that the chief concern of the saints should be to obtain spiritual gifts, still it becomes them to see that they seek without blame, according to our Lord's command, their common bread. For from the fact that He bids them ask for bread, that is daily food, it seems that He implies that they should possess nothing, but rather practise an honourable poverty. For it is not the part of those who have bread to seek it, but rather of those who are oppressed with want. BASIL ; As if He said, For thy daily bread, namely, that which serves for our daily wants, trust not to thyself, but fly to God for it, making known to Him the necessities of thy nature. CHRYS. We must then require of God the necessities of life ; not varieties of meats, and spiced wines, and the other things

Side notes: App. Serm. 84. super- substan- tialem. Heb. 13, 8. Basil. in Reg. brev. ad inter. 252. Chrys. Hom. 23. in Matt.

which please the palate, while they load thy stomach and disturb thy mind, but bread which is able to support the bodily substance, that is to say, which is sufficient only for the day, that we may take no thought of the morrow. But we make only one petition about things of sense, that the present life may not trouble us.

Greg. Orat. Dom. Serm. 5. GREG. NYSS. Having taught us to take confidence through good works, He next teaches us to implore the remission of our offences, for it follows, *And forgive us our sins.*

Tit. in Matt. TIT. BOST. This also was necessarily added, for no one is found without sin, that we should not be hindered from the holy participation on account of man's guilt. For whereas we are bound to render unto Christ all manner of holiness, who maketh His Spirit to dwell in us, we are to be blamed if we keep not our temples clean for Him. But this defect is supplied by the goodness of God, remitting to human frailty the severe punishment of sin. And this act is done justly by the just God, when we forgive as it were our debtors, those, namely, who have injured us, and have not restored what was due. Hence it follows, *For we also forgive every one that is indebted to us.* CYRIL; For He wishes, if I may so speak, to make God the imitator of the patience which men practise, that the kindness which they have shewn to their fellowservants, they should in like manner seek to receive in equal balance from God, who recompenses to each man justly, and knows how to have mercy upon all men. CHRYS. Considering then these things, we ought to shew mercy to our debtors. For they are to us if we are wise the cause of our greatest pardon; and though we perform only a few things, we shall find many. For we owe many and great debts to the Lord, of which if the least part should be exacted from us, we should soon perish.

ubi sup. PSEUDO-AUG. But what is the debt except sin? If thou hadst not received, thou wouldest not owe money to another. And therefore sin is imputed to you. For thou hadst money with which thou wert born rich, and made after the likeness and image of God, but thou hast lost what thou then hadst. As when thou puttest on pride thou losest the gold of humility, thou hast receipted the devil's debt which was not necessary; the enemy held the bond, but the Lord crucified it, and cancelled it with His blood. But the Lord is able, who has taken away our sins and forgiven our debts, to guard us against the snares of the devil, who is wont to produce sin in us. Hence it follows, *And lead us not into temptation*, such as we are not able to bear, but like the wrestler we wish only such temptation as the condition of man can sustain. TIT. BOST. For it is imposible not to be tempted by the devil, but we make this prayer that we may not be abandoned to our temptations. Now that which happens by Divine permission, God is sometimes in Scripture said to do. And in this way by hindering not the increase of temptation which is above our strength, he leads us into temptation. MAX. Or, the Lord commands us to pray, *Lead us not into temptation*, that is, let us not have experience of lustful and self-induced temptations. But James teaches those who contend only for the truth, not to be unnerved by involuntary and troublesome temptations, saying, *My brethren, count it all joy when ye fall into divers temptations.* Tit. ubi sup.

in Orat. Dom.

James 1, 2.

BASIL; It does not however become us to seek by our prayers bodily afflictions. For Christ has universally commanded men every where to pray that they enter not into temptation. But when one has already entered, it is fitting to ask from the Lord the power of enduring, that we may have fulfilled in us those words, *He that endureth to the end shall be saved.* AUG. But what Matthew has placed at the end, *But deliver us from evil*, Luke has not mentioned, that we might understand it belongs to the former, which was spoken of temptation. He therefore says, *But deliver us*, not, "And deliver us," clearly proving this to be but one petition, "Do not this, but this." But let every one know that he is therein delivered from evil, when he is not brought into temptation. PSEUDO-AUG. For each man seeks to be delivered from evil, that is, from his enemies and sin, but he who gives himself up to God, fears not the devil, for *if God is for us, who can be against us?* Basil. in reg. brev. ad inter. 221.

Mat. 10, 22.
Aug. in Enchirid. c. 116.

ubi sup.

Rom. 8, 31.

5. And he said unto them, Which of you shall have a friend, and shall go unto him at midnight, and say unto him, Friend, lend me three loaves;

6. For a friend of mine in his journey is come to me, and I have nothing to set before him?

7. And he from within shall answer and say, Trouble me not : the door is now shut, and my children are with me in bed ; I cannot rise and give thee.

8. I say unto you, Though he will not rise and give him, because he is his friend, yet because of his importunity he will rise and give him as many as he needeth.

CYRIL; The Saviour had before taught, in answer to the request of His apostles, how men ought to pray. But it might happen that those who had received this wholesome teaching, poured forth their prayers indeed according to the form given to them, but carelessly and languidly, and then when they were not heard in the first or second prayer, left off praying. That this then might not be our case, he shews by means of a parable, that cowardice in our prayers is hurtful, but it is of great advantage to have patience in them. Hence it is said, *And he says unto them, Which of you shall have a friend.* THEOPHYL. God is that friend, who loveth all men, and wills that all should be saved. AMBROSE; Who is a greater friend to us, than He who delivered up His body for us ? Now we have here another kind of command given us, that at all times, not only in the day, but at night, prayers should be offered up. For it follows, *And shall go into him at midnight.* As David did when he said, *At midnight I will rise and give thanks unto thee.* For he had no fear of awakening them from sleep, whom he knew to be ever watching. For if David who was occupied also in the necessary affairs of a kingdom was so holy, that seven times in the day he gave praise to God, what ought we to do, who ought so much the more to pray, as we more frequently sin, through the weakness of our mind and body ? But if thou lovest the Lord thy God, thou wilt be able to gain favour, not only for thyself, but others. For it follows, *And say unto him, Friend, lend me three loaves, &c.* AUG. But what are these three loaves but the food of the heavenly mystery ? For it may be that one has had a friend asking for what he cannot supply him with, and then finds that he has not what he is compelled to give. A friend then

Ps. 119, 62.

Ps. 119, 164.

Aug. Serm. 105.

comes to you on his journey, that is, in this present life, in which all are travelling on as strangers, and no one remains possessor, but to every man is told, *Pass on, O stranger, give* Ecclus. *place to him that is coming.* Or perhaps some friend of²⁹, ²⁷. yours comes from a bad road, (that is, an evil life,) wearied and not finding the truth, by hearing and receiving which he may become happy. He comes to thee as to a Christian, and says, " Give me a reason," asking perhaps what you from the simplicity of your faith are ignorant of, and not having wherewith to satisfy his hunger, are compelled to seek it in the Lord's books. For perhaps what he asked is contained in the book, but obscure. You are not permitted to ask Paul himself, or Peter, or any prophet, for all that family is now resting with their Lord, and the ignorance of the world is very great, that is, it is midnight, and your friend who is urgent from hunger presses this, not contented with a simple faith; must he then be abandoned? Go therefore to the Lord Himself with whom the family is sleeping, *Knock, and pray;* of whom it is added, *And he from within shall answer and say, Trouble me not.* He delays to give, wishing that you should the more earnestly desire what is delayed, lest by being given at once it should grow common. BASIL; For perhaps He delays purposely, to redouble your Basil. earnestness and coming to him, and that you may know $\frac{\text{Const.}}{\text{Mon.}}$ what the gift of God is, and may anxiously guard what is c. 1. given. For whatever a man acquires with much pains he strives to keep safe, lest with the loss of that he should lose his labour likewise.

GLOSS. He does not then take away the liberty of asking, Gloss. but is the more anxious to kindle the desire of praying, by ⁰ʳᵈⁱⁿ. shewing the difficulty of obtaining that we ask for. For it follows, *The door is now shut.* AMBROSE; This is the door which Paul also requests may be opened to him, Col.4,3. beseeching to be assisted not only by his own prayers, but those also of the people, that a door of utterance may be opened to him to speak the mystery of Christ. And perhaps that is the door which John saw open, and it was said to him, Rev. 4, *Come up hither, and I will shew thee things which must be* 1. *hereafter.* AUG. The time then referred to is that of the $\frac{\text{Aug.Qu.}}{\text{Ev. l. ii.}}$ famine of the word, when the understanding is shut up, and $\frac{\text{qu. 21.}}{\text{Amos 8,}}$ 11.

they who dealt out the wisdom of the Gospel as it were bread,
preached throughout the world, are now in their secret rest with
the Lord.   And this it is which is added, *And my children
are with me in bed.*   GREG. NYSS. Well does he call those,
who by the arms of righteousness have claimed to themselves freedom from passion, shewing that the good which
by practice we have acquired, had been from the beginning
laid up in our nature.   For when any one renouncing the
flesh, by living in the exercise of a virtuous life, has
overcome passion, then he becomes as a child, and is
insensible to the passions.   But by the bed we understand
Gloss. ordin. the rest of Christ.   GLOSS. And because of what has gone
before he adds, *I cannot rise and give thee,* which must have
Aug. de Quæst. Ev. lib. ii.qu.21. reference to the difficulty of obtaining.   AUG. Or else, the
friend to whom the visit is made at midnight, for the loan of
the three loaves, is evidently meant for an allegory, just
as a person set in the midst of trouble might ask God
that He would give him to understand the Trinity, by which
he may console the troubles of this present life.   For his
distress is the midnight in which he is compelled to be so
urgent in his request for the three.   Now by the three
loaves it is signified, that the Trinity is of one substance.
But the friend coming from his journey is understood the
desire of man, which ought to obey reason, but was
obedient to the custom of the world, which he calls the way,
from all things passing along it.   Now when man is converted to God, that desire also is reclaimed from custom.
But if not consoled by that inward joy arising from the
spiritual doctrine which declares the Trinity of the Creator,
he is in great straits who is pressed down by earthly sorrows,
seeing that from all outward delights he is commanded to
abstain, and within there is no refreshment from the delight
of spiritual doctrine.   And yet it is effected by prayer, that
he who desires should receive understanding from God, even
though there be no one by whom wisdom should be preached.
For it follows, *And if that man shall continue, &c.*   The
argument is drawn from the less to the greater.   For, if a
friend rises from his bed, and gives not from the force of
friendship, but from weariness, how much more does God give
who without weariness gives most abundantly whatever we ask?

AUG. But when thou shalt have obtained the three loaves, Aug. that is, the food and knowledge of the Trinity, thou hast ubi sup. both the source of life and of food. Fear not. Cease not. For that bread will not come to an end, but will put an end to your want. Learn and teach. Live and eat.

THEOPHYL. Or else, The midnight is the end of life, at which many come to God. But the friend is the Angel who receives the soul. Or, the midnight is the depth of temptations, in which he who has fallen, seeks from God three loaves, the relief of the wants of his body, soul, and spirit; through whom we run into no danger in our temptations. But the friend who comes from his journey is God Himself, who tries by temptations him who has nothing to set before him who is weakened in temptation. But when He says, *And the door is shut*, we must understand that we ought to be prepared before temptations. But after that we have fallen into them, the gate of preparation is shut, and being found unprepared, unless God keep us, we are in danger.

9. And I say unto you, Ask, and it shall be given you; seek, and ye shall find; knock, and it shall be opened unto you.

10. For every one that asketh receiveth; and he that seeketh findeth; and to him that knocketh it shall be opened.

11. If a son shall ask bread of any of you that is a father, will he give him a stone? or if he ask a fish, will he for a fish give him a serpent?

12. Or if he shall ask an egg, will he offer him a scorpion?

13. If ye then, being evil, know how to give good gifts unto your children: how much more shall your heavenly Father give the Holy Spirit to them that ask him?

AUG. Having laid aside the metaphor, our Lord added an Aug. exhortation, and expressly urged us to ask, seek, and knock, ubi sup.

until we receive what we are seeking. Hence he says, *And I say unto you, Ask, and it shall be given you.* CYRIL; The words, *I say unto you*, have the force of an oath. For God doth not lie, but whenever He makes known any thing to His hearers with an oath, he manifests the inexcusable littleness of our faith. CHRYS. Now by asking, He means prayer, but by seeking, zeal and anxiety, as He adds, *Seek, and ye shall find.* For those things which are sought require great care. And this is particularly the case with God. For there are many things which block up our senses. As then we search for lost gold, so let us anxiously seek after God. He shews also, that though He does not forthwith open the gates, we must yet wait. Hence he adds, *Knock, and it shall be opened unto you;* for if you continue seeking, you shall surely receive. For this reason, and as the door shut makes you knock, therefore he did not at once consent that you might entreat. GREEK EX. Or by the word *knock* perhaps he means seeking effectually, for one knocks with the hand, but the hand is the sign of a good work. Or these three may be distinguished in another way. For it is the beginning of virtue to ask to know the way of truth. But the second step is to seek how we must go by that way. The third step is when a man has reached the virtue to knock at the door, that he may enter upon the wide field of knowledge. All these things a man acquires by prayer. Or to ask indeed is to pray, but to seek is by good works to do things becoming our prayers. And to knock is to continue in prayer without ceasing. AUG. But He would not so encourage us to ask were He not willing to give. Let human slothfulness blush, He is more willing to give than we to receive.

AMBROSE; Now he who promises any thing ought to convey a hope of the thing promised, that obedience may follow commands, faith, promises. And therefore he adds, *For every one that asketh receiveth.* ORIGEN; But some one may seek to know, how it comes that they who pray are not heard? To which we must answer, that whoso sets about seeking in the right way, omitting none of those things which avail to the obtaining of our requests, shall really receive what he has prayed to be given him. But if a man turns away from the object of a right petition,

Chrys.
Hom.
23. in
Matt.

Severus
Antioch.

Aug.
Serm.
105.

and asks not as it becomes him, he does not ask. And therefore it is, that when he does not receive, as is here promised, there is no falsehood. For so also when a master says, " Whoever will come to me, he shall receive the gift of instruction;" we understand it to imply a person going in real earnest to a master, that he may zealously and diligently devote himself to his teaching.   Hence too James says, *Ye ask and receive not,* James 4, *because ye ask amiss,* namely, for the sake of vain pleasures. [3.] But some one will say, Nay, when men ask to obtain divine knowledge, and to recover their virtue they do not obtain? To which we must answer, that they sought not to receive the good things for themselves, but that thereby they might reap praise.

BASIL; If also any one from indolence surrenders himself Basil. to his desires, and betrays himself into the hands of his in Const. enemies, God neither assists him nor hears him, because by c. 1. sin he has alienated himself from God.   It becomes then a man to offer whatever belongs to him, but to cry to God to assist him.   Now we must ask for the Divine assistance not slackly, nor with a mind wavering to and fro, because such a one will not only not obtain what it seeks, but will the rather provoke God to anger.   For if a man standing before a prince has his eye fixed within and without, lest perchance he should be punished, how much more before God ought he to stand watchful and trembling? But if when awakened by sin you are unable to pray stedfastly to the utmost of your power, check yourself, that when you stand before God you may direct your mind to Him.   And God pardons you, because not from indifference, but infirmity, you cannot appear in His presence as you ought.   If then you thus command yourself, do not depart until you receive. For whenever you ask and receive not, it is because your request was improperly made, either without faith, or lightly, or for things which are not good for you, or because you left off praying.   But some frequently make the objection, " Why pray we?   Is God then ignorant of what we have need?" He knows undoubtedly, and gives us richly all temporal things even before we ask.   But we must first desire good works, and the kingdom of heaven; and then having desired, ask in faith and patience, bringing into our prayers whatever is good for us, convicted of no offence by our own conscience.

AMBROSE; The argument then persuading to frequent prayer, is the hope of obtaining what we pray for. The ground of persuasion was first in the command, afterwards it is contained in that example which He sets forth, adding, *If a son shall ask bread of any of you, will he give him a stone? &c.* CYRIL; In these words our Saviour gives us a very necessary piece of instruction. For oftentimes we rashly, from the impulse of pleasure, give way to hurtful desires. When we ask any such thing from God, we shall not obtain it. To shew this, He brings an obvious example from those things which are before our eyes, in our daily experience. For when thy son asks of thee bread, thou givest it him gladly, because he seeks a wholesome food. But when from want of understanding he asks for a stone to eat, thou givest it him not, but rather hinderest him from satisfying his hurtful desire. So that the sense may be, But which of you asking his father for bread, (which the father gives,) will he give him a stone? (that is, if he asked it.) There is the same argument also in the serpent and the fish ; of which he adds, *Or if he asks a fish, will he for a fish give him a serpent?* And in like manner in the egg and scorpion, of which he adds, *Or if he ask an egg, will he offer him a scorpion?*

ORIGEN; Consider then this, if the bread be not indeed the food of the soul in knowledge, without which it can not be saved, as, for example, the well planned rule of a just life. But the fish is the love of instruction, as to know the constitution of the world, and the effects of the elements, and whatever else besides wisdom treats of. Therefore God does not in the place of bread offer a stone, which the devil wished Christ to eat, nor in the place of a fish does He give a serpent, which the Ethiopians eat who are unworthy to eat fishes. Nor generally in the place of what is nourishing does he give what is not eatable and injurious, which relates to the scorpion and egg.

Aug. de
Quæst.
Ev. lib.
ii.qu. 22. AUG. Or by the bread is meant charity, because we have a greater desire of it, and it is so necessary, that without it all other things are nothing, as the table without bread is mean.

Opposed to which is hardness of heart, which he compared
to a stone. But by the fish is signified the belief in invisible
things, either from the waters of baptism, or because it is
taken out of invisible places which the eye cannot reach.
Because also faith, though tossed about by the waves of this
world, is not destroyed, it is rightly compared to a fish, in
opposition to which he has placed the serpent on account of
the poison of deceit, which by evil persuasion had its first
seed in the first man. Or, by the egg is understood hope. For
the egg is the young not yet formed, but hoped for through
cherishing, opposed to which he has placed the scorpion,
whose poisoned sting is to be dreaded behind; as the contrary
to hope is to look back, since the hope of the future reaches
forward to those things which are before. AUG. What great
things the world speaks to thee, and roars them behind thy
back to make thee look behind! O unclean world, why
clamourest thou! Why attempt to turn him away! Thou
wouldest detain him when thou art perishing, what wouldest
thou if thou wert abiding for ever? Whom wouldest thou
not deceive with sweetness, when bitter thou canst infuse
false food?

CYRIL; Now from the example just given he concludes,
If then ye being evil, (i. e. having a mind capable of wickedness, and not uniform and settled in good, as God,) *know how
to give good gifts; how much more shall your heavenly
Father?* BEDE; Or, he calls the lovers of the world evil,
who give those things which they judge good according to
their sense, which are also good in their nature, and are
useful to aid imperfect life. Hence he adds, *Know how to
give good gifts to your children.* The Apostles even, who
by the merit of their election had exceeded the goodness of
mankind in general, are said to be evil in comparison with
Divine goodness, since nothing is of itself good but God
alone. But that which is added, *How much more shall your
heavenly Father give the Holy Spirit to them that ask him,*
for which Matthew has written, *will give good things to them
that ask him,* shews that the Holy Spirit is the fulness of
God's gifts, since all the advantages which are received from
the grace of God's gifts flow from that source. ATHAN.
Now unless the Holy Spirit were of the substance of God,

Aug. Serm. 105.

Athan. Dial. 1. de Trin.

Who alone is good, He would by no means be called good, since our Lord refused to be called good, inasmuch as He was Aug. Serm. 105. made man. AUG. Therefore, O covetous man, what seekest thou? or if thou seekest any thing else, what will suffice thee to whom the Lord is not sufficient?

14. And he was casting out a devil, and it was dumb. And it came to pass, when the devil was gone out, the dumb spake; and the people wondered.

15. But some of them said, He casteth out devils through Beelzebub the chief of the devils.

16. And others, tempting him, sought of him a sign from heaven.

Gloss. non occ. GLOSS. The Lord had promised that the Holy Spirit should be given to those that asked for it; the blessed effects whereof He indeed clearly shews in the following miracle. Hence it follows, *And Jesus was casting out a devil, and it was dumb.* THEOPHYL. Now he is called κωφὸς, as commonly meaning one who does not speak. It is also used for one who does not hear, but more properly who neither hears nor speaks. But he who has not heard from his birth necessarily cannot speak. For we speak those things which we are taught to speak by hearing. If however one has lost his hearing from a disease that has come upon him, there is nothing to hinder him from speaking. But He who was brought before the Lord was both dumb in speech, Tit. in Matt. and deaf in hearing. TIT. BOST. Now He calls the devil deaf or dumb, as being the cause of this calamity, that the Divine word should not be heard. For the devil, by taking away the quickness of human feeling, blunts the hearing of our soul. Christ therefore comes that He might cast out the devil, and that we might hear the word of truth. For He healed one that He might create a universal foretaste of man's salvation. Hence it follows, *And when he had cast out the devil, the dumb spake.*

BEDE; But that demoniac is related by Matthew to have been not only dumb, but blind. Three miracles then were performed at the same time on one man. The blind see, the

dumb speaks, and he that was possessed by a devil is set free.
The like is daily accomplished in the conversion of believers,
so that the devil being first cast out, they see the light, and
then those mouths which were before silent are loosened to
speak the praises of God.   CYRIL; Now when the miracle was
performed, the multitude extolled Him with loud praises, and
the glory which was due to God.   As it follows, *And the
people wondered.*   BEDE; But since the multitudes who
were thought ignorant always marvelled at our Lord's actions,
the Scribes and Pharisees took pains to deny them, or to pervert them by an artful interpretation, as though they were not
the work of a Divine power, but of an unclean spirit.   Hence
it follows, *But some of them said, He casteth out devils
through Beelzebub the prince of the devils.*   Beelzebub was
the God Accaron.   For Beel is indeed Baal himself.   But
Zebub means a fly.   Now he is called Beelzebub as the
man of flies, from whose most foul practices the chief of the
devils was so named.   CYRIL; But others by similar darts
of envy sought from Him a sign from heaven.   As it follows,
And others, tempting him, sought of him a sign from heaven.
As if they said, " Although thou hast cast out a devil from
the man, this is no proof however of Divine power.   For
we have not yet seen any thing like to the miracles of former
times.   Moses led the people through the midst of the _{Exod.} ^{14.}
sea, and Joshua his successor stayed the sun in Gibeon. ^{14.} _{Josh.10,}
But thou hast shewn us none of these things."   For to _{13.}
seek signs from heaven shewed that the speaker was at
that time influenced by some feeling of this kind towards
Christ.

17. But he, knowing their thoughts, said unto
them, Every kingdom divided against itself is brought
to desolation ; and a house divided against a house
falleth.

18. If Satan also be divided against himself, how
shall his kingdom stand ? because ye say that I cast
out devils through Beelzebub.

19. And if I by Beelzebub cast out devils, by

whom do your sons cast them out? therefore shall they be your judges.

20. But if I with the finger of God cast out devils, no doubt the kingdom of God is come upon you.

Chrys.
Hom.
41. in
Matt.

CHRYS. The suspicion of the Pharisees being utterly without reason, they dared not divulge it for fear of the multitude, but pondered it in their minds. Hence it is said, *But he, knowing their thoughts, said unto them, Every kingdom divided against itself will be brought to desolation.* BEDE; He answered not their words but their thoughts, that so at least they might be compelled to believe in His power, who saw

Chrys.
ubi sup.

into the secrets of the heart. CHRYS. He did not answer them from the Scriptures, since they gave no heed to them, explaining them away falsely; but he answers them from things of every day occurrence. For a house and a city if it be divided is quickly scattered to nothing; and likewise a kingdom, than which nothing is stronger. For the harmony of the inhabitants maintains houses and kingdoms. If then, says He, I cast out devils by means of a devil, there is dissension among them, and their power perishes. Hence He adds, *But if Satan be divided against himself, how shall he stand?* For Satan resists not himself, nor hurts his soldiers, but rather strengthens his kingdom. It is then by Divine power alone that I crush Satan under my feet. AMBROSE; Herein also He shews His own kingdom to be undivided and everlasting. Those then who possess no hope in Christ, but think that He casts out devils through the chief of the devils, their kingdom, He says, is not everlasting. This also has reference to the Jewish people. For how can the kingdom of the Jews be everlasting, when by the people of the law Jesus is denied, who is promised by the law? Thus in part does the faith of the Jewish people impugn itself; the glory of the wicked is divided, by division is destroyed. And therefore the kingdom of the Church shall remain for ever, because its faith is undivided in one body. BEDE; The kingdom also of the Father, Son, and Holy Spirit, is not divided, because it is sealed with an eternal stability. Let then the Arians cease to say that the Son is inferior to the Father, but the

Holy Spirit inferior to the Son, since whose kingdom is one, their power is one also.

CHRYS. This then is the first answer; the second which Chrys. relates to His disciples He gives as follows, *And if I by Beel-* Hom. *zebub cast out devils, by whom do your sons cast them out?* Matt. He says not, " My disciples," but *your sons*, wishing to soothe their wrath.   CYRIL; For the disciples of Christ were Jews, and sprung from Jews according to the flesh, and they had obtained from Christ power over unclean spirits, and delivered those who were oppressed by them in Christ's name.   Seeing then that your sons subdue Satan in My name, is it not very madness to say that I have My power from Beelzebub? Ye are then condemned by the faith of your children.   Hence He adds, *Therefore shall they be your judges.*   CHRYS. For Chrys. since they who come forth from you are obedient unto Me, ut sup. it is plain that they will condemn those who do the contrary.

BEDE; Or else, By the sons of the Jews He means the exorcists of that nation, who cast out devils by the invocation of God.   As if He says, If the casting out of devils by your sons is ascribed to God, not to devils, why in My case has not the same work the same cause?   Therefore shall they be your judges, not in authority to exercise judgment, but in act, since they assign to God the casting out of devils, you to Beelzebub, the chief of the devils.

CYRIL; Since then what you say bears upon it the mark of calumny, it is plain that by the Spirit of God I cast out devils. Hence He adds, *But if I by the finger of God cast out devils, no doubt the kingdom of God is come upon you.*   AUG. Aug de cons.Ev. That Luke speaks of the *finger of God*, where Matthew has l.ii.c.38. said, *the Spirit*, does not take away from their agreement in sense, but it rather teaches us a lesson, that we may know what meaning to give to the *finger of God*, whenever we read it in the Scriptures.   AUG. Now the Holy Spirit is called the Aug. de finger of God, because of the distribution of gifts which are Ev. l. ii. given through Him, to every one his own gift, whether he be qu. 17. of men or angels.   For in none of our members is division more apparent than in our fingers.   CYRIL; Or the Holy Spirit is called the finger of God for this reason.   The Son was said Ps. 98, to be the hand and arm of the Father, for the Father [1.] worketh all things by Him.   As then the finger is not separate from the hand, but by nature a part of it; so the Holy Spirit is consubstantially united to the Son, and through Him the Son does all things. AMBROSE; Nor would you think in the compacting together of our limbs any division of power to be made, for there can be no division in an undivided thing. And therefore the appellation of finger must be referred to the form of unity, not to the distinction of power. ATHAN. But at this time our Lord does not hesitate because of His humanity to speak of Himself as inferior to the Holy Spirit, saying, that He cast out devils by Him, as though the human nature was not sufficient for the casting out of devils without the power of the Holy Spirit. CYRIL; And therefore it is justly said, *The kingdom of God is come upon you*, that is, " If I as a man cast out devils by the Spirit of God, human nature is enriched through Me, and the kingdom of God is come."

Athan. Orat. 2. con. Arian.

CHRYS. But it is said, *upon you*, that He might draw them to Him; as if He said, If prosperity comes to you, why do you despise your good things? AMBROSE; At the same time He shews that it is a regal power which the Holy Spirit possesses, in whom is the kingdom of God, and that we in whom the Spirit dwells are a royal house. TIT. BOST. Or He says, *The kingdom of God is come upon you*, signifying, " is come against you, not for you." For dreadful is the second coming of Christ to faithless Christians.

Chrys. Hom. 41. ut sup.

Tit. in Matt.

21. When a strong man armed keepeth his palace, his goods are in peace :

22. But when a stronger than he shall come upon him and overcome him, he taketh from him all his armour wherein he trusted, and divideth his spoils.

23. He that is not with me is against me : and he that gathereth not with me scattereth.

CYRIL; As it was necessary for many reasons to refute the cavils of His opponents, our Lord now makes use of a very plain example, by which He proves to those who will consider it that He overcomes the power of the world, by a power inherent in Himself, saying, *When a strong man armed keepeth his palace.* CHRYS. He calls the devil *a strong man*, not because Chrys. he is naturally so, but referring to his ancient dominion, of $^{\text{Hom.}}_{41. \text{ in}}$ which our weakness was the cause. CYRIL; For he used before Matt. the coming of the Saviour to seize with great violence upon the flocks of another, that is, God, and carry them as it were to his own fold.

THEOPHYL. The Devil's arms are all kinds of sins, trusting in which he prevailed against men. BEDE; But the world he calls his palace, which lieth in wickedness, wherein up to 1 John our Saviour's coming he enjoyed supreme power, because he $^{5, 19.}$ rested in the hearts of unbelievers without any opposition. But with a stronger and mightier power Christ has conquered, and by delivering all men has cast him out. Hence it is added, *But if a stronger than he shall come upon him, and overcome, &c.* CYRIL; For as soon as the Word of the Most High God, the Giver of all strength, and the Lord of Hosts, was made man, He attacked him, and took away his arms. BEDE; His arms then are the craft and the wiles of spiritual wickedness, but his spoils are the men themselves, who have been deceived by him.

CYRIL; For the Jews who had been a long time entrapped by him into ignorance of God and sin, have been called out by the holy Apostles to the knowledge of the truth, and presented to God the Father, through faith in the Son. BASIL; Christ also divides the spoil, shewing the faithful watch which angels keep over the salvation of men. BEDE; As conqueror too Christ divides the spoils, which is a sign of triumph, for leading captivity captive He gave gifts to men, ordaining some Apostles, some Evangelists, some Prophets, and some Ephes. Pastors and Teachers. $^{4, 8. 11.}$

CHRYS. Next we have the fourth answer, where it is added, Chrys. *He who is not with me is against me;* as if He says, I wish $^{\text{ubi sup.}}$ to present men to God, but Satan the contrary. How then would he who does not work with Me, but scatters what is Mine, become so united with Me, as with Me to cast out devils? It follows, *And he who gathereth not with me, scattereth.* CYRIL; As if He said, I came to gather together the sons of God whom he hath scattered. And Satan himself as he is not with Me, tries to scatter those which I have gathered and saved. How then does he whom I use all

Chrys.
Hom.
41. in
Matt. My efforts to resist, supply Me with power? Chrys. But if he who does not work with Me is My adversary, how much more he who opposes Me? It seems however to me that he here under a figure refers to the Jews, ranging them with the devil. For they also acted against, and scattered those whom He gathered together.

24. When the unclean spirit is gone out of a man, he walketh through dry places, seeking rest; and finding none, he saith, I will return unto my house whence I came out.

25. And when he cometh, he findeth it swept and garnished.

26. Then goeth he, and taketh to him seven other spirits more wicked than himself; and they enter in, and dwell there: and the last state of that man is worse than the first.

Cyril; After what had gone before, our Lord proceeds to shew how it was that the Jewish people had sunk to these opinions concerning Christ, saying, *When the unclean spirit is gone out of a man, &c.* For that this example relates to Matt.
12, 45. the Jews, Matthew has explained when he says, *Even so shall it be also unto this wicked generation.* For all the time that they were living in Egypt in the practice of the Egyptians, there dwelt in them an evil spirit, which was drawn out of them when they sacrificed the lamb as a type of Christ, and were sprinkled with its blood, and so escaped the destroyer.

Ambrose; The comparison then is between one man and the whole Jewish people, from whom through the Law the unclean spirit had been cast out. But because in the Gentiles, whose hearts were first barren, but afterwards in baptism moistened with the dew of the Spirit, the devil could find no rest because of their faith in Christ, (for to the unclean spirits Christ is a flaming fire,) he then returned to the Jewish people. Hence it follows, *And finding none, he saith, I will return to my house whence I came.*

ORIGEN; That is, to those who are of Israel, whom he saw possessing nothing divine in them, but desolate, and vacant for him to take up his abode there; and so it follows, *And when he came, he findeth it swept and garnished.* AMBROSE; For Israel being adorned with a mere outward and superficial beauty, remains inwardly the more polluted in her heart. For she never quenched or allayed her fires in the water of the sacred fountain, and rightly did the unclean spirit return to her, bringing with him seven other spirits more wicked than himself. Hence it follows, *And he goeth and taketh with him seven other spirits more wicked than himself, and they enter in and dwell there.* Seeing that in truth she has sacrilegiously profaned the seven weeks of the Law, (i. e. from Easter to Pentecost,) and the mystery of the eighth day. Therefore as upon us is multiplied the seven-fold gifts of the Spirit, so upon them falls the whole accumulated attack of the unclean spirits. For the number seven is frequently taken to mean the whole.

CHRYS. Now the evil spirits who dwell in the souls of the Jews, are worse than those in former times. For then the Jews raged against the Prophets, now they lift up their hands against the Lord of the Prophets, and therefore suffered worse things from Vespasian and Titus than in Egypt and Babylon. Hence it follows, *And the last state of that man is worse than the former.* Then too they had with them the Providence of God, and the grace of the Holy Spirit; but now they are deprived even of this protection, so that there is now a greater lack of virtue, and their sorrows are more intense, and the tyranny of the evil spirits more terrible. Chrys. Hom. 43. in Matt.

CYRIL; The last state also is worse than the first, according to the words of the Apostle, *It were better not to have known the way of truth, than after they have known it to turn back from it.* BEDE; This may also be taken to refer to certain heretics or schismatics, or even to a bad Catholic, from whom at the time of his baptism the evil spirit had gone out. And he wanders about in dry places, that is, his crafty device is to try the hearts of the faithful, which have been purged of all unstable and transient knowledge, if he can plant in them any where the footsteps of his iniquity. But he says, *I will return to my house whence I came out.* 2 Pet. 2, 21.

And here we must beware lest the sin which we supposed extinguished in us, by our neglect overcome us unawares. But he finds his house swept and garnished, that is, purified by the grace of baptism from the stain of sin, yet replenished with no diligence in good works. By the seven evil spirits which he takes to himself, he signifies all the vices. And they are called more wicked, because he will have not only those vices which are opposed to the seven spiritual virtues, but also by his hypocrisy he will pretend to have the virtues themselves.

Chrys.
ut sup.

CHRYS. Let us receive the words which follow, as said not only to them, but also to ourselves, *And the last state of that man shall be worse than the first;* for if enlightened and released from our former sins we again return to the same course of wickedness, a heavier punishment will await our latter sins.

BEDE; It may also be simply understood, that our Lord added these words to shew the distinction between the works of Satan and His own, that in truth He is ever hastening to cleanse what has been defiled, Satan to defile with still greater pollution what has been cleansed.

27. And it came to pass, as he spake these things, a certain woman of the company lifted up her voice, and said unto him, Blessed is the womb that bare thee, and the paps which thou hast sucked.

28. But he said, Yea rather, blessed are they that hear the word of God, and keep it.

BEDE; While the Scribes and Pharisees were tempting our Lord, and uttering blasphemies against Him, a certain woman with great boldness confessed His incarnation, as it follows, *And it came to pass, as he spake these things, a certain woman of the company lifted up her voice, and said unto him, Blessed is the womb that bare thee, &c.* by which she refutes both the calumnies of the rulers present, and the unbelief of future heretics. For as then by blaspheming the works of the Holy Spirit, the Jews denied the true Son of

God, so in after times the heretics, by denying that the Ever-virgin Mary, by the cooperating power of the Holy Spirit, ministered of the substance of her flesh to the birth of the only-begotten Son, have said, that we ought not to confess Him who was the Son of man to be truly of the same substance with the Father. But if the flesh of the Word of God, who was born according to the flesh, is declared alien to the flesh of His Virgin Mother, what cause is there why the womb which bare Him and the paps which gave Him suck are pronounced blessed? By what reasoning do they suppose Him to be nourished by her milk, from whose seed they deny Him to be conceived? Whereas according to the physicians, from one and the same fountain both streams are proved to flow. But the woman pronounces blessed not only her who was thought worthy to give birth from her body to the Word of God, but those also who have desired by the hearing of faith spiritually to conceive the same Word, and by diligence in good works, either in their own or the hearts of their neighbours, to bring it forth and nourish it; for it follows, *But he said, Yea rather, blessed are they that hear the word of God, and keep it.*

CHRYS. In this answer He sought not to disown His mother, but to shew that His birth would have profited her nothing, had she not been really fruitful in works and faith. But if it profited Mary nothing that Christ derived His birth from her, without the inward virtue of her heart, much less will it avail us to have a virtuous father, brother, or son, while we ourselves are strangers to virtue. *(Chrys. Hom. 44. in Matt.)*

BEDE; But she was the mother of God, and therefore indeed blessed, in that she was made the temporal minister of the Word becoming incarnate; yet therefore much more blessed that she remained the eternal keeper of the same ever to be beloved Word. But this expression startles the wise men of the Jews, who sought not to hear and keep the word of God, but to deny and blaspheme it.

29. And when the people were gathered thick together, he began to say, This is an evil genera-

tion : they seek a sign; and there shall no sign be given it, but the sign of Jonas the prophet.

30. For as Jonas was a sign unto the Ninevites, so shall also the Son of man be to this generation.

31. The queen of the south shall rise up in the judgment with the men of this generation, and condemn them ; for she came from the utmost parts of the earth to hear the wisdom of Solomon; and, behold, a greater than Solomon is here.

32. The men of Nineve shall rise up in the judgment with this generation, and shall condemn it : for they repented at the preaching of Jonas; and, behold, a greater than Jonas is here.

BEDE; Our Lord had been assailed with two kinds of questions, for some accused Him of casting out devils through Beelzebub, to whom up to this point His answer was addressed; and others tempting Him, sought from Him a sign from heaven, and these He now proceeds to answer. As it follows, *And when the people were gathered thick together, he began to say, This is an evil generation, &c.* AMBROSE; That you may know that the people of the Synagogue are treated with dishonour, while the blessedness of the Church is increased.   But as Jonas was a sign to the Ninevites, so also will the Son of man be to the Jews.   Hence it is added, *They seek a sign ; and there shall no sign be given them but the sign of Jonas the prophet.*   BASIL; A sign is a thing brought openly to view, containing in itself the manifestation of something hidden, as the sign of Jonas represents the descent to hell, the ascension of Christ, and His resurrection from the dead.   Hence it is added, *For as Jonas was a sign to the Ninevites, so shall also the Son of man be to this generation.*   He gives them a sign, not from heaven, because they were unworthy to see it, but from the lowest depths of hell; a sign, namely, of His incarnation, not of His divinity; of His passion, not of His glorification.

AMBROSE; Now as the sign of Jonas is a type of our Lord's passion, so also is it a testimony of the grievous sins

Basil. in Esai. 7.

which the Jews have committed. We may remark at once both the mighty voice of warning, and the declaration of mercy. For by the example of the Ninevites both a punishment is denounced, and a remedy promised. Hence even the Jews ought not to despair of pardon, if they will but practise repentance. THEOPHYL. Now Jonas after he came forth from the whale's belly converts the men of Nineveh by his preaching, but when Christ rose again, the Jewish nation believed not. So there was a sentence already passed upon them, of which there follows a second example, as it is said, *The queen of the south shall rise up in the judgment with the men of this generation, and condemn them.* BEDE; Not certainly by any authority to judge, but by the contrast of a better deed. As it follows, *For she came from the utmost parts of the earth to hear the wisdom of Solomon; and, behold, a greater than Solomon is here.* *Here* in this place is not the pronoun, but the adverb of place, that is, " there is one present among you who is incomparably superior to Solomon." He said not, " I am greater than Solomon," that he might teach us to be humble, though fruitful in spiritual graces. As if he said, " The barbarian woman hastened to hear Solomon, taking so long a journey to be instructed in the knowledge of visible living creatures, and the virtues of herbs. But ye when ye stand by and hear Wisdom herself teaching you invisible and heavenly things, and confirming her words with signs and wonders, are strangers to the word, and senselessly disregard the miracles."

BEDE; But if the queen of the South, who doubtless is of the elect, shall rise up in judgment together with the wicked, we have a proof of the one resurrection of all men, good as well as bad, and that not according to Jewish fables to happen a thousand years before the judgment, but at the judgment itself. AMBROSE; Herein also while condemning the Jewish people, He strongly expresses the mystery of the Church, which in the queen of the South, through the desire of obtaining wisdom, is gathered together from the uttermost parts of the whole earth, to hear the words of the Peacemaking Solomon; a queen plainly whose kingdom is undivided, rising up from different and distant nations into one body. GREG. NYSS. Now as she was queen of the Ethiopians, and in a far distant country, so in the beginning Greg. Hom. 7. Cant.

the Church of the Gentiles was in darkness, and far off from
the knowledge of God. But when Christ the Prince of peace
shone forth, the Jews being still in darkness, thither came
the Gentiles, and offered to Christ the frankincense of
piety, the gold of divine knowledge, and precious stones,
that is, obedience to His commands. THEOPHYL. Or because
the South is praised in Scripture as warm and life-giving,
therefore the soul reigning in the south, that is, in all spiritual
conversation, comes to hear the wisdom of Solomon, the
Prince of peace, the Lord our God, (i. e. is raised up to
contemplate Him,) to whom no one shall come except
he reign in a good life. But He brings next an example
from the Ninevites, saying, *The men of Nineveh shall rise
up in judgment with this generation, and shall condemn it.*
Chrys. CHRYS. The judgment of condemnation comes from men
non occ. like or unlike to those who are condemned. From like,
for instance, as in the parable of the ten virgins, but from
unlike, when the Ninevites condemn those who lived at the
time of Christ, that so their condemnation might be the
more remarkable. For the Ninevites indeed were barbarians,
Hom.
43. in but these Jews. The one enjoying the prophetic teaching,
Matt. the other having never received the divine word. To the
former came a servant, to the latter the Master, of whom the
one foretold destruction, the other preached the kingdom of
heaven. To all men then was it known that the Jews ought
rather to have believed, but the contrary happened; therefore
he adds, *For they repented at the preaching of Jonas, and,
behold, a greater than Jonas is here.* AMBROSE; Now in a
mystery, the Church consists of two things, either ignorance
of sin, which has reference mainly to the queen of the South,
or ceasing to sin, which relates indeed to the repentant
Ninevites. For repentance blots out the offence, wisdom
guards against it.
Aug.
de Cons. AUG. Luke indeed relates this in the same place as
Ev. lib. Matthew, but in a somewhat different order. But who does
ii. c. 39. not see that it is an idle question, in what order our Lord
said those things, seeing that we ought to learn by the most
precious authority of the Evangelist, that there is no falsehood. But not every man will repeat another's words in the
same order in which they proceeded from his mouth, seeing

that the order itself makes no difference with respect to the fact, whether it be so or not.

33. No man, when he hath lighted a candle, putteth it in a secret place, neither under a bushel, but on a candlestick, that they which come in may see the light.

34. The light of the body is the eye: therefore when thine eye is single, thy whole body also is full of light; but when thine eye is evil, thy body also is full of darkness.

35. Take heed therefore that the light which is in thee be not darkness.

36. If thy whole body therefore be full of light, having no part dark, the whole shall be full of light, as when the bright shining of a candle doth give thee light.

CYRIL; The Jews said, that our Lord performed His miracles not for faith, i. e. that they might believe on Him, but to gain the applause of the spectators, i. e. that He might have more followers. He refutes therefore this calumny, saying, *No man, when he hath lighted a candle, putteth it in a secret place, neither under a bushel, but on a candlestick.* BEDE; Our Lord here speaks of Himself, shewing that although He had said above that no sign should be given to this wicked generation but the sign of Jonas, yet the brightness of His light should by no means be hid from the faithful. He Himself indeed lights the candle, who filled the vessel of our nature with the fire of His divinity; and this candle surely He wished neither to hide from believers, nor to place under a bushel, that is, enclose it in the measure of the law, or confine it within the limits of the single nation of the Jews. But He placed it upon a candlestick, that is, the Church, for He has imprinted on our foreheads the faith of His incarnation, that they who with a true faith wish to enter the Church, might be able to see clearly the light of the

truth. Lastly, He bids them remember to cleanse and purify
not only their works, but their thoughts, and the intentions
of the heart. For it follows, *The light of the body is the eye.*
AMBROSE; Either faith is the light, as it is written, *Thy word,*
O Lord, is a lantern to my feet. For the word of God is
our faith. But a lantern cannot shine except it has received
its quality from something else. Hence also the powers of our
mind and senses are enlightened, that the piece of money which
had been lost may be found. Let no one then place faith
under the law, for the law is bound by certain limits, grace is
unlimited; the law obscures, grace makes clear. THEOPHYL.
Or else, because the Jews, seeing the miracles, accused them
out of the malice of their heart, therefore our Lord tells
them, that, receiving the light, that is, their understanding,
from God, they were so darkened with envy, as not to
recognise His miracles and mercies. But to this end
received we our understanding from God, that we should
place it upon a candlestick, that others also who are entering
in may see the light. The wise man indeed has already entered,
but the learner is still walking. As if He said to the Pharisees,
You ought to use your understanding to know the miracles,
and declare them to others, seeing that what you see are the
works not of Beelzebub, but the Son of God. Therefore,
keeping up the meaning, He adds, *The light of the body is the*
eye. ORIGEN; For He gives the name of the eye especially
to our understanding, but the whole soul, although not
corporeal, He metaphorically calls the body. For the whole
soul is enlightened by the understanding.

THEOPHYL. But as if the eye of the body be light the
body will be light, but if dark the body will be dark also, so
is it with the understanding in relation to the soul. Hence it
follows, *If thine eye be single, thy whole body will be full*
of light; but if evil, thy whole body will be full of
darkness. ORIGEN; For the understanding from its very
beginning desires only singleness, containing no dissimulation,
or guile, or division in itself. CHRYS. If then we have
corrupted the understanding, which is able to let loose the
passions, we have done violence to the whole soul, and suffer
dreadful darkness, being blinded by the perversion of our
understanding. Therefore adds he, *Take heed, therefore,*

Ps. 119,
105.

Chrys.
Hom.
20. in
Matt.

that the light which is in thee be not darkness. He speaks of a darkness which may be perceived, but which has its origin within itself, and which we every where carry about with us, the eye of the soul being put out. Concerning the power of this light He goes on to say, *If thy whole body therefore be full of light, &c. &c.* ORIGEN; That is, If thy material body, when the light of a candle shines upon it, is made full of light, so that not one of thy members is any longer in darkness; much more when thou sinnest not, shall thy whole spiritual body be so full of light, that its brightness may be compared to the shining of a candle, while the light which was in the body, and which used to be darkness, is directed whithersoever the understanding may command. GREG. NAZ. Or else; The light and eye of the Church is the Bishop. It is necessary then that as the body is rightly directed as long as the eye keeps itself pure, but goes wrong when it becomes corrupt, so also with respect to the Prelate, according to what his state may be, must the Church in like manner suffer shipwreck, or be saved. *Greg. Epist. 41.*

GREG. Or else; By the name body each particular action is understood which follows its own intention, as it were the eye of the spectators. Therefore it is said, *The light of the body is the eye,* because by the ray of a good intention the deserving parts of an action receive light. If then thy eye be single, thy whole body will be full of light, for if we intend rightly in singleness of heart, we accomplish a good work, even though it seem not to be good. And if thy eye be evil, thy whole body will be full of darkness, because when with a crooked intention even a right thing is done, although it appears to glitter in men's sight, yet before the bar of the internal judge it is covered with darkness. Hence too it is rightly added, *Take heed therefore that the light which is in thee be not darkness.* For if what we think we do well we cloud by a bad intention, how many are the evils themselves which even when we do them we know to be evil? BEDE; Now when He adds, *If thy whole body therefore, &c.* by the whole of our body He means all our works. If then thou hast done a good work with a good intention, having in thy conscience nothing approaching to a dark thought, *Greg. 28. Mor. c. 12.*

though it chance that thy neighbour is injured by thy
good actions, nevertheless for thy singleness of heart shalt
thou be rewarded with grace here, and with glorious light
hereafter; which he signifies, adding, *And as the bright
shining of a candle shall it give thee light.* These words
were especially directed against the hypocrisy of the Pharisees, who sought for signs that they might catch him.

37. And as he spake, a certain Pharisee besought
him to dine with him, and he went in, and sat down
to meat.

38. And when the Pharisee saw it, he marvelled
that he had not first washed before dinner.

39. And the Lord said unto him, Now do ye
Pharisees make clean the outside of the cup and the
platter; but your inward part is full of ravening and
wickedness.

40. Ye fools, did not he that made that which is
without make that which is within also?

41. But rather give alms of such things as ye have;
and, behold, all things are clean unto you.

42. But woe unto you, Pharisees! for ye tithe
mint and rue and all manner of herbs, and pass over
judgment and the love of God: these ought ye to
have done, and not to leave the other undone.

43. Woe unto you, Pharisees! for ye love the
uppermost seats in the synagogues, and greetings in
the markets.

44. Woe unto you, Scribes and Pharisees, hypocrites! for ye are as graves which appear not, and
the men that walk over them are not aware of them.

Cyril; The Pharisee, while our Lord still continued on
speaking, invites Him to his own house. As it is said,
*And while he was speaking, a certain Pharisee besought
him to dine with him.* Bede; Luke expressly says, *And
as he spake these things,* to shew that He had not quite

finished what He had purposed to say, but was somewhat interrupted by the Pharisee asking Him to dine. Aug. For in order to relate this, Luke has made a variation from Matthew, at that place where both had mentioned what our Lord said concerning the sign of Jonah, and the queen of the south, and the unclean spirit; after which discourse Matthew says, *While he yet talked to the people, behold his mother and his brethren stood without desiring to speak to him;* but Luke having also in that discourse of our Lord related some of our Lord's sayings which Matthew omitted, now departs from the order which he had hitherto kept with Matthew.

Aug. de Con. Evan. lib. ii. c. 40.

BEDE; Accordingly, after that it was told Him that His mother and brethren stood without, and He said, *For he that doeth the will of God, the same is my brother, and sister, and mother,* we are given to understand that He by the request of the Pharisee went to the dinner.

CYRIL; For Christ, knowing the wickedness of those Pharisees, Himself purposely condescends to be occupied in admonishing them, after the manner of the best physicians, who bring remedies of their own making to those who are dangerously ill. Hence it follows, *And he went in and sat down to meat.* But what gave occasion for the words of Christ was, that the ignorant Pharisees were offended, that while men thought Him to be a great man and a prophet, He conformed not to their unreasonable customs. Therefore it is added, *But the Pharisee began to think and say within himself, Why had he not first washed before dinner?*

AUG. For every day before dinner the Pharisees washed themselves with water, as if a daily washing could be a cleansing of the heart. But the Pharisee thought within himself, yet did not give utterance to a word; nevertheless, He heard who perceived the secrets of the heart. Hence it follows, *And the Lord said unto him, Now do ye Pharisees make clean the outside of the cup and the platter; but your inward part is full of ravening and wickedness.*

Aug. Serm. 106.

CYRIL; Now our Lord might also have used other words to admonish the foolish Pharisee, but he seizes the opportunity and framed his reproof from the things that were ready before him. At the hour, namely, of meals He takes for His example the cup and the platter, pointing out that it became the sincere servants of God to be washed and clean, not only from bodily impurity, but also from that which lies concealed within the power of the soul, just as any of the vessels which are used for the table ought to be free from all inward defilement.

AMBROSE; Now mark that our bodies are signified by the mention of earthly and fragile things, which when let fall a short distance are broken to pieces, and those things which the mind meditates within, it easily expresses through the senses and actions of the body, just as those things which the cup contains within make a glitter without. Hence also hereafter, by the word cup doubtless the passion of the body is spoken of. You perceive then, that not the outside of the cup and platter defiles us, but the inner parts. For he said, *But your inward part is full of ravening and wickedness.*

Aug.
Serm.
106.
AUG. But how was it that He spared not the man by whom He was invited? Yea rather, He spared him by reproof, that when corrected He might spare him in the judgment. Further, He shews us that baptism also which is once given cleanses by faith; but faith is something within, not without. The Pharisees despised faith, and used washings which were without; while within they remained full of pollution. The Lord condemns this, saying, *Ye fools, did not he that made that which is without make that which is within also?* BEDE; As if He says, He who made both natures of man, will have each to be cleansed. This is against the Manicheans, who think the soul only was created by God, but the flesh by the devil. It is also against those who abominate the sins of the flesh, such as fornication, theft, and the like; while those of the Spirit, which are no less condemned by the Apostle, they disregard as trifling.

AMBROSE; Now our Lord as a good Master taught us how we ought to purify our bodies from defilement, saying, *But rather give alms of such things as ye have over: and, behold, all things are clean unto you.* You see what the remedies are; almsgiving cleanseth us, the word of God cleanseth us, John 15, 3. according to that which is written, *Now ye are clean through the word which I have spoken unto you.*

Cypr. de
Op. et
Eleem.
CYPRIAN; The Merciful bids us to shew mercy; and because

He seeks to save those whom He has redeemed at a great price,
He teaches that they who have been defiled after the grace
of baptism may again be made clean.

CHRYS. Now He says, *give alms*, not injury. For alms- ^{Chrys.}
giving is that which is free from all injury. It makes all ^{72. in}
things clean, and is more excellent than fasting; which ^{Joan.}
though it be the more painful, the other is the more
profitable. It enlightens the soul, enriches it, and makes it
good and beautiful. He who resolves to have compassion
on the needy, will sooner cease from sin. For as the
physician who is in the habit of healing the diseased is
easily grieved by the misfortunes of others; so we, if we
have devoted ourselves to the relief of others, shall easily
despise things present, and be raised up to heaven. The
unction of almsgiving then is no slight good, since it is
capable of being applied to every wound.

BEDE; He speaks of " what is over and above" our ^{quod}
necessary food and clothing. For you are not commanded ^{super-est.}
to give alms so as to consume yourself by want, but that after
satisfying your wants, you should supply the poor to the
utmost of your power. Or it must be taken in this way. Do that
which remains within your power, that is, which is the only
remedy remaining to those who have been hitherto engaged in
so much wickedness; give alms. Which word applies to every
thing which is done with profitable compassion. For not he
alone gives alms who gives food to the hungry and things of
that kind, but he also who gives pardon to the sinner, and
prays for him, and reproves him, visiting him with
some correcting punishment. THEOPHYL. Or He means,
" That which is uppermost." For wealth rules the covetous
man's heart.

AMBROSE; The whole then of this beautiful discourse
is directed to this end, that while it invites us to the study of
simplicity, it should condemn the luxury and worldliness of
the Jews. And yet even they are promised the abolition
of their sins if they will follow mercy.

AUG. But if they cannot be cleansed except they believe ^{Aug.}
on Him who cleanses the heart by faith, what is this which ^{Serm.}^{106.}
He says, *Give alms, and behold all things are clean to you?*
Let us give heed, and perhaps He Himself explains it to us.

For the Jews withdrew a tenth part from all their produce, and gave it in alms, which rarely a Christian does. Therefore they mocked Him, for saying this to them as to men who did not give alms. God knowing this adds, *But woe unto you, Pharisees! for ye tithe mint and rue and all manner of herbs, and pass over judgment and the love of God.* This then is not giving alms. For to give alms is to shew mercy. If thou art wise, begin with thyself: for how art thou merciful to another, if cruel to thyself? Hear the Scripture, which says unto thee, *Have mercy on thy own soul, and please God.* Return unto thy conscience, thou that livest in evil or unbelief, and then thou findest thy soul begging, or perhaps struck dumb with want. In judgment and love give alms to thy soul. What is judgment? Do what is displeasing to thyself. What is charity? Love God, love thy neighbour. If thou neglectest this alms, love as much you like, thou doest nothing, since thou doest it not to thyself.

Ecclus. 30, 23.

CYRIL; Or He says it by way of censure upon the Pharisees, who ordered those precepts only to be strictly observed by their people, which were the cause of fruitful returns to themselves. Hence they omitted not even the smallest herbs, but despised the work of inspiring love to God, and the just awarding of judgment. THEOPHYL. For because they despised God, treating sacred things with indifference, He commands them to have love to God; but by judgment He implies the love of our neighbour. For when a man judges his neighbour justly, it proceeds from his love to him.

AMBROSE; Or judgment, because they do not bring to examination every thing that they do; charity, because they love not God with their heart. But that He might not make us zealous of the faith, to the neglect of good works, He sums up the perfection of a good man in a few words, *these ought ye to have done, and not to leave the other undone.* CHRYS. Where indeed the subject treated was the Jewish cleansing, He altogether passed it by, but as the tithe is a kind of almsgiving, and the time was not yet come for absolutely destroying the customs of the law, therefore He says, *these ought ye to have done.*

Chrys. Hom. 73. in Matt.

AMBROSE; He reproves also the arrogance of the boasting Jews in seeking the preeminence: for it follows, *Woe unto you,*

Pharisees, for ye love the uppermost seats in the synagogues,
&c. CYRIL; By means of those things for which He blames
us He makes us better. For He would have us be free from
ambition, and not desire after vain show rather than the
reality, which the Pharisees were then doing. For the
greetings of men, and the rule over them, do not move us
to be really useful, for these things fall to men though they
be not good men. Therefore he adds, *Woe unto you, who*
are as graves which appear not. For in wishing to receive
greetings from men and to exercise authority over them, that
they might be accounted great, they differ not from hidden
graves, which glitter indeed with outward ornaments, but
within are full of all uncleanness. AMBROSE; And like
graves which appear not, they deceive by their outside
beauty, and by their look impose upon the passers by;
as it follows, *And the men that walk over them are not*
aware of them; so much that in truth, though they give
outward promise of what is beautiful, inwardly they enclose
all manner of pollution.

CHRYS. But that the Pharisees were so, cannot be won- Chrys.
dered at. But if we who are counted worthy to be the 73.
temples of God suddenly become graves full only of corruption, this is indeed the lowest wretchedness.

CYRIL; Now here the apostate Julian says, that we must Cyril.
avoid graves which Christ says are unclean; but he knew Julian.
not the force of our Saviour's words, for He did not command lib. 10.
us to depart from the graves, but likened to them the
hypocritical people of the Pharisees.

45. Then answered one of the Lawyers, and said
unto him, Master, thus saying thou reproachest us
also.

46. And he said, Woe unto you also, ye Lawyers!
for ye lade men with burdens grievous to be borne,
and ye yourselves touch not the burdens with one of
your fingers.

47. Woe unto you! for ye build the sepulchres of
the prophets, and your fathers killed them.

48. Truly ye bear witness that ye allow the deeds of your fathers: for they indeed killed them, and ye build their sepulchres.

49. Therefore also said the wisdom of God, I will send them prophets and apostles, and some of them they shall slay and persecute:

50. That the blood of all the prophets, which was shed from the foundation of the world, may be required of this generation;

51. From the blood of Abel unto the blood of Zacharias, which perished between the altar and the temple: verily I say unto you, It shall be required of this generation.

52. Woe unto you, Lawyers! for ye have taken away the key of knowledge: ye enter not in yourselves, and them that were entering in ye hindered.

53. And as he said these things unto them, the Scribes and Pharisees began to urge him vehemently, and to provoke him to speak of many things:

54. Laying wait for him, and seeking to catch something out of his mouth, that they might accuse him.

CYRIL; A reproof which exalts the meek is generally hateful to the proud man. When therefore our Saviour was blaming the Pharisees for transgressing from the right path, the body of Lawyers were struck with consternation. Hence it is said, *Then answered one of the Lawyers, and said unto him, Master, thus saying thou reproachest us also.* BEDE; In what a grievous state is that conscience, which hearing the word of God thinks it a reproach against itself, and in the account of the punishment of the wicked perceives its own condemnation.

THEOPHYL. Now the Lawyers were different from the Pharisees. For the Pharisees being separated from the rest had the appearance of a religious sect; but those skilled in the Law were the Scribes and Doctors who solved legal questions. CYRIL; But Christ brings a severe charge against the Lawyers, and subdues their foolish pride, as it follows, *And he said, Woe unto you also, ye Lawyers, for ye lade men, &c.* He brings forward an obvious example for their direction. The Law was burdensome to the Jews as the disciples of Christ confess, but these Lawyers binding together legal burdens which could not be borne, placed them upon those under them, taking care themselves to have no toil whatever. THEOPHYL. As often also as the teacher does what he teaches, he lightens the load, offering himself for an example. But when he does none of the things which he teaches others, the loads appear heavy to those who learn his teaching, as being what even their teacher is not able to bear.

BEDE; Now they are rightly told that they would not touch the burdens of the Law even with one of their fingers, that is, they fulfil not in the slightest point that law which they pretend to keep and transmit to the keeping of others, contrary to the practice of their fathers, without faith and the grace of Christ.

GREG. NYSS. So also are there now many severe judges of sinners, yet weak combatants; burdensome imposers of laws, yet weak bearers of burdens; who wish neither to approach nor to touch strictness of life, though they sternly exact it from their subjects.

CYRIL; Having then condemned the burdensome dealing of the Lawyer, He brings a general charge against all the chief men of the Jews, saying, *Woe to you who build the tombs of the prophets, and your fathers killed them.* AMBROSE; This is a good answer to the foolish superstition of the Jews, who in building the tombs of the prophets condemned the deeds of their fathers, but by rivalling their fathers' wickedness, throw back the sentence upon themselves. For not the building but the imitation of their deeds is looked upon as a crime. Therefore He adds, *Truly ye bear witness that ye allow, &c.*

BEDE; They pretended indeed, in order to win the favour of the multitude, that they were shocked at the unbelief of their fathers, since by splendidly honouring the memories of the prophets who were slain by them they condemned their deeds.

But in their very actions they testify how much they coincide with their fathers' wickedness, by treating with insult that Lord whom the prophets foretold. Hence it is added, *Therefore also said the wisdom of God, I will send them prophets and apostles, and some of them they shall slay and persecute.* AMBROSE; The wisdom of God is Christ. The words indeed in Matthew are, *Behold I send unto you prophets and wise men.* BEDE; But if the same Wisdom of God sent prophets and Apostles, let heretics cease to assign to Christ a beginning from the Virgin; let them no longer declare one God of the Law and Prophets, another of the New Testament. For although the Apostolic Scripture often calls by the name of prophets not only those who foretell the coming Incarnation of Christ, but those also who foretell the future joys of the kingdom of heaven, yet I should never suppose that these were to be placed before the Apostles in the order of enumeration.

Athan.
Apol. 1.
de fuga
sua.
ATHAN. Now if they kill, the death of the slain will cry out the louder against them; if they pursue, they send forth memorials of their iniquity, for flight makes the pursuit of the sufferers to redound to the great disgrace of the pursuers. For no one flees from the merciful and gentle, but rather from the cruel and evil-minded man. And therefore it follows, *That the blood of all the prophets who have been slain from the foundation of the world may be required of this generation.* BEDE; It is asked, How comes it that the blood of all the prophets and just men is required of the single generation of the Jews; whereas many of the saints, both before the Incarnation and after, have been slain by other nations? But it is the manner of the Scriptures frequently to reckon two generations of men, one of the good, and the other of the evil. CYRIL; Although then He says pointedly of this generation, He expresses not merely those who were then standing by Him and listening, but every manslayer. For like is attri-
Chrys.
Hom.
74. in
Matt.
buted to like. CHRYS. But if He means that the Jews are about to suffer worse things, this will not be undeserved, for they have dared to do worse than all. And they have been corrected by none of their past calamities, but when they saw others sin, and punished, they were not made better, but did likewise; yet it will not be that one shall suffer punishment for the sins of others.

.THEOPHYL. But our Lord shews that the Jews have inhe-
rited the malice of Cain, since he adds, *From the blood of
Abel, to the blood of Zacharias, &c.* Abel, inasmuch as he
was slain by Cain; but Zacharias, whom they slew between
the temple and the altar, some say was the Zacharias of old
time, the son of Jehoiadah the Priest. BEDE; Why He
begins *from the blood of Abel*, who was the first martyr, we
need not wonder; but why, *to the blood of Zacharias*, is a
question, since many were slain after him even up to our
Lord's birth, and soon after His birth the Innocents, unless
perhaps it was because Abel was a shepherd, Zacharias a
Priest. And the one was killed in the field, the other in the
court of the temple, martyrs of each class, that is, under
their names are shadowed both laymen, and those engaged
in the office of the altar.

GREG. NYSS. But some say that Zacharias, the father of
John, by the spirit of prophecy forecasting the mystery of the
immaculate virginity of the mother of God, in no wise separated her from the part of the temple set apart for virgins,
wishing to shew that it was in the power of the Creator of all
things to manifest a new birth, while he did not deprive the
mother of the glory of her virginity. Now this part was
between the altar and the temple, in which was placed the
brazen altar, where for this reason they slew him. It is said
also, that when they heard the King of the world was about to
come, from fear of subjection they designedly attacked him who
bore witness to His coming, and slew the priest in the temple.
GREEK EX. But others give another reason for the destruction
of Zacharias. For at the murder of the children the blessed
John was to be slain with the rest of the same age, but Elisabeth, snatching up her son from the midst of the slaughter,
sought the desert. And so when Herod's soldiers could not
find Elisabeth and the child, they turn their wrath against
Zacharias, killing him as he was ministering in the temple.

It follows, *Woe to you, lawyers, for ye have taken away the
key of knowledge.* BASIL; This word *woe*, which is uttered
with pain intolerable, is suited to those who were shortly after
to be cast out into grievous punishment. CYRIL; Now we
say, the law itself is the key of knowledge. For it was
both a shadow and a figure of the righteousness of Christ,

Greg.
Orat. in
Diem
Nat.
Christi.

Geome-
ter.

Basil. in
Esai. 1.

therefore it became the Lawyers, as instructors of the Law of
Moses and the words of the Prophets, to reveal in a certain
measure to the Jewish people the knowledge of Christ.
This they did not, but on the contrary detracted from the
divine miracles, and spoke against His teaching, *Why hear
ye him?* So then they took away the key of knowledge.
Hence it follows, *Ye entered not in yourselves, and them that
were entered in ye hindered.* But faith also is the key of
knowledge.   For by faith comes also the knowledge of

Isa.7,9. truth, according to that of Isaiah, *Unless ye have believed,*
LXX. *ye will not understand.* The Lawyers then have taken away
the key of knowledge, not permitting men to believe in Christ.

Aug. de AUG. But the key of knowledge is also the humility of Christ,
qu. Ev.
l.ii.q.23. which they would neither themselves understand, nor let be
understood by others. AMBROSE; Those also are even now
condemned under the name of Jews, and made subject to future
punishment, who, while usurping to themselves the teaching
of divine knowledge, both hinder others, and do not themselves
acknowledge that which they profess.

Aug. de   AUG. Now all these things Matthew records to have been
con. Ev.
lib. ii. said after our Lord had come into Jerusalem. But Luke re-
c. 75. lates them here, when our Lord was yet on His journey to
Jerusalem. From which they appear to me to be similar
discourses, of which ·Matthew has given one, Luke the
other.

BEDE; But how true were the charges of unbelief, hypocrisy, and impiety, brought against the Pharisees and Lawyers
they themselves testify, striving not to repent, but to entrap
the Teacher of truth; for it follows, *And as he said these
things to them, the Pharisees and Lawyers began to urge
him vehemently.* CYRIL; Now this urging is taken to mean
pressing upon Him, or threatening Him, or waxing furious
against Him. But they began to interrupt His words in
many ways, as it follows, *And to force him to speak of
many things.* THEOPHYL. For when several are questioning
a man on different subjects, since he can not reply to all at
once, foolish people think he is doubting. This also
was part of their wicked design against Him; but they
sought also in another way to control His power of
speech, namely, by provoking Him to say something by

which He might be condemned; whence it follows, *Laying in wait for him, and seeking to catch something out of his mouth, that they might accuse him.* Having first spoken of " forcing," Luke now says to catch or seize something from His mouth; at one time indeed they asked Him concerning the Law, that they might convict as a blasphemer Him who accused Moses; but at another time concerning Cæsar, that they might accuse Him as a traitor and rebel against the majesty of Cæsar.

1. In the mean time, when there were gathered together an innumerable multitude of people, insomuch that they trode one upon another, he began to say unto his disciples first of all, Beware ye of the leaven of the Pharisees, which is hypocrisy.

2. For there is nothing covered, that shall not be revealed; neither hid, that shall not be known.

3. Therefore whatsoever ye have spoken in darkness shall be heard in the light; and that which ye have spoken in the ear in closets shall be proclaimed upon the housetops.

THEOPHYL. The Pharisees sought indeed to catch Jesus in His talk, that they might lead away the people from Him. But this design of theirs is reversed. For the people came all the more unto Him gathered together by thousands, and so desirous to attach themselves to Christ, that they pressed one upon another. So mighty a thing is truth, so feeble every where deceit. Whence it is said, *And when there were gathered together a great multitude, insomuch that they trode upon one another, he began to say unto his disciples, Beware ye of the leaven of the Pharisees, which is hypocrisy.* CYRIL; For they were false accusers; therefore Christ warned His disciples against them. GREG. NAZ. When leaven is praised it is as composing the bread of life, but when blamed it signifies a lasting and bitter maliciousness. THEOPHYL. He calls their hypocrisy leaven, as perverting and corrupting the intentions of the men in whom it has sprung up. For nothing so changes the characters of men as hypocrisy. BEDE; For as a little leaven leaveneth a whole lump of meal, so hypocrisy will rob the mind of all the purity and integrity of its virtues. AMBROSE; Our Lord has introduced

1 Cor. 5, 6.

a most forcible argument for preserving simplicity, and being
zealous for the faith, that we should not after the
manner of faithless Jews put one thing in practice, while in
words we pretend another, namely, that at the last day the
hidden thoughts accusing or else excusing one another, shall be
seen to reveal the secrets of our mind.   Whence it is added,
There is nothing hid which shall not be revealed.   ORIGEN;
He either then says this concerning that time when God shall
judge the secrets of men, or He says it because however much
a man may endeavour to hide the good deeds of another
by discredit, good of its own nature cannot be concealed.
CHRYS. As if He says to His disciples, Although now some Chrys.
call you deceivers and wizards, time shall reveal all things and Hom.
34. in
convict them of calumny, while it makes known your virtue. Matt.
Therefore whatsoever things I have spoken to you in the
small corner of Palestine, these boldly and with open brow,
casting away all fear, proclaim to the whole world.   And
therefore He adds, *Whatsoever ye have spoken in darkness
shall be heard in light.*   BEDE; Or He says this, because all
the things which the Apostles of old spoke and suffered
amid the darkness of oppression and the gloom of the
prison, are now that the Church is made known through
the world and their acts are read, publicly proclaimed.
The words, *shall be proclaimed on the housetops*, are
spoken according to the manner of the country of Palestine,
where they are accustomed to live on the housetops.   For
their roofs were not after our way raised to a point, but flat
shaped, and level at the top.   Therefore He says, *proclaimed
on the housetops;* that is, spoken openly in the hearing of all
men.   THEOPHYL. Or this is addressed to the Pharisees; as
if He said, O Pharisees, what you have spoken in darkness,
that is, all your endeavours to tempt me in the secrets of
your hearts, shall be heard in the light, for I am the light, and
in My light shall be known whatsoever your darkness devises.
And what you have spoken in the ear and in closets, that is,
whatsoever in whispers you have poured into one another's
ears, shall be proclaimed on the housetops, that is, was as
audible to me as if it had been cried aloud on the housetops.
Herein also you may understand that the light is the
Gospel, but the housetop the lofty souls of the Apostles.

But whatever things the Pharisees plotted together, were afterwards divulged and heard in the light of the Gospel, the great Herald, the Holy Spirit, presiding over the souls of the Apostles.

4. And I say unto you my friends, Be not afraid of them that kill the body, and after that have no more that they can do.

5. But I will forewarn you whom ye shall fear: Fear him, which after he hath killed hath power to cast into hell; yea, I say unto you, Fear him.

6. Are not five sparrows sold for two farthings, and not one of them is forgotten before God?

7. But even the very hairs of your head are all numbered. Fear not therefore: ye are of more value than many sparrows.

AMBROSE; Since unbelief springs from two causes, either from a deeply-seated malice or a sudden fear; lest any one from terror should be compelled to deny the God whom he acknowledges in his heart, He well adds, *And I say unto you my friends, Be not afraid of them that kill the body, &c.* CYRIL; For it is not absolutely to every one that this discourse seems to apply, but to those who love God with their whole heart to whom it belongs to say, *Who shall separate us from the love of Christ?* But they who are not such, are tottering, and ready to fall down. Moreover our Lord says, *Greater love hath no man than this, that a man lay down his life for his friends.* How then is it not most ungrateful to Christ not to repay Him what we receive? AMBROSE; He tells us also, that that death is not terrible for which at a far more costly rate of interest immortality is to be purchased.

CYRIL; We must then consider that crowns and honours are prepared for the labours of those upon whom men are continually venting forth their indignation, and to them the death of the body is the end of their persecutions. Whence He adds, *And after this have nothing more that they can do.* BEDE; Their rage then is but useless raving, who cast the

Rom. 8, 3.

John 15, 13.

lifeless limbs of martyrs to be torn in pieces by wild beasts and birds, seeing that they can in no wise prevent the omnipotence of God from quickening and bringing them to life again. CHRYS. Observe how our Lord makes His disciples superior to all, by exhorting them to despise that very death which is terrible to all. At the same time also he brings them proofs of the immortality of the soul: adding, *I will forewarn you whom ye shall fear: fear him, which after he hath killed hath power to cast into hell.* AMBROSE; For our natural death is not the end of punishment: and therefore He concludes that death is the cessation of bodily punishment, but the punishment of the soul is everlasting. And God alone is to be feared, to whose power nature prescribes not, but is herself subject; adding, *Yea, I say unto you, Fear him.* THEOPHYL. Here observe, that upon sinners death is sent as a punishment, since they are here tormented by destruction, and afterwards thrust down into hell. But if you will sift the words you will understand something farther. For He says not, "Who casts into hell," but *has power to cast.* For not every one dying in sin is forthwith thrust down into hell, but there is sometimes pardon given for the sake of the offerings and prayers which are made for the dead '.

AMBROSE; Our Lord then had instilled the virtue of simplicity, had awakened a courageous spirit. Their faith alone was wavering, and well did He strengthen it by adding with respect to things of less value, *Are not five sparrows sold for two farthings? and not one of them is forgotten before God.* As if He said, If God forgets not the sparrows, how can He man? BEDE; The dipondius is a coin of the lightest weight, and equal to two asses. GLOSS. Now that which in number is one is in weight an ass, but that which is two is a dipondius. AMBROSE; But perhaps some one will say, How is it that the Apostle says, *Does the Lord care for oxen?* whereas an ox is of more value than a sparrow; but to care for is one thing, to have knowledge another.

Chrys. Hom. 22. in Matt.

Gloss. ordin.

1 Cor. 9, 9.

' This opinion of Theophylact's is different from the declared doctrines both of the Roman and Greek Churches, and the general language of the Fathers. See Bellarmine de Purg. lib. ii. c. 1. Coccius, lib. x. art. 4. Chrysost. Phil. i. 24. Trans. p. 38, note e. Hom. de Stat. Tr. p. 130. note c. and Tracts for the Times, No. lxxii. p. 32.

ORIGEN; Literally, hereby is signified the quickness of
the Divine foresight, which reaches even to the least things.
But mystically, the five sparrows justly represent the spiritual
senses, which have perception of high and heavenly things: beholding God, hearing the Divine voice, tasting of the bread of life,
smelling the perfume of Christ's anointing, handling the Word
of Life.   And these being sold for two farthings, that is, being
lightly esteemed by those who count as perishing whatever
is of the Spirit, are not forgotten before God.   But God is
said to be forgetful of some because of their iniquities.
THEOPHYL. Or these five senses are sold for two farthings,
that is, the New and Old Testament, and are therefore not
forgotten by God.   Of those whose senses are given up to
the word of life that they may be fit for the spiritual food,
the Lord is ever mindful.   AMBROSE; Or else; A good
sparrow is one which nature has furnished with the power of
flying; for nature has given us the grace of flying, pleasure
has taken it away, which loads with meats the soul of the
wicked, and moulds it towards the nature of a fleshly
mass.   The five senses of the body then, if they seek the
food of earthly alloy, cannot fly back to the fruits of higher
actions.   A bad sparrow therefore is one which has lost its
habit of flying through the fault of earthly grovelling; such
are those sparrows which are sold for two farthings, namely,
at the price of worldly luxury.   For the enemy sets up his,
as it were, captive slaves, at the very lowest price.   But the
Lord, being the fit judge of His own work, has redeemed
at a great price us, His noble servants, whom He hath made in
His own image.   CYRIL; It is His care then diligently
to know the life of the saints.   Whence it follows, *But the hairs
of your heads are all numbered;* by which He means, that of
all things which relate to them He has most accurate knowledge, for the numbering manifests the minuteness of the care
exercised.   AMBROSE; Lastly, the numbering of the hairs is
not to be taken with reference to the act of reckoning, but
to the capability of knowing.   Yet they are well said to be
numbered, because those things which we wish to preserve
we number.

CYRIL; Now mystically, indeed, the head of a man is his
understanding, but his hairs the thoughts, which are open to

the eye of God. THEOPHYL. Or, by the head of each of the faithful, you must understand a conversation meet for Christ, but by his hair, the works of bodily mortification which are numbered by God, and are worthy of the Divine regard. AMBROSE; If then such is the majesty of God, that a single sparrow or the number of our hair is not beside His knowledge, how unworthy is it to suppose that the Lord is either ignorant of the hearts of the faithful, or despises them so as to account them of less value. Hence He proceeds to conclude, *Fear not then, ye are of more value than many sparrows.* BEDE; We must not read, *Ye are more,* which relates to the comparison of number, but ye are of more pluris value, that is, of greater estimation in the sight of God. estis ATHAN. Now I ask the Arians, if God, as if disdaining to make all other things, made only His Son, but deputed all things to His Son; how is it that He extends His providence even to such trifling things as our hair, and the sparrows? For upon whatever things He exercises His providence, of these is He the Creator by His own word.

8. Also I say unto you, Whosoever shall confess me before men, him shall the Son of man also confess before the angels of God:

9. But he that denieth me before men shall be denied before the angels of God.

10. And whosoever shall speak a word against the Son of man, it shall be forgiven him: but unto him that blasphemeth against the Holy Ghost it shall not be forgiven.

11. And when they bring you unto the synagogues, and unto magistrates, and powers, take ye no thought how or what thing ye shall answer, or what ye shall say:

12. For the Holy Ghost shall teach you in the same hour what ye ought to say.

BEDE; It was said above, that every hidden work and word is to be revealed, but He now declares that this revelation is to take place in the presence of the heavenly city and the eternal Judge and King; saying, *But I say unto you, Whosoever shall confess me, &c.* AMBROSE; He has also well introduced faith, stimulating us to its confession, and to faith itself He has placed virtue as a foundation. For as faith is the incentive to fortitude, so is fortitude the strong

Chrys. Hom. 34. in Matt.
support of faith. CHRYS. The Lord is not then content with an inward faith, but requires an outward confession, urging us to confidence and greater love. And since this is useful for all, He speaks generally, saying, *Whosoever shall confess me, &c.*

Rom. 10, 9.
CYRIL; Now Paul says, *If thou wilt confess with thy mouth the Lord Jesus, and believe in thy heart that God raised him from the dead, thou shalt be saved.* The whole mystery of Christ is conveyed in these words. For we must first confess that the Word born of God the Father, that is, the only-begotten Son of His substance, is Lord of all, not as one who had gained His Lordship from without and by stealth, but who is in truth by His nature Lord, as well as the Father. Next we must confess that God raised Him from the dead, who was Himself truly made man, and suffered in the flesh for us; for such He rose from the dead. Whoever then will so confess Christ before men, namely, as God and the Lord, Christ will confess him before the angels of God at that time when He shall descend with the holy angels in the glory of His Father at the end of the world.

EUSEB. But what will be more glorious than to have the only-begotten Word of God Himself to bear witness in our behalf at the divine judgment, and by His own love to draw forth as a recompense for confession, a declaration upon that soul to whom He bears witness. For not as abiding without him to whom He bears witness, but as dwelling in him and filling him with light, He will give His testimony. But having confirmed them with good hope by so great promises, He again rouses them by more alarming threats, saying, *But he that denieth me before men, shall be denied before the Angels of God.*

Chrys. ubi sup.
CHRYS. Both in condemnation a greater punishment is announced, and in blessing a greater reward; as if He said, Now you confess and deny, but I then, for a far greater recompense of good and evil awaits them in the world to come. EUSEB.

He rightly declares this threatening, in order that none should refuse to confess Him by reason of the punishment, which is to be denied by the Son of God, to be disowned by Wisdom, to fall away from life, to be deprived of light, and to lose every blessing; but all these things to suffer before God the Father who is in heaven, and the Angels of God.

CYRIL; Now they who deny are first indeed those who in time of persecution renounce the faith. Besides these, there are heretical teachers also, and their disciples. CHRYS. There are other modes also of denying which St. Paul describes, saying, *They profess that they know God, but in works they deny him.* And again, *If any provide not for his own, and specially for those of his own house, he hath denied the faith, and is worse than an infidel.* Also, *Flee from covetousness, which is idolatry.* Since then there are so many modes of denial, it is plain that there are many likewise of confession, which whosoever has practised, shall hear that most blessed voice with which Christ greets all who have confessed Him. But mark the precaution of the words. For in the Greek he says, *Whosoever shall confess* in Me, shewing that not by his own strength, but by the aid of grace from above, a man confesses Christ. But of him who denies, He said not " in Me," but *me.* For though being destitute of grace he denies, he is nevertheless condemned, because the destitution is owing to him who is forsaken, or he is forsaken for his own fault. BEDE; But lest from what He says, that those who have denied Him are to be denied, it should be supposed that the condition of all was alike, that is, both of those who deny deliberately, and those who deny from infirmity or ignorance, He immediately added, *And whosoever shall speak a word against the Son of Man, it shall be forgiven him.* CYRIL; But if our Saviour means to imply, that if any injurious word is spoken by us against a common man, we shall obtain pardon if we repent, there is no difficulty in the passage, for since God is by nature merciful, He restores those who are willing to repent. But if the words are referred to Christ how is he not to be condemned who speaks a word against Him?

AMBROSE; Truly by the Son of Man we understand Christ, Who by the Holy Spirit was born of a virgin, seeing that His only parent on earth is the Virgin. What then, is the Holy

Tit. 1, 16.
1 Tim.5, 8.
Col.5, 3.

Spirit greater than Christ, that they who sin against Christ should obtain pardon, while they who offend against the Holy Spirit are not thought worthy to obtain it? But where there is unity of power there is no question of comparison.

Athan.
Ep. 4.
ad Se-
rap.
ATHAN. The ancients indeed, the learned Origen and the great Theognostus, describe this to be the blasphemy against the Holy Ghost, when they who have been counted worthy of the gift of the Holy Spirit in Baptism, fall back into sin. For they say that for this reason they can not obtain pardon; Heb. 6, 4. as Paul says, *It is impossible for those who have been made partakers of the Holy Ghost to renew them again, &c.*

But each adds his own explanation. For Origen gives this as his reason; God the Father indeed penetrates and contains all things, but the power of the Son extends to rational things only; the Holy Spirit is only in those who partake of Him in the gift of Baptism. When then catechumens and heathens sin, they sin against the Son who abideth in them, yet they may obtain pardon when they become worthy of the gift of regeneration. But when the baptized commit sin, he says that their offence touches the Spirit, after coming to whom they have sinned, and therefore their condemnation must be irrevocable.

But Theognostus says, that he who has gone beyond both the first and second threshold deserves less punishment, but he who has also passed the third, shall no more receive pardon. By the first and second threshold, he speaks of the doctrine of the Father and the Son, but by the third the partaking John16, 13. of the Holy Spirit. According to St. John, *When the Spirit of truth is come, he will lead you into all truth.* Not as though the doctrine of the Spirit was above that of the Son, but because the Son condescends to those who are imperfect, but the Spirit is the seal of those who are perfect. If then not because the Spirit is above the Son, blasphemy against the Spirit is unpardonable; but because remission of sin is indeed to the imperfect, but no excuse remains to the perfect, therefore since the Son is in the Father, He is in those in whom the Father and the Spirit are not absent, for the Holy Trinity cannot be divided. Besides this, if all things were made by the Son, and all things consist in Him, He will Himself be truly in all; so that it must needs be, that he who sinneth against the

Son, sinneth against the Father also, and against the Holy
Spirit. But holy Baptism is given in the name of the
Father, and the Son, and the Holy Spirit. And so they that
sin after baptism commit blasphemy against the holy Trinity.
But if the Pharisees had not received baptism, how did He
condemn them as if they had spoken blasphemy against the
Holy Spirit, of which they were not yet partakers, especially since He did not accuse them simply of sin, but of blasphemy? But these differ, for he who sins transgresses the
Law, but he who blasphemes offends against the Deity Himself. But again, if to those who sin after baptism there is no
remission of the punishment of their offences, how does the
Apostle pardon the penitent at Corinth; but he travails in
birth of the backsliding Galatians until Christ be formed
again in them.

2 Cor.
11, 10.
Gal. 4,
19.

And why also do we oppose Novatus, who does away with
repentance after baptism? The Apostle to the Hebrews does
not thus reject the repentance of sinners, but lest they should
suppose that as according to the rites of the Law, under
the veil of repentance there could be many and daily baptisms,
he therefore warns them indeed to repent, but tells them that
there could be only one renewal, namely, by Baptism. But
with such considerations I return to the dispensation which is οἰκονο-
in Christ, who being God was made man; as very God raised μίαν
the dead; as clothed with the flesh, thirsted, laboured, suffered.
When any then, looking to human things, see the Lord athirst
or in suffering, and speak against the Saviour as if against a
man, they sin indeed, yet may speedily on repentance receive
pardon, alleging as excuse the weakness of His body. And
again when any, beholding the works of Deity, doubt concerning the nature of the body, they also sin grievously. But
these too if they repent may be quickly pardoned, seeing that
they have an excuse in the greatness of the works. But
when they refer the works of God to the Devil, justly do they
undergo the irrevocable sentence, because they have judged
God to be the Devil, and the true God to have nothing more
in His works than the evil spirits. To this unbelief then the
Pharisees had come. For when the Saviour manifested the
works of the Father, raising the dead, giving sight to the
blind, and such like deeds, they said that these were the

works of Beelzebub. As well might they say, looking at the order of the world and the providence exercised over it, that the world was created by Beelzebub. As long then as regarding human things they erred in knowledge, saying, *Is not this the carpenter's son, and how knoweth this man things which he never learnt?* He suffered them as sinning against the Son of man; but when they wax more furious, saying that the works of God are the works of Beelzebub, He no longer endured them. For thus also He endured their fathers so long as their murmurings were for bread and water; but when having found a calf, they impute to it the divine mercies they had received, they were punished. At first indeed multitudes of them were slain, afterwards He said indeed, *Nevertheless, in the day when I visit I will visit their sin upon them.* Such then is the sentence passed upon the Pharisees, that in the flame prepared for the devil they shall be together with him everlastingly consumed. Not then to make comparison between a blasphemy spoken against Himself and the Holy Spirit said He these things, as if the Spirit were the greater, but each blasphemy being uttered against Him, He shews the one to be greater, the other less. For looking at Him as man they reviled Him, and said that His works were those of Beelzebub.

Exod. 32, 34.

AMBROSE; Thus it is thought by some that we should believe both the Son and the Holy Spirit to be the same Christ, preserving the distinction of Persons with the unity of the substance, since Christ both God and man is one Spirit, as it is written, *The Spirit before our face, Christ the Lord;* the same Spirit is holy, for both the Father is holy, and the Son holy, and the Spirit holy. If then Christ is each, what difference is there except we know that it is not lawful for us to deny the divinity of Christ? BEDE; Or else; Whoso saith that the works of the Holy Spirit are those of Beelzebub, it shall not be forgiven him either in the present world, or in that which is to come. Not that we deny that if he could come to repentance he could be forgiven by God, but that we believe that such a blasphemer as by the necessity of his deserts he would never come to forgiveness, so neither to the fruits themselves of a worthy repentance; according to that, *He hath blinded their eyes, so that they*

Lam. 4, 20.

Isa. 6, 10.

should not be converted, and I should heal them. CYRIL;
But if the Holy Spirit were a creature, and not of the divine
substance of the Father and the Son, how does an injury
committed against Him entail upon it so great a punishment
as is denounced against those that blaspheme against God?
BEDE; Nor however are all they who say that the Spirit is
not holy, or is not God, but is inferior to the Father and the
Son, involved in the crime of unpardonable blasphemy, because they are led to do it through human ignorance, not a
demoniacal hatred, as the rulers of the Jews were. AUG. Or
if it were here said, " Who hath spoken any blasphemy whatever against the Holy Spirit," we ought then to understand
thereby " all blasphemy ;" but because it was said, *who blasphemeth against the Holy Spirit,* let it be understood of him
that blasphemed not in any way, but in such a manner
that it can never be pardoned him. For so when it was said,
The Lord tempteth no man, that is not spoken of every, but only
of a certain kind of temptation. Now what that kind of blasphemy against the Holy Spirit is, let us see. The first blessing of believers is forgiveness of sins in the Holy Spirit. Against
this free gift the impenitent heart speaks. Impenitence itself
therefore is blasphemy against the Spirit, which is neither
forgiven in this world, nor in that which is to come; for repentance gains that forgiveness in this world which is to avail
in the world to come. CYRIL; But the Lord after having
inspired such great fear, and prepared men to resist those
who depart from a right confession, commanded them
for the rest to take no care what they should answer, because
for those who are faithfully disposed, the Holy Spirit frames
fit words, as their teacher, and dwelling within them. Whence
it follows, *And when they shall bring you into synagogues,
take no thought how or what ye shall answer.* GLOSS.
Now he says, *how,* with respect to the manner of speaking,
what, with respect to the manner of intention. How ye shall
answer to those who ask, or what ye shall say to those who
wish to learn. BEDE; For when we are led for Christ's sake
before judges, we ought to offer only our will for Christ, but
in answering, the Holy Spirit will supply His grace, as it is
added, *For the Holy Spirit will teach you, &c.* CHRYS. But
elsewhere it is said, *Be ready to answer every one who*

Margin notes:
Aug. Serm. 71.
James 1, 13.
Gloss. inter.
Chrys. Hom. 33. in Matt.

shall ask you for a reason of the hope that is in you. When
indeed a contest or strife arises among friends, He bids us
take thought, but when there are the terrors of a court of
justice and fear on every side, He gives His own strength so
as to inspire boldness and utterance, but not dismay.   THEO-
PHYL. Since then our weakness is twofold, and either from
fear of punishment we shun martyrdom, or because we are
ignorant and can not give a reason of our faith, he has excluded both; the fear of punishment in that He said,
Fear not them which kill the body, but the fear of ignorance, when He said, *Take no thought how or what ye shall
answer, &c.*

13. And one of the company said unto him, Master,
speak to my brother, that he divide the inheritance
with me.

14. And he said unto him, Man, who made me a
judge or a divider over you?

15. And he said unto them, Take heed, and beware of covetousness : for a man's life consisteth not
in the abundance of the things which he possesseth.

AMBROSE; The whole of the former passage is given to
prepare us for undergoing suffering for confessing the Lord, or
for contempt of death, or for the hope of reward, or for denun-
ciation of the punishment that will await him to whom pardon
will never be granted. And since covetousness is generally
wont to try virtue, for destroying this also, a precept and example is added, as it is said, *And one of the company said to
him, Speak to my brother, that he divide the inheritance with
me.* THEOPHYL. As these two brothers were contending
concerning the division of their paternal inheritance, it follows,
that one meant to defraud the other; but our Lord teaches us
that we ought not to be set on earthly things, and rebukes
him that called Him to the division of inheritance; as it
follows, *And he said unto him, Man, who made me a judge or
a divider over you?* BEDE; He who wills to impose the trouble
of division of lands upon the Master who is commending the
joys of heavenly peace, is rightly called man, according to

that, *whereas there is envying, strife, and divisions among* 1 Cor. 3, *you, are ye not men?* 3.

CYRIL; Now the Son of God, when He was made like unto us, was appointed by God the Father to be King and Prince upon his holy Mount of Sion, to make known the Divine command.   AMBROSE; Well then does He avoid earthly things who had descended for the sake of divine things, and deigns not to be a judge of strifes and arbiter of laws, having the judgment of the quick and dead and the recompensing of works.   You should consider then, not what you seek, but from whom you ask it; and you should not eagerly suppose that the greater are to be disturbed by the less.   Therefore is this brother deservedly disappointed who desired to occupy the steward of heavenly things with corruptible, seeing that between brothers no judge should intervene, but natural affection should be the umpire to divide the patrimony, although immortality not riches should be the patrimony which men should wait for.

BEDE; He takes occasion from this foolish petitioner to fortify both the multitudes and His disciples alike by precept and example against the plague of covetousness.   Whence it follows, *He said to them, Take heed, and beware of all covetousness;* and he says, *of all,* because some things seem to be honestly done, but the internal judge decides with what intention they are done.   CYRIL; Or he says, *of all covetousness,* that is, great and little.   For covetousness is unprofitable, as the Lord says, *Ye shall build houses of hewn stone,* Amos *and shall not dwell in them.*   And elsewhere, *Yea ten acres* 5, 11. *of vineyards shall yield one bath, and the seed of an homer* Isa. 5, *shall yield an ephah.*   But also in another way it is unprofitable, as he shews, adding, *For a man's life consisteth not in the abundance, &c.*   THEOPHYL. This our Lord says to rebuke the motives of the covetous, who seem to heap up riches as if they were going to live for a long time.   But will wealth ever make thee long lived?   Why then dost thou manifestly undergo evils for the sake of an uncertain rest?   For it is doubtful whether thou oughtest to attain to an old age, for the sake of which thou art collecting treasures.

16. And he spake a parable unto them, saying,

The ground of a certain rich man brought forth plentifully:

17. And he thought within himself, saying, What shall I do, because I have no room where to bestow my fruits?

18. And he said, This will I do: I will pull down my barns, and build greater; and there will I bestow all my fruits and my goods.

19. And I will say to my soul, Soul, thou hast much goods laid up for many years; take thine ease, eat, drink, and be merry.

20. But God said unto him, Thou fool, this night thy soul shall be required of thee: then whose shall those things be, which thou hast provided?

21. So is he that layeth up treasure for himself, and is not rich toward God.

THEOPHYL. Having said that the life of man is not extended by abundance of wealth, he adds a parable to induce belief in this, as it follows, *And he spake a parable unto them, saying, The ground of a certain rich man brought forth plentifully.*

Basil. in Hom. de Avar. BASIL; Not indeed about to reap any good from his plenty of fruits, but that the mercy of God might the more appear, which extends its goodness even to the bad; sending down His rain upon the just and the unjust. But what are the things wherewith this man repays his Benefactor? He remembered not his fellow-creatures, nor deemed that he ought to give of his superfluities to the needy. His barns indeed bursting from the abundance of his stores, yet was his greedy mind by no means satisfied. He was unwilling to put up with his old ones because of his covetousness, and not able to undertake new ones because of the number, for his counsels were imperfect, and his care barren. Hence it follows, *And he thought.* His complaint is like that of the poor. Does not the man oppressed with want say, What shall I do, whence can I get food, whence clothing? Such things also the rich man utters. For his mind is distressed on account of his fruits pouring out from his storehouse, lest perchance when they have come forth they should profit the poor; like the glutton who had rather burst from eating, than give any thing of what remains to the starving. GREG. O adversity, the child of plenty. For saying, *What shall I do,* he surely betokens, that, oppressed by the success of his wishes, he labours as it were under a load of goods. BASIL; It was easy for him to say, I will open my barn, I will call together the needy, but he has no thought of want, only of amassing; for it follows, *And he said, This will I do, I will pull down my barns.* Thou doest well, for the storehouses of iniquity are worthy of destruction. Pull down thy barns, from which no one receives comfort. He adds, *I will build greater.* But if thou shalt complete these, wilt thou again destroy them? What more foolish than labouring on for ever. Thy barns, if thou wilt, are the home of the poor. But thou wilt say, *Whom do I wrong by keeping what is my own?* For it follows also, *And there will I bestow all my fruits and my goods.* Tell me what is thine, from whence didst thou get it and bring it into life? As he who anticipates the public games, injures those who are coming by appropriating to himself what is appointed for the common use, so likewise the rich who regard as their own the common things which they have forestalled. For if every one receiving what is sufficient for his own necessity would leave what remains to the needy, there would be no rich or poor.

CYRIL; Observe also in another respect the folly of his words, when he says, *I will gather all my fruits,* as if he thought that he had not obtained them from God, but that they were the fruits of his own labours. BASIL; But if thou confessest that those things have come to thee from God, is God then unjust in distributing to us unequally. Why dost thou abound while another begs? unless that thou shouldest gain the rewards of a good stewardship, and be honoured with the meed of patience. Art not thou then a robber, for counting as thine own what thou hast received to distribute? It is the bread of the famished which thou receivest, the garment of the naked which thou hoardest in thy chest, the shoe of the barefooted which rots in thy possession, the money of the pennyless which thou hast buried in the earth. Wherefore then dost thou injure so many to whom thou

Margin notes: Greg. Mor. 15, c. 13. Basil. ubi sup. Basil. ubi sup.

Chrys. Hom. 8. in 2 ad Tim. mightest be a benefactor. CHRYS. But in this he errs, that he thinks those things good which are indifferent. For there are some things good, some evil, some between the two. The good are chastity, and humility, and the like, which when a man chooses he becomes good. But opposed to these are the evil, which when a man chooses he becomes bad; and there are the neutral, as riches, which at one time indeed are directed to good, as to almsgiving, at other times to evil, as to covetousness. And in like manner poverty at one time leads to blasphemy, at another to wisdom, according to the disposition of the user.

CYRIL; The rich man then builds barns which last not, but decay, and what is still more foolish, reckons for himself upon a long life; for it follows, *And I will say unto my soul, Soul, thou hast much goods laid up for many years.* But, O rich man, thou hast indeed fruits in thy barns, but as for many years Athan. non occ. whence canst thou obtain them? ATHAN. Now if any one lives so as to die daily, seeing that our life is naturally uncertain, he will not sin, for the greater fear destroys very much pleasure, but the rich man on the contrary, promising to himself length of life, seeks after pleasures, for he says, *Rest,* that is, from toil, *eat, drink, and be merry,* that is, with Basil. ubi sup. great luxury. BASIL; Thou art so careless with respect to the goods of the soul, that thou ascribest the meats of the body to the soul. If indeed it has virtue, if it is fruitful in good works, if it clings to God, it possesses many goods, and rejoices with a worthy joy. But because thou art altogether carnal and subject to the passions, thou speakest from thy Chrys. Hom. 39, 8. in 1 ad Cor. belly, not from thy soul. CHRYS. Now it behoves us not to indulge in delights which fattening the body make lean the soul, and bring a heavy burden upon it, and spread darkness over it, and a thick covering, because in pleasure our governing part which is the soul becomes the slave, but the subject part, namely the body, rules. But the body is in need not of luxuries but of food, that it may be nourished, not that it may be racked and melt away. For not to the soul alone are pleasures hurtful, but to the body itself, because from being a strong body it becomes weak, from being healthy diseased, from being active slothful, from being beautiful unshapely, and from youthful old.

BASIL; But he was permitted to deliberate in every thing, Basil.
Hom. in
loc. and to manifest his purpose, that he might receive a sentence such as his inclinations deserved. But while he speaks in secret, his words are weighed in heaven, from whence the answers come to him. For it follows, *But God said unto him, Thou fool, this night thy soul shall they require of thee.* Hear the name of folly, which most properly belongs to thee which not man has imposed, but God Himself. GREG. The Greg.
22. Mor.
c. 2. same night he was taken away, who had expected many years, that he indeed who had in gathering stores for himself looked a long time forward, should not see even the next day. CHRYS. Chrys.
Concio.
2. de
Lazar. *They shall require of thee,* for perhaps certain dread powers were sent to require it, since if when going from city to city we want a guide, much more will the soul when released from the body, and passing to a future life, need direction. On this account many times the soul rises and sinks into the deep again, when it ought to depart from the body. For the consciousness of our sins is ever pricking us, but most of all when we are going to be dragged before the awful tribunal. For when the whole accumulation of crimes is brought up again, and placed before the eyes, it astounds the mind. And as prisoners are always indeed sorrowful, but particularly at the time when they are going to be brought before the judge; so also the soul at this time is greatly tormented by sin and afflicted, but much more after it has been removed. GREG. But in Greg.
ubi sup. the night the soul was taken away which had gone forth in the darkness of its heart, being unwilling to have the light of consideration, so as to foresee what it might suffer. But He adds, *Then whose shall those things be which thou hast provided?* CHRYS. For here shalt thou leave those things, and not Chrys.
Hom.
23. in
Gen. only reap no advantage from them, but carry a load of sins upon thy own shoulders. And these things which thou hast laid up will for the most part come into the hands of enemies, but of thee shall an account of them be required. It follows, *So is he that layeth up treasure for himself, and is not rich toward God.* BEDE; For such a one is a fool, and will be taken off in the night. He then who wishes to be rich toward God, will not lay up treasures for himself, but distribute his possessions to the poor. AMBROSE; For in vain he

amasses wealth who knows not how to use it. Neither are
these things ours which we cannot take away with us. Virtue
alone is the companion of the dead, mercy alone follows us,
which gains for the dead an everlasting habitation.

22. And he said unto his disciples, Therefore I say
unto you, Take no thought for your life, what ye
shall eat: neither for the body, what ye shall put
on.

23. The life is more than meat, and the body is
more than raiment.

THEOPHYL. The Lord carries us onward by degrees to a
more perfect teaching. For He taught us above to beware
of covetousness, and He added the parable of the rich man,
intimating thereby that the fool is he who desires more than
is enough. Then as His discourse goes on, He forbids us
to be anxious even about necessary things, plucking out the
very root of covetousness; whence he says, *Therefore I say
unto you, Take no thought.* As if He said, Since he is a fool,
who awards to himself a longer measure of life, and is thereby
rendered more covetous; be not ye careful for your soul, what
ye shall eat, not that the intellectual soul eats, but because there
seems no other way for the soul to dwell united to the body except by being nourished. Or because it is a part of the ani-
mate body to receive nourishment, he fitly ascribes nourishment
to the soul. For the soul is called also a nutritive power, as it
is so understood. Be not then anxious for the nourishing
part of the soul, what ye shall eat. But a dead body may
also be clothed, therefore he adds, *Nor for your body, what
ye shall put on.* CHRYS. Now the words, *Take no thought,*
are not the same as do no work, but, " Have not your minds
fixed on earthly things." For it so happens, that the man
who is working takes no thought. CYRIL.; Now the soul is
more excellent than food, and the body than clothing. Therefore
He adds, *The life is more than meat, &c.* As if He said, " God
who has implanted that which is greater, how will He not
give that which is less?" Let not our attention then be

Chrys.
Hom.
21. in
Matt.

stayed upon trifling things, nor our understanding serve to
seek for food and raiment, but rather think on whatever saves
the soul, and raises it to the kingdom of heaven. AMBROSE;
Now nothing is more likely to produce conviction in believers that God can give us all things, than the fact, that
the ethereal spirit perpetuates the vital union of the soul
and body in close fellowship, without our exertion, and the
healthgiving use of food does not fail until the last day of
death has arrived. Since then the soul is clothed with the
body as with a garment, and the body is kept alive by the
vigour of the soul, it is absurd to suppose that a supply of
food will be wanting to us, who are in possession of the
everlasting substance of life.

24. Consider the ravens: for they neither sow nor
reap; which neither have storehouse nor barn; and
God feedeth them : how much more are ye better than
the fowls ?

25. And which of you with taking thought can add
to his stature one cubit ?

26. If ye then be not able to do that thing which
is least, why take ye thought for the rest ?

CYRIL; As before in raising our minds to spiritual boldness,
He assured us by the example of the birds, which are counted
of little worth, saying, *Ye are of more value than many sparrows ;* so now also from the instance of birds, He conveys to
us a firm and undoubting trust, saying, *Consider the ravens,
for they neither sow nor reap, which neither have storehouse
nor barn, and God feedeth them; how much more are ye
better than fowls?* BEDE ; That is, ye are more precious,
because a rational animal like man is of a higher order in
the nature of things than irrational things, as the birds
are.

AMBROSE : But it is a great thing to follow up this example
in faith. For to the birds of the air who have no labour of
tilling, no produce from the fruitfulness of crops, Divine Providence grants an unfailing sustenance. It is true then that
the cause of our poverty seems to be covetousness. For they

have for this reason a toilless and abundant use of food, because they think not of claiming to themselves by any special right fruits given for common food. We have lost what things were common by claiming them as our own· For neither is any thing a man's own, where nothing is perpetual, nor is supply certain when the end is uncertain.

CYRIL; Now whereas our Lord might have taken an example from the men who have cared least about earthly things, such as Elias, Moses, and John, and the like, He made mention of the birds, following the Old Testament, which sends us to the bee and the ant, and others of the same kind, in whom the Creator has implanted certain natural dispositions. THEOPHYL. Now the reason that he omits mention of the other birds, and speaks only of the ravens, is, that the young of the ravens are by an especial providence fed by God. For the ravens produce indeed, but do not feed, but neglect their young, to whom in a marvellous manner from the air their food comes, brought as it were by the wind, which they receive having their mouths open, and so are nourished. Perhaps also such things were spoken by synecdoche, i. e. the whole signified by a part. Hence in Matthew our Lord refers to the birds of the air, but here more particularly to the ravens, as being more greedy and ravenous than others.

Matt. 6, 26.

EUSEB. By the ravens also he signifies something else, for the birds which pick up seeds have a ready source of food, but those that feed on flesh as the ravens do have more difficulty in getting it. Yet birds of this kind suffer from no lack of food, because the providence of God extends every where ; but he brings to the same purpose also a third argument, saying, *And which of you by taking thought can add to his stature ?*

CHRYS. Observe, that when God has once given a soul, it abides the same, but the body is taking growth daily. Passing over then the soul as not receiving increase, he makes mention only of the body, giving us to understand that it is not increased by food alone, but by the Divine Providence, from the fact that no one by receiving nourishment can add any thing to his stature. It is therefore concluded, *If ye then be not able to do that thing which is least, take no thought for the rest.* EUSEB. If no one has by his own skill con-

Chrys. Hom. 21. in Matt.

trived a bodily stature for himself, but can not add even the shortest delay to the prefixed limit of his time of life, why should we be vainly anxious about the necessaries of life? BEDE; To Him then leave the care of directing the body, by whose aid you see it to come to pass that you have a body of such a stature.

AUG. But in speaking concerning increasing the stature of the body, He refers to that which is least, that is, to God, to make bodies.

Aug de Qu. Ev. l. ii. qu. 28.

27. Consider the lilies how they grow: they toil not, they spin not; and yet I say unto you, that Solomon in all his glory was not arrayed like one of these.

28. If then God so clothe the grass, which is to day in the field, and to morrow is cast into the oven; how much more will he clothe you, O ye of little faith?

29. And seek not ye what ye shall eat, or what ye shall drink, neither be ye of doubtful mind.

30. For all these things do the nations of the world seek after: and your Father knoweth that ye have need of these things.

31. But rather seek ye the kingdom of God; and all these things shall be added unto you.

CHRYS. As our Lord had before given instruction about food, so now also about raiment, saying, *Consider the lilies of the field how they grow; they toil not, neither do they spin,* that is, to make themselves clothing. Now as above when our Lord said, *the birds sow not,* He did not reprove sowing, but all superfluous trouble; so when He said, *They toil not, neither do they spin,* He does not put an end to work, but to all anxiety about it.

EUSEB. But if a man wishes to be adorned with precious raiment, let him observe closely how even down to the flowers which spring from the earth God extends His manifold

Chrys. Hom. 22. in Matt.

wisdom, adorning them with divers colours, so adapting to the delicate membranes of the flowers dyes far superior to gold and purple, that under no luxurious king, not even Solomon himself, who was renowned among the ancients for his riches as for his wisdom and pleasures, has so exquisite a work been devised; and hence it follows, *But I say unto you, that Solomon in all his glory was not arrayed like one of these.*

Chrys. Hom. 22. in Matt.

CHRYS. He does not here employ the example of the birds, making mention of a swan or a peacock, but the lilies, for he wishes to give force to the argument on both sides, that is to say, both from the meanness of the things which have obtained such honour, and from the excellence of the honour conferred upon them; and hence a little after He does not call them lilies, but *grass*, as it is added, *If then God so clothe the grass, which to-day is*, He says not, which to-morrow is not, but *to-morrow is cast into the oven;* nor does He say simply, God clothe, but He says, *God so clothe*, which has much meaning, and adds, *how much more you*, which expresses His estimation and care of the human race. Lastly, when it behoves Him to find fault, He deals here also with mildness, reproving them not for unbelief, but for littleness of faith, adding, *O ye of little faith*, that He may so the more rouse us up to believe in His words, that we should not only take no thought about our apparel, but not even admire elegance in dress. CYRIL; For it is sufficient to the prudent for the sake of necessity only, to have a suitable garment, and moderate food, not exceeding what is enough. To the saints it is sufficient even to have those spiritual delights which are in Christ, and the glory that comes after. AMBROSE; Nor does it seem of light moment, that a flower is either compared to man, or even almost more than to man is preferred to Solomon, to make us conceive the glory expressed, from the brightness of the colour to be that of the heavenly angels; who are truly the flowers of the other world, since by their brightness the world is adorned, and they breathe forth the pure odour of sanctification, who shackled by no cares, employed in no toilsome task, cherish the grace of the Divine bounty towards them, and the gifts of their heavenly nature. Therefore well also is Solomon here described to be clothed in his own glory, and in another

place to be veiled, because the frailty of his bodily nature he
clothed as it were by the powers of his mind to the glory of
his works. But the Angels, whose diviner nature remains free
from bodily injury, are rightly preferred, although he be the
greatest man. We should not however despair of God's mercy
to us, to whom by the grace of His resurrection He promises
the likeness of angels.

CYRIL; Now it were strange for the disciples, who ought
to set before others the rule and pattern of life, to fall into
those things, which it was their duty to advise men to renounce;
and therefore our Lord adds, *And seek not what ye shall
eat, &c.* Herein also our Lord strongly recommends the
study of holy preaching, bidding His disciples to cast away all
human cares.

BEDE; It must however be observed, that He says not, Do
not seek or take thought about meat, or drink, or raiment, but
what ye shall eat or drink, in which He seems to me to reprove those who, despising the common food and clothing,
seek for themselves either more delicate or coarser food
and clothing than theirs with whom they live.

GREG. NYSS. Some have obtained dominion and honours
and riches by praying for them, how then dost thou forbid
us to seek such things in prayer? And indeed that all these
things belong to the Divine counsel is plain to every one, yet
are they conferred by God upon those that seek them,
in order that by learning that God listens to our lower petitions,
we may be raised to the desire of higher things; just as we
see in children, who as soon as they are born cling to their
mother's breasts, but when the child grows up it despises
the milk, and seeks after a necklace or some such thing with
which the eye is delighted; and again when the mind has advanced together with the body, giving up all childish desires,
he seeks from his parents those things which are adapted to a
perfect life.

AUG. Now having forbidden all thought about food, he
next goes on to warn men not to be puffed up, saying, *Neither
be ye lifted up*, for man first seeks these things to satisfy
his wants, but when he is filled, he begins to be puffed up
concerning them. This is just as if a wounded man should
boast that he had many plasters in his house, whereas it

(margin notes: Greg. in Orat. Dom. Serm. 1.   Aug. de Qu. Ev. l. ii. qu. 29. nolite in sublime tolli μὴ μι-τεωρίζ-)

were well for him that he had no wounds, and needed not even one plaster. THEOPHYL. Or by being lifted up he means nothing else but an unsteady motion of the mind, meditating first one thing, then another, and jumping from this to that, and imagining lofty things. BASIL; And that you may understand an elation of this kind, remember the vanity of your own youth; if at any time while by yourself you have thought about life and promotions, passing rapidly from one dignity to another, have grasped riches, have built palaces, benefitted friends, been revenged upon enemies. Now such abstraction is sin, for to have our delights fixed upon useless things, leads away from the truth. Hence He goes on to add, *For all these things do the nations of the* Greg. *world seek after, &c.* GREG. NYSS. For to be careful about ubi sup. visible things is the part of those who possess no hope of a future life, no fear of judgment to come. BASIL; But with respect to the necessaries of life, He adds, *And your Father* Chrys. *knoweth that ye have need of these things.* CHRYS. He said Hom. not " God," but *your Father*, to incite them to greater con- 22. in Matt. fidence. For who is a father, and would not allow the want of his children to be supplied? But He adds another thing also; for you could not say that He is indeed a father, yet knoweth not that we are in need of these things. For He who has created our nature, knoweth its wants.

AMBROSE; But He goes on to shew, that neither at the present time, nor hereafter, will grace be lacking to the faithful, if only they who desire heavenly things seek not earthly; for it is unworthy for men to care for meats, who fight for a kingdom. The king knoweth wherewithal he shall support and clothe his own family. Therefore it follows, *But seek ye first the kingdom of God, and all these things shall* Chrys. *be added unto you.* CHRYS. Now Christ promises not only ubi sup. a kingdom, but also riches with it; for if we rescue from cares those who neglecting their own concerns are diligent about ours, much more will God. BEDE; For He declares that there is one thing which is primarily given, another which is superadded; that we ought to make eternity our aim, the present life our business.

32. Fear not, little flock; for it is your Father's good pleasure to give you the kingdom.

33. Sell that ye have, and give alms; provide yourselves bags which wax not old, a treasure in the heavens that faileth not, where no thief approacheth, neither moth corrupteth.

34. For where your treasure is, there will your heart be also.

GLOSS. Our Lord having removed the care of temporal things from the hearts of His disciples, now banishes fear from them, from which superfluous cares proceed, saying, *Fear not, &c.* THEOPHYL. By the little flock, our Lord signifies those who are willing to become His disciples, or because in this world the Saints seem little because of their voluntary poverty, or because they are outnumbered by the multitude of Angels, who incomparably exceed all that we can boast of. The name *little* our Lord gives to the company of the elect, either from comparison with the greater number of the reprobate, or rather because of their devout humility.

CYRIL; But why they ought not to fear, He shews, adding, *for it is your Father's good pleasure;* as if He says, How shall He who gives such precious things be wearied in shewing mercy towards you? For although His flock is little both in nature and number and renown, yet the goodness of the Father has granted even to this little flock the lot of heavenly spirits, that is, the kingdom of heaven. Therefore that you may possess the kingdom of heaven, despise this world's wealth. Hence it is added, *Sell that ye have, &c.* BEDE; As if He says, Fear not lest they who warfare for the kingdom of God, should be in want of the necessaries of this life. But sell that ye have for alms' sake, which then is done worthily, when a man having once for his Lord's sake forsaken all that he hath, nevertheless afterwards labours with his hands that he may be able both to gain his living, and give alms. CHRYS. For there is no sin which almsgiving does not avail to blot out. It is a salve adapted to every wound. But almsgiving has to do not only with money, but with all matters also

Gloss. non occ.

Chrys. Hom. 25. in Act.

wherein man succours man, as when the physician heals,

Greg. Orat.14. and the wise man gives counsel. GREG. NAZ. Now I fear lest you should think deeds of mercy to be not necessary to you, but voluntary. I also thought so, but was alarmed at the goats placed on the left hand, not because they robbed, but did

Chrys. ubi sup. not minister unto Christ among the poor. CHRYS. For without alms it is impossible to see the kingdom. For as a fountain if it keeps its waters within itself grows foul, so also rich men when they retain every thing in their possession.

Basil. reg. brev. ad int. 92. BASIL; But some one will ask, upon what grounds ought we to sell that which we have? Is it that these things are by nature hurtful, or because of the temptation to our souls? To this we must answer, first, that every thing existing in the world if it were in itself evil, would be no creation

1 Tim. 4, 4. of God, for *every creation of God is good.* And next, that our Lord's command teaches us not to cast away as evil what we possess, but to distribute, saying, *and give alms.*

CYRIL; Now perhaps this command is irksome to the rich, yet to those who are of a sound mind, it is not unprofitable, for their treasure is the kingdom of heaven. Hence it follows, *Provide for yourselves bags which wax not old, &c.* BEDE; That is, by doing alms, the reward of which abideth for ever; which must not be taken as a command that no money be kept by the saints either for their own, or the use of

Matt. 4, 12. John 12, 6. the poor, since we read that our Lord Himself, to whom the angels ministered, had a bag in which he kept the offerings of the faithful; but that God should not be obeyed for the sake of such things, and righteousness be not forsaken from fear of poverty. GREG. NYSS. But He bids us lay up our visible and earthly treasures where the power of corruption does not reach, and hence He adds, *a treasure that faileth not, &c.*

THEOPHYL. As if He said, " Here the moth corrupts, but there is no corruption in heaven." Then because there are some things which the moth does not corrupt, He goes on to speak of the thief. For gold the moth corrupts not, but the thief takes away.

BEDE; Whether then should it be simply understood, that money kept faileth, but given away to our neighbour bears everlasting fruit in heaven; or, that the treasure of good works, if it be stored up for the sake of earthly advantage, is soon corrupted and perishes; but if it be laid up solely from heavenly motives, neither outwardly by the favour of men, as by the thief which steals from without, nor inwardly by vainglory, as by the moth which devours within, can it be defiled. GLOSS. Or, the thieves are heretics and evil spirits, who are bent upon depriving us of spiritual things. The moth which secretly frets the garments is envy, which mars good desires, and bursts the bonds of charity.

THEOPHYL. Moreover, because all things are not taken away by theft, He adds a more excellent reason, and one which admits of no objection whatever, saying, *For where your treasure is, there will your hearts be also ;* as if He says, " Suppose that neither moth corrupts nor thief takes away, yet this very thing, namely, to have the heart fixed in a buried treasure, and to sink to the earth a divine work, that is, the soul, how great a punishment it deserves." EUSEB. For every man naturally dwells upon that which is the object of his desire, and thither he directs all his thoughts, where he supposes his whole interest to rest. If any one then has his whole mind and affections, which he calls the heart, set on things of this present life, he lives in earthly things. But if he has given his mind to heavenly things, there will his mind be ; so that he seems with his body only to live with men, but with his mind to have already reached the heavenly mansion. BEDE; Now this must not only be felt concerning love of money, but all the passions. Luxurious feasts are treasures; also the sports of the gay and the desires of the lover.

35. Let your loins be girded about, and your lights burning ;

36. And ye yourselves like unto men that wait for their lord, when he will return from the wedding; that when he cometh and knocketh, they may open unto him immediately.

37. Blessed are those servants, whom the lord when he cometh shall find watching: verily I say unto you, that he shall gird himself, and make them to sit down to meat, and will come forth and serve them.

38. And if he shall come in the second watch, or in the third watch, and find them so, blessed are those servants.

39. And this know, that if the goodman of the house had known what hour the thief would come, he would have watched, and not have suffered his house to be broken through.

40. Be ye therefore ready also : for the Son of man cometh at an hour when ye think not.

THEOPHYL. Our Lord having taught His disciples moderation, taking from them all care and conceit of this life, now leads them on to serve and obey, saying, *Let your loins be girded,* that is, always ready to do the work of your Lord, *and your lamps burning,* that is, do not lead a life in darkness, but have with you the light of reason, shewing you what to do and what to avoid. For this world is the night, but they have their loins girded, who follow a practical or active life. For such is the condition of servants who must have with them also lamps burning; that is, the gift of discernment, that the active man may be able to distinguish not only what he ought to do, but in what way; otherwise men rush down the precipice of pride. But we must observe, that He first orders *our loins to be girded,* secondly, *our lamps to be burning.* For first indeed comes action, then reflection, which is an enlightening of the mind. Let us then strive to exercise the virtues, that we may have two lamps burning, that is, the conception of the mind ever shining forth in the soul, by which we are ourselves enlightened, and learning, whereby we enlighten others. MAXIM. Or, he teaches us to keep our lamps burning, by prayer and contemplation and spiritual love. CYRIL; Or, to be girded, signifies activity and readiness to undergo evils from regard to Divine love. But the burning of the lamp signifies that we should not suffer any to live in the darkness of ignorance. GREG. Or else, we gird our loins when by continence we control the lusts of the flesh. For the lust of men is in their loins, and of women in their womb; by the name of loins, therefore, from the principal sex, lust is signified. But

Greg. Hom. 13. in Evang.

because it is a small thing not to do evil, unless also men strive to labour in good works, it is added, *And your lamps burning in your hands ;* for we hold burning lamps in our hands, when by good works we shew forth bright examples to our neighbours. AUG. Or, He teaches us also to gird our loins for the sake of keeping ourselves from the love of the things of this world, and to have our lamps burning, that this thing may be done with a true end and right intention. GREG. But if a man has both of these, whosoever he be, nothing remains for him but that he should place his whole expectation on the coming of the Redeemer. Therefore it is added, *And be ye like to men that wait for their Lord, when he will return from the wedding, &c.* For our Lord went to the wedding, when ascending up into heaven as the Bridegroom He joined to Himself the heavenly multitude of angels. THEOPHYL. Daily also in the heavens He betroths the souls of the Saints, whom Paul or another offers to Him, as a chaste virgin. But He returns from the celebration of the heavenly marriage, perhaps to all at the end of the whole world, when He shall come from heaven in the glory of the Father; perhaps also every hour standing suddenly present at the death of each individual. CYRIL; Now consider that He comes from the wedding as from a festival, which God is ever keeping; for nothing can cause sadness to the Incorruptible Nature. GREG. NYSS. Or else, when the wedding was celebrated and the Church received into the secret bridal chamber, the angels were expecting the return of the King to His own natural blessedness. And after their example we order our life, that as they living together without evil, are prepared to welcome their Lord's return, so we also, keeping watch at the door, should make ourselves ready to obey Him when He comes knocking ; for it follows, *that when he cometh and knocketh, they may open to him immediately.*

GREG. For He comes when He hastens to judgment, but He knocks, when already by the pain of sickness He denotes that death is at hand; to whom we immediately open if we receive Him with love. For he who trembles to depart from the body, has no wish to open to the Judge knocking, and dreads to see that Judge whom he remembers to have despised. But he who rests secure concerning his hope and works, immediately opens to Him that knocks ; for when he is aware of the

Aug. de Qu. Ev. lib. ii. q. 25.

Greg. ubi sup.

2 Cor. 11, 2.

Greg. Hom.11. in Cant.

Greg. ubi sup.

time of death drawing near, he grows joyful, because of the glory of his reward; and hence it is added, *Blessed are the servants whom the Lord when he cometh shall find watching.* He watches who keeps the eyes of his mind open to behold the true light; who by his works maintains that which he beholds, who drives from himself the darkness of sloth and carelessness.

Greg. ubi sup. GREG. NYSS. For the sake then of keeping watch, our Lord advised above that our loins should be girded, and our lamps burning, for light when placed before the eyes drives away sleep. The loins also when tied with a girdle, make the body incapable of sleep. For he who is girt about with chastity, and illuminated by a pure conscience, continues wakeful.

CYRIL; When then our Lord coming shall find us awake and girded, having our hearts enlightened, He will then pronounce us blessed, for it follows, *Verily I say unto you, that he shall gird himself;* from which we perceive that He will recompense us in like manner, seeing that He will gird Himself with those that are girded. ORIGEN; For He will be girded about His loins with righteousness. GREG. By which He girds Himself, that is, prepares for judgment. THEOPHYL. Or, He will gird Himself, in that He imparts not the whole fulness of blessings, but confines it within a certain measure. For who can comprehend God how great He is? Therefore are the Seraphims said to veil their countenance, because of the excellence of the Divine brightness. It follows, *and will make them to sit down;* for as a man sitting down causes his whole body to rest, so in the future coming the Saints will have complete rest; for here they have not rest for the body, but there together with their souls their spiritual bodies partaking of immortality will rejoice in perfect rest. CYRIL; He will then make them to sit down as a refreshment to the weary, setting before them spiritual enjoyments, and ordering a sumptuous table of His gifts.

Isn. 11, 5.
Greg. Hom. 13. in Ev.

DIONYSIUS AR. The " sitting down" is taken to be the repose from many labours, a life without annoyance, the divine conversation of those that dwell in the region of light enriched with all holy affections, and an abundant pouring forth of all gifts, whereby they are filled with joy. For the reason why Jesus makes them to sit down, is that He might give them perpetual rest, and distribute to them blessings without number. Therefore it follows, *And will pass over and serve them.*

Dion. in Ep. ad Tit.

transiens.

THEOPHYL. That is, Give back to them, as it were, an equal return, that as they served Him, so also He will serve them. GREG. But He is said to be *passing over*, when He returns Greg. from the judgment to His kingdom. Or the Lord passes to Hom. 13. in us after the judgment, and raises us from the form of His Ev. humanity to a contemplation of His divinity.

CYRIL; Our Lord knew the proneness of human infirmity to sin, but because He is merciful, He does not allow us to despair, but rather has compassion, and gives us repentance as a saving remedy. And therefore He adds, *And if he shall come in the second watch, &c.* For they who keep watch on the walls of cities, or observe the attacks of the enemy, divide the night into three or four watches. GREG. The first watch Greg. then is the earliest time of our life, that is, childhood, the ubi sup. second youth and manhood, but the third represents old age. He then who is unwilling to watch in the first, let him keep even the second. And he who is unwilling in the second, let him not lose the remedies of the third watch, that he who has neglected conversion in childhood, may at least in the time of youth or old age recover himself. CYRIL; Of the first watch, however, he makes no mention, for childhood is not punished by God, but obtains pardon; but the second and third age owe obedience to God, and the leading of an honest life according to His will. GREEK Ex. Or, to the first Severus. watch belong those who live more carefully, as having gained the first step, but to the second, those who keep the measure of a moderate conversation, but to the third, those who are below these. And the same must be supposed of the fourth, and if it should so happen also of the fifth. For there are different measures of life, and a good rewarder metes out to every man according to his deserts. THEOPHYL. Or since the watches are the hours of the night which lull men to sleep, you must understand that there are also in our life certain hours which make us happy if we are found awake. Does any one seize your goods? Are your children dead? Are you accused? But if at these times you have done nothing against the commandments of God, He will find you watching in the second and third watch, that is, at the evil time, which brings destructive sleep to idle souls.

GREG. But to shake off the sloth of our minds, even our Greg. ubi sup.

external losses are by a similitude set before us. For it is added, *And this know, that if the goodman of the house had known what hour the thief would come.* THEOPHYL. Some understand this thief to be the devil, the house, the soul, the goodman of the house, man. This interpretation, however, does not seem to agree with what follows. For the Lord's coming is compared to the thief as suddenly at hand, according to the word of the Apostle, *The day of the Lord so cometh as a thief in the night.* And hence also it is here added, *Be ye also ready, for the Son of man cometh at an hour when ye think not.* GREG. Or else; unknown to the master the thief breaks into the house, because while the spirit sleeps instead of guarding itself, death comes unexpectedly, and breaks into the dwelling place of our flesh. But he would resist the thief if he were watching, because being on his guard against the coming of the Judge, who secretly seizes his soul, he would by repentance go to meet Him, lest he should perish impenitent. But the last hour our Lord wishes to be unknown to us, in order as we cannot foresee it, we may be unceasingly preparing for it.

1 Thess. 5, 2.

Greg. Hom. 13.inEv.

41. Then Peter said unto him, Lord, speakest thou this parable unto us, or even to all?

42. And the Lord said, Who then is that faithful and wise steward, whom his lord shall make ruler over his household, to give them their portion of meat in due season?

43. Blessed is that servant, whom his lord when he cometh shall find so doing.

44. Of a truth I say unto you, that he will make him ruler over all that he hath.

45. But and if that servant say in his heart, My lord delayeth his coming; and shall begin to beat the menservants and maidens, and to eat and drink, and to be drunken;

46. The lord of that servant will come in a day when he looketh not for him, and at an hour when

he is not aware, and will cut him in sunder, and will appoint him his portion with the unbelievers.

THEOPHYL. Peter, to whom the Church had already been committed, as having the care of all things, inquires whether our Lord put forth this parable to all. As it follows, *Then Peter said unto him, Lord, speakest thou this parable unto us, or even unto all?* BEDE; Our Lord had taught two things in the preceding parable unto all, even that He would come suddenly, and that they ought to be ready and waiting for Him. But it is not very plain concerning which of these, or whether both, Peter asked the question, or whom he compared to himself and his companions, when he said, *Speakest thou to us, or to all?* Yet in truth by these words, *us* and *all*, he must be supposed to mean none other than the Apostles, and those like to the Apostles, and all other faithful men; or Christians, and unbelievers; or those who dying separately, that is, singly, both unwillingly indeed and willingly, receive the coming of their Judge, and those who when the universal judgment comes are to be found alive in the flesh. Now it is marvellous if Peter doubted that all must live soberly, piously, and justly, who wait for a blessed hope, or that the judgment will to each and all be unexpected. It therefore remains to be supposed, that knowing these two things, he asked about that which he might not know, namely, whether those sublime commands of a heavenly life in which He bade us sell what we have and provide bags which wax not old, and watch with our loins girded, and lamps burning, belonged to the Apostles only, and those like unto them, or to all who were to be saved.

CYRIL; Now to the courageous rightly belong the great and difficult of God's holy commandments, but to those who have not yet attained to such virtue, belong those things from which all difficulty is excluded. Our Lord therefore uses a very obvious example, to shew that the above-mentioned command is suited to those who have been admitted into the rank of disciples, for it follows, *And the Lord said, Who then is that faithful steward?* AMBROSE; Or else, the form of the first command is a general one adapted to all, but the following example seems to be proposed to the stewards, that is, the priests; and therefore it follows, *And the Lord said, Who then is that faithful and wise steward, whom his Lord shall make ruler over his household, to give them their portion of meat in due season?*

THEOPHYL. The above-mentioned parable relates to all the faithful in common, but now hear what suits the Apostles and teachers. For I ask, where will be found the steward, that possesses in himself faithfulness and wisdom? for as in the management of goods, whether a man be careless yet faithful to his master, or else wise yet unfaithful, the things of the master perish; so also in the things of God there is need of faithfulness and wisdom. For I have known many servants of God, and faithful men, who because they were unable to manage ecclesiastical affairs, have destroyed not only possessions, but souls, exercising towards sinners indiscreet virtue by extravagant rules of penance or unseasonable indulgence.

Chrys.
Hom.
77. in
Matt.
CHRYS. But our Lord here asks the question not as ignorant, who was a faithful and wise steward, but wishing to imply the rareness of such, and the greatness of this kind of chief government.

THEOPHYL. Whosoever then has been found a faithful and wise steward, let him bear rule over the Lord's household, that he may give them their portion of meat in due season, either the word of doctrine by which their souls are fed, or

Aug. de
Qu. Ev.
l.ii.c.26.
the example of works by which their life is fashioned. AUG. Now he says *portion*, because of suiting His measure to the capacity of his several hearers.

Isid.l. 3.
Ep. 170.
ISIDORE; It was added also *in their due season*, because a benefit not conferred at its proper time is rendered vain, and loses the name of a benefit. The same bread is not equally coveted by the hungry man, and him that is satisfied. But with respect to this servant's reward for his stewardship, He adds, *Blessed is that servant whom his Lord when he*

Basil. in
Procem.
in reg.
fus.
cometh shall find so doing. BASIL; He says not, ' doing,' as if by chance, but *so doing*. For not only conquest is honourable, but to contend lawfully, which is to perform each thing as we have been commanded. CYRIL; Thus the faithful and wise servant prudently giving out in due season

the servants' food, that is, their spiritual meat, will be blessed according to the Saviour's word, in that he will obtain still greater things, and will be thought worthy of the rewards which are due to friends. Hence it follows, *Of a truth I say unto you, that he will make him ruler over all that he hath.* BEDE; For whatever difference there is in the merits of good hearers and good teachers, such also there is in their rewards; for the one whom when He cometh He finds watching, He will make to sit down; but the others whom He finds faithful and wise stewards, He will place over all that He hath, that is, over all the joys of the kingdom of heaven, not certainly that they alone shall have power over them, but that they shall more abundantly than the other saints enjoy eternal possession of them.

THEOPHYL. Or, *he will make him ruler over all that he hath,* not only over His own household, but that earthly things as well as heavenly shall obey him. As it was with Joshua the son of Nun, and Elias, the one commanding the sun, the other the clouds; and all the Saints as God's friends use the things of God. Whosoever also passes his life virtuously, and has kept in due submission his servants, that is, anger and desire, supplies to them their portion of food in due season; to anger indeed that he may feel it against those who hate God, but to desire that he may exercise the necessary provision for the flesh, ordering it unto God. Such an one, I say, will be set over all things which the Lord hath, being thought worthy to look into all things by the light of contemplation.

CHRYS. But our Lord not only by the honours kept in store for the good, but by threats of punishment upon the bad, leads the hearer to correction, as it follows, *But if that servant shall say in his heart, My Lord delayeth his coming.* BEDE; Observe that it is counted among the vices of a bad servant that he thought the coming of his Lord slow, yet it is not numbered among the virtues of the good that he hoped it would come quickly, but only that he ministered faithfully. There is nothing then better than to submit patiently to be ignorant of that which can not be known, but to strive only that we be found worthy. Chrys. Hom. 77. in Matt.

THEOPHYL. Now from not considering the time of our departure, there proceed many evils. For surely if we thought that our Lord was coming, and that the end of our life was at hand, we should sin the less. Hence it follows, *And shall begin to strike the man servants and maidens, and to eat and drink and be drunken.* BEDE; In this servant is declared the condemnation of all evil rulers, who, forsaking the fear of the Lord, not only give themselves up to pleasures, but also provoke with injuries those who are put under them. Although these words may be also understood figuratively, meaning to corrupt the hearts of the weak by an evil example; *and to eat, drink, and be drunken,* to be absorbed in the vices and allurements of the world, which overthrow the mind of man. But concerning his punishment it is added, *The Lord of that servant will come in a day when he looketh not for him,* that is, the day of his judgment or death, and will cut him in

Basil. in lib. de Sp. San. c. 16.

sunder. BASIL; The body indeed is not divided, so that one part indeed should be exposed to torments, the other escape. For this is a fable, nor is it a part of just judgment when the whole has offended that half only should suffer punishment; nor is the soul cut in sunder, seeing that the whole possesses a guilty consciousness, and cooperates with the body to work evil; but its division is the eternal severing of the soul from the Spirit. For now although the grace of the Spirit is not in the unworthy, yet it seems ever to be at hand expecting their turning to salvation, but at that time it will be altogether cut off from the soul. The Holy Spirit then is the prize of the just, and the chief condemnation of sinners, since they who are unworthy will lose Him. BEDE; Or He will cut him in sunder, by separating him from the communion of the faithful, and dismissing him to those who have never attained unto the faith. Hence it follows, *And will appoint him his portion with the unbelievers;* for *he who has no care for his own, and those of his own house, has denied the faith, and is worse than an infidel.* THEOPHYL. Rightly also shall the unbelieving steward receive his portion with the unbelievers, because he was without true faith.

1 Tim. 5, 8.

47. And that servant, which knew his lord's will, and prepared not himself, neither did according to his will, shall be beaten with many stripes.

48. But he that knew not, and did commit things worthy of stripes, shall be beaten with few stripes. For unto whomsoever much is given, of him shall be much required: and to whom men have committed much, of him they will ask the more.

THEOPHYL. Our Lord here points to something still greater and more terrible, for the unfaithful steward shall not only be deprived of the grace he had, so that it should profit him nothing in escaping punishment, but the greatness of his dignity shall the rather become a cause of his condemnation. Hence it is said, *And that servant who knew his lord's will and did it not, shall be beaten with many stripes.* CHRYS. For all things are not judged alike in all, but greater knowledge is an occasion of greater punishment. Therefore shall the Priest, committing the same sin with the people, suffer a far heavier penalty. _{Chrys. Hom. 26. in Matt.}

CYRIL; For the man of understanding who has given up his will to baser things will shamelessly implore pardon, because he has committed an inexcusable sin, departing as it were maliciously from the will of God, but the rude or unlearned man will more reasonably ask for pardon of the avenger. Hence it is added, *But he that knew not, and did commit things worthy of stripes, shall be beaten with few stripes.* THEOPHYL. Here some object, saying, He is deservedly punished who, knowing the will of His Lord, pursues it not; but why is the ignorant punished? Because when he might have known, he would not, but being himself slothful, was the cause of his own ignorance.

BASIL; But you will say, If the one indeed received many stripes, and the other few, how do some say He assigns no end to punishments? But we must know, that what is here said assigns neither measure nor end of punishments, but their differences. For a man may deserve unquenchable fire, to either a slight or more intense degree of heat, and the worm that dieth not with greater or more violent gnawings. THEOPHYL. But he goes on to shew why teachers and learned men deserve a severer punishment, as it is said, *For unto whomsoever much is given, of him shall be much required.* _{Basil. in reg. brev. 267.}

Teachers indeed are given the grace to perform miracles, but entrusted the grace of speech and learning. But not in that which is given, He says, is any thing more to be sought, but in that which is entrusted or deposited; for the grace of the word needs increase. But from a teacher more is required, for he should not lie idle, but improve the talent of the word. BEDE; Or else, much is often given also to certain individuals, upon whom is bestowed the knowledge of God's will, and the means of performing what they know; much also is given to him to whom, together with his own salvation, is committed the care also of feeding our Lord's flock. Upon those then who are gifted with more abundant grace a heavier penalty falls; but the mildest punishment of all will be theirs, who, beyond the guilt they originally contracted, have added none besides; and in all who have added, theirs will be the more tolerable who have committed fewest iniquities.

49. I am come to send fire on the earth; and what will I, if it be already kindled?

50. But I have a baptism to be baptized with; and how am I straitened till it be accomplished!

51. Suppose ye that I am come to give peace on earth? I tell you, Nay; but rather division:

52. For from henceforth there shall be five in one house divided, three against two, and two against three.

53. The father shall be divided against the son, and the son against the father; the mother against the daughter, and the daughter against the mother; the mother in law against her daughter in law, and the daughter in law against her mother in law.

AMBROSE; To stewards, that is, to Priests, the preceding words seem to have been addressed, that they may thereby know that hereafter a heavier punishment awaits them, if, intent upon the world's pleasures, they have neglected the charge of their Lord's household, and the people entrusted to their care. But as it profiteth little to be recalled from error by the fear of punishment, and far greater is the privilege of charity and love, our Lord therefore kindles in men the desire of acquiring the divine nature, saying, *I came to send fire on earth*, not indeed that He is the Consumer of good men, but the Author of good will, who purifies the golden vessels of the Lord's house, but burns up the straw and stubble. CYRIL.; Now it is the way of holy Scripture to use sometimes the term *fire*, of holy and divine words. For as they who know how to purify gold and silver, destroy the dross by fire, so the Saviour by the teaching of the Gospel in the power of the Spirit cleanses the minds of those who believe in Him. This then is that wholesome and useful fire by which the inhabitants of earth, in a manner cold and dead through sin, revive to a life of piety. CHRYS. For by the earth He now means not that which we tread under our feet, but that which was fashioned by His hands, namely, man, upon whom the Lord pours out fire for the consuming of sins, and the renewing of souls. TIT. BOST. And we must here believe that Christ came down from heaven. For if He had come from earth to earth, He would not say, *I came to send fire upon the earth*. CYRIL; But our Lord was hastening the kindling of the fire, and hence it follows, *And what will I, save that it be kindled*[a]*?* For already some of the Jews believed, of whom the first were the holy Apostles, but the fire once lighted in Judæa was about to take possession of the whole world, yet not till after the dispensation of His Passion had been accomplished. Hence it follows, *But I have a baptism to be baptized with.* For before the holy cross and His resurrection from the dead, in Judæa only was the news told of His preaching and miracles; but after that the Jews in their rage had slain the Prince of life, then commanded He His Apostles, saying, *Go and teach all nations.* GREG. Or else, fire is sent upon the earth, when by the fiery breath of the Holy Spirit, the earthly mind has all its carnal desires burnt up, but inflamed with spiritual love, bewails the evil it has done; and so the earth is burnt, when the conscience accusing itself, the heart of the sinner is consumed in the sorrow of repentance.

nisi ut accendatur

Matt. 28, 19. Greg. in Ezech. lib. i. Hom. 2.

---

[a] Nisi ut, is the reading of the Vulg. and Germ. versions, and nisi of several   others. See Scholz in loc.

BEDE; But He adds, *I have a baptism to be baptized with,* that is, I have first to be sprinkled with the drops of My own Blood, and then to inflame the hearts of believers by the fire of the Spirit.

AMBROSE; But so great was our Lord's condescension, that He tells us He has a desire of inspiring us with devotion, of accomplishing perfection in us, and of hastening His passion for us; as it follows, *And how am I straitened till it be accomplished?* BEDE; Some manuscripts have, "And how am I coangor anguished," that is, grieved. For though He had in Himself nothing to grieve Him, yet was He afflicted by our woes, and at the time of death He betrayed the anguish which He underwent not from the fear of His death, but from the delay of our redemption. For he who is troubled until he reaches perfection, is secure of perfection, for the condition of bodily affections not the dread of death offends him. For he who has put on the body must suffer all things which are of the body, hunger, thirst, vexation, sorrow; but the Divine nature knows no change from such feelings. At the same time He also shews, that in the conflict of suffering consists the death of the body, peace of mind has no struggle with grief.

BEDE; But the manner in which after the baptism of His passion and the coming of the spiritual fire the earth will be burnt, He declares as follows, *Suppose ye that I am to Eph. 2, give peace, &c.* CYRIL; What sayest thou, O Lord? Didst 14. thou not come to give peace, Who art made peace for us? Col. 1, 20. making peace by Thy cross with things in earth and things John 14, in heaven; Who saidst, *My peace I give unto you.* But it 27. is plain that peace is indeed a good, but sometimes hurtful, and separating us from the love of God, that is, when by it we unite with those who keep away from God. And for this reason we teach the faithful to avoid earthly bonds. Hence it follows, *For from henceforth there shall be five in one house divided, three against two, &c.* AMBROSE; Though the connexion would seem to be of six persons, father and son, mother and daughter, mother in law and daughter in law, yet are they five, for the mother and the mother in law may be taken as the same, since she who is the mother of the son, is Chrys. the mother in law of his wife. CHRYS. Now hereby He non occ.

declared a future event, for it so happened in the same house
that there have been believers whose fathers wished to bring
them to unbelief; but the power of Christ's doctrines has so
prevailed, that fathers were left by sons, mothers by daughters,
and children by parents.   For the faithful in Christ were content not only to despise their own, but at the same time also
to suffer all things as long as they were not without the worship of their faith.   But if He were mere man, how would it
have occurred to Him to conceive it possible that He should
be more loved by fathers than their children were, by children
than their fathers, by husbands than their wives, and they too
not in one house or a hundred, but throughout the world?
And not only did he predict this, but accomplish it in deed.

AMBROSE; Now in a mystical sense the one house is one
man, but by two we often mean the soul and the body.
But if two things meet together, each one has its part;
there is one which obeys, another which rules.   But there
are three conditions of the soul, one concerned with reason,
another with desire, the third with anger.   Two then are
divided against three, and three against two.   For by the
coming of Christ, man who was material became rational.   We
were carnal and earthly, God sent His Spirit into our hearts, Gal. 4,
and we became spiritual children.   We may also say, that in 6.
the house there are five others, that is, smell, touch, taste, sight,
and hearing.   If then with respect to those things which we
hear or see, separating the sense of sight and hearing, we shut
out the worthless pleasures of the body which we take in by
our taste, touch, and smell, we divide two against three, because the mind is not carried away by the allurements of vice.
Or if we understand the five bodily senses, already are the
vices and sins of the body divided among themselves.   The
flesh and the soul may also seem separated from the smell,
touch, and taste of pleasure, for while the stronger sex of reason
is impelled, as it were, to manly affections, the flesh strives to
keep the reason more effeminate.   Out of these then there
spring up the motions of different desires, but when the soul
returns to itself it renounces the degenerate offspring.   The
flesh also bewails that it is fastened down by its desires (which
it has borne to itself,) as by the thorns of the world.   But
pleasure is a kind of daughter in law of the body and soul, and

is wedded to the motions of foul desire. As long then as there remained in one house the vices conspiring together with one consent, there seemed to be no division; but when Christ sent fire upon the earth which should burn out the offences of the heart, or the sword which should pierce the very secrets of the heart, then the flesh and the soul renewed by the mysteries of regeneration cast off the bond of connection with their offspring. So that parents are divided against their children, while the intemperate man gets rid of his intemperate desires, and the soul has no more fellowship with crime. Children also are divided against parents when men having become regenerate renounce their old vices, and younger pleasure flies from the rule of piety, as from the discipline of a strict house. BEDE; Or in another way. By three are signified those who have faith in the Trinity, by two the unbelievers who depart from the unity of the faith. But the father is the devil, whose children we were by following him, but when that heavenly fire came down, it separated us from one another, and shewed us another Father who is in heaven. The mother is the Synagogue, the daughter is the Primitive Church, who had to bear the persecution of that same synagogue, from whom she derived her birth, and whom she did herself in the truth of the faith contradict. The mother in law is the Synagogue, the daughter in law the Gentile Church, for Christ the husband of the Church is the son of the Synagogue, according to the flesh. The Synagogue then was divided both against its daughter in law, and its daughter, persecuting believers of each people. But they also were divided against their mother in law and mother, because they wished to abolish the circumcision of the flesh.

54. And he said also to the people, When ye see a cloud rise out of the west, straightway ye say, There cometh a shower; and so it is.

55. And when ye see the south wind blow, ye say, There will be heat; and it cometh to pass.

56. Ye hypocrites, ye can discern the face of the sky and of the earth; but how is it that ye do not discern this time?

57. Yea, and why even of yourselves judge ye not what is right?

THEOPHYL. When He spoke about preaching, and called it a sword, His hearers may have been troubled, not knowing what He meant. And therefore our Lord adds, that as men determine the state of the weather by certain signs, so ought they to know His coming. And this is what he means by saying, *When ye see a cloud rise out of the west, straightway ye say, There cometh a shower. And when ye see the south wind blowing, ye say, There will be heat, &c.* As if He says, Your words and works shew me to be opposed to you. Ye may therefore suppose that I came not to give peace, but the storm and whirlwind. For I am a cloud, and I come out of the west, that is, from human nature; which has been long since clothed with the thick darkness of sin. I came also to send fire, that is, to stir up heat. For I am the strong south wind, opposed to the northern coldness. BEDE; Or, they who from the change of the elements can easily when they like predetermine the state of the weather, might if they wished also understand the time of our Lord's coming from the words of the Prophets. CYRIL; For the prophets have in many ways foretold the mystery of Christ; it became them therefore, if they were wise, to stretch their prospect beyond to the future, nor will ignorance of the time to come avail them after the present life. For there will be wind and rain, and a future punishment by fire; and this is signified when it is said, *A shower cometh.* It became them also not to be ignorant of the time of salvation, that is, the coming of the Saviour, through whom perfect piety entered into the world. And this is meant when it is said, *Ye say that there will be heat.* Whence it follows in censure of them, *Ye hypocrites, ye can discern the face of the sky and the earth, but how is it that ye do not discern this time?*

BASIL; Now we must observe, that conjectures concerning the stars are necessary to the life of man, as long as we do not push our searches into their signs beyond due limits. For it is possible to discover some things with respect to coming rain, still more concerning heat and the force of the winds, whether partial or universal, stormy or gentle. But

Basil. in Hexam. Hom. 6, 4.

the great advantage that is rendered to life by these conjectures is known to every one. For it is of importance to the sailor to prognosticate the dangers of storms, to the traveller the changes of the weather, to the husbandman the abundant supply of his fruits.

BEDE; But lest any of the people should allege their ignorance of the prophetical books as a reason why they could not discern the courses of the times, He carefully adds, *And why even of yourselves judge ye not what is right*, shewing them that although unlearned they might still by their natural ability discern Him, who did works such as none other man did, to be above man, and to be God, and that therefore after the injustice of this world, the just judgment of the creation would come. ORIGEN; But had it not been implanted in our nature to judge what is right, our Lord would never have said this.

58. When thou goest with thine adversary to the magistrate, as thou art in the way, give diligence that thou mayest be delivered from him; lest he hale thee to the judge, and the judge deliver thee to the officer, and the officer cast thee into prison.

59. I tell thee, thou shalt not depart thence, till thou hast paid the very last mite.

THEOPHYL. Our Lord having described a rightful difference, next teaches us a rightful reconciliation, saying, *When thou goest with thine adversary to the magistrate, as thou art in the way, give diligence that thou mayest be delivered from him, &c.* As if He says, When thine adversary is bringing thee to judgment, give diligence, that is, try every method, to be released from him. Or give diligence, that is, although thou hast nothing, borrow in order that thou may be released from him, lest he summon thee before the judge, as it follows, *Lest he hale thee to the judge, and the judge deliver thee to the officer, and the officer cast thee into prison.* CYRIL; Where thou wilt suffer want until thou payest the last farthing; and this is what He adds, *I say unto you, thou shalt not depart hence.*

CHRYS. It seems to me that He is speaking of the present Chrys. judges, and of the way to the present judgment, and of the Hom. 16. in prison of this world. For by these things which are visible Matt. and at hand, ignorant men are wont to gain improvement. For often He gives a lesson, not only from future good and evil but from present, for the sake of His ruder hearers. AMBROSE; Or our adversary is the devil, who lays his baits for sin, that he may have those his partners in punishment who were his accomplices in crime; our adversary is also every vicious practice. Lastly, our adversary is an evil conscience, which affects us both in this world, and will accuse and betray us in the next. Let us then give heed, while we are in this life's course, that we may be delivered from every bad act as from an evil enemy. Nay, while we are going with our adversary to the magistrate, as we are in the way, we should condemn our fault. But who is the magistrate, but He in whose hands is all power? But the Magistrate delivers the guilty to the Judge, that is, to Him, to whom He gives the power over the quick and dead, namely, Jesus Christ, through Whom the secrets are made manifest, and the punishment of wicked works awarded. He delivers to the officer, and the officer casts into prison, for He says, *Bind him hand and* Matt. *foot, and cast him into outer darkness.* And he shews that 22, 12. His officers are the angels, of whom he says, *The angels shall* Matt. *come forth, and sever the wicked from among the just, and* 13, 49. *shall cast them into the furnace of fire;* but it is added, *I tell thee, thou shalt not depart thence till thou hast paid the very last mite.* For as they who pay money on interest do not get rid of the debt of interest before that the amount of the whole principal is paid even up to the least sum in every kind of payment, so by the compensation of love and the other acts, or by each particular kind of satisfaction the punishment of sin is cancelled. ORIGEN; Or else, He here introduces four characters, the adversary, the magistrate, the officer, and the judge. But with Matthew the character of the magistrate is left out, and instead of the officer *a servant* is introduced. They differ also in that the one has written *a farthing,* the other *a mite,* but each has called it the *last.* Now we say that all men have present with them two angels, a bad one who encourages them to wicked deeds, a good one who persuades all that is best. Now the former, our adversary whenever we sin rejoices, knowing that he has an occasion for exultations and boasting with the prince of the world, who sent him. But in the Greek, " the adversary" is written with the article, to signify that he is one out of many, seeing that each individual is under the ruler of his nation. Give diligence then that you may be delivered from your adversary, or from the ruler to whom the adversary drags you, by having wisdom, justice, fortitude, and temperance. But if you have given diligence, let it be in Him who says, *I am the life*, otherwise the adversary will hale thee to the judge. Now he says, *hale*, to point out that they are forced unwillingly to condemnation. But I know no other judge but our Lord Jesus Christ who delivers to the officer. Each of us have our own officers; the officers exercise rule over us, if we owe any thing. If I paid every man every thing, I come to the officers and answer with a fearless heart, " I owe them nothing." But if I am a debtor, the officer will cast me into prison, nor will he suffer me to go out from thence until I have paid every debt. For the officer has no power to let me off even a farthing. He who forgave one debtor five hundred pence and another fifty, was the Lord, but the exactor is not the master, but one appointed by the master to demand the debts. But the last mite he calls slight and small, for our sins are either heavy or slight. Happy then is he who sinneth not, and next in happiness he who has sinned slightly. Even among slight sins there is diversity, otherwise he would not say until he has paid the *last* mite. For if he owes a little, he shall not come out till he pays the last mite. But he who has been guilty of a great debt, will have endless ages for his payment.

John 14, 6.

Luke 7, 41.

BEDE; Or else, our adversary in the way is the word of God, which opposes our carnal desires in this life; from which he is delivered who is subject to its precepts. Else he will be delivered to the judge, for of contempt of God's word the sinner will be accounted guilty in the judgment of the judge. The judge will deliver him to the officer, that is, the evil spirit for punishment. He will then be cast into prison, that is, to hell, where because he will ever have to pay the penalty by suffering, but never by paying it obtain pardon, he will never come out from thence, but with that most terrible serpent the devil, will expiate everlasting punishment.

1. There were present at that season some that told him of the Galilæans, whose blood Pilate had mingled with their sacrifices.

2. And Jesus answering said unto them, Suppose ye that these Galilæans were sinners above all the Galilæans, because they suffered such things?

3. I tell you, Nay: but, except ye repent, ye shall all likewise perish.

4. Or those eighteen, upon whom the tower in Siloam fell, and slew them, think ye that they were sinners above all men that dwelt in Jerusalem?

5. I tell you, Nay: but, except ye repent, ye shall all likewise perish.

GLOSS. As He had been speaking of the punishments of sinners, the story is fitly told Him of the punishment of certain particular sinners, from which He takes occasion to denounce vengeance also against other sinners: as it is said, *There were present at that season some that told him of the Galilæans, whose blood Pilate had mingled with their sacrifices.*

CYRIL; For these were followers of the opinions of Judas of Galilee, of whom Luke makes mention in the Acts of the Apostles, who said, that we ought to call no man master. Great numbers of them refusing to acknowledge Cæsar as their master, were therefore punished by Pilate. They said also that men ought not to offer God any sacrifices that were not ordained in the law of Moses, and so forbade to offer the sacrifices appointed by the people for the safety of the

Acts 5, 7.

Emperor and the Roman people. Pilate then, being enraged against the Galilæans, ordered them to be slain in the midst of the very victims which they thought they might offer according to the custom of their law; so that the blood of the offerers was mingled with that of the victims offered. Now it being generally believed that these Galilæans were most justly punished, as sowing offences among the people, the rulers, eager to excite against Him the hatred of the people, relate these things to the Saviour, wishing to discover what He thought about them. But He, admitting them to be sinners, does not however judge them to have suffered such things, as though they were worse than those who suffered not. Whence it follows, *And he answered and said unto them, Suppose ye that these Galilæans were sinners above all the Galilæans, &c.*

CHRYS. For God punishes some sinners by cutting off their iniquities, and appointing to them hereafter a lighter punishment, or perhaps even entirely releasing them, and correcting those who are living in wickedness by their punishment. Again, he does not punish others, that if they take heed to themselves by repentance they may escape both the present penalty and future punishment, but if they continue in their sins, suffer still greater torment. TIT. BOST. And he here plainly shews, that whatever judgments are passed for the punishment of the guilty, happen not only by the authority of the judges, but the will of God. Whether therefore the judge punishes upon the strict grounds of conscience, or has some other object in his condemnation, we must ascribe the work to the Divine appointment. *(Chrys. de Laz. Conc. 3.)*

CYRIL.; To save therefore the multitudes, from the intestine seditions, which were excited for the sake of religion, He adds, *but unless ye repent*, and unless ye cease to conspire against your rulers, for which ye have no divine guidance, *ye shall all likewise perish*, and your blood shall be united to that of your sacrifices. CHRYS. And herein he shews that He permitted them to suffer such things, that the heirs of the kingdom yet living might be dismayed by the dangers of others. " What then," you will say, " is this man punished, that I might become better?" Nay, but he is punished for his own crimes, and hence arises an opportunity of salvation to *(Chrys. ubi sup.)*

those who see it. BEDE; But because they repented not in
the fortieth year of our Lord's Passion, the Romans coming,
(whom Pilate represented, as belonging to their nation,) and beginning from Galilee, (whence our Lord's preaching had begun,)
utterly destroyed that wicked nation, and defiled with human
blood not only the courts of the temples, where they were
wont to offer sacrifices, but also the inner parts of the doors,
(where there was no entrance to the Galileans.)

Chrys.
ubi sup. CHRYS. Again, there had been eighteen others crushed to
death by the falling of a tower, of whom He adds the same
things, as it follows, *Or those eighteen upon whom the tower
of Siloam fell and slew them, think ye that they were sinners
above all men that dwelt in Jerusalem? I tell you, Nay,*
For he does not punish all in this life, giving them a time meet
for repentance. Nor however does he reserve all for future punishment, lest men should deny His providence. TIT. BOST.
Now one tower is compared to the whole city, that the destruction of a part may alarm the whole. Hence it is added,
But, except ye repent, ye shall all likewise perish; as if He
said, The whole city shall shortly be smitten if the inhabitants continue in impenitence.

AMBROSE; In those whose blood Pilate mingled with
the sacrifices, there seems to be a certain mystical type,
which concerns all who by the compulsion of the Devil offer
not a pure sacrifice, whose prayer is for a sin, as it was written of Judas, who when he was amongst the sacrifices devised the betrayal of our Lord's blood.

Ps. 109,
7.

BEDE; For Pilate, who is interpreted, "The mouth of the
hammerer," signifies the devil ever ready to strike. The
blood expresses sin, the sacrifices good actions. Pilate then
mingles the blood of the Galilæans with their sacrifices when
the devil stains the alms and other good works of the faithful
either by carnal indulgence, or by courting the praise of men,
or any other defilement. Those men of Jerusalem also who
were crushed by the falling of the tower, signify that the
Jews who refuse to repent will perish within their own walls.
Nor without meaning is the number eighteen given, (which
number among the Greeks is made up of I and H, that is, of
the same letters with which the name of Jesus begins.) And
it signifies that the Jews were chiefly to perish, because

they would not receive the name of the Saviour. That tower represents Him who is *the tower of strength.* And this is rightly in Siloam, which is interpreted, " sent;" for it signifies Him who, sent by the Father, came into the world, and who shall grind to powder all on whom He falls.

6. He spake also this parable; A certain man had a fig tree planted in his vineyard; and he came and sought fruit thereon, and found none.

7. Then said he unto the dresser of his vineyard, Behold, these three years I come seeking fruit on this fig tree, and find none; cut it down: why cumbereth it the ground?

8. And he answering said unto him, Lord, let it alone this year also, till I shall dig about it, and dung it:

9. And if it bear fruit, well: and if not, then after that thou shalt cut it down.

TIT. BOST. The Jews were boasting, that while the eighteen had perished, they all remained unhurt. He therefore sets before them the parable of the fig tree, for it follows, *He spake also this parable; A certain man had a fig tree planted in his vineyard.* AMBROSE; There was a vineyard of the Lord of hosts, which He gave for a spoil to the Gentiles. And the comparison of the fig tree to the synagogue is well chosen, because as that tree abounds with wide and spreading foliage, and deceives the hopes of its possessor with the vain expectation of promised fruit, so also in the synagogue, while its teachers are unfruitful in good works, yet magnify themselves with words as with abundant leaves, the empty shadow of the law stretches far and wide. This tree also is the only one which puts forth fruit in place of flowers. And the fruit falls, that other fruit may succeed; yet some few of the former remain, and do not fall. For the first people of the synagogue fell off as a useless fruit, in order that out of the fruitfulness of the old religion might arise the new people of the Church;

yet they who were the first out of Israel whom a branch of a stronger nature bore, under the shadow of the law and the cross, in the bosom of both, stained with a double juice after the example of a ripening fig, surpassed all others in the grace of most excellent fruits; to whom it is said, *You shall sit upon twelve thrones.* Some however think the fig tree to be a figure not of the synagogue, but of wickedness and treachery; yet these differ in nothing from what has gone before, except that they choose the genus instead of the species.

BEDE; The Lord Himself who established the synagogue by Moses, came born in the flesh, and frequently teaching in the synagogue, sought for the fruits of faith, but in the hearts of the Pharisees found none; therefore it follows, *And came seeking fruit on it, and found none.*

AMBROSE; But our Lord sought, not because He was ignorant that the fig tree had no fruit, but that He might shew in a figure that the synagogue ought by this time to have fruit. Lastly, from what follows, He teaches that He Himself came not before the time who came after three years. For so it is said, *Then said he to the dresser of the vineyard, Behold, these three years I come seeking fruit on this fig tree, and find none.* He came to Abraham, He came to Moses, He came to Mary, that is, He came in the seal of the covenant, He came in the law, He came in the body. We recognise His coming by His gifts; at one time purification, at another sanctification, at another justification. Circumcision purified, the law sanctified, grace justified. The Jewish people then could not be purified because they had not the circumcision of the heart, but of the body; nor be sanctified, because ignorant of the meaning of the law, they followed carnal things rather than spiritual; nor justified, because not working repentance for their offences, they knew nothing of grace. Rightly then was there no fruit found in the synagogue, and consequently it is ordered to be cut down; for it follows, *Cut it down, why cumbereth it the ground?* But the merciful dresser, perhaps meaning him on whom the Church is founded, foreseeing that another would be sent to the Gentiles, but he himself to them who were of the circumcision, piously intercedes that it may not be cut off; trusting to his calling, that the Jewish people also might be saved through the Church. Hence it follows, *And*

he answering said unto him, Lord, let it alone this year also.
He soon perceived hardness of heart and pride to be the
causes of the barrenness of the Jews.   He knew therefore how
to discipline, who knew how to censure faults.   Therefore adds
He, *till I shall dig about it.*   He promises that the hardness
of their hearts shall be dug about by the Apostles' spades, lest
a heap of earth cover up and obscure the root of wisdom.
And He adds, *and dung it,* that is, by the grace of humility, by
which even the fig is thought to become fruitful toward the
Gospel of Christ.   Hence He adds, *And if it bear fruit, well,*
that is, it shall be well, *but if not, then after that thou shalt
cut it down.*   BEDE; Which indeed came to pass under the
Romans, by whom the Jewish nation was cut off, and thrust
out from the land of promise.

AUG. Or, in another sense, the fig tree is the race of mankind. Aug.
For the first man after he had sinned concealed with fig leaves ubi sup.
his nakedness, that is, the members from which we derive
our birth.   THEOPHYL. But each one of us also is a fig tree
planted in the vineyard of God, that is, in the Church, or in
the world.

GREG. But our Lord came three times to the fig tree, Greg.
because He sought after man's nature before the law, under Hom.
the law, and under grace, by waiting, admonishing, visiting; Evang.
but yet He complains that for three years he found no fruit,
for there are some wicked men whose hearts are neither corrected by the law of nature breathed into them, nor instructed
by precepts, nor converted by the miracles of His incarnation.
THEOPHYL. Our nature yields no fruit though three times
sought for; once indeed when we transgressed the commandment in paradise; the second time, when they made the molten
calf under the law; thirdly, when they rejected the Saviour.
But that three years' time must be understood to mean also
the three ages of life, boyhood, manhood, and old age.

GREG. But with great fear and trembling should we hear Greg.
the word which follows, *Cut it down, why cumbereth it the* ubi sup.
ground.   For every one according to his measure, in whatsoever station of life he is, except he shew forth the fruits
of good works, like an unfruitful tree, cumbereth the ground;
for wherever he is himself placed, he there denies to another
the opportunity of working.

De Pœ-
nit. PSEUDO-BASIL; For it is the part of God's mercy not silently to inflict punishment, but to send forth threatenings to recall the sinner to repentance, as He did to the men of Nineveh, and now to the dresser of the vineyard, saying, *Cut it down,* exciting him indeed to the care of it, and stirring up the barren soil to bring forth the proper fruits. GREG. NAZ. Let us not then strike suddenly, but overcome by gentleness, lest we cut down the fig tree still able to bear fruit, which the care perhaps of a skilful dresser will restore. Hence it is also here added, *And he answering said unto him, Lord, let alone, &c.*

Greg.
Orat.
32.

Greg.
31. in
Ev. GREG. By the dresser of the vineyard is represented the order of Bishops, who, by ruling over the Church, take care of our Lord's vineyard. THEOPHYL. Or the master of the household is God the Father, the dresser is Christ, who will not have the fig tree cut down as barren, as if saying to the Father, Although through the Law and the Prophets they gave no fruit of repentance, I will water them with My sufferings and teaching, and perhaps they will yield us fruits of obedience.

Aug.
ubi sup. AUG. Or, the husbandman who intercedes is every holy man who within the Church prays for them that are without the Church, saying, *O Lord, O Lord, let it alone this year,* that is, for that time vouchsafed under grace, *until I dig about it.* To dig about it, is to teach humility and patience, for the ground which has been dug is lowly. The dung signifies the soiled garments, but they bring forth fruit. The soiled garment of the dresser, is the grief and mourning of sinners; for they who do penance and do it truly are in soiled garments.

Greg.
ubi sup. GREG. Or, the sins of the flesh are called the dung. From this then the tree revives to bear fruit again, for from the remembrance of sin the soul quickens itself to good works. But there are very many who hear reproof, and yet despise the return to repentance; wherefore it is added, *And if it bear fruit, well.*

Aug.
ubi sup. AUG. That is, it will be well, *but if not, then after that thou shalt cut it down;* namely, when Thou shalt come to judge the quick and the dead. In the mean time it is now spared. GREG. But he who will not by correction grow rich

Greg.
ubi sup.

unto fruitfulness, falls to that place from whence he is no more able to rise again by repentance.

10. And he was teaching in one of the synagogues on the sabbath.

11. And, behold, there was a woman which had a spirit of infirmity eighteen years, and was bowed together, and could in no wise lift up herself.

12. And when Jesus saw her, he called her to him, and said unto her, Woman, thou art loosed from thine infirmity.

13. And he laid his hands on her: and immediately she was made straight, and glorified God.

14. And the ruler of the synagogue answered with indignation, because that Jesus had healed on the sabbath day, and said unto the people, There are six days in which men ought to work: in them therefore come and be healed, and not on the sabbath day.

15. The Lord then answered him, and said, Thou hypocrite, doth not each one of you on the sabbath loose his ox or his ass from the stall, and lead him away to watering?

16. And ought not this woman, being a daughter of Abraham, whom Satan hath bound, lo, these eighteen years, be loosed from this bond on the sabbath day?

17. And when he had said these things, all his adversaries were ashamed: and all the people rejoiced for all the glorious things that were done by him.

AMBROSE; He soon explained that He had been speaking of the synagogue, shewing, that He truly came to it, who preached in it, as it is said, *And he was teaching in one of the synagogues.* CHRYS. He teaches indeed not separately, but in the synagogues; calmly, neither wavering in any thing, nor determining aught against the law of Moses; on the Sabbath also, because the Jews were then engaged in the hearing of the law.

CYRIL; Now that the Incarnation of the Word was manifested to destroy corruption and death, and the hatred of the devil against us, is plain from the actual events; for it follows, *And behold there was a woman which had a spirit of infirmity, &c.* He says *spirit of infirmity*, because the woman suffered from the cruelty of the devil, forsaken by God because of her own crimes or for the transgression of Adam, on account of which the bodies of men incur infirmity and death. But God gives this power to the Devil, to the end that men when pressed down by the weight of their adversity might betake them to better things. He points out the nature of her infirmity, saying, *And was bowed together, and could in no wise lift up herself.* BASIL; Because the head of the brutes is bent down towards the ground and looks upon the earth, but the head of man was made erect towards the heaven, his eyes tending upward. For it becomes us to seek what is above, and with our sight to pierce beyond earthly things.

Basil. Hom. 9. in Hex.

CYRIL; But our Lord, to shew that His coming into this world was to be the loosing of human infirmities, healed this woman. Hence it follows, *And when Jesus saw her, he called her to him, and said unto her, Woman, thou art loosed from thine infirmity.* A word most suitable to God, full of heavenly majesty; for by His royal assent He dispels the disease. He also laid His hands upon her, for it follows, *He laid his hands on her, and immediately she was made straight, and glorified God.* We should here answer, that the Divine power had put on the sacred flesh. For it was the flesh of God Himself, and of no other, as if the Son of Man existed apart from the Son of God, as some have falsely thought. But the ungrateful ruler of the synagogue, when he saw the woman, who before was creeping on the ground, now by Christ's single touch made upright, and relating the mighty works of God, sullies his zeal for the glory of the Lord with envy, and condemns the miracle, that he might appear to be jealous for the Sabbath.

As it follows, *And the ruler of the synagogue answered with indignation, because that Jesus had healed on the sabbath-day, and said unto the people, There are six days in which men ought to work, and not on the sabbath-day.* He would have those who are dispersed about on the other days, and engaged in their own works, not come on the Sabbath to see and admire our Lord's miracles, lest by chance they should believe. But the law has not forbidden all manual work on the Sabbath-day, and has it forbidden that which is done by a word or the mouth? Cease then both to eat and drink and speak and sing. And if thou readest not the law, how is it a Sabbath to thee? But supposing the law has forbidden manual works, how is it a manual work to raise a woman upright by a word?

AMBROSE; Lastly, God rested from the works of the world not from holy works, for His working is constant and everlasting; as the Son says, *My Father worketh until now,* John 5, *and I work;* that after the likeness of God our worldly, not 17. our religious, works should cease. Accordingly our Lord pointedly answered him, as it follows, *Thou hypocrite, doth not each one of you on the sabbath-day loose his ox or his ass? &c.*

BASIL; The hypocrite is one who on the stage assumes a Basil. different character from his own. So also in this life some Hom. 1. men carry one thing in their heart, and shew another on the de Jej. surface to the world. CHRYS. Well then does he call the ruler of the synagogue a hypocrite, for he had the appearance of an observer of the law, but in his heart was a crafty and envious man. For it troubles him not that the Sabbath is broken, but that Christ is glorified. Now observe, that whenever Christ orders a *work* to be done, (as when He ordered the man sick of the palsy to take up his bed,) He raises His words to something higher, convincing men by the majesty of the Father, as He says, *My Father worketh* John 5, *until now, and I work.* But in this place, as doing every 17. thing by *word,* He adds nothing further, refuting their calumny by the very things which they themselves did. CYRIL; Now the ruler of the synagogue is convicted a hypocrite, in that he leads his cattle to watering on the Sabbath-day, but this woman, not more by birth than by

faith the daughter of Abraham, he thought unworthy to be
loosed from the chain of her infirmity.   Therefore He adds,
*And ought not this woman, being a daughter of Abraham,
whom Satan has bound, lo, these eighteen years, to be loosed
from this bond on the sabbath-day?*   The ruler preferred
that this woman should like the beasts rather look upon the
earth than receive her natural stature, provided that Christ
was not magnified.   But they had nothing to answer; they
themselves unanswerably condemned themselves.   Hence
it follows, *And when he had said these things, all his
adversaries were ashamed.*   But the people, reaping great
good from His miracles, rejoiced at the signs which they
saw, as it follows, *And all the people rejoiced.*   For the
glory of His works vanquished every scruple in them who
sought Him not with corrupt hearts.

Greg.
Hom.
31. in
Evang.

GREG.   Mystically the unfruitful fig tree signifies the woman
that was bowed down.   For human nature of its own will
rushes into sin, and as it would not bring forth the fruit of
obedience, has lost the state of uprightness.   The same fig
tree preserved signifies the woman made upright.   AMBROSE;
Or the fig tree represents the synagogue; afterwards in the in-
firm woman there follows as it were a figure of the Church,
which having fulfilled the measure of the law and the resurrection, and now raised up on high in that eternal resting place,
can no more experience the frailty of our weak inclinations.
Nor could this woman be healed except she had fulfilled the
law and grace.   For in ten sentences is contained the perfection of the law, and in the number eight the fulness of the

Greg.
ut sup.

resurrection.   GREG.   Or else; man was made on the sixth
day, and on the same sixth day were all the works of the
Lord finished, but the number six multiplied three times
makes eighteen.   Because then man who was made on the
sixth day was unwilling to do perfect works, but before the
law, under the law, and at the beginning of grace, was

Aug.
Serm.
110.

weak, the woman was bowed down eighteen years.   AUG.
That which the three years signified in the tree, the
eighteen did in the woman, for three times six is eighteen.   But
she was crooked and could not look up, for in vain she heard

Greg.
ut sup.

the words, *lift up your hearts.*   GREG.   For every sinner who
thinketh earthly things, not seeking those that are in heaven,

is unable to look up.   For while pursuing his baser desires,
he declines from the uprightness of his state ; or his heart
is bent crooked, and he ever looks upon that which he
unceasingly thinks about.   The Lord called her and made
her upright, for He enlightened her and succoured her.
He sometimes calls but does not make upright, for when
we are enlightened by grace, we ofttimes see what should be
done, but because of sin do not practise it.   For habitual sin
binds down the mind, so that it cannot rise to uprightness.
It makes attempts and fails, because when it has long stood
by its own will, when the will is lacking, it falls.

AMBROSE ; Now this miracle is a sign of the coming
sabbath, when every one who has fulfilled the law and grace,
shall by the mercy of God put off the toils of this weak body.
But why did He not mention any more animals, save to shew
that the time would come when the Jewish and Gentile
nations should quench their bodily thirst, and this world's
heat in the fulness of the fountain of the Lord, and so
through the calling forth of two nations, the Church should
be saved.   BEDE ; But the daughter of Abraham is every
faithful soul, or the Church gathered out of both nations into
the unity of the faith.   There is the same mystery then in the
ox or ass being loosed and led to water, as in the daughter
of Abraham being released from the bondage of our affections.

18. Then said he, Unto what is the kingdom of
God like ? and whereunto shall I resemble it ?

19. It is like a grain of mustard seed, which a
man took, and cast into his garden ; and it grew, and
waxed a great tree ; and the fowls of the air lodged
in the branches of it.

20. And again he said, Whereunto shall I liken
the kingdom of God ?

21. It is like leaven, which a woman took and
hid in three measures of meal, till the whole was
leavened.

GLOSS. While His adversaries were ashamed, and the
people rejoiced, at the glorious things that were done by

Christ, He proceeds to explain the progress of the Gospel under certain similitudes, as it follows, *Then said he, Unto what is the kingdom of God like? It is like a grain of mustard seed, &c.* AMBROSE; In another place, a grain of mustard seed is introduced where it is compared to faith. If then the mustard seed is the kingdom of God, and faith is as the grain of mustard seed; faith is truly the kingdom of heaven, which is within us. A grain of mustard seed is indeed a mean and trifling thing, but as soon as it is crushed, it pours forth its power. And faith at first seems simple, but when it is buffeted by adversity, pours forth the grace of its virtue. The martyrs are grains of mustard seed. They have about them the sweet odour of faith, but it is hidden. Persecution comes; they are smitten by the sword; and to the farthest boundaries of the whole world they have scattered the seeds of their martyrdom. The Lord Himself also is a grain of mustard seed; He wished to be bruised that we might see that we are *a sweet savour of Christ.* He wishes to be sown as a grain of mustard seed, which when a man takes he puts it into his garden. For Christ was taken and buried in a garden, where also He rose again and became a tree, as it follows, *And it waxed into a great tree.* For our Lord is a grain when He is buried in the earth, a tree when He is lifted up into the heaven. He is also a tree overshadowing the world, as it follows, *And the fowls of the air rested in his branches;* that is, the heavenly powers and they whoever (for their spiritual deeds) have been thought worthy to fly forth. Peter is a branch, Paul is a branch, into whose arms, by certain hidden ways of disputation, we who were afar off now fly, having taken up the wings of the virtues. Sow then Christ in thy garden; a garden is truly a place full of flowers, wherein the grace of thy work may blossom, and the manifold odour of thy different virtues be breathed forth. Wherever is the fruit of the seed, there is Christ. CYRIL; Or else; The kingdom of God is the Gospel, through which we gain the power of reigning with Christ. As then the mustard seed is surpassed in size by the seeds of other herbs, yet so increases as to become the shelter of many birds; so also the life-giving doctrine was at first in the possession only of a few, but afterwards spread itself abroad.

Marginal references:
Mat. 17, 19.
Luke 17, 21.
2 Cor. 2, 15.

BEDE; Now the *man*, is Christ, the *garden*, His Church, to be cultivated by His discipline. He is well said to have taken the grain, because the gifts which He together with the Father gave to us from His divinity, He took from His humanity. But the preaching of the Gospel grew and was disseminated throughout the whole world. It grows also in the mind of every believer, for no one is suddenly made perfect. But in its growth, not like the grass, (which soon withers,) but it rises up like the trees. The branches of this tree are the manifold doctrines, on which the chaste souls, soaring upwards on the wings of virtue, build and repose.

THEOPHYL. Or, any man receiving a grain of mustard seed, that is, the word of the Gospel, and sowing it in the garden of his soul, makes it a great tree, so as to bring forth branches, and the birds of the air (that is, they who soar above the earth) rest in the branches, (that is, in sublime contemplation.) For Paul received the instruction of Ananias Acts 9, as it were a small grain, but planting it in his garden, he 17. brought forth many good doctrines, in which they dwell who have high heavenly thoughts, as Dionysius, Hierotheus, and many others.

He next likens the kingdom of God to leaven, for it follows, *And again he says, Whereunto shall I liken it? It is like to leaven, &c.* AMBROSE; Many think Christ is the leaven, for leaven which is made from meal, excels its kind in strength, not in appearance. So also Christ (according to the Fathers) shone forth above others equal in body, but unapproachable in excellence. The Holy Church therefore represents the type of the woman, of whom it is added, *Which a woman took and hid in three measures of meal, till the whole was* sata. *leavened.* BEDE; The Satum is a kind of measure in use in the province of Palestine, holding about a bushel and a half. AMBROSE; But we are the meal of the woman which hide the Lord Jesus in the secrets of our hearts, until the heat of heavenly wisdom penetrates our innermost recesses. And since He says it was hid in three measures, it seems fitting that we should believe the Son of God to have been hid in the Law, veiled in the Prophets, manifested in the preaching of the Gospel. Here however I am invited to proceed farther, because our Lord Himself has taught us, that the leaven is the spiritual teaching of the Church. Now the Church sanctifies with its spiritual leaven the man who is renewed in body, soul, and spirit, seeing that these three are united in a certain equal measure of desire, and there breathes forth a complete harmony of the will. If then in this life the three measures abide in the same person until they are leavened and become one, there will be hereafter an incorruptible communion with them that love Christ.

THEOPHYL. Or, for the woman you must understand the soul; but the three measures, its three parts, the reasoning part, the affections, and the desires. If then any one has hidden in these three the word of God, he will make the whole spiritual, so as not by his reason to lie in argument, nor by his anger or desire to be transported beyond control, but to be conformed to the word of God.

Aug.
Serm.
111.

AUG. Or, the three measures of meal are the race of mankind, which was restored out of the three sons of Noah. The woman who hid the leaven is the wisdom of God. EUSEBIUS; Or else, by the leaven our Lord means the Holy . Spirit, the Sower proceeding (as it were) from the seed, which is the word of God. But the three measures of meal, signify the knowledge of the Father, and the Son, and the Holy Spirit, which the woman, that is, Divine wisdom, and the Holy Spirit, impart. BEDE; Or, by the leaven He speaks of love, which kindles and stirs up the heart; the woman, that is, the Church, hides the leaven of love in three measures, because she bids us love God with all our hearts, all our minds, and all our strength. And this until the whole is leavened, that is, until love moves the whole soul into the perfection of itself, which begins here, but will be completed hereafter.

22. And he went through the cities and villages, teaching, and journeying toward Jerusalem.

23. Then said one unto him, Lord, are there few that be saved? And he said unto them,

24. Strive to enter in at the strait gate: for many, I say unto you, will seek to enter in, and shall not be able.

25. When once the master of the house is risen up, and hath shut to the door, and ye begin to stand without, and to knock at the door, saying, Lord, Lord, open unto us; and he shall answer and say unto you, I know you not whence ye are :

26. Then shall ye begin to say, We have eaten and drunk in thy presence, and thou hast taught in our streets.

27. But he shall say, I tell you, I know you not whence ye are; depart from me, all ye workers of iniquity.

28. There shall be weeping and gnashing of teeth, when ye shall see Abraham, and Isaac, and Jacob, and all the prophets, in the kingdom of God, and you yourselves thrust out.

29. And they shall come from the east, and from the west, and from the north, and from the south, and shall sit down in the kingdom of God.

30. And, behold, there are last which shall be first, and there are first which shall be last.

GLOSS. Having spoken in parables concerning the increase of the teaching of the Gospel, he every where endeavours to spread it by preaching. Hence it is said, *And he went through the cities and villages.* THEOPHYL. For he did not visit the small places only, as they do who wish to deceive the simple, nor the cities only, as they who are fond of show, and seek their own glory; but as their common Lord and Father providing for all, He went about every where. Nor again did He visit the country towns only, avoiding Jerusalem, as if He feared the cavils of the lawyers, or death, which might follow therefrom; and hence he adds, *And journeying towards Jerusalem.* For where there were many sick, there the Physician chiefly shewed Himself. It follows, *Then said one unto him, Lord, are there few that be saved?* GLOSS. This question seems to have reference to what had gone before. For in the parable which was given above, He had said,

that the birds of the air rested on its branches, by which it
might be supposed that there would be many who would
obtain the rest of salvation.   And because one had asked the
question for all, the Lord does not answer him individually,
as it follows, *And he said unto them, Strive to enter in at the*
Basil. in *strait gate.*   BASIL; For as in earthly life the departure
reg. ad
int. 240. from right is exceeding broad, so he who goes out of the
path which leads to the kingdom of heaven, finds himself
int. 241. in a vast extent of error.   But the right way is narrow, the
slightest turning aside being full of danger, whether to the
right or to the left, as on a bridge, where he who slips on
either side is thrown into the river.

CYRIL; The narrow gate also represents the toils and
sufferings of the saints.   For as a victory in battle bears witness
to the strength of the soldiers, so a courageous endurance
Chrys. of labours and temptations will make a man strong.   CHRYS.
24, 40.
in Matt. What then is that which our Lord says elsewhere, *My yoke*
Matt. *is easy, and my burden is light?*   There is indeed no con-
11, 33. tradiction, but the one was said because of the nature of
temptations, the other with respect to the feeling of those
who overcame them.   For whatever is troublesome to our
nature may be considered easy when we undertake it heartily.
Besides also, though the way of salvation is narrow at its
entrance, yet through it we come into a large space, but
Greg. on the contrary the broad way leadeth to destruction.   GREG.
Mor. 11.
c. 50. Now when He was about to speak of the entrance of the
narrow gate, He said first, *strive,* for unless the mind struggles
manfully, the wave of the world is not overcome, by which
the soul is ever thrown back again into the deep.

CYRIL; Now our Lord does not seem to satisfy him who
asked whether there are few that be saved, when He declares
the way by which man may become righteous.   But it must
be observed, that it was our Saviour's custom to answer those
who asked Him, not according as they might judge right, as
often as they put to Him useless questions, but with regard
to what might be profitable to His hearers.   And what
advantage would it have been to His hearers to know
whether there should be many or few who would be saved.
But it was more necessary to know the way by which man
may come to salvation.   Purposely then He says nothing

in answer to the idle question, but turns His discourse to a more important subject.

AUG. Or else, our Lord confirmed the words He heard, Aug. that is, by saying that there are few who are saved, for few Serm. enter by the strait gate, but in another place He says this 111. very thing, *Narrow is the way which leadeth unto life, and* Matt. 7, *few there are who enter into it.* Therefore He adds, *For* 14. *many I say unto you shall seek to enter;* BEDE; Urged thereto by their love of safety, yet shall not be able, frightened by the roughness of the road.

BASIL; For the soul wavers to and fro, at one time choosing Basil. virtue when it considers eternity, at another preferring Hom. in pleasures when it looks to the present. Here it beholds Psalm ease, or the delights of the flesh, there its subjection or 1, 5. captive bondage; here drunkenness, there sobriety; here wanton mirth, there overflowing of tears; here dancing, there praying; here the sound of the pipe, there weeping; here lust, there chastity. AUG. Now our Lord in no wise con- Aug. tradicts Himself when He says, *that there are few who* Serm. *enter in at the strait gate,* and elsewhere, *Many shall* Matt. 8, *come from the east and the west;* for there are few in com- 11. parison with those who are lost, many when united with the angels. Scarcely do they seem a grain when the threshing floor is swept, but so great a mass will come forth from this floor, that it will fill the granary of heaven.

CYRIL; But that they who cannot enter are regarded with wrath, He has shewn by an obvious example, as follows, *When once the master of the house has risen up, &c.* as if when the master of the house who has called many to the banquet has entered in with his guests, and shut to the door, then shall come afterwards men knocking. BEDE; The master of the house is Christ, who since as very God He is every where, is already said to be within those whom though He is in heaven He gladdens with His visible presence, but is as it were without to those whom while contending in this pilgrimage, He helps in secret. But He will enter in when He shall bring the whole Church to the contemplation of Himself. He will shut the door when He shall take away from the reprobate all room for repentance. Who standing without will knock, that is, separated from the righteous

will in vain implore that mercy which they have despised.
Therefore it follows, *And he will answer and say to you,*
I know you not whence ye are. GREG. For God not to
know is for Him to reject, as also a man who speaks the truth
is said not to know how to lie, for he disdains to sin by telling
a lie, not that if he wished to lie he knew not how, but that
from love of truth he scorns to speak what is false.   Therefore
the light of truth knows not the darkness which it condemns.
It follows, *Then shall ye begin to say, We have eaten and*
drunk in thy presence, &c.   CYRIL; This refers to the
Israelites, who, according to the practice of their law, when
offering victims to God, eat and are merry.   They heard
also in the synagogues the books of Moses, who in his
writings delivered not his own words, but the words of God.
THEOPHYL. Or it is said to the Israelites, simply because
Christ was born of them according to the flesh, and they ate
and drank with Him, and heard Him preaching.   But these
things also apply to Christians.   For we eat the body of
Christ and drink His blood as often as we approach the
mystic table, and He teaches in the streets of our souls,
which are open to receive Him.   BEDE; Or mystically, he
eats and drinks in the Lord's presence who eagerly receives
the food of the word.   Hence it is added for explanation,
Thou hast taught in our streets.   For Scripture in its more
obscure places is food, since by being expounded it is as
it were broken and swallowed.   In the clearer places it is
drink, where it is taken down just as it is found.   But at a
feast the banquet does not delight him whom the piety of
faith commends not.   The knowledge of the Scriptures does not
make him known to God, whom the iniquity of his works
proves to be unworthy; as it follows, *And he will say unto*
you, I know not whence ye are; depart from me.

BASIL; He perhaps speaks to those whom the Apostle
describes in his own person, saying, *If I speak with the*
tongues of men and of angels, and have all knowledge, and
give all my goods to feed the poor, but have not charity,
it profiteth me nothing.   For whatever is done not from
regard to the love of God, but to gain praise from men,
obtains no praise from God.   THEOPHYL. Observe also that
they are objects of wrath in whose street the Lord teaches.

Side notes:
Greg.
Moral.
2. c. 5.

Basil.
reg.
brev. ad
int. 282.

If then we have heard Him teaching not in the streets, but in poor and lowly hearts, we shall not be regarded with wrath. BEDE; But the twofold punishment of hell is here described, that is, the feeling cold and heat. For weeping is wont to be excited by heat, gnashing of teeth by cold. Or gnashing of teeth betrays the feeling of indignation, that he who repents too late, is too late angry with himself. GLOSS; Or the teeth will gnash which here delighted in eating, the eyes will weep which here wandered with desire. By each He represents the real resurrection of the wicked. THEOPHYL. This also refers to the Israelites with whom He was speaking, who receive from this their severest blow, that the Gentiles have rest with the fathers, while they themselves are shut out. Hence He adds, *When you shall see Abraham, Isaac, and Jacob, in the kingdom of God, &c.* EUSEB. For the Fathers above mentioned, before the times of the Law, forsaking the sins of many gods to follow the Gospel way, received the knowledge of the most high God; to whom many of the Gentiles were conformed through a similar manner of life, but their children suffered estrangement from the Gospel rules; and herein it follows, *And behold they are last which shall be first, and they are first which shall be last.* CYRIL; For to the Jews who held the first place have the Gentiles been preferred.

THEOPHYL. But we as it seems are the first who have received from our very cradles the rudiments of Christian teaching, and perhaps shall be last in respect of the heathens who have believed at the end of life. BEDE; Many also at first burning with zeal, afterwards grow cold; many at first cold, on a sudden become warm; many despised in this world, will be glorified in the world to come; others renowned among men, will in the end be condemned.

31. The same day there came certain of the Pharisees, saying unto him, Get thee out, and depart hence : for Herod will kill thee.

32. And he said unto them, Go ye, and tell that fox, Behold, I cast out devils, and I do cures to

day and to morrow, and the third day I shall be perfected.

33. Nevertheless I must walk to day, and to morrow, and the day following: for it cannot be that a prophet perish out of Jerusalem.

34. O Jerusalem, Jerusalem, which killest the prophets, and stonest them that are sent unto thee; how often would I have gathered thy children together, as a hen doth gather her brood under her wings, and ye would not!

35. Behold, your house is left unto you desolate: and verily I say unto you, Ye shall not see me, until the time come when ye shall say, Blessed is he that cometh in the name of the Lord.

CYRIL; The preceding words of our Lord roused the Pharisees to anger. For they perceived that the people were now smitten in their hearts, and eagerly receiving His faith. For fear then of losing their office as rulers of the people, and lacking their gains, with pretended love for Him, they persuade Him to depart from hence, as it is said, *The same day there came certain of the Pharisees, saying unto him, Get thee out and depart hence, for Herod will kill thee:* but Christ, who searcheth the heart and the reins, answers them meekly and under figure. Hence it follows, *And he said unto them, Go ye and tell that fox.* BEDE; Because of his wiles and stratagems He calls Herod a fox, which is an animal full of craft, concealing itself in a ditch because of snares, having a noisome smell, never walking in straight paths, all which things belong to heretics, of whom Herod is a type, who endeavours to destroy Christ (that is, the humility of the Christian faith) in the hearts of believers.

CYRIL; Or else the discourse seems to change here, and not to refer so much to the character of Herod as some think, as to the lies of the Pharisees. For He almost represents the Pharisees themselves to be standing near, when He said, *Go tell this fox,* as it is in the Greek. Therefore he commanded them to say that which might rouse the multitude of

Pharisees. *Behold*, said He, *I cast out devils, and I do cures to day and to morrow, and on the third day I shall be perfected.* He promises to do what was displeasing to the Jews, namely, to command the evil spirits, and deliver the sick from disease, until in His own person He should undergo the suffering of the cross. But because the Pharisees thought that He who was the Lord of hosts, feared the hand of Herod. He refutes this, saying, *Nevertheless I must walk to day and to morrow, and the day following.* When He says *must*, He by no means implies a necessity imposed upon Him, but rather that He walked where He liked according to the inclination of His will, until He should come to the end of the dreadful cross, the time of which Christ shews to be now drawing near, when He says, *To day and to morrow.* THEOPHYL. As if He says, What think ye of My death? Behold, a little while, and it will come to pass. But by the words, *To day and to morrow*, are signified many days; as we also are wont to say in common conversation, " To day and to morrow such a thing takes place," not that it happens in that interval of time. And to explain more clearly the words of the Gospel, you must not understand them to be, *I must walk to day and to morrow*, but place a stop after *to day and to morrow*, then add, *and walk on the day following*, as frequently in reckoning we are accustomed to say, " The Lord's day and the day after, and on the third I will go out," as if by reckoning two, to denote the third. So also our Lord speaks as if calculating, I must do so to day, and so to morrow, and then afterward on the third day I must go to Jerusalem.

AUG. Or these things are understood to have been spoken mystically by Him, so as to refer to His body, which is the Church. For devils are cast out when the Gentiles having forsaken their superstition, believe in Him. And cures are perfected when according to His commands, after having renounced the devil and this world until the end of the resurrection, (by which as it were the third day will be completed,) the Church shall be perfected in angelical fulness by the immortality also of the body. Aug. con. Julian. lib. 6. c. 19.

THEOPHYL. But because they said unto Him, *Depart from hence, for Herod seeks to kill thee*, speaking in Galilee where Herod reigned, He shews that not in Galilee, but in Jerusalem it had been fore-ordained that He should suffer. Hence it follows, *For it can not be that a prophet perish out of Jerusalem.* When thou hearest, *It can not be* (or it is not fitting) *that a prophet should perish out of Jerusalem,* think not that any violent constraint was imposed upon the Jews, but He says this seasonably with reference to their eager desire after blood; just as if any one seeing a most savage robber, should say, the road on which this robber lurks can not be without bloodshed to travellers. So also no where else but in the abode of robbers must the Lord of the prophets perish. For accustomed to the blood of His prophets, they will also kill the Lord; as it follows, *O Jerusalem, Jerusalem, which killest the prophets.*

BEDE; In calling upon Jerusalem, He addresses not the stones and buildings of the city, but the dwellers therein, and He weeps over it with the affection of a father. CHRYS. For the twice repeated word betokens compassion or very great love. For the Lord speaks, if we may say it, as a lover would to his mistress who despised him, and was therefore about to be punished. GREEK EX. But the repetition of the name also shews the rebuke to be severe. For she who knew God, how does she persecute God's ministers? CYRIL; Now that they were unmindful of the Divine blessings He proves as follows, *How often would I have gathered thy children together as a hen doth gather her brood under her wings, and ye would not.* He led them by the hand of Moses out of all wisdom, He warns them by His prophets, He wished to have them under His wings, (i. e. under the shelter of His power,) but they deprived themselves of these choice blessings, through their ingratitude. AUG. As many as I gathered together, it was done by my all prevailing will, yet thy unwillingness, for thou wert ever ungrateful. BEDE; Now He who aptly had called Herod a fox, who was plotting His death, compares Himself to a bird, for foxes are ever lying in wait for birds.

BASIL; He compared also the sons of Jerusalem to birds in the net, as if He said, Birds who are used to fly in the air are caught by the treacherous devices of the catchers, but thou shalt be as a chicken in want of another's protection; when thy mother then has fled away, thou art taken from thy nest

Chrys. Hom. 75. in Matt.

Severus.

Aug. Enchir. 97.

Basil. in Esaiam c. 16. §. 301.

as too weak to defend thyself, too feeble to fly; as it follows, *Behold, your house is left unto you desolate.* BEDE; The city itself which He had called the nest, He now calls the house of the Jews; for when our Lord was slain, the Romans came, and plundering it as a deserted nest, took away both their place, nation, and kingdom. THEOPHYL. Or your house, (that is, temple,) as if He says, As long as there was virtue in you, it was my temple, but after that you made it a den of thieves, it was no more my house but yours. Or by house He meant the whole Jewish nation, according to the Psalm, *O house of Jacob, bless ye the Lord,* by which he shews that ^{Psalm} it was He Himself who governed them, and took them out ^{135, 20.} of the hand of their enemies. It follows, *And verily I say unto you, &c.* AUG. There seems nothing opposed to ^{Aug.} St. Luke's narrative, in what the multitudes said when ^{de Cons.} ^{Ev. lib.} our Lord came to Jerusalem, *Blessed is he who cometh in* ^{2. c. 72.} *the name of the Lord,* for He had not as yet come thither, ^{Mat. 21,} ^{9.} nor had this yet been spoken. CYRIL; For our Lord had departed from Jerusalem, as it were abandoning those who were unworthy of His presence, and afterwards returned to Jerusalem, having performed many miracles, when that crowd meets Him, saying, *Osanna to the Son of David, blessed is he that cometh in the name of the Lord.* AUG. ^{Aug.} But as Luke does not say to what place our Lord went ^{de Cons.} ^{Ev. ubi} from thence, so that He should not come except at that time, ^{sup.} (for when this was spoken He was journeying onward until He should come to Jerusalem,) He means therefore to refer to that coming of His, when He should appear in glory. THEOPHYL. For then also will they unwillingly confess Him to be their Lord and Saviour, when there shall be no departure hence. But in saying, *Ye shall not see me until he shall come, &c.* does not signify that present hour, but the time of His cross; as if He says, When ye have crucified Me, ye shall no more see Me until I come again. AUG. Luke ^{Aug.} must be understood then as wishing to anticipate here, before ^{ubi sup.} his narrative brought our Lord to Jerusalem, or to make Him when approaching the same city, give an answer to those who told Him to beware of Herod, like to that which Matthew says He gave when He had already reached

Jerusalem.   BEDE; Ye shall not see, that is, unless ye
have worked repentance, and confessed Me to be the Son
of the Father Almighty, ye shall not see My face at the
second coming.

1. And it came to pass, as he went into the house of one of the chief Pharisees to eat bread on the sabbath day, that they watched him.

2. And, behold, there was a certain man before him which had the dropsy.

3. And Jesus answering spake unto the Lawyers and Pharisees, saying, Is it lawful to heal on the sabbath day?

4. And they held their peace. And he took him, and healed him, and let him go;

5. And answered them, saying, Which of you shall have an ass or an ox fallen into a pit, and will not straightway pull him out on the sabbath day?

6. And they could not answer him again to these things.

CYRIL; Although our Lord knew the malice of the Pharisees, yet He became their guest, that He might benefit by His words and miracles those who were present. Whence it follows, *And it came to pass, as he went into the house of one of the chief Pharisees to eat bread on the sabbath day, that they watched him;* to see whether He would despise the observance of the law, or do any thing that was forbidden on the sabbath day. When then the man with the dropsy came into the midst of them, He rebukes by a question the insolence of the Pharisees, who wished to detect Him; as it is said, *And, behold, there was a certain man before him which had the dropsy. And Jesus answering, &c.*

BEDE; When it is said that *Jesus answered*, there is a
reference to the words which went before, *And they watched
him.* For the Lord knew the thoughts of men. THEOPHYL.
But by His question He exposes their folly. For while God
Gen. 2, blessed the sabbath, they forbade to do good on the sabbath;
1. but the day which does not admit the works of the good is
accursed.

BEDE; But they who were asked, are rightly silent, for
they perceived that whatever they said, would be against
themselves. For if it is lawful to heal on the sabbath day,
why did they watch the Saviour whether He would heal?
If it is not lawful, why do they take care of their cattle on
the sabbath? Hence it follows, *But they held their peace.*

CYRIL; Disregarding then the snares of the Jews, He cures
the dropsical, who from fear of the Pharisees did not ask to
be healed on account of the sabbath, but only stood up, that
when Jesus beheld him, He might have compassion on him
and heal him. And the Lord knowing this, asked not whether
he wished to be made whole, but forthwith healed him.
Whence it follows; *And he took him, and healed him, and
let him go.* Wherein our Lord took no thought not to offend
the Pharisees, but only that He might benefit him who
needed healing. For it becomes us, when a great good is
the result, not to care if fools take offence. CYRIL; But
seeing the Pharisees awkwardly silent, Christ baffles their
determined impudence by some important considerations.
As it follows; *And he answered and said unto them, Which
of you shall have an ass or an ox fallen into a pit, and will
not straightway pull him out on the sabbath day?* THEOPHYL.
As though He said, If the law forbids to have mercy on the
sabbath-day, have no care of thy son when in danger on the
sabbath-day. But why speak I of a son, when thou dost not
even neglect an ox if thou seest it in danger?

BEDE; By these words He so refutes His watchers, the
Pharisees, as to condemn them also of covetousness, who in
the deliverance of animals consult their own desire of wealth.
How much more then ought Christ to deliver a man, who is
Aug. de much better than cattle! AUG. Now He has aptly compared
Quæst.
Evan. the dropsical man to an animal which has fallen into a ditch,
lib. 2. (for he is troubled by water,) as He compared that woman,
cap. 29.

whom He spoke of as bound, and whom He Himself loosed, to a beast which is let loose to be led to water. BEDE; By a suitable example then He settles the question, shewing that they violate the sabbath by a work of covetousness, who contend that he does so by a work of charity. Hence it follows, *And they could not answer him again to these things.* Mystically, the dropsical man is compared to him who is weighed down by an overflowing stream of carnal pleasures. For the disease of dropsy derives the name from a watery humour. AUG. Or we rightly compare the dropsical man to a covetous rich man. For as the former, the more he increases ^{Aug. ubi sup.} in unnatural moisture the greater his thirst; so also the other, the more abundant his riches, which he does not employ well, the more ardently he desires them.

GREG. Rightly then is the dropsical man healed in the Pharisees' presence, for by the bodily infirmity of the one, ^{Greg. 14 Mor. c. 6.} is expressed the mental disease of the other. BEDE; In this example also He well refers to the ox and the ass; so as to represent either the wise and the foolish, or both nations; that is, the Jew oppressed by the burden of the law, the Gentile not subject to reason. For the Lord rescues from the pit of concupiscence all who are sunk therein.

7. And he put forth a parable to those which were bidden, when he marked how they chose out the chief rooms; saying unto them,

8. When thou art bidden of any man to a wedding, sit not down in the highest room; lest a more honourable man than thou be bidden of him;

9. And he that bade thee and him come and say to thee, Give this man place; and thou begin with shame to take the lowest room.

10. But when thou art bidden, go and sit down in the lowest room; that when he that bade thee cometh, he may say unto thee, Friend, go up higher: then shalt thou have worship in the presence of them that sit at meat with thee.

11. For whosoever exalteth himself shall be abased; and he that humbleth himself shall be exalted.

AMBROSE; First the dropsical man is cured, in whom the abundant discharges of the flesh crushed down the powers of the soul, quenched the ardour of the Spirit. Next, humility is taught, when at the nuptial feast the desire of the highest place is forbidden. As it is said, *And he spake, Sit not down in the highest room.* CYRIL; For to rush forward hastily to honours which are not fitting for us, indicates rashness· and casts a slur upon our actions. Hence it follows, *lest* Chrys. non occ. *a more honourable man than thou be invited, &c.* CHRYS. And so the seeker of honour obtained not that which he coveted, but suffered a defeat, and busying himself how he might be loaded with honours, is treated with dishonour. And because nothing is of so much worth as modesty, He leads His hearer to the opposite of this; not only forbidding him to seek the highest place, but bidding him search for the lowest. As it follows; *But when thou art bidden, go and sit down in the lowest room.* CYRIL; For if a man wishes not to be set before others, he obtains this honour according to the divine word. As it follows; *That when he that bade thee cometh, he may say unto thee, Friend, go up higher.* In these words He does not harshly chide, but gently admonishes; for a word of advice is enough for the wise. And thus for their humility men are crowned with honours; as it follows, *Then shalt thou have worship.*

Basil. in reg. fus. ad inter. 12. BASIL; To take then the lowest place at a feast, according to our Lord's command, is becoming to every man, but again to rush contentiously after this is to be condemned as a breach of order and cause of tumult; and a strife raised about it, will place you on a level with those who dispute concerning the highest place. Wherefore, as our Lord here says, it becomes him who makes the feast to arrange the order of sitting down. Thus in patience and love should we mutually bear ourselves, following all things decently according to order, not for external appearance or public display; nor should we seem to study or affect humility by violent contradiction, but rather gain it by condescension or by patience. For resistance or opposition is a far stronger token of pride than taking the first seat at meat, when we obtain it by authority.

THEOPHYL. Now let no one deem the above precepts of Christ to be trifling, and unworthy of the sublimity and grandeur of the Word of God. For you would not call him a merciful physician who professed to heal the gout, but refused to cure a scar on the finger or a tooth-ache. Besides, how can that passion of vainglory appear slight, which moved or agitated those who sought the first seats. It became then the Master of humility to cut off every branch of the bad root. But observe this also, that when the supper was ready, and the wretched guests were contending for precedency before the eyes of the Saviour, there was a fit occasion for advice.

CYRIL; Having shewn therefore from so slight an example the degradation of the ambitious and the exaltation of the humbleminded, He adds a great thing to a little, pronouncing a general sentence, as it follows, *For every one who exalts himself shall be abased, and he that humbleth himself shall be exalted.* This is spoken according to the divine judgment, not after human experience, in which they who desire after glory obtain it, while others who humble themselves remain inglorious.

THEOPHYL. Moreover, he is not to be respected in the end, nor by all men, who thrusts himself into honours; but while by some he is honoured, by others he is disparaged, and sometimes even by the very men who outwardly honour him. BEDE; But as the Evangelist calls this admonition a parable, we must briefly examine what is its mystical meaning. Whosoever being bidden has come to the marriage feast of Christ's Church, being united to the members of the Church by faith, let him not exalt himself as higher than others by boasting of his merits. For he will have to give place to one more honourable who is bidden afterwards, seeing that he is overtaken by the activity of those who followed him, and with shame he occupies the lowest place, now that knowing better things of the others he brings low whatever high thoughts he once had of his own works. But a man sits in the lowest place according to that verse, *The greater thou art,* Eccles. *humble thyself in all things.* But the Lord when He cometh, 3, 18.

whomsoever He shall find humble, blessing him with the name of friend, He will command him to go up higher. For whoever humbleth himself as a little child, he is the greatest in the kingdom of heaven. But it is well said, *Then shalt thou have glory*, that thou mayest not begin to seek now what is kept for thee in the end. It may also be understood, even in this life, for daily does God come to His marriage feast, despising the proud; and often giving to the humble such great gifts of His Spirit, that the assembly of those who sit at meat, i. e. the faithful, glorify them in wonder. But in the general conclusion which is added, it is plainly declared that the preceding discourse of our Lord must be understood typically. For not every one who exalts himself before men is abased; nor is he who humbleth himself in their sight, exalted by them. But whoever exalteth himself because of his merits, the Lord shall bring low, and him who humbleth himself on account of his mercies, shall He exalt.

12. Then said he also to him that bade him, When thou makest a dinner or a supper, call not thy friends, nor thy brethren, neither thy kinsmen, nor thy rich neighbours; lest they also bid thee again, and a recompence be made thee.

13. But when thou makest a feast, call the poor, the maimed, the lame, the blind :

14. And thou shalt be blessed; for they cannot recompense thee: for thou shalt be recompensed at the resurrection of the just.

THEOPHYL. The supper being composed of two parties, the invited and the inviter, and having already exhorted the invited to humility, He next rewards by His advice the inviter, guarding him against making a feast to gain the favour of men. Hence it is said, *Then said he also to him that bade him, When thou makest a dinner or a supper, call not thy friends.*

Chrys. Hom. 1, 3. in ep. Col.

CHRYS. Many are the sources from which friendships are

made. Leaving out all unlawful ones, we shall speak only of
those which are natural and moral; the natural are, for instance, between father and son, brother and brother, and
such like; which He meant, saying, *Nor thy brethren,
nor thy kinsmen;* the moral, when a man has become your
guest or neighbour; and with reference to these He says, *nor
thy neighbours.*

BEDE; Brothers then, and friends, and the rich, are not
forbidden, as though it were a crime to entertain one another,
but this, like all the other necessary intercourse among men,
is shewn to fail in meriting the reward of everlasting life; as
it follows, *Lest perchance they also bid thee again, and a recompense be made thee.* He says not, " and sin be committed
against thee." And the like to this He speaks in another
place, *And if ye do good to those who do good to you, what* Luke 6,
thank have ye? There are however certain mutual feastings [33.]
of brothers and neighbours, which not only incur a retribution in this life, but also condemnation hereafter. And these
are celebrated by the general gathering together of all, or the
hospitality in turn of each one of the company; and they meet
together that they may perpetrate foul deeds, and through
excess of wine be provoked to all kinds of lustful pleasure.
CHRYS. Let us not then bestow kindness on others under the
hope of return. For this is a cold motive, and hence it is that
such a friendship soon vanishes. But if you invite the poor,
God, who never forgets, will be your debtor, as it follows, *But
when ye make a feast, call the poor, the maimed, the lame, and
the blind.* CHRYS. For the humbler our brother is, so much Chrys.
the more does Christ come through him and visit us. For he [Hom. 45. in]
who entertains a great man does it often from vainglory. And [Act.]
elsewhere, But very often interest is his object, that through
such a one he may gain promotion. I could indeed mention
many who for this pay court to the most distinguished of the
nobles, that through their assistance they may obtain the
greater favour from the prince. Let us not then ask those
who can recompense us, as it follows, *And thou shalt be
blessed, for they cannot recompense thee.* And let us not be
troubled when we receive no return of a kindness, but when
we do; for if we have received it we shall receive nothing
more, but if man does not repay us, God will. As it follows,

For thou shalt be recompensed at the resurrection of the just.
BEDE; And though all rise again, yet it is called the resurrection of the just, because in the resurrection they doubt
not that they are blessed. Whoever then bids the poor to
his feast shall receive a reward hereafter. But he who invites his friends, brothers, and the rich, has received his
reward. But if he does this for God's sake after the example of
the sons of Job, God, who Himself commanded all the duties of
brotherly love, will reward him. CHRYS. But thou sayest, *the
poor are unclean and filthy.* Wash him, and make him to sit
with thee at table. If he has dirty garments, give him clean ones.
Christ comes to thee through him, and dost thou stand trifling?
GREG. NYSS. Do not then let them lie as though they were
nothing worth. Reflect who they are, and thou wilt discover
their preciousness. They have put on the image of the
Saviour. Heirs of future blessings, bearing the keys of the
kingdom, able accusers and excusers, not speaking themselves,
but examined by the judge.

Chrys.
Hom.
45. in
Act.   CHRYS. It would become thee then to receive them above
in the best chamber, but if thou shrinkest, at least admit Christ
below, where are the menials and servants. Let the poor
man be at least thy door keeper. For where there is alms, the
devil durst not enter. And if thou sittest not down with
them, at any rate send them the dishes from thy table.
ORIGEN; But mystically, he who shuns vain-glory calls to a
spiritual banquet the poor, that is, the ignorant, that he may
enrich them; the weak, that is, those with offended consciences,
that he may heal them; the lame, that is, those who have
wandered from reason, that he may make their paths straight;
the blind, that is, those who discern not the truth, that they
may behold the true light. But it is said, *They cannot recompense thee,* i. e. they know not how to return an answer.

15. And when one of them that sat at meat with
him heard these things, he said unto him, Blessed
is he that shall eat bread in the kingdom of God.

16. Then said he unto him, A certain man made a
great supper, and bade many:

17. And sent his servant at supper time to say to them that were bidden, Come; for all things are now ready.

18. And they all with one consent began to make excuse. The first said unto him, I have bought a piece of ground, and I must needs go and see it : I pray thee have me excused.

19. And another said, I have bought five yoke of oxen, and I go to prove them: I pray thee have me excused.

20. And another said, I have married a wife, and therefore I cannot come.

21. So that servant came, and shewed his lord these things. Then the master of the house being angry said to his servant, Go out quickly into the streets and lanes of the city, and bring in hither the poor, and the maimed, and the halt, and the blind.

22. And the servant said, Lord, it is done as thou hast commanded, and yet there is room.

23. And the lord said unto the servant, Go out into the highways and hedges, and compel them to come in, that my house may be filled.

24. For I say unto you, That none of those men which were bidden shall taste of my supper.

EUSEB. Our Lord had just before taught us to prepare our feasts for those who cannot repay, seeing that we shall have our reward at the resurrection of the just. Some one then, supposing the resurrection of the just to be one and the same with the kingdom of God, commends the above-mentioned recompense; for it follows, *When one of them that sat at meat with him heard these things, he said unto him, Blessed is he that shall eat bread in the kingdom of God.* CYRIL.; That man was carnal, and a careless hearer of the things which Christ delivered, for he thought the reward of the saints was to be bodily. AUG. Or because he sighed for Aug. Serm. 112.

something afar off, and that bread which he desired lay
before him. For who is that Bread of the kingdom of God
John 6, but He who says, *I am the living bread which came down*
51. *from heaven?* Open not thy mouth, but thy heart.

BEDE; But because some receive this bread by faith
merely, as if by smelling, but its sweetness they loathe to
really touch with their mouths, our Lord by the following
parable condemns the dulness of those men to be unworthy of
the heavenly banquet. For it follows, *But he said unto him, A*
certain man made a great supper, and bade many. CYRIL;
This man represents God the Father just as images are formed
to give the resemblance of power. For as often as God
wishes to declare His avenging power, He is called by the
names of bear, leopard, lion, and others of the same kind;
but when He wishes to express mercy, by the name of man. The
Maker of all things, therefore, and Father of Glory, or the
Lord, prepared the great supper which was finished in Christ.

For in these latter times, and as it were the setting of our
world, the Son of God has shone upon us, and enduring
death for our sakes, has given us His own body to eat. Hence
also the lamb was sacrificed in the evening according to the
Mosaic law. Rightly then was the banquet which was pre-
Greg.
Hom.
36. in
Evan. pared in Christ called a supper. GREG. Or he made a great
supper, as having prepared for us the full enjoyment of eternal
sweetness. He bade many, but few came, because sometimes
they who themselves are subject to him by faith, by their
lives oppose his eternal banquet. And this is generally the
difference between the delights of the body and the soul,
that fleshly delights when not possessed provoke a longing
desire for them, but when possessed and devoured, the eater
soon turns from satiety to loathing; spiritual delights, on the
other hand, when not possessed are loathed, when possessed
the more desired. But heavenly mercy recalls those despised delights to the eyes of our memory, and in order that
we should drive away our disgust, bids us to the feast. Hence
it follows, *And he sent his servant, &c.* CYRIL; That servant who was sent is Christ Himself, who being by nature
God and the true Son of God, emptied Himself, and took
upon Him the form of a servant. But He was sent at supper
time. For not in the beginning did the Word take upon Him

our nature, but in the last time; and he adds, *For all things
are ready.* For the Father prepared in Christ the good
things bestowed upon the world through Him, the removal of
sins, the participation of the Holy Spirit, the glory of adoption. To these Christ bade men by the teaching of the Gospel.
AUG. Or else, the Man is the Mediator between God and Aug.
man, Christ Jesus; He sent that they who were bidden might^{ubi sup.}
come, i. e. those who were called by the prophets whom He
had sent; who in the former times invited to the supper
of Christ, were often sent to the people of Israel, often bade
them to come at supper time. They received the inviters, refused the supper. They received the prophets and killed Christ,
and thus ignorantly prepared for us the supper. The supper
being now ready, i. e. Christ being sacrificed, the Apostles
were sent to those, to whom prophets had been sent before.
GREG. By this servant then who is sent by the master of the
family to bid to supper, the order of preachers is signified.
But it is often the case that a powerful person has a despised
servant, and when his Lord orders any thing through him,
the servant speaking is not despised, because respect for the
master who sends him is still kept up in the heart. Our
Lord then offers what he ought to be asked for, not ask others
to receive. He wishes to give what could scarcely be hoped
for; yet all begin at once to make excuse, for it follows,
And they all began with one consent to make excuse. Behold a rich man invites, and the poor hasten to come. We are
invited to the banquet of God, and we make excuse. AUG. Aug.
Now there were three excuses, of which it is added, *The first*^{ubi sup.}
*said unto him, I have bought a piece of ground, and I must
needs go and see it.* The bought piece of ground denotes
government. Therefore pride is the first vice reproved. For
the first man wished to rule, not willing to have a master.
GREG. Or by the piece of ground is meant worldly substance. Greg.
Therefore he goes out to see it who thinks only of outward^{ubi sup.}
things for the sake of his living. AMBROSE; Thus it is that
the worn out soldier is appointed to serve degraded offices,
as he who intent upon things below buys for himself
earthly possessions, can not enter into the kingdom of
heaven. Our Lord says, *Sell all that thou hast, and follow me.*
It follows, *And another said, I have bought five yoke of*

Aug.
Serm.
112. *oxen, and I go to prove them.* Aug. The five yoke of oxen are taken to be the five senses of the flesh; in the eyes sight, in the ears hearing, in the nostrils smelling, in the mouth taste, in all the members touch. But the yoke is more easily apparent in the three first senses; two eyes, two ears, two nostrils. Here are three yoke. And in the mouth is the sense of taste which is found to be a kind of double, in that nothing is sensible to the taste, which is not touched both by the tongue and palate. The pleasure of the flesh which belongs to the touch is secretly doubled. It is both outward and inward. But they are called yoke of oxen, because through those senses of the flesh earthly things are pursued. For the oxen till the ground, but men at a distance from faith, given up to earthly things, refuse to believe in any thing, but what they arrive at by means of the five-fold sense of the body. " I believe nothing but what I see." If such were our thoughts, we should be hindered from the supper by those five yoke of oxen. But that you may understand that it is not the delight of the five senses which charms and conveys pleasure, but that a certain curiosity is denoted, he says not, *I have bought five yoke of oxen, and* go to feed them, but *go to prove them.*

Greg.
in Hom.
56. in
Ev. Greg. By the bodily senses also because they cannot comprehend things within, but take cognizance only of what is without, curiosity is rightly represented, which while it seeks to shake off a life which is strange to it, not knowing its own secret life, desires to dwell upon things without. But we must observe, that the one who for his farm, and the other who to prove his five yoke of oxen, excuse themselves from the supper of their Inviter, mix up with their excuse the words of humility. For when they say, I pray thee, and then disdain to come, the word sounds of humility, but the action is pride. It follows, *And this said, I have married* Aug.
ubi sup. *a wife, and therefore I cannot come.* Aug. That is, the delight of the flesh which hinders many, I wish it were outward and not inward. For he who said, I have married a wife, taking pleasure in the delights of the flesh, excuses himself from the supper; let such a one take heed lest he die from inward hunger.

Basil; But he says, *I cannot come*, because that the

human mind when it is degenerating to worldly pleasures, is feeble in attending to the things of God. GREG. Greg.
But although marriage is good, and appointed by Divine Pro- Hom.
vidence for the propagation of children, some seek therein 36.
not fruitfulness of offspring, but the lust of pleasure. And
so by means of a righteous thing may not unfitly an unrighteous thing be represented. AMBROSE; Or marriage is not
blamed; but purity is held up to greater honour, since the
unmarried woman careth for the things of the Lord, that she 1 Cor. 7,
may be holy in body and spirit, but she that is married 34.
careth for the things of the world.

AUG. Now John when he said, *all that is in the world is* Aug.
the lust of the flesh, and the lust of the eyes, and the pride of ubi sup.
life, began from the point where the Gospel ended. The 1 John
lust of the flesh, *I have married a wife;* the lust of the eyes, 2, 16.
I have bought five yoke of oxen; the pride of life, *I have bought
a farm.* But proceeding from a part to the whole, the five
senses have been spoken of under the eyes alone, which hold
the chief place among the five senses. Because though properly the sight belongs to the eyes, we are in the habit of
ascribing the act of seeing to all the five senses.

CYRIL; But whom can we suppose these to be who refused
to come for the reason just mentioned, but the rulers of the
Jews, whom throughout the sacred history we find to have
been often reproved for these things? ORIGEN; Or else, they
who have bought a piece of ground and reject or refuse the
supper, are they who have taken other doctrines of divinity,
but have despised the word which they possessed. But he
who has bought five yoke of oxen is he who neglects his
intellectual nature, and follows the things of sense, therefore
he cannot comprehend a spiritual nature. But he who has
married a wife is he who is joined to the flesh, a lover of 1 Tim.
pleasure rather than of God. AMBROSE; Or let us suppose that 3, 4.
three classes of men are excluded from partaking of that supper,
Gentiles, Jews, Heretics. The Jews by their fleshly service
impose upon themselves the yoke of the law, for the five yoke
are the yoke of the Ten Commandments, of which it is said,
And he declared unto you his covenant, which he commanded Deut. 4,
you to perform, even ten commandments; and he wrote them 13.
upon two tables of stone. That is, the commands of the De-

calogue. Or the five yoke are the five books of the old law.

Eph. 5, 3. But heresy indeed, like Eve with a woman's obstinacy, tries the affection of faith. And the Apostle says that we must Col. 3,5. Heb. 13, 5. flee from covetousness, lest entangled in the customs of the Gentiles we be unable to come to the kingdom of Christ. 1 Tim. 6, 11. Therefore both he who has bought a farm is a stranger to the kingdom, and he who has chosen the yoke of the law rather than the gift of grace, and he also who excuses himself because he has married a wife.

Aug. in Gen. ad lit. c. 19. It follows, *And the servant returned, and told these things to his Lord.* AUG. Not for the sake of knowing inferior beings does God require messengers, as though He gained aught from them, for He knows all things stedfastly and unchangeably. But he has messengers for our sakes and their own, because to be present with God, and stand before Him so as to consult Him about His subjects, and obey His heavenly commandments, is good for them in the order of their own nature.

CYRIL; But with the rulers of the Jews who refused their John 7, 48. call, as they themselves confessed, *Have any of the rulers believed on him ?* the Master of the household was wroth, as with them that deserved His indignation and anger; whence it Pseudo-Basil. app. Hom. in Ps.37. follows, *Then the master of the house being angry, &c.* PSEUDO-BASIL; Not that the passion of anger belongs to the Divine substance, but an operation such as in us is caused by anger, is called the anger and indignation of God. CYRIL; Thus it was that the master of the house is said to have been enraged with the chiefs of the Jews, and in their stead were called men taken from out of the Jewish multitude, and of weak and impotent Acts 2, 41. 44. minds. For at Peter's preaching, first indeed three thousand, then five thousand believed, and afterwards much people; whence it follows, *He said unto his servant, Go out straightway into the streets and lanes of the city, and bring in hither the poor, and the maimed, and the halt, and the blind.* AMBROSE; He invites the poor, the weak, and the blind, to shew that weakness of body shuts out no one from the kingdom of heaven, and that he is guilty of fewer sins who lacks the incitement to sin; or that the infirmities of sin are forgiven through the mercy of God. Therefore he sends to the streets, that from the broader ways they may come to the narrow way.

Greg. Hom. 36. Because then the proud refuse to come, the *poor* are

chosen, since they are called weak and poor who are weak in
their own judgment of themselves, for there are poor, and yet
as it were strong, who though lying in poverty are proud; the
blind are they who have no brightness of understanding; the
lame are they who have walked not uprightly in their works.
But since the faults of these are expressed in the weakness
of their members, as those were sinners who when bidden
refused to come, so also are these who are invited and come;
but the proud sinners are rejected, the humble are chosen.
God then chooses those whom the world despises, because
for the most part the very act of contempt recals a man to
himself. And men so much the sooner hear the voice of
God, as they have nothing in this world to take pleasure in.
When then the Lord calls certain from the streets and lanes
to supper, He denotes that people who had learnt to observe
in the city the constant practice of the law. But the multitude who believed of the people of Israel did not fill the
places of the upper feast room. Hence it follows, *And the
servant said, Lord, it is done as thou hast commanded, and
yet there is room.* For already had great numbers of the
Jews entered, but yet there was room in the kingdom for the
abundance of the Gentiles to be received. Therefore it is
added, *And the Lord said unto the servant, Go out into the
highways and hedges, and compel them to come in, that my
house may be filled.* When He commanded His guests to be
collected from the wayside and the hedges, He sought for a
rural people, that is, the Gentiles. AMBROSE ; Or, He sends
to the highways and about the hedges, because they are fit
for the kingdom of God, who, not absorbed in the desire for
present goods, are hastening on to the future, set in a
certain fixed path of good will. And who like a hedge
which separates the cultivated ground from the uncultivated,
and keeps off the incursion of the cattle, know how to distinguish good and evil, and to hold up the shield of faith
against the temptations of spiritual wickedness.

AUG. The Gentiles came from the streets and lanes, the Aug.
heretics come from the hedges. For they who make a hedge Serm.
112.
seek for a division; let them be drawn away from the hedges,
plucked asunder from the thorns. But they are unwilling to
be compelled. By our own will, say they, will we enter.

2 L 2

Compel them to enter, He says. Let necessity be used from without, thence arises a will.

Greg. in
Hom.
36. GREG. They then who, broken down by the calamities of this world, return to the love of God, are compelled to enter. But very terrible is the sentence which comes next. *For I say unto you, That none of those men which were bidden shall taste of my supper.* Let no one then despise the call, lest if when bidden he make excuse, when he wishes to enter he shall not be able.

25. And there went great multitudes with him : and he turned, and said unto them,

26. If any man come to me, and hate not his father, and mother, and wife, and children, and brethren, and sisters, yea, and his own life also, he cannot be my disciple.

27. And whosoever doth not bear his cross, and come after me, cannot be my disciple.

Greg. in
Hom.
37. in
Ev. GREG. The mind is kindled, when it hears of heavenly rewards, and already desires to be there, where it hopes to enjoy them without ceasing; but great rewards cannot be reached except by great labours. Therefore it is said, *And there went great multitudes with him: and he turned to them, and said, &c.*

THEOPHYL. For because many of those that accompanied Him followed not with their whole heart, but lukewarmly, He shews what kind of a man his disciple ought to be.

Greg. in
Hom.
ut sup. GREG. But it may be asked, how are we bid to hate our parents and our relations in the flesh, who are commanded to love even our enemies? But if we weigh the force of the command we are able to do both, by rightly distinguishing them so as both to love those who are united to us by the bond of the flesh, and whom we acknowledge our relations, and by hating and avoiding not to know those whom we find our enemies in the way of God. For he is as it were loved by hatred, who in his carnal wisdom, pouring into our ears his evil sayings, is not heard. AMBROSE; For if for thy Matt.
12, 48.
Mark 3,
33. sake the Lord renounces His own mother, saying, *Who is*

my mother? and who are my brethren? why dost thou deserve to be preferred to thy Lord? But the Lord will have us neither be ignorant of nature, nor be her slaves, but so to submit to nature, that we reverence the Author of nature, and depart not from God out of love to our parents. GREG. Now to shew that this hatred towards relations proceeds not from inclination or passion, but from love, our Lord adds, *yea, and his own life also.* It is plain therefore that a man ought to hate his neighbour, by loving as himself him who hated him. For then we rightly hate our own soul when we indulge not its carnal desires, when we subdue its appetites, and wrestle against its pleasures. That which by being despised is brought to a better condition, is as it were loved by hatred. CYRIL; But life must not be renounced, which both in the body and the soul the blessed Paul also preserved, that yet living in the body he might preach Christ. But when it was necessary to despise life so that he might finish his course, he counts not his life dear unto him.

Greg. in Hom. ut sup.

Acts 20, 24.

GREG. How the hatred of life ought to be shewn He declares as follows; *Whosoever bears not his cross, &c.* CHRYS. He means not that we should place a beam of wood on our shoulders, but that we should ever have death before our eyes. As also Paul died daily and despised death. BASIL; By bearing the cross also he announced the death of his Lord, saying, *The world is crucified to me, and I to the world,* which we also anticipate at our very baptism, in which our old man is crucified, that the body of sin may be destroyed. GREG. Or because the cross is so called from torturing. In two ways we bear our Lord's cross, either when by abstinence we afflict our bodies, or when through compassion of our neighbour we think all his necessities our own. But because some exercise abstinence of the flesh not for God's sake but for vain-glory, and shew compassion, not spiritually but carnally, it is rightly added, *And cometh after me.* For to bear His cross and come after the Lord, is to use abstinence of the flesh, or compassion to our neighbour, from the desire of an eternal gain.

Greg. in Hom. ut sup.

1 Cor. 15, 31.

Gal. 6, 14.

Greg. in Hom. 37. in Ev.

28. For which of you, intending to build a tower,

sitteth not down first, and counteth the cost, whether he have sufficient to finish it?

29. Lest haply, after he hath laid the foundation, and is not able to finish it, all that behold it begin to mock him,

30. Saying, This man began to build, and was not able to finish.

31. Or what king, going to make war against another king, sitteth not down first, and consulteth whether he be able with ten thousand to meet him that cometh against him with twenty thousand?

32. Or else, while the other is yet a great way off, he sendeth an ambassage, and desireth conditions of peace.

33. So likewise, whosoever he be of you that forsaketh not all that he hath, he cannot be my disciple.

Greg. 37. in Ev.

GREG. Because He had been giving high and lofty precepts, immediately follows the comparison of building a tower, when it is said, *For which of you intending to build a tower does not first count &c.* For every thing that we do should be preceded by anxious consideration. If then we desire to build a tower of humility, we ought first to brace ourselves against the ills of this world. BASIL; Or the tower is a lofty watch-tower fitted for the guardianship of the city and the discovery of the enemy's approach. In like manner was our understanding given us to preserve the good, to guard against the evil. For the building up whereof the Lord bids us sit down and count our means if we have sufficient to finish. GREG. NYSS. For we must be ever pressing onward that we may reach the end of each difficult undertaking by successive increases of the commandments of God, and so to the completion of the divine work. For neither is one stone the whole fabric of the tower, nor does a single command lead to the perfection of the soul. But we must lay the foundation, and according to the Apostle, thereupon must be placed store of gold, silver, and precious stones. Whence it is added, *Lest haply after he hath laid the foundation, &c.*

Basil. in Esai. 2.

Greg. lib. de Virg. 18.

1 Cor.3, 12.

THEOPHYL. For we ought not to lay a foundation, i. e. begin to follow Christ, and not bring the work to an end, as those of whom St. John writes, *That many of his disciples went back-* John 6, *ward.* Or by the foundation understand the word of teaching, as 66. for instance concerning abstinence. There is need therefore of the above-mentioned foundation, that the building up of our works be established, a tower of strength from the face of the Ps.60,3. enemy. Otherwise, man is laughed at by those who see him, men as well as devils. GREG. For when occupied in good Greg. works, unless we watch carefully against the evil spirits, we ubi sup. find those our mockers who are persuading us to evil. But another comparison is added proceeding from the less to the greater, in order that from the least things the greatest may be estimated. For it follows, *Or what king, going to make war against another king, sitteth not down first, and consulteth whether he be able with ten thousand to meet him that cometh against him with twenty thousand?* CYRIL; *For we fight* Eph. 6, *against spiritual wickedness in high places;* but there presses 12. upon us a multitude also of other enemies, fleshly lust, the law of sin raging in our members, and various passions, that is, a dreadful multitude of enemies. AUG. Or the ten thousand of him who is going to fight with the king who has twenty, signify the simplicity of the Christian about to contend with the subtlety of the devil. THEOPHYL. The king is sin reigning in our mortal body ; but our understand- Rom. 6, ing also was created king. If then he wishes to fight against 12. sin, let him consider with his whole mind. For the devils are the satellites of sin, which being twenty thousand, seem to surpass in number our ten thousand, because that being spiritual compared to us who are corporeal, they are come to have much greater strength.

AUG. But as with respect to the unfinished tower, he alarms Aug. us by the reproaches of those who say, *The man began to build,* nt sup. *and was not able to finish,* so with regard to the king with whom the battle was to be, he reproved even peace, adding, *Or else, while the other is yet a great way off, he sendeth an ambassage, and desireth conditions of peace;* signifying that those also who forsake all they possess cannot endure from the devil the threats of even coming temptations, and make peace with him by consenting unto him to commit

Greg.
in Hom.
ut sup. sin. GREG. Or else, in that awful trial we come not to the judgment a match for our king, for ten thousand are against twenty thousand, two against one. He comes with a double army against a single. For while we are scarcely prepared in deeds only, he sifts us at once both in thought and deed. While then he is yet afar off, who though still present in judgment, is not seen, let us send him an embassy, our tears, our works of mercy, the propitiatory victim. This is our message which appeases the coming king.

AUG. Now to what these comparisons refer, He on the same occasion sufficiently explained, when he said, *So like-wise whosoever he be of you that forsaketh not all that he hath, he cannot be my disciple.* The cost therefore of build-ing the tower, and the strength of the ten thousand against the king who has twenty thousand, mean nothing else than that each one should forsake all that he hath. The foregoing introduction tallies then with the final conclusion. For in the saying that a man forsakes all that he hath, is contained also that he hates his father and mother, his wife and children, brothers and sisters, yea and his own wife also. For all these things are a man's own, which entangle him, and hinder him from obtaining not those particular possessions which will pass away with time, but those common blessings which will abide for ever.

BASIL; But our Lord's intention in the above-mentioned example is not indeed to afford occasion or give liberty to any one to become His disciple or not, as indeed it is lawful not to begin a foundation, or not to treat of peace, but to shew the impossibility of pleasing God, amidst those things which distract the soul, and in which it is in danger of becoming an easy prey to the snares and wiles of the devil. BEDE; But there is a difference between renouncing all things and leav-ing all things. For it is the way of few perfect men to leave all things, that is, to cast behind them the cares of the world, but it is the part of all the faithful to renounce all things, that is, so to hold the things of the world as by them not to be held in the world.

34. Salt is good: but if the salt have lost his savour, wherewith shall it be seasoned ?

35. It is neither fit for the land, nor yet for the dunghill; but men cast it out. He that hath ears to hear, let him hear.

BEDE; He had said above that the tower of virtue was not only to be begun, but also to be completed, and to this belongs the following, *Salt is good.* It is a good thing to season the secrets of the heart with the salt of spiritual wisdom, nay with the Apostles to become *the salt of the earth.* For salt in substance consists of water and air, having a slight mixture of earth, but it dries up the fluent nature of corrupt bodies so as to preserve them from decay. Fitly then He compares His disciples to salt, inasmuch as they are regenerated by water and the Spirit; and as living altogether spiritually and not according to the flesh, they after the manner of salt change the corrupt life of men who live on the earth, and by their own virtuous lives delight and season their followers.

Matt. 5, 14.

THEOPHYL. But not only those who are gifted with the grace of teachers, but private individuals also He requires to become like salt, useful to those around them. But if he who is to be useful to others becomes reprobate, he cannot be profited, as it follows, *But if the salt has lost his savour, wherewith shall it be seasoned?* BEDE; As if He says, " If a man who has once been enlightened by the seasoning of truth, falls back into apostacy, by what other teacher shall he be corrected, seeing that the sweetness of wisdom which he tasted he has cast away, alarmed by the troubles or allured by the attractions of the world; hence it follows, *It is neither fit for the land, nor yet for the dunghill, &c.* For salt when it has ceased to be fit for seasoning food and drying flesh, will be good for nothing. For neither is it useful to the land, which when it is cast thereon is hindered from bearing, nor for the dunghill to benefit the dressing of the land. So he who after knowledge of the truth falls back, is neither able to bring forth the fruit of good works himself, nor to instruct others; but he must be cast out of doors, that is, must be separated from the unity of the Church. THEOPHYL. But because His discourse was in parables and dark sayings, our Lord, in order to rouse His hearers that they might not receive indifferently

what was said of the salt, adds, *He that hath ears to hear,*
let him hear, that is, as he has wisdom let him understand.
For we must take the ears here as the perceptive power of the
mind and capacity of understanding. BEDE ; Let him hear
also not by despising, but by doing what he has learnt.

CHAP. XV.

1. Then drew near unto him all the Publicans and sinners for to hear him.

2. And the Pharisees and Scribes murmured, saying, This man receiveth sinners, and eateth with them.

3. And he spake this parable unto them, saying,

4. What man of you, having an hundred sheep, if he lose one of them, doth not leave the ninety and nine in the wilderness, and go after that which is lost, until he find it?

5. And when he hath found it, he layeth it on his shoulders, rejoicing.

6. And when he cometh home, he calleth together his friends and neighbours, saying unto them, Rejoice with me; for I have found my sheep which was lost.

7. I say unto you, that likewise joy shall be in heaven over one sinner that repenteth, more than over ninety and nine just persons, which need no repentance.

AMBROSE; Thou hadst learnt by what went before not to be occupied by the business of this world, not to prefer transitory things to eternal. But because the frailty of man can not keep a firm step in so slippery a world, the good Physician has shewn thee a remedy even after falling; the merciful Judge has not denied the hope of pardon; hence it is added, *Then drew near unto him all the publicans.* GLOSS. That is, those who collect or farm the public taxes, Gloss. interlin.

and who make a business of following after worldly gain.
THEOPHYL. For this was His wont, for the sake whereof
He had taken upon Him the flesh, to receive sinners as the
physician those that are sick. But the Pharisees, the really
guilty, returned murmurs for this act of mercy, as it follows,
And the Pharisees and Scribes murmured, saying, &c.

Greg. in
Hom.
34. in
Evang.

GREG. From which we may gather, that true justice feels
compassion, false justice scorn, although the just are wont
rightly to repel sinners. But there is one act proceeding
from the swelling of pride, another from the zeal for discipline. For the just, though without they spare not rebukes
for the sake of discipline, within cherish sweetness from
charity. In their own minds they set above themselves
those whom they correct, whereby they keep both them
under by discipline, and themselves by humility. But, on
the contrary, they who from false justice are wont to pride
themselves, despise all others, and never in mercy condescend
to the weak; and thinking themselves not to be sinners,
are so much the worse sinners. Of such were the Pharisees,
who condemning our Lord because He received sinners,
with parched hearts reviled the very fountain of mercy.
But because they were so sick that they knew not of their
sickness, to the end that they might know what they were,
the heavenly Physician answers them with mild applications.
For it follows, *And he spake this parable unto them, say-*
ing, What man of you having an hundred sheep, and if he
lose one of them, does not go after it, &c. He gave a comparison which man might recognise in himself, though it
referred to the Creator of men. For since a hundred is a
perfect number, He Himself had a hundred sheep, seeing
that He possessed the nature of the holy angels and men.
Hence he adds, *Having an hundred sheep.*

CYRIL; We may hence understand the extent of our
Saviour's kingdom. For He says there are a hundred sheep,
bringing to a perfect sum the number of rational creatures
subject to Him. For the number hundred is perfect, being
composed of ten decades. But out of these one has wandered,
namely, the race of man which inhabits earth. AMBROSE;
Rich then is that Shepherd of whom we all are a hundredth
part; and hence it follows, *And if he lose one of them, does*

he not leave &c. GREG. One sheep then perished when man
by sinning left the pastures of life. But in the wilderness
the ninety and nine remained, because the number of the
rational creatures, that is to say of Angels and men who were
formed to see God, was lessened when man perished; and
hence it follows, *Does he not leave the ninety and nine in the*
wilderness, because in truth he left the companies of the
Angels in heaven. But man then forsook heaven when he
sinned. And that the whole body of the sheep might be perfectly made up again in heaven, the lost man was sought for
on earth; as it follows, *And go after that &c.* CYRIL.; But
was He then angry with the rest, and moved by kindness
only to one? By no means. For they are in safety, the right
hand of the Most Mighty being their defence. It behoved
Him rather to pity the perishing, that the remaining number might not seem imperfect. For the one being brought
back, the hundred regains its own proper form. AUG. Or He
spoke of those ninety and nine whom He left in the wilderness,
signifying the proud, who bear solitude as it were in their mind,
in that they wish to appear themselves alone, to whom unity
is wanting for perfection. For when a man is torn from
unity, it is by pride; since desiring to be his own master, he
follows not that One which is God, but to that One God ordains
all who are reconciled by repentance, which is obtained by humility. GREG. NYSS. But when the shepherd had found the
sheep, he did not punish it, he did not get it to the flock by
driving it, but by placing it upon his shoulder, and carrying it
gently, he united it to his flock. Hence it follows, *And when he*
hath found it, he layeth it upon his shoulders rejoicing.
GREG. He placed the sheep upon his shoulders, for taking
man's nature upon Him he bore our sins. But having found
the sheep, he returns home; for our Shepherd having restored
man, returns to his heavenly kingdom. And hence it follows,
And coming he collects together his friends and neighbours,
saying to them, Rejoice with me, for I have found my sheep
which was lost. By His friends and neighbours He means the
companies of Angels, who are His friends because they are
keeping His will in their own stedfastness; they are also His
neighbours, because by their own constant waiting upon Him
they enjoy the brightness of His sight. THEOPHYL. The heavenly

Aug. de
Quæst.
Ev.lib.2.
qu. 32.

Greg.
Hom.de
Mul.
Pecc.

Greg. in
Hom.
34.
1 Pet.2,
24.
Isai. 53.

powers thus are called sheep, because every created nature as compared with God is as the beasts, but inasmuch as it is rational, they are called friends and neighbours.

Greg. in Hom. 34. GREG. And we must observe that He says not, " Rejoice with the sheep that is found," but *with me*, because truly our life is His joy, and when we are brought home to heaven we fill up the festivity of His joy. AMBROSE; Now the angels, inasmuch as they are intelligent beings, do not unreasonably rejoice at the redemption of men, as it follows, *I say unto you, that likewise joy shall be in heaven over one sinner that repenteth, more than over ninety and nine just persons who need no repentance.* Let this serve as an incentive to goodness, for a man to believe that his conversion will be pleasing to the assembled angels, whose favour he Greg. ubi sup. ought to court, or whose displeasure to fear. GREG. But he allows there is more joy in heaven over the converted sinner, than over the just who remain stedfast; for the latter for the most part, not feeling themselves oppressed by the weight of their sins, stand indeed in the way of righteousness, but still do not anxiously sigh after the heavenly country, frequently being slow to perform good works, from their confidence in themselves that they have committed no grievous sins. But, on the other hand, sometimes those who remember certain iniquities that they have committed, being pricked to the heart, from their very grief grow inflamed towards the love of God; and because they consider they have wandered from God, make up for their former losses by the succeeding gains. Greater then is the joy in heaven, just as the leader in battle loves that soldier more who having turned from flight, bravely pursues the enemy, than him who never turned his back and never did a brave act. So the husbandman rather loves that land which after bearing thorns yields abundant fruit, than that which never had thorns, and never gave him a plentiful crop. But in the mean time we must be aware that there are very many just men in whose life there is so much joy, that no penitence of sinners however great can in any way be preferred to them. Whence we may gather what great joy it causes to God when the just man humbly mourns, if it produces joy in heaven when the unrighteous by his repentance condemns the evil that he has done.

8. Either what woman having ten pieces of silver, if she lose one piece, doth not light a candle, and sweep the house, and seek diligently till she find it?

9. And when she hath found it, she calleth her friends and her neighbours together, saying, Rejoice with me; for I have found the piece which I had lost.

10. Likewise, I say unto you, there is joy in the presence of the angels of God over one sinner that repenteth.

CHRYS. By the preceding parable, in which the race of mankind was spoken of as a wandering sheep, we were shewn to be the creatures of the most high God, *who has made us, and not we ourselves, and we are the sheep of his pasture.* But now is added a second parable, in which the race of man is compared to a piece of silver which was lost, by which he shews that we were made according to the royal likeness and image, that is to say, of the most high God. For the piece of silver is a coin having the impress of the king's image, as it is said, *Or what woman having ten pieces of silver, if she lose one, &c.* GREG. He who is signified by the shepherd, is also by the woman. For it is God Himself, God and the wisdom of God, but the Lord has formed the nature of angels and men to know Him, and has created them after His likeness. The woman then had ten pieces of silver, because there are nine orders of angels, but that the number of the elect might be filled up, man the tenth was created. AUG. Or by the nine pieces of silver, as by the ninety and nine sheep, He represents those who trusting in themselves, prefer themselves to sinners returning to salvation. For there is one wanting to nine to make it ten, and to ninety-nine to make it a hundred. To that One He ordains all who are reconciled by repentance. GREG. And because there is an image impressed on the piece of silver, the woman lost the piece of silver when man (who was created after the image of God) by sinning departed from the likeness of his Creator. And this is what is added, *If she lose one piece, doth she not light a candle.* The woman lighted a candle because the

Chrys.
non occ.

Ps. 95,
7.

Greg.
Hom.
34. in
Ev.

Aug. de
Quæst.
Ev. lib.
2. qu.
33.

Greg.
ut sup.

wisdom of God appeared in man. For the candle is a light in an earthen vessel, but the light in an earthen vessel is the Godhead in the flesh. But the candle being lit, it *evertit* follows, *And disturbs the house.* Because verily no sooner had his Divinity shone forth through the flesh, than all our consciences were appalled. Which word of disturbance differs not from that which is read in other manuscripts, *everrit* *sweeps,* because the corrupt mind if it be not first overthrown through fear, is not cleansed from its habitual faults. But when the house is broken up, the piece of silver is found, for it follows, *And seeks diligently till she find it ;* for truly when the conscience of man is disturbed, the likeness of the Creator is restored in man.

Greg. Orat. xlv. 26.
GREG. NAZ. But the piece of silver being found, He makes the heavenly powers partakers of the joy whom He made the ministers of His dispensation, and so it follows, *And when she had found it, she calls together her friends and neighbours.*

Greg. in Hom. 23. ut sup.
GREG. For the heavenly powers are nigh unto Divine wisdom, inasmuch as they approach Him through the grace of continual vision. THEOPHYL. Either they are friends as performing His will, but neighbours as being spiritual; or perhaps His friends are all the heavenly powers, but His neighbours those that come near to Him, as Thrones, Cherubims, and Seraphims.

Greg. lib. de Virgin. c. 12.
GREG. NYSS. Or else ; this I suppose is what our Lord sets before us in the search after the lost piece of silver, that no advantage attaches to us from the external virtues which He calls pieces of silver, although all of them be ours, as long as that one is lacking to the widowed soul, by which in truth it obtains the brightness of the Divine image. Wherefore He first bids us light a candle, that is to say, the divine word which brings hidden things to light, or perhaps the torch of repentance. But in his own house, that is, in himself and his own conscience, must a man seek for the lost piece of silver, that is, the royal image, which is not entirely defaced, but is hid under the dirt, which signifies its corruption of the flesh, and this being diligently wiped away, that is, washed out by a well-spent life, that which was sought for shines forth. Therefore ought she who has found it to rejoice, and to call to partake of her joy the neighbours, (that is, the com-

panion virtues,) reason, desire, and anger, and whatever powers are observed round the soul, which she teaches to rejoice in the Lord.   Then concluding the parable, He adds, *There is joy in the presence of the angels over one sinner that repenteth.*   GREG. To work repentance is to mourn Greg. over past sins, and not to commit things to be mourned over. in Hom. For he who weeps over some things so as yet to commit others, 34. ut still knows not how to work repentance, or is a hypocrite; he sup. must also reflect that by so doing he satisfies not his Creator, since he who had done what was forbidden, must cut off himself even from what is lawful, and so should blame himself in the least things who remembers that he has offended in the greatest.

11. And he said, A certain man had two sons:

12. And the younger of them said to his father, Father, give me the portion of goods that falleth to me.   And he divided unto them his living.

13. And not many days after the younger son gathered all together, and took his journey into a far country, and there wasted his substance with riotous living.

14. And when he had spent all, there arose a mighty famine in that land; and he began to be in want.

15. And he went and joined himself to a citizen of that country; and he sent him into his fields to feed swine.

16. And he would fain have filled his belly with the husks that the swine did eat: and no man gave unto him.

AMBROSE; St. Luke has given three parables successively; the sheep which was lost and found, the piece of silver which was lost and found, the son who was dead and came to life again, in order that invited by a threefold remedy, we might heal our wounds.   Christ as the Shepherd bears thee on His own body, the Church as the woman seeks for thee, God as the Father receives thee, the first, pity, the second, intercession, the third, reconciliation.

CHRYS There is also in the above-mentioned parable a rule of distinction with reference to the characters or dispositions of the sinners. The father receives his penitent son, exercising the freedom of his will, so as to know from whence he had fallen; and the shepherd seeks for the sheep that wanders and knows not how to return, and carries it on his shoulders, comparing to an irrational animal the foolish man, who, taken by another's guile, had wandered like a sheep. This parable is then set forth as follows; *But he said, A certain man had two sons.* There are some who say of these two sons, that the elder is the angels, but the younger, man, who departed on a long journey, when he fell from heaven and paradise to earth; and they adapt what follows with reference to the fall or condition of Adam. This interpretation seems indeed a lenient one, but I know not if it be true. For the younger son came to repentance of his own accord, remembering the past plenty of his father's house, but the Lord coming called the race of man to repentance, because he saw that to return of their own accord to whence they had fallen had never been in their thoughts; and the elder son is vexed at the return and safety of his brother, whereas the Lord says, *There is joy in heaven over one sinner repenting.* CYRIL; But some say that by the elder son is signified Israel according to the flesh, but by the other who left his father, the multitude of the Gentiles.

AUG. This man then having two sons is understood to be God having two nations, as if they were two roots of the human race; and the one composed of those who have remained in the worship of God, the other, of those who have ever deserted God to worship idols. From the very beginning then of the creation of mankind the elder son has reference to the worship of the one God, but the younger seeks that the part of the substance which fell to him should be given him by his father. Hence it follows, *And the younger of them said unto his father, Give me the portion of goods which falleth to me;* just as the soul delighted with its own power seeks that which belongs to it, to live, to understand, to remember, to excel in quickness of intellect, all which are the gifts of God, but it has received them in its own power by free will. Hence it follows, *And he divided unto them his substance.* THEOPHYL. The substance of man is the capacity of reason which is accompanied by free will, and in like manner whatever God has given us shall be accounted for our substance, as the heaven, the earth, and universal nature, the Law and the Prophets.

AMBROSE; Now you see that the Divine patrimony is given to them that seek; nor think it wrong in the father that he gave it to the younger, for no age is weak in the kingdom of God; faith is not weighed down by years. He at least counted himself sufficient who asked, And I wish he had not departed from his father, nor had the hindrance of age. For it follows, *And not many days after, the younger son gathered all together, and took his journey into a far country.* CHRYS. The younger son set out into a distant country, not locally departing from God, who is every where present, but in heart. For the sinner flees from God that he may stand afar off. AUG. Whoever wishes to be so like to God as to ascribe his strength to Him, let him not depart from Him, but rather cleave to Him that he may preserve the likeness and image in which he was made. But if he perversely wishes to imitate God, that as God has no one by whom He is governed, so should he desire to exercise his own power as to live under no rules, what remains for him but that having lost all heat he should grow cold and senseless, and, departing from truth, vanish away.

AUG. But that which is said to have taken place not many days after, namely, that gathering all together he set out abroad into a far country, which is forgetfulness of God, signifies that not long after the institution of the human race, the soul of man chose of its free will to take with it a certain power of its nature, and to desert Him by whom it was created, trusting in its own strength, which it wastes the more rapidly as it has abandoned Him who gave it. Hence it follows, *And there wasted his substance in riotous living.* But he calls a riotous or prodigal life one that loves to spend and lavish itself with outward show, while exhausting itself within, since every one follows those things which pass on to something else, and forsakes Him who is closest to himself. As it follows,

Chrys. ut sup.

Aug. in Ps. 70. Ps. 59, 9.

Aug. de Quæst Ev. lib. ii. qu. 33.

And when he had spent all, there arose a great famine in that land. The famine is the want of the word of truth.

It follows, *And he began to be in want.* Fitly did he begin to be in want who abandoned the treasures of the wisdom and the knowledge of God, and the unfathomableness of the heavenly riches. It follows, *And he went and joined himself to a citizen of that country.* AUG. One of the citizens of that country was a certain prince of the air belonging to the army of the devil, whose fields signify the manner of his power, concerning which it follows, *And he sent him into the field to feed swine.* The swine are the unclean spirits which are under him. BEDE; But to feed swine is to work those things in which the unclean spirits delight. It follows, *And he would have filled his belly with the husks which the swine did eat.* The husk is a sort of bean, empty within, soft outside, by which the body is not refreshed, but filled, so that it rather loads than nourishes. AUG. The husks then with which the swine were fed are the teaching of the world, which cries loudly of vanity; according to which in various prose and verse men repeat the praises of the idols, and fables belonging to the gods of the Gentiles, wherewith the devils are delighted. Hence when he would fain have filled himself, he wished to find therein something stable and upright which might relate to a happy life, and he could not; as it follows, *And no one gave to him.*

CYRIL; But since the Jews are frequently reproved in holy Scripture for their many crimes, how agree with this people the words of the elder son, saying, *Lo, these many years do I serve thee, neither transgressed I at any time thy commandment.* This then is the meaning of the parable. The Pharisees and Scribes reproved Him because He received sinners; He set forth the parable in which He calls God the man who is the father of the two sons, (that is, the righteous and the sinners,) of whom the first degree is of the righteous who follow righteousness from the beginning, the second is of those men who are brought back by repentance to righteousness. BASIL; Besides, it belongs more to the character of the aged to have an old man's mind and gravity, than his hoar hairs, nor is he blamed who is young in age, but it is the young in habits who lives

Marginal notes:
Aug. ubi sup.

Aug. ubi sup.

Jer. 2, 5. Isa. 29, 13.

Basil. Esai. 3, 23.

according to his passions. TIT. BOST. The younger son then went away not yet matured in mind, and seeks from his father the part of his inheritance which fell to him, that in truth he might not serve of necessity. For we are rational animals endowed with free will.

CHRYS. Now the Scripture says, that the father divided Chrys. equally between his two sons his substance, that is, the ^ut sup. knowledge of good and evil, which is a true and everlasting possession to the soul that uses it well. The substance of reason which flows from God to men at their earliest birth, is given equally to all who come into this world, but after the intercourse that follows, each one is found to possess more or less of the substance; since one believing that which he has received to be from his father, preserves it as his patrimony, another abuses it as something that may be wasted away, by the liberty of his own possession. But the freedom of will is shewn in that the father neither kept back the son who wished to depart, nor forced the other to go that desired to remain, lest he should seem rather the author of the evil that followed. But the youngest son went afar off, not by changing his place, but by turning aside his heart. Hence it follows, *He took a journey into a far country.* AMBROSE; For what is more afar off than to depart from one's self, to be separate not by country but by habits. For he who severs himself from Christ is an exile from his country, and a citizen of this world. Fitly then does he waste his patrimony who departs from the Church. TIT. BOST. Hence too was the prodigal denominated one who wasted his substance, that is, his right understanding, the teaching of chastity, the knowledge of the truth, the recollections of his father, the sense of creation.

AMBROSE; Now there came to pass in that country a famine not of food but of good works and virtues, which is the more wretched fast. For he who departs from the word of God is hungry, because man does not live on bread Matt. 4, alone, but on every word of God. And he who departs from ^4. his treasures is in want. Therefore began he to be in want and to suffer hunger, because nothing satisfies a prodigal mind. He went away therefore, and attached himself to one of the citizens. For he who is attached, is in a snare. And that citizen seems to be a prince of the world. Lastly, he is sent

Luke 14, 18. to his farm which he bought who excused himself from the kingdom. BEDE; For to be sent to the farm is to be enthralled by the desire of worldly substance. AMBROSE; But Matt. 8. Mark 2. Luke 8. he feeds those swine into whom the devil sought to enter, living in filth and pollution. THEOPHYL. There then he feeds, who surpassed others in vice, such as are panders, arch-robbers, arch-publicans, who teach others their abominable works.

Chrys. ut sup. CHRYS. Or he who is destitute of spiritual riches, as wisdom and understanding, is said to feed swine, that is, to nourish in his soul sordid and unclean thoughts, and he devours the material food of evil conversation, sweet indeed to him who lacks good works, because every work of carnal pleasure seems sweet to the depraved, while it inwardly unnerves and destroys the powers of the soul. Food of this kind, as being swines' food and hurtfully sweet, that is, the allurements of fleshly delights, the Scripture describes by the name of husks. AMBROSE; But he desired to fill his belly with the husks. For the sensual care for nothing else but to fill their bellies. THEOPHYL. To whom no one gives a sufficiency of evil; for he is afar from God who lives on such things, and the devils do their best that a satiety of evil should never come. GLOSS. Or no one gave to him, because when the devil makes any one his own, he procures no further abundance for him, knowing him to be dead.

17. And when he came to himself, he said, How many hired servants of my father's have bread enough and to spare, and I perish with hunger!

18. I will arise and go to my father, and will say unto him, Father, I have sinned against heaven, and before thee,

19. And am no more worthy to be called thy son: make me as one of thy hired servants.

20. And he arose, and came to his father. But when he was yet a great way off, his father saw him, and had compassion, and ran, and fell on his neck, and kissed him.

21. And the son said unto him, Father, I have sinned against heaven, and in thy sight, and am no more worthy to be called thy son.

22. But the father said to his servants, Bring forth the best robe, and put it on him; and put a ring on his hand, and shoes on his feet:

23. And bring hither the fatted calf, and kill it; and let us eat, and be merry:

24. For this my son was dead, and is alive again; he was lost, and is found. And they began to be merry.

GREG. NYSS. The younger son had despised his father when first he departed, and had wasted his father's money. But when in course of time he was broken down by hardship, having become a hired servant, and eating the same food with the swine, he returned, chastened, to his father's house. Hence it is said, *And when he came to himself, he said, How many hired servants of my father's have bread enough and to spare, but I perish with hunger.* AMBROSE; He rightly returns to himself, because he departed from himself. For he who returns to God restores himself to himself, and he who departs from Christ rejects himself from himself. AUG. But he returned to himself, when from those things which without unprofitably entice and seduce, he brought back his mind to the inward recesses of his conscience.

BASIL; There are three different distinct kinds of obedience. For either from fear of punishment we avoid evil and are servilely disposed; or looking to the gain of a reward we perform what is commanded, like to mercenaries; or we obey the law for the sake of good itself and our love to Him who gave it, and so savour of the mind of children. AMBROSE; For the son who has the pledge of the Holy Spirit in his heart seeks not the gain of an earthly reward, but preserves the right of an heir. These are also good husbandmen, to whom the vineyard is let out. They abound not in husks, but bread. AUG. But whence could he know this who had that great forgetfulness of God, which exists

Margin notes: Greg. Orat. in mul.pec. cat. — Aug. de Quæst. Ev. lib. ii.qu.33. — Matt. 20, 41. — Aug. ubi sup.

in all idolaters, unless it was the reflection of one returning to his right understanding, when the Gospel was preached. Already might such a soul see that many preach the truth, among whom there were some not led by the love of the truth itself, but the desire of getting worldly profit, who yet do not preach another Gospel like the heretics. Therefore are they rightly called mercenaries. For in the same house there are men who handle the same bread of the word, yet are not called to an eternal inheritance, but hire themselves for a temporal reward.

Chrys.
Hom.de
Patre et
duobus
Filiis.

CHRYS. After that he had suffered in a foreign land all such things as the wicked deserve, constrained by the necessity of his misfortunes, that is, by hunger and want, he becomes sensible of what had been his ruin, who through fault of his own will had thrown himself from his father to strangers, from home to exile, from riches to want, from abundance and luxury to famine; and he significantly adds, *But I am here perishing with hunger.* As though he said; I am not a stranger, but the son of a good father, and the brother of an obedient son; I who am free and noble am become more wretched than the hired servants, sunk from the highest eminence of exalted rank, to the lowest degra-

Greg.
ubi sup.

dation. GREG. NYSS. But he returned not to his former happiness before that coming to himself he had experienced the presence of overpowering bitterness, and resolved the words

Aug.
ubi sup.

of repentance, which are added, *I will arise.* AUG. For he was lying down. *And I will go,* for he was a long way off. *To my father,* because he was under a master of swine. But the other words are those of one meditating repentance in confession of sin, but not yet working it. For he does not now speak to his father, but promises that he will speak when he shall come. You must understand then that this "coming to the father" must now be taken for being established in the Church by faith, where there may yet be a lawful and effectual confession of sins. He says then that he will say to his father, *Father.* AMBROSE; How merciful! He, though offended, disdains not to hear the name of Father. *I have sinned;* this is the first confession of sin to the Author of nature, the Ruler of mercy, the Judge of faith. But though God knows all things, He yet waits for the voice of thy confession. For with the mouth confession is made to salvation, since he lightens the load of error, who himself throweth the weight upon himself, and shuts out the hatred of accusation, who anticipates the accuser by confessing. In vain would you hide from Him whom nothing escapes; and you may safely discover what you know to be already known. Confess the rather that Christ may intercede for thee, the Church plead for thee, the people weep over thee: nor fear that thou wilt not obtain; thy Advocate promises pardon, thy Patron favour, thy Deliverer promises thee the reconciliation of thy Father's affection. But he adds, *Against heaven and before thee.*

CHRYS. When he says, *Before thee,* he shews that this father must be understood as God. For God alone beholds all things, from Whom neither the simple thoughts of the heart can be hidden. Chrys. ubi sup.

AUG. But whether was this *sin against heaven,* the same as that which is *before thee;* so that he described by the name of heaven his father's supremacy. *I have sinned against heaven,* i. e. before the souls of the saints; but *before thee* in the very sanctuary of my conscience. Aug. de Quæst. Evan. l. ii. qu. 33.

CHRYS. Or by heaven in this place may be understood Christ. For he who sins against heaven, which although above us is yet a visible element, is the same as he who sins against man, whom the Son of God took into Himself for our salvation. AMBROSE; Or by these words are signified the heavenly gifts of the Spirit impaired by the sin of the soul, or because from the bosom of his mother Jerusalem which is in heaven, he ought never to depart. But being cast down, he must by no means exalt himself. Hence he adds, *I am no more worthy to be called thy son.* And that he might be raised up by the merit of his humility, he adds, *Make me as one of thy hired servants.* Chrys. ut sup.

BEDE; To the affection of a son, who doubts not that all things which are his father's are his, he by no means lays claim, but desires the condition of a hired servant, as now about to serve for a reward. But he admits that not even this could he deserve except by his father's approbation.

GREG. NYSS. Now this prodigal son, the Holy Spirit has engraved upon our hearts, that we may be instructed how we Greg. ubi sup.

ought to deplore the sins of our soul. CHRYS. Who after that he said, *I will go to my father,* (which brought all good things,) tarried not, but took the whole journey; for it follows, *And he arose, and came to his father.* Let us do likewise, and not be wearied with the length of the way, for if we are willing, the return will become swift and easy, provided that we desert sin, which led us out from our father's house. But the father pitieth those who return.

Aug.
ubi sup. For it is added, *And when he was yet afar off.* AUG. For before that he perceived God afar off, when he was yet piously seeking him, his father saw him. For the ungodly and proud, God is well said not to see, as not having them before his eyes. For men are not commonly said to be before the eyes of any one except those who are beloved.

Chrys.
Hom.
10. in
Ep.
Rom.
Greg.
ubi sup. CHRYS. Now the father perceiving his penitence did not wait to receive the words of his confession, but anticipates his supplication, *and had compassion on him,* as it is added, and was moved with pity. GREG. NYSS. His meditating confession so won his father to him, that he went out to meet him, and kissed his neck; for it follows, *and ran, and fell on his neck, and kissed him.* This signifies the yoke of reason imposed on the mouth of man by Evangelical tra-

Chrys.
Hom. de
Patre
et duob.
Fil. dition, which annulled the observance of the law. CHRYS. For what else means it that *he ran,* but that we through the hindrance of our sins cannot by our own virtue reach to God. But because God is able to come to the weak, *he fell on his neck.* The mouth is kissed, as that from which has proceeded the confession of the penitent, springing from the heart, which the father gladly received.

AMBROSE; He runs then to meet thee, because He hears thee within meditating the secrets of thy heart, and when thou wert yet afar off, He runs lest any one should stop Him. He embraces also, (for in the running there is fore-knowledge, in the embrace mercy,) and as if by a certain impulse of paternal affection, falls upon thy neck, that he may raise up him that is cast down, and bring back again to heaven him that was loaded with sins and bent down to the earth. I had rather then be a son than a sheep. For the sheep is found by the shepherd, the son is honoured by the father.

Aug.
ubi sup. AUG. Or running he fell upon his neck; because the Father

abandoned not His Only-Begotten Son, in whom He has ever been running after our distant wanderings. *For God was in* 2 Cor. 5, *Christ reconciling the world unto himself.* But to fall upon 19. his neck is to lower to his embrace His own Arm, which is the Lord Jesus Christ. But to be comforted by the word of God's grace unto the hope of pardon of our sins, this is to return after a long journey to obtain from a father the kiss of love. But already planted in the Church, he begins to confess his sins, nor says he all that he promised he would say. For it follows, *And his son said unto him, &c.* He wishes that to be done by grace, of which he confesses himself unworthy by any merits of his own. He does not add what he had said, when meditating beforehand, *Make me as one of thy hired servants.* For when he had not bread, he desired to be even a hired servant, which after the kiss of his father he now most nobly disdained. CHRYS. The father Chrys. does not direct his words to his son, but speaks to his non occ. steward, for he who repents, prays indeed, but receives no answer in word, yet beholds mercy effectual in operation. For it follows, *But the father said unto his servants, Bring forth the best robe, and put it on him.* THEOPHYL. By the servants (or angels) you may understand administering spirits, or priests who by baptism and the word of teaching clothe the soul with Christ Himself. *For as many* Gal. 3, *of us as have been baptized in Christ have put on Christ.* 27. AUG. Or the best robe is the dignity which Adam lost; Aug. de the servants who bring it are the preachers of reconciliation. Quæst. Ev. l. ii. AMBROSE; Or the robe is the cloke of wisdom, by which the q. 33. Apostle covers the nakedness of the body. But he received the best wisdom; for there is one wisdom which knew not the mystery. The ring is the seal of our unfeigned faith, and the impression of truth; concerning which it follows, *And put a ring on his hand.* BEDE; That is, his working, that by works faith may shine forth, and by faith his works be strengthened. AUG. Or the ring on Aug. the hand is a pledge of the Holy Spirit, because of the ut sup. participation of grace, which is well signified by the finger. CHRYS. Or he orders the ring to be given, which is Chrys. the symbol of the seal of salvation, or rather the badge of ubi sup. betrothment, and pledge of the nuptials with which Christ

espouses His Church. Since the soul that recovers is united
by this ring of faith to Christ.

Aug.
ubi sup. AUG. But the *shoes on the feet* are the preparation
for preaching the Gospel, in order not to touch earthly
Chrys.
Hom. de
Patre et
duobus
Filiis. things. CHRYS. Or he bids them put shoes on his feet,
either for the sake of covering the soles of his feet that he may
walk firm along the slippery path of the world, or for the mortification of his members. For the course of our life is called
in the Scriptures a foot, and a kind of mortification takes
place in shoes; inasmuch as they are made of the skins of
dead animals. He adds also, that the fatted calf must be
killed for the celebration of the feast. For it follows,
And bring the fatted calf, that is, the Lord Jesus Christ,
whom he calls a calf, because of the sacrifice of a body without spot; but he called it fatted, because it is rich and costly,
inasmuch as it is sufficient for the salvation of the whole
world. But the Father did not Himself sacrifice the calf, but
gave it to be sacrificed to others. For the Father permitting,
the Son consenting thereto by men was crucified. AUG. Or,
Aug.
ubi sup. the fatted calf is our Lord Himself in the flesh loaded with
insults. But in that the Father commands them to bring it,
what else is this but that they preach Him, and by declaring
Him cause to revive, yet unconsumed by hunger, the bowels
of the hungry son? He also bids them kill Him, alluding to
His death. For He is then killed to each man who believes
Him slain. It follows, *And let us eat.* AMBROSE; Rightly
the flesh of the calf, because it is the priestly victim which
was offered for sin. But he introduces him feasting, when
he says, *Be merry;* to shew that the food of the Father is
our salvation; the joy of the Father the redemption of our
Chrys.
ut sup. sins. CHRYS. For the father himself rejoices in the return
of his son, and feasts on the calf, because the Creator,
rejoicing in the acquisition of a believing people, feasts
on the fruit of His mercy by the sacrifice of His Son.
Hence it follows, *For this my son was dead, and is alive
again.* AMBROSE; He is dead who was. Therefore the
Gentiles are not, the Christian is. Here however might be
understood one individual of the human race; Adam was,
and in him we all were. Adam perished, and in him we all
have perished. Man then is restored in that Man who has

died. It might also seem to be spoken of one working
repentance, because he dies not who has not at one time
lived. And the Gentiles indeed when they have believed
are made alive again by grace. But he who has fallen
recovers by repentance. THEOPHYL. As then with respect
to the condition of his sins, he had been despaired of; so in
regard to human nature, which is changeable and can be
turned from vice to virtue, he is said to be lost. For it is
less to be lost than to die. But every one who is recalled
and turned from sin, partaking of the fatted calf, becomes an
occasion of joy to his father and his servants, that is, the
angels and priests. Hence it follows, *And they all began
to be merry.* AUG. Those banquets are now celebrated, Aug.
the Church being enlarged and extended throughout the ubi sup.
whole world. For that calf in our Lord's body and blood
is both offered up to the Father, and feeds the whole
house.

25. Now his elder son was in the field : and as he
came and drew nigh to the house, he heard musick
and dancing.

26. And he called one of the servants, and asked
what these things meant.

27. And he said unto him, Thy brother is come ;
and thy father hath killed the fatted calf, because he
hath received him safe and sound.

28. And he was angry, and would not go
in : therefore came his father out, and intreated
him.

29. And he answering said to his father, Lo, these
many years do I serve thee, neither transgressed I at
any time thy commandment : and yet thou never
gavest me a kid, that I might make merry with my
friends :

30. But as soon as this thy son was come, which
hath devoured thy living with harlots, thou hast killed
for him the fatted calf.

31. And he said unto him, Son, thou art ever with me, and all that I have is thine.

32. It was meet that we should make merry, and be glad : for this thy brother was dead, and is alive again ; and was lost, and is found.

BEDE; While the Scribes and Pharisees were murmuring about His receiving sinners, our Saviour put three parables to them successively. In the two first He hints at the joy He has with the angels in the salvation of penitents. But in the third He not only declares His own joy and that of His angels, but He also blames the murmurings of those who were envious. For He says, *Now his elder son was in the field.* AUG. The elder son is the people of Israel, not indeed gone into a distant country, yet not in the house, but in the field, that is, in the paternal wealth of the Law and the Prophets, choosing to work earthly things. But coming from the field he began to draw nigh to the house, that is, the labour of his servile works being condemned by the same Scriptures, he was looking upon the liberty of the Church. Whence it follows ; *And as he came and drew nigh to the house, he heard music and dancing;* that is, men filled with the Holy Spirit, with harmonious voices preaching the Gospel. It follows, *And he called one of the servants, &c.* that is, he takes one of the prophets to read, and as he searches in it, . asks in a manner, why are those feasts celebrated in the Church at which he finds himself present? His Father's servant, the prophet, answers him. For it follows ; *And he said unto him, Thy brother is come, &c.* As if he should say, Thy brother was in the farthest parts of the earth, but hence the greater rejoicing of those *who sing a new song,* because *His praise is from the end of the earth ;* and for his sake who was afar off, was slain the Man who knows how to bear our infirmities, for they who have not been told of Him have seen Him.

Aug. ubi sup.

Is. 42, 10.

See Isa. 53, 4; 52, 15.

AMBROSE; But the younger son, that is the Gentile people, is envied by Israel as the elder brother, the privilege of his father's blessing. Which the Jews did because Christ sat down to meat with the Gentiles, as it follows ; *And he was angry, and would not go in, &c.*

AUG. He is angry even also now, and still is unwilling to enter. When then the fulness of the Gentiles shall have come in, His father will go out at the fit time that all Israel also may be saved, as it follows, *therefore came his father out and entreated him.* For there shall be at some time an open calling of the Jews to the salvation of the Gospel. Which manifestation of calling he calls the going out of the father to entreat the elder son.   Next the answer of the elder son involves two questions; for it follows, *And he answering said to his father, Lo these many years do I serve thee, neither transgressed I at any time thy commandment.* With respect to the commandment not transgressed, it at once occurs, that it was not spoken of every command, but of that most essential one, that is, that he was seen to worship no other God but one, the Creator of all.   Nor is that son to be understood to represent all Israelites, but those who have never turned from God to idols.   For although he might desire earthly things, yet sought he them from God alone, though in common with sinners.   Hence it is said, *I was as a beast before thee, and I am always with thee.* But who is the kid which he never received to make merry upon? for it follows, *Thou never gavest me a kid, &c.* Under the name of a kid the sinner may be signified.

AMBROSE; The Jew requires a kid, the Christian a lamb, and therefore is Barabbas released to them, to us a lamb is sacrificed. Which thing also is seen in the kid, because the Jews have lost the ancient rite of sacrifice. Or they who seek for a kid wait for Antichrist. AUG. But I do not see the object of this interpretation, for it is very absurd for him to whom it is afterwards said, *Thou art ever with me,* to have wished for this from his father, i. e. to believe in Antichrist. Nor altogether can we rightly understand any of the Jews who are to believe in Antichrist to be that son.

And how could he feast upon that kid which is Antichrist who did not believe in him? But if to feast upon the slain kid, is the same as to rejoice at the destruction of Antichrist, how does the son whom the father did not entertain say that this was never given him, seeing that all the sons will rejoice at his destruction? His complaint then is, that the Lord Himself was denied him to feast upon, because he deems Him a sinner.

Rom. 11, 26.

Ps. 7, 22.

For since He is a kid to that nation which regards Him as a violater and profaner of the Sabbath, it was not meet that they should be made merry at his banquet. But his words *with my friends* are understood according to the relation of the chiefs with the people, or of the people of Jerusalem with the other nations of Judæa. JEROME; Or he says, *Thou never gavest me a kid*, that is, no blood of prophet or priest has delivered us from the Roman power.

Hier. in Ep. 21. ad Da- masum.

AMBROSE; Now the shameless son is like to the Pharisee justifying himself. Because he had kept the law in the letter, he wickedly accused his brother for having wasted his father's substance with harlots. For it follows, *But as soon as this thy son is come, who hath devoured thy living, &c.* AUG. The harlots are the superstitions of the Gentiles, with whom he wastes his substance, who having left the true marriage of the true God, goes a whoring after evil spirits from foul desire. JEROME; Now in that which he says, *Thou hast killed for him the fatted calf*, he confesses that Christ has come, but envy has no wish to be saved. AUG. But the father does not rebuke him as a liar, but commending his stedfastness with him invites him to the perfection of a better and happier rejoicing. Hence it follows, *But he said to him, Son, thou art ever with me.* JEROME; Or after having said, "This is boasting, not truth," the father does not agree with him, but restrains him in another way, saying, *Thou art with me*, by the law under which thou art bound; not as though he had not sinned, but because God continually drew him back by chastening. Nor is it wonderful that he lies to his father who hates his brother. AMBROSE; But the kind father was still desirous to save him, saying, *Thou art ever with me*, either as a Jew in the law, or as the righteous man in communion with Him.

Aug. ubi sup.

Hier. ubi sup.

Hier. ubi sup.

Aug. ubi sup.

AUG. But what means he that he adds, *And all that I have is thine*, as if they were not his brother's also? But it is thus that all things are looked at by perfect and immortal children, that each is the possession of all, and all of each. For as desire obtains nothing without want, so charity nothing with want. But how all things? Must then God be supposed to have subjected the angels also to the possession of such a son? If you so take possession as that the possessor of a thing is its lord, certainly not all things. For we shall not be the lords, but the companions of angels. Again, if possession is thus understood, how do we rightly say that our souls possess truth? I see no reason why we may not truly and properly say so. For we do not so speak as to call our souls the mistresses of truth. Or if by the term possession we are hindered from this sense, let that also be set aside. For the father says not, " Thou possessest all things," but *All that I have is thine*, still not as if thou wert its lord. For that which is our property may be either food for our families, or ornament, or something of the kind. And surely, when he can rightly call his father his own, I do not see why he may not also rightly call his own what belongs to his father, only in different ways. For when we shall have obtained that blessedness, the higher things will be ours to look upon, equal things ours to have fellowship with, the lower things ours to rule. Let then the elder brother join most safely in the rejoicing. AMBROSE; For if he ceases to envy, he will feel all things to be his, either as the Jew possessing the sacraments of the Old Testament, or as a baptized person those of the New also. THEOPHYL. Or to take the whole differently; the character of the son who seems to complain is put for all those who are offended at the sudden advances and salvation of the perfect, as David introduces one who took offence at the peace of sinners. TIT. BOST. The elder son then as a husbandman was engaged in husbandry, digging not the land, but the field of the soul, and planting trees of salvation, that is to say, the virtues. THEOPHYL. Or he was in the field, that is, in the world, pampering his own flesh, that he might be filled with bread, and sowing in tears that he might reap in joy, but when he found what was being done, he was unwilling to enter into the common joy. CHRYS. But it is asked, whether one who grieves at the prosperity of others is affected by the passion of envy. We must answer, that no Saint grieves at such things; but rather looks upon the good things of others as his own. Now we must not take every thing contained in the parable literally, but bringing out the meaning which the author had in view, search for nothing farther. This parable then was written to the end that sinners should not despair of returning, knowing that they

Chrys. Hom. 64. in Matt.

shall obtain great things. Therefore he introduces others so troubled at these good things as to be consumed with envy, but those who return, treated with such great honour as to become themselves an object of envy to others. THEOPHYL. Or by this parable our Lord reproves the will of the Pharisees, whom according to the argument he terms *just*, as if to say, Let it be that you are truly just, having transgressed none of the commandments, must we then for this reason refuse to admit those who turn away from their iniquities?

Hier.
ubi sup.
Rom. 7,
24. JEROME; Or, in another way, all justice in comparison of the justice of God is injustice. Therefore Paul says, *Who shall deliver me from the body of this death?* and hence were Matt.
20, 24. the Apostles moved with anger at the request of the sons of Zebedee. CYRIL; Which we also ourselves sometimes feel; for some live a most excellent and perfect life, another ofttime even in his old age is converted to God, or perhaps when just about to close his last day, through God's mercy washes away his guilt. But this mercy some men reject from restless timidity of mind, not counting upon the will of our Saviour, who rejoices in the salvation of those who are perishing. THEOPHYL. The son then says to the father, For nothing I left a life of sorrow, ever harassed by sinners who were my enemies, and never hast thou for my sake ordered a kid to be slain, (that is, a sinner who persecuted me,) that I might enjoy myself for 1 Kings
19, 14. a little. Such a kid was Ahab to Elijah, who said, *Lord, they have killed thy prophets.* AMBROSE; Or else, This brother is described so as to be said to come from the farm, that is, engaged in worldly occupations, so ignorant of the things of the Spirit of God, as at last to complain that a kid had never been slain for him. For not for envy, but for the pardon of the world, was the Lamb sacrificed. The envious seeks a kid, the innocent a lamb, to be sacrificed for it. Therefore also is he called the elder, because a man soon grows old through envy. Therefore too he stands without, because his malice excludes him; therefore could he not hear the dancing and music, that is, not the wanton fascinations of the stage, but the harmonious song of a people, resounding with the sweet pleasantness of joy for a sinner saved. For they who seem to themselves righteous are angry when pardon is granted to one confessing his sins.

Who art thou that speakest against thy Lord, that he should not, for example, forgive a fault, when thou pardonest whom thou wilt?   But we ought to favour forgiving sin after repentance, lest while grudging pardon to another, we ourselves obtain it not from our Lord.   Let us not envy those who return from a distant country, seeing that we ourselves also were afar off.

1. And he said unto his disciples, There was a certain rich man, which had a steward; and the same was accused unto him that he had wasted his goods.

2. And he called him, and said unto him, How is it that I hear this of thee? give an account of thy stewardship; for thou mayest be no longer steward.

3. Then the steward said within himself, What shall I do? for my lord taketh away from me the stewardship: I cannot dig; to beg I am ashamed.

4. I am resolved what to do, that, when I am put out of the stewardship, they may receive me into their houses.

5. So he called every one of his lord's debtors unto him, and said unto the first, How much owest thou unto my lord?

6. And he said, An hundred measures of oil. And he said unto him, Take thy bill, and sit down quickly, and write fifty.

7. Then said he to another, And how much owest thou? And he said, An hundred measures of wheat. And he said unto him, Take thy bill, and write fourscore.

BEDE; Having rebuked in three parables those who murmured because He received penitents, our Saviour shortly after subjoins a fourth and a fifth on almsgiving and frugality, because it is also the fittest order in preaching that almsgiving should be added after repentance. Hence it follows, *And he said unto his disciples, There was a certain rich man.* PSEUDO-CHRYS. There is a certain erroneous opinion inherent in mankind, which increases evil and lessens good. It is the feeling that all the good things we possess in the course of our life we possess as lords over them, and accordingly we seize them as our especial goods. But it is quite the contrary. For we are placed in this life not as lords in our own house, but as guests and strangers, led whither we would not, and at a time we think not of. He who is now rich, suddenly becomes a beggar. Therefore whoever thou art, know thyself to be a dispenser of the things of others, and that the privileges granted thee are for a brief and passing use. Cast away then from thy soul the pride of power, and put on the humility and modesty of a steward. BEDE; The bailiff is the manager of the farm, therefore he takes his name from the farm. But the steward, or director of the household, is the overseer of money as well as fruits, and of every thing his master possesses. AMBROSE; From this we learn then, that we are not ourselves the masters, but rather the stewards of the property of others. THEOPHYL. Next, that when we exercise not the management of our wealth according to our Lord's pleasure, but abuse our trust to our own pleasures, we are guilty stewards. Hence it follows, *And he was accused to him.* PSEUDO-CHRYS. Meanwhile he is taken and thrust out of his stewardship; for it follows, *And he called him, and said unto him, What is this that I hear of thee? give an account of thy stewardship, for thou canst be no longer steward.* Day after day by the events which take place our Lord cries aloud to us the same thing, shewing us a man at midday rejoicing in health, before the evening cold and lifeless; another expiring in the midst of a meal. And in various ways we go out from our stewardship; but the faithful steward, who has confidence concerning his management, desires with Paul *to depart and be with Christ.* But he whose wishes are on earth is troubled at his departing. Hence it is added of this steward, *Then the steward said within himself, What shall I do, for my Lord taketh away from me the stewardship? I cannot dig, to beg I am ashamed.* Weakness in action is the fault of a slothful life. For no one

Marginal notes: Hom. de Divite. — Bede, ex Hieron. — villicus œconomus. — ut sup. — Phil. 1, 23.

would shrink who had been accustomed to apply himself to labour. But if we take the parable allegorically, after our departure hence there is no more time for working; the present life contains the practice of what is commanded, the future, consolation. If thou hast done nothing here, in vain then art thou careful for the future, nor wilt thou gain any thing by begging. The foolish virgins are an instance of this, who unwisely begged of the wise, but returned empty. For every one puts on his daily life as his inner garment; it is not possible for him to put it off or exchange it with another. But the wicked steward aptly contrived the remission of debts, to provide for himself an escape from his misfortunes among his fellow-servants; for it follows, *I am resolved what to do, that when I am put out of the stewardship, they may receive me into their houses.* For as often as a man, perceiving his end approaching, lightens by a kind deed the load of his sins, (either by forgiving a debtor his debts, or by giving abundance to the poor,) dispensing those things which are his Lord's, he conciliates to himself many friends, who will afford him before the judge a real testimony, not by words, but by the demonstration of good works, nay moreover will provide for him by their testimony a resting-place of consolation. But nothing is our own, all things are in the power of God. Hence it follows, *So he called every one of his Lord's debtors unto him, and said unto the first, How much owest thou unto my Lord? And he said, A hundred casks of oil.* BEDE; A cadus in Greek is a vessel containing three urns. It follows, *And he said unto him, Take thy bill, and sit down quickly, and write fifty,* forgiving him the half. It follows, *Then said he to another, And how much owest thou? And he said, An hundred measures of wheat.* A corus is made up of thirty bushels. *And he said unto him, Take thy bill, and write fourscore,* forgiving him a fifth part. It may be then simply taken as follows: whosoever relieves the want of a poor man, either by supplying half or a fifth part, will be blessed with the reward of his mercy. AUG. Or because out of the hundred measures of oil, he caused fifty to be written down by the debtors, and of the hundred measures of wheat, fourscore, the meaning thereof is this, that those things which every Jew performs toward the Priests and

Matt. 25, 8.

Aug. de Qu. Ev. l. ii. qu. 34.

Levites should be the more attendant in the Church of Christ, that whereas they give a tenth, Christians should give a half, as Zaccheus gave of his goods, or at least by giving two tenths, that is, a fifth, exceed the payments of the Jews. Luke 19, 8.

8. And the lord commended the unjust steward, because he had done wisely: for the children of this world are in their generation wiser than the children of light.

9. And I say unto you, Make to yourselves friends of the mammon of unrighteousness; that, when ye fail, they may receive you into everlasting habitations.

10. He that is faithful in that which is least is faithful also in much: and he that is unjust in the least is unjust also in much.

11. If therefore ye have not been faithful in the unrighteous mammon, who will commit to your trust the true riches?

12. And if ye have not been faithful in that which is another man's, who shall give you that which is your own?

13. No servant can serve two masters: for either he will hate the one, and love the other; or else he will hold to the one, and despise the other. Ye cannot serve God and mammon.

Aug. The steward whom his Lord cast out of his stewardship is nevertheless commended because he provided himself against the future. As it follows, *And the Lord commended the unjust steward, because he had done wisely;* we ought not however to take the whole for our imitation. For we should never act deceitfully against our Lord in order that from the fraud itself we may give alms. Aug. ubi sup.

Origen; But because the Gentiles say that wisdom is a virtue, and define it to be the experience of what is good, Origen. in Prov. i. 1.

evil, and indifferent, or the knowledge of what is and what
is not to be done, we must consider whether this word
Prov. 3, signifies many things, or one. For it is said that God by
19.
wisdom prepared the heavens. Now it is plain that wisdom
is good, because the Lord by wisdom prepared the heavens.
It is said also in Genesis, according to the LXX, that the
serpent was the wisest animal, wherein he does not make
wisdom a virtue, but evil-minded cunning. And it is in this
sense that the Lord commended the steward that he had
done wisely, that is, cunningly and evilly. And perhaps
the word *commended* was spoken not in the sense of real
commendation, but in a lower sense; as when we speak of
a man being commended in slight and indifferent matters, and
in a certain measure clashings and sharpness of wit are ad-
Aug. mired, by which the power of the mind is drawn out. Aug.
ubi sup. On the other hand this parable is spoken, that we should
understand that if the steward who acted deceitfully, could
be praised by his lord, how much more they please God who
do their works according to His commandment.

ORIGEN; The children of this world also are not called
wiser but more prudent than the children of light, and this
not absolutely and simply, but in their generation. For it
follows, *For the children of this world are in their generation*
wiser than the children of light, &c. BEDE; The children
of light and the children of this world are spoken of in
the same manner as the children of the kingdom, and the
children of hell. For whatever works a man does, he is
also termed their son. THEOPHYL. By the children of this
world then He means those who mind the good things which
are on the earth; by the children of light, those who beholding
the divine love, employ themselves with spiritual treasures.
But it is found indeed in the management of human affairs,
that we prudently order our own things, and busily set ourselves to work, in order that when we depart we may have
a refuge for our life; but when we ought to direct the things
of God, we take no forethought for what shall be our lot
hereafter.

Greg. GREG. In order then that after death they may find
18. Mor.
cap. 18. something in their own hand, let men before death place
their riches in the hands of the poor. Hence it follows,

And I say to you, Make to yourselves friends of the mammon of unrighteousness, &c. AUG. That which the Hebrews Aug. Serm. 113.
call *mammon*, in Latin is " riches." As if He said, " Make
to yourselves friends of the riches of unrighteousness." Now
some misunderstanding this, seize upon the things of others,
and so give something to the poor, and think that they are
doing what is commanded. That interpretation must be Prov. 3, 9. LXX.
corrected into, Give alms of your righteous labours. For you
will not corrupt Christ your Judge. If from the plunder of a
poor man, you were to give any thing to the judge that he
might decide for you, and that judge should decide for you,
such is the force of justice, that you would be ill pleased in
yourself. Do not then make to yourself such a God. God
is the fountain of Justice, give not your alms then from
interest and usury. I speak to the faithful, to whom we
dispense the body of Christ. But if you have such money,
it is of evil that you have it. Be no longer doers of evil.
Zaccheus said, *Half my goods I give to the poor.* See how Luke 19, 8.
he runs who runs to make friends of the mammon of unrighteousness; and not to be held guilty from any quarter, he
says, *I If have taken any thing from any one, I restore fourfold.* According to another interpretation, the mammon of
unrighteousness are all the riches of the world, whenever they
come. For if you seek the true riches, there are some in
which Job when naked abounded, when he had his heart full
towards God. The others are called riches from unrighteousness; because they are not true riches, for they are full of
poverty, and ever liable to chances. For if they were true
riches, they would give you security.

AUG. Or the riches of unrighteousness are so called, be- Aug. de Quæst. Ev. l. ii. q. 34.
cause they are not riches except to the unrighteous, and
such as rest in their hopes and the fulness of their
happiness. But when these things are possessed by the
righteous, they have indeed so much money, but no riches
are theirs but heavenly and spiritual. AMBROSE; Or he
spoke of the unrighteous Mammon, because by the various
enticements of riches covetousness corrupts our hearts, that we
may be willing to obey riches. BASIL; Or if thou hast Basil. Hom. de Avar.
succeeded to a patrimony, thou receivest what has been
amassed by the unrighteous; for in a number of pre-

decessors some one must needs be found who has unjustly usurped the property of others. But suppose that thy father has not been guilty of exaction, whence hast thou thy money? If indeed thou answerest, " From myself;" thou art ignorant of God, not having the knowledge of thy Creator; but if, " From God," tell me the reason for Ps.2*,1. which thou receivedst it. *Is not the earth and the fulness thereof the Lord's?* If then whatever is ours belongs to our common Lord, so will it also belong to our fellow-servant.

THEOPHYL. Those then are called the riches of unrighteousness which the Lord has given for the necessities of our brethren and fellow-servants, but we spend upon ourselves. It became us then, from the beginning, to give all things to the poor, but because we have become the stewards of unrighteousness, wickedly retaining what was appointed for the aid of others, we must not surely remain in this cruelty, but distribute to the poor, that we may be received by them into everlasting habitations. For it follows, *That, when ye fail, they may receive you into everlasting habitations.*

Greg.
21. Mor.
cap. 14. GREG. But if through their friendship we obtain everlasting habitations, we ought to calculate that when we give we rather offer presents to patrons, than bestow benefits upon the needy.

Aug.
Serm.
113. AUG. For who are they that shall have everlasting habitations but the saints of God? and who are they that are to be received by them into everlasting habitations but they who administer to their want, and whatsoever they have need of, gladly supply. They are those little ones of Christ, who have forsaken all that belonged to them and followed Him; and whatsoever they had have given to the poor, that they might serve God without earthly shackles, and freeing their shoulders from the burdens of the world, might raise them aloft as with wings.

Aug. de
Quæst.
Ev. l. ii.
q. 34. AUG. We must not then understand those by whom we wish to be received into everlasting habitations to be as it were debtors of God; seeing that the just and holy are signified in this place, who cause those to enter in, who administered to their necessity of their own worldly goods. AMBROSE; Or else, make to yourselves friends of the mammon of un-

righteousness, that by giving to the poor we may purchase the favour of angels and all the saints. CHRYS. Mark also that He said not, " that they may receive you into their own habitations." For it is not they who receive you. Therefore when He said, *Make to yourselves friends,* he added, *of the mammon of unrighteousness,* to shew, that their friendship will not alone protect us unless good works accompany us, unless we righteously cast away all riches unrighteously amassed. The most skilful then of all arts is that of almsgiving. For it builds not for us houses of mud, but lays up in store an everlasting life. Now in each of the arts one needs the support of another; but when we ought to shew mercy, we need nothing else but the will alone.

CYRIL; Thus then Christ taught those who abound in riches, earnestly to love the friendship of the poor, and to have treasure in heaven. But He knew the sloth of the human mind, how that they who court riches bestow no work of charity upon the needy. That to such men there results no profit of spiritual gifts, He shews by obvious examples, adding, *He that is faithful in that which is least is faithful also in much; and he that is unjust in the least is unjust also in much.* Now our Lord opens to us the eye of the heart, explaining what He had said, adding, *If therefore ye have not been faithful in the unrighteous mammon, who will commit to your trust the true riches?* That which is least then is the mammon of unrighteousness, that is, earthly riches, which seem nothing to those that are heavenly wise. I think then that a man is faithful in a little, when he imparts aid to those who are bowed down with sorrow. If then we have been unfaithful in a little thing, how shall we obtain from hence the true riches, that is, the fruitful gift of Divine grace, impressing the image of God on the human soul? But that our Lord's words incline to this meaning is plain from the following; for He says, *And if ye have not been faithful in that which is another man's, who shall give you that which is your own?* AMBROSE; Riches are foreign to us, because they are something beyond nature, they are not born with us, and they do not pass away with us. But Christ is ours, because He is the life of man. Lastly, He came unto His own.

THEOPHYL. Thus then hitherto He has taught us how faithfully we ought to dispose of our wealth. But because the management of our wealth according to God is no otherwise obtained than by the indifference of a mind unaffected towards riches, He adds, *No man can serve two masters.* AMBROSE; Not because the Lord is two, but one. For although there are who serve mammon, yet he knoweth no rights of lordship; but has himself placed upon himself a yoke of servitude. There is one Lord, because there is one God. Hence it is evident, that the power of the Father and the Son is one: and He assigns a reason, thus saying, *For either he will hate the one, and love the other; or else he will hold to the one, and despise the other.* AUG. But these things were not spoken indifferently or at random. For no one when asked whether he loves the devil, answers that he loves him, but rather that he hates him; but all generally proclaim that they love God. *Therefore either he will hate the one,* (that is, the devil,) *and love the other,* (that is, God;) *or will hold to the one,* (that is, the devil, when he pursues as it were temporal wants,) *and will despise the other,* (that is, God,) as when men frequently neglect His threats for their desires, who because of His goodness flatter themselves that they will have impunity.

Aug. de Qu. Ev. lib. ii. q. 36.

CYRIL; But the conclusion of the whole discourse is what follows, *Ye cannot serve God and mammon.* Let us then transfer all our devotions to the one, forsaking riches. BEDE; Let then the covetous hear this, that we can not at the same time serve Christ and riches; and yet He said not, " Who has riches," but, who serves riches; for he who is the servant of riches, watches them as a servant; but he who has shaken off the yoke of servitude, dispenses them as a master; but he who serves mammon, verily serves him who is set over those earthly things as the reward of his iniquity, and is called *the prince of this world.*

Bede ex Hier.

John 12, 31. 2 Cor. 4, 4.

14. And the Pharisees also, who were covetous, heard all these things : and they derided him.

15. And he said unto them, Ye are they which justify yourselves before men; but God knoweth

your hearts: for that which is highly esteemed among men is abomination in the sight of God.

16. The Law and the Prophets were until John: since that time the kingdom of God is preached, and every man presseth into it.

17. And it is easier for heaven and earth to pass, than one tittle of the law to fail.

18. Whosoever putteth away his wife, and marrieth another, committeth adultery : and whosoever marrieth her that is put away from her husband committeth adultery.

BEDE; Christ had told the Pharisees not to boast of their own righteousness, but to receive penitent sinners, and to redeem their sins by almsgiving. But they derided the Preacher of mercy, humility, and frugality; as it is said, *And the Pharisees also, who were covetous, heard these things; and derided him:* it may be for two reasons, either because He commanded what was not sufficiently profitable, or cast blame upon their past superfluous actions. THEOPHYL. But the Lord detecting in them a hidden malice, proves that they make a pretence of righteousness. Therefore it is added, *And he said unto them, Ye are they which justify yourselves before men.* BEDE; They justify themselves before men who despise sinners as in a weak and hopeless condition, but fancy themselves to be perfect and not to need the remedy of almsgiving; but how justly the depth of deadly pride is to be condemned, He sees who will enlighten the hidden places of darkness. Hence it follows, *But God knoweth your hearts.* THEOPHYL. And therefore ye are an abomination to Him because of your arrogance, and love of seeking after the praise of men; as He adds, *For that which is highly esteemed among men is abomination in the sight of God.*

BEDE; Now the Pharisees derided our Saviour disputing against covetousness, as if He taught things contrary to the Law and the Prophets, in which many very rich men are said to have pleased God; but Moses also himself promised

Deut.
28, 11. that the people whom he ruled, if they followed the Law, should abound in all earthly goods. These the Lord answers by shewing that between the Law and the Gospel, as in these promises so also in the commands, there is not the slightest difference. Hence He adds, *The Law and the Prophets were until John.* AMBROSE; Not that the Law failed, but that the preaching of the Gospel began; for that which is inferior seems to be completed when a better

Chrys.
Hom.
37. in
Matt.
Pseudo-
Chrys.
Hom.
19. op.
imp. succeeds. CHRYS. He hereby disposes them readily to believe on Him, because if as far as John's time all things were complete, I am He who am come. For the Prophets had not ceased unless I had come; but you will say, "how" were the Prophets until John, since there have been many more Prophets in the New than the Old Testament. But He spoke of those prophets who foretold Christ's coming.

EUSEB. Now the ancient prophets knew the preaching of the kingdom of heaven, but none of them had expressly announced it to the Jewish people, because the Jews having a childish understanding were unequal to the preaching of what is infinite. But John first openly preached that the kingdom of heaven was at hand, as well as also the remission of sins by the laver of regeneration. Hence it follows, *Since that time the kingdom of heaven is preached, and every one presseth into it.* AMBROSE; For the Law delivered many things according to nature, as being more indulgent to our natural desires, that it might call us to the pursuit of righteousness. Christ breaks through nature as cutting off even our natural pleasures. But therefore we keep under nature, that it should not sink us down to earthly things, but raise us to heavenly. EUSEB. A great struggle befals men in their ascent to heaven. For that men clothed with mortal flesh should be able to subdue pleasure and every unlawful appetite, desiring to imitate the life of angels, must be compassed with violence. But who that looking upon those who labour earnestly in the service of God, and almost put to death their flesh, will not in reality confess that they do violence to the kingdom

Aug. de
Quæst.
Ev. l. ii.
q. 87. of heaven. AUG. They also do violence to the kingdom of heaven, in that they not only despise all temporal things,

but also the tongues of those who desire their doing so.
This the Evangelist added, when he said that Jesus was
derided when He spoke of despising earthly riches.

BEDE; But lest they should suppose that in His words,
the Law and the Prophets were until John, He preached the
destruction of the Law or the Prophets, He obviates such a
notion, adding, *And it is easier for heaven and earth to pass,
than one tittle of the law should fail.* For it is written, the
fashion of this world passeth away. But of the Law, not
even the very extreme point of one letter, that is, not even
the least things are destitute of spiritual sacraments. And
yet the Law and the Prophets were until John, because that
could always be prophesied as about to come, which by the
preaching of John it was clear had come. But that which
He spoke beforehand concerning the perpetual inviolability
of the Law, He confirms by one testimony taken therefrom for
the sake of example, saying, *Whosoever putteth away his
wife, and marrieth another, committeth adultery: and whosoever marrieth her that is put away from her husband, committeth adultery;* that from this one instance they should
learn that He came not to destroy but to fulfil the commands
of the Law. THEOPHYL. For that to the imperfect the Law
spoke imperfectly is plain from what he says to the hard
hearts of the Jews, " If a man hate his wife, let him put her
away," because since they were murderers and rejoiced in
blood, they had no pity even upon those who were united to
them, so that they slew their sons and daughters for devils.
But now there is need of a more perfect doctrine. Wherefore I say, that if a man puts away his wife, having no
excuse of fornication, he commits adultery, and he who
marrieth another commits adultery.

AMBROSE; But we must first speak, I think, of the law of
marriage, that we may afterwards discuss the forbidding of
divorce. Some think that all marriage is sanctioned by God,
because it is written, *Whom God hath joined, let not man
put asunder.* How then does the Apostle say, *If the
unbelieving depart, let him depart?* Herein he shews that
the marriage of all is not from God. For neither by God's
approval are Christians joined with Gentiles. Do not then
put away thy wife, lest thou deny God to be the Author of

1 Cor. 7, 31.

Deut. 24, 1.

Matt. 19, 6. Mark 10, 9. 1 Cor. 7, 15.

thy union. For if others, much more oughtest thou to bear
with and correct the behaviour of thy wife. And if she is
sent away pregnant with children, it is a hard thing to shut
out the parent and keep the pledge; so as to add to the
parents' disgrace the loss also of filial affection. Harder still
if because of the mother thou drivest away the children also.
Wouldest thou suffer in thy lifetime thy children to be under
a step-father, or when the mother was alive to be under a
step-mother? How dangerous to expose to error the tender
age of a young wife. How wicked to desert in old age one,
the flower of whose growth thou hast blighted. Suppose that
being divorced she does not marry, this also ought to be
displeasing to you, to whom though an adulterer, she keeps
her troth. Suppose she marries, her necessity is thy crime,
and that which thou supposest marriage, is adultery.

But to understand it morally. Having just before set
forth that the kingdom of God is preached, and said that one
tittle could not fall from the Law, He added, *Whosoever putteth
away his wife, &c.* Christ is the husband; whomsoever
then God has brought to His son, let not persecution sever,
nor lust entice, nor philosophy spoil, nor heretics taint,
nor Jew seduce. Adulterers are all such as desire to corrupt
truth, faith, and wisdom.

19. There was a certain rich man, which was
clothed in purple and fine linen, and fared sumptuously every day:

20. And there was a certain beggar named Lazarus, which was laid at his gate, full of sores,

21. And desiring to be fed with the crumbs which
fell from the rich man's table: moreover the dogs
came and licked his sores.

BEDE; Our Lord had just before advised the making
friends of the Mammon of unrighteousness, which the Pharisees derided. He next confirms by examples what he had
set before them, saying, *There was a certain rich man, &c.*
CHRYS. There was, not is, because he had passed away as a

flecting shadow. AMBROSE ; But not all poverty is holy, or
all riches criminal, but as luxury disgraces riches, so does
holiness commend poverty.

It follows, *And he was clothed in purple and fine linen.* bysso.
BEDE ; Purple, the colour of the royal robe, is obtained
from sea shells, which are scraped with a knife. Byssus
is a kind of white and very fine linen. GREG. Now Greg.
if the wearing of fine and precious robes were not a fault, Hom.
40. in
the word of God would never have so carefully expressed Ev.
this. For no one seeks costly garments except for vain-
glory, that he may seem more honourable than others ; for
no one wishes to be clothed with such, where he cannot be
seen by others. CHRYS. Ashes, dust, and earth he covered Chrys.
with purple, and silk ; or ashes, dust, and earth bore upon ut sup.
them purple and silk. As his garments were, so was also his
food. Therefore with us also as our food is, such let our
clothing be. Hence it follows, *And he fared sumptuously
every day.* GREG. And here we must narrowly watch our- Greg.
selves, seeing that banquets can scarcely be celebrated blame- Hom.
40. in
lessly, for almost always luxury accompanies feasting ; and Ev.
when the body is swallowed up in the delight of refreshing
itself, the heart relaxes to empty joys.

It follows, *And there was a certain beggar named Lazarus.*
AMBRQSE ; This seems rather a narrative than a parable,
since the name is also expressed. CHRYS. But a parable is Chrys.
that in which an example is given, while the names are ut sup.
omitted. Lazarus is interpreted, " one who was assisted."
For he was poor, and the Lord helped him. CYRIL ; Or else ;
This discourse concerning the rich man and Lazarus was
written after the manner of a comparison in a parable, to
declare that they who abound in earthly riches, unless they
will relieve the necessities of the poor, shall meet with a
heavy condemnation. But the tradition of the Jews relates
that there was at that time in Jerusalem a certain Lazarus
who was afflicted with extreme poverty and sickness, whom
our Lord remembering, introduces him into the example for
the sake of adding greater point to His words.

GREG. We must observe also, that among the heathen the Greg.
names of poor men are more likely to be known than of rich. Moral.
l. c. 8.
Now our Lord mentions the name of the poor, but not

the name of the rich, because God knows and approves the humble, but not the proud. But that the poor man might be more approved, poverty and sickness were at the same time consuming him; as it follows, *who was laid at his gate full of sores.* PSEUDO-CHRYS. He lay at his gate for this reason, that the rich might not say, I never saw him, no one told me; for he saw him both going out and returning. The poor is full of sores, that so he might set forth in his own body the cruelty of the rich. Thou seest the death of thy body lying before the gate, and thou pitiest not. If thou regardest not the commands of God, at least have compassion on thy own state, and fear lest also thou become such as he. But sickness has some comfort if it receives help. How great then was the punishment in that body, in which with such wounds he remembered not the pain of his sores, but only his hunger; for it follows, *desiring to be fed with the crumbs, &c.* As if he said, What thou throwest away from thy table, afford for alms, make thy losses gain.

Hom.
de Div.

AMBROSE; But the insolence and pride of the wealthy is manifested afterwards by the clearest tokens, for it follows, *and no one gave to him.* For so unmindful are they of the condition of mankind, that as if placed above nature they derive from the wretchedness of the poor an incitement to their own pleasure, they laugh at the destitute, they mock the needy, and rob those whom they ought to pity. AUG. For the covetousness of the rich is insatiable, it neither fears God nor regards man, spares not a father, keeps not its fealty to a friend, oppresses the widow, attacks the property of a ward.

Aug.
Serm.
367.

GREG. Moreover the poor man saw the rich as he went forth surrounded by flatterers, while he himself lay in sickness and want, visited by no one. For that no one came to visit him, the dogs witness, who fearlessly licked his sores, for it follows, *moreover the dogs came and licked his sores.* PSEUDO-CHRYS. Those sores which no man deigned to wash and dress, the beasts tenderly lick.

Greg.
in Ev.
Hom.
40.

ut sup.

GREG. By one thing Almighty God displayed two judgments. He permitted Lazarus to lie before the rich man's gate, both that the wicked rich man might increase the vengeance of his condemnation, and the poor man by his trials

Greg.
ubi sup.

enhance his reward; the one saw daily him on whom he should shew mercy, the other that for which he might be approved.

22. And it came to pass, that the beggar died, and was carried by the angels into Abraham's bosom: the rich man also died, and was buried;

23. And in hell he lift up his eyes, being in torments, and seeth Abraham afar off, and Lazarus in his bosom.

24. And he cried and said, Father Abraham, have mercy on me, and send Lazarus, that he may dip the tip of his finger in water, and cool my tongue; for I am tormented in this flame.

25. But Abraham said, Son, remember that thou in thy lifetime receivedst thy good things, and likewise Lazarus evil things: but now he is comforted, and thou art tormented.

26. And beside all this, between us and you there is a great gulf fixed: so that they which would pass from hence to you cannot; neither can they pass to us, that would come from thence.

PSEUDO-CHRYS. We have heard how both fared on earth, *ubi sup.* let us see what their condition is among the dead. That which was temporal has passed away; that which follows is eternal. Both died; the one angels receive, the other torments; for it is said, *And it came to pass, that the beggar died, and was carried by the angels, &c.* Those great sufferings are suddenly exchanged for bliss. He is carried after all his labours, because he had fainted, or at least that he might not tire by walking; and he was carried by angels. One angel was not sufficient to carry the poor man, but many come, that they may make a joyful band, each angel rejoicing to touch so great a burden. Gladly do they thus encumber themselves, that so they may bring men to the kingdom of heaven. But he was carried into Abraham's bosom, that he ____ might be embraced and cherished by him ; *Abraham's bosom* is Paradise.　And the ministering angels carried the poor man, and placed him in Abraham's bosom, because though he lay despised, he yet despaired not nor blasphemed, saying, This rich man living in wickedness is happy and suffers no tribulation, but I cannot get even food to supply my wants.

Aug.
de Orig.
Anim.
4. 16.
AUG. Now as to your thinking Abraham's bosom to be any thing bodily, I am afraid lest you should be thought to treat so weighty a matter rather lightly than seriously.　For you could never be guilty of such folly, as to suppose the corporeal bosom of one man able to hold so many souls, nay, to use your own words, so many bodies as the Angels carry thither as they did Lazarus.　But perhaps you imagine that one soul to have alone deserved to come to that bosom.　If you would not fall into a childish mistake, you must understand Abraham's bosom to be a retired and hidden resting-place where Abraham is; and therefore called Abraham's, not that it is his alone, but because he is the father of many nations, and placed first, that others might imitate his preeminence of faith.

Greg.
in Hom.
40.
GREG. When the two men were below on earth, that is, the poor and the rich, there was one above who saw into their hearts, and by trials exercised the poor man to glory, by endurance awaited the rich man to punishment.　Hence it follows, *The rich man also died.*
Chrys.
Hom. 6.
in 2 a d
Cor.
CHRYS. He died then indeed in body, but his soul was dead before.　For he did none of the works of the soul.　All that warmth which issues from the love of our neighbour had fled, and he was
Chrys.
Conc.
2. de
Lazaro.
more dead than his body.　But no one is spoken of as having ministered to the rich man's burial as to that of Lazarus. Because when he lived pleasantly in the broad road, he had many busy flatterers; when he came to his end, all forsook him. For it simply follows, *and was buried in hell.* 　But his soul also when living was buried, enshrined in its body as it were in a tomb.　AUG. The burial in hell is the lowest depth of torment which after this life devours the proud and unmerciful.

In Esai.
5.
PSEUDO-BASIL. Hell is a certain common place in the interior of the earth, shaded on all sides and dark, in which there is a kind of opening stretching downward, through which lies the

descent of the souls who are condemned to perdition. PSEUDO- Chrys.
Op.imp.
Hom.
53.
Matt. 8,
22. 25.
CHRYS. Or as the prisons of kings are placed at a distance
without, so also hell is somewhere far off without the world,
and hence it is called the outer darkness.

THEOPHYL. But some say that hell is the passing from
the visible to the invisible, and the unfashioning of the soul.
For as long as the soul of the sinner is in the body, it is visible
by means of its own operations. But when it flies out of
the body, it becomes shapeless.

CHRYS. As it made the poor man's affliction heavier while Chrys.
Conc.
2. de
Lazaro.
he lived to lie before the rich man's gate, and to behold the
prosperity of others, so when the rich man was dead it added
to his desolation, that he lay in hell and saw the happiness
of Lazarus, feeling not only by the nature of His own torments, but also by the comparison of Lazarus's honour, his
own punishment the more intolerable. Hence it follows, *But
lifting up his eyes.* He lifted up his eyes that he might look
on him, not despise him; for Lazarus was above, he below.
Many angels carried Lazarus; he was seized by endless torments. Therefore it is not said, *being in* torment, but *torments.* For he was wholly in torments, his eyes alone were free,
so that he might behold the joy of another. His eyes are
allowed to be free that he may be the more tortured, not
having that which another has. The riches of others are the
torments of those who are in poverty.

GREG. Now if Abraham sate below, the rich man placed Greg.
lib. 4.
Mor. c.
29.
in torments would not see him. For they who have followed
the path to the heavenly country, when they leave the flesh,
are kept back by the gates of hell; not that punishment smites
them as sinners, but that resting in some more remote places,
(for the intercession of the Mediator was not yet come,) the
guilt of their first fault prevents them from entering the
kingdom.

CHRYS. There were many poor righteous men, but he who Chrys.
ad Hom.
2. in ep.
Phil.
Chrys.
Conc.
de Laz.
lay at his door met his sight to add to his woe. For it
follows, *And Lazarus in his bosom.* It may here be observed,
that all who are offended by us are exposed to our view.
But the rich man sees Lazarus not with any other righteous
man, but in Abraham's bosom. For Abraham was full of
love, but the man is convicted of cruelty. Abraham sitting

before his door followed after those that passed by, and brought them into his house, the other turned away even

Greg. Hom. 40. in Ev. them that abode within his gate. GREG. And this rich man forsooth, now fixed in his doom, seeks as his patron him to whom in this life he would not shew mercy. THEOPHYL. He does not however direct his words to Lazarus, but to Abraham, because he was perhaps ashamed, and thought Lazarus would remember his injuries; but he judged of him from

Hom. de Div. himself. Hence it follows, *And he cried and said.* PSEUDO-CHRYS. Great punishments give forth a great cry. *Father Abraham.* As if he said, I call thee father by nature, as the son who wasted his living, although by my own fault I have lost thee as a father. *Have mercy on me.* In vain thou workest repentance, when there is no place for repentance; thy torments drive thee to act the penitent, not the desires of thy soul. He who is in the kingdom of heaven, I know not whether he can have compassion on him who is in hell. The Creator pitieth His creature. There came one Physician who was to heal all; others could not heal. *Send Lazarus.* Thou errest, wretched man. Abraham cannot send, but he can receive. *To dip the tip of his finger in water.* Thou wouldest not deign to look upon Lazarus, and now thou desirest his finger. What thou seekest now, thou oughtest to have done to him when alive. Thou art in want of water, who before despisedst delicate food. Mark the conscience of the sinner; he durst not ask for the whole of the finger. We are instructed also

Chrys. Conc. 2. de Laz. how good a thing it is not to trust in riches. See the rich man in need of the poor who was before starving. Things are changed, and it is now made known to all who was rich and who was poor. For as in the theatres, when it grows towards evening, and the spectators depart, then going out, and laying aside their dresses, they who seemed kings and generals are seen as they really are, the sons of gardeners and fig-sellers. So also when death is come, and the spectacle is over, and all the masks of poverty and riches are put off, by their works alone are men judged, which are truly rich, which poor, which are

Greg. ut sup. worthy of honour, which of dishonour. GREG. For that rich man who would not give to the poor man even the scraps of his table, being in hell came to beg for even the least thing. For he sought for a drop of water, who refused to

give a crumb of bread. BASIL; But he receives a meet reward, fire and the torments of hell; the parched tongue; for
the tuneful lyre, wailing; for drink, the intense longing for a
drop; for curious or wanton spectacles, profound darkness; for
busy flattery, the undying worm. Hence it follows, *That he
may cool my tongue, for I am tormented in the flame.* CHRYS. Chrys.
ubi sup.
But not because he was rich was he tormented, but because
he was not merciful. GREG. We may gather from this, with
what torments he will be punished who robs another, if he is
smitten with the condemnation to hell, who does not distribute
what is his own. AMBROSE; He is tormented also because
to the luxurious man it is a punishment to be without his
pleasures; water is also a refreshment to the soul which is
set fast in sorrow. GREG. But what means it, that when in torments he desires his tongue to be cooled, except that at his
feasts having sinned in talking, now by the justice of retribution, his tongue was in fierce flame; for talkativeness is generally rife at the banquet. CHRYS. His tongue too had spoken
many proud things. Where the sin is, there is the punishment;
and because the tongue offended much, it is the more tormented.
CHRYS. Or, in that he wishes his tongue to be cooled, when
he was altogether burning in the flame, that is signified which
is written, *Death and life are in the hands of the tongue,* Prov.
18, 21.
and *with the mouth confession is made to salvation;* Rom.
10, 10.
which from pride he did not do, but the tip of the finger
means the very least work in which a man is assisted by the
Holy Spirit.

AUG. Thou sayest that the members of the soul are here Aug.
de Orig.
described, and by the eye thou wouldest have the whole Anim.
head understood, because he was said to lift up his eyes; 4. 16.
by the tongue, the jaws; by the finger, the hand. But what
is the reason that those names of members when spoken of
God do not to thy mind imply a body, but when of the soul
they do? It is that when spoken of the creature they are to
be taken literally, but when of the Creator metaphorically
and figuratively. Wilt thou then give us bodily wings, seeing
that not the Creator, but man, that is, the creature, says, *If I* Ps. 139,
9.
take not the wings in the morning? Besides, if the rich
man had a bodily tongue, because he said, *to cool my
tongue,* in us also who live in the flesh, the tongue itself has

Prov.
18, 21.
bodily hands, for it is written, *Death and life are in the hands of the tongue.*

Greg.
Orat. 5.
de Beat.
GREG. NYSS. As the most excellent of mirrors represents an image of the face, just such as the face itself which is opposite to it, a joyful image of that which is joyful, a sorrowful of that which is sorrowful; so also is the just judgment of God adapted to our dispositions. Wherefore the rich man because he pitied not the poor as he lay at his gate, when he needs mercy for himself, is not heard, for it follows, *And Abraham said unto him, Son, &c.*

Chrys.
Conc.
2, 3. de
Lazaro.
CHRYS. Behold the kindness of the Patriarch; he calls him son, (which may express his tenderness,) yet gives no aid to him who had deprived himself of cure. Therefore he says, *Remember*, that is, consider the past, forget not that thou delightedst in thy riches, and *thou receivedst good things in thy life*, that is, such as thou thoughtest to be good. Thou couldest not both have triumphed on earth, and triumph here. Riches can not be true both on earth and below. It follows, *And Lazarus likewise evil things;* not that Lazarus thought them evil, but he spoke this according to the opinion of the rich man, who thought poverty, and hunger, and severe sickness, evils. When the heaviness of sickness harasses us, let us think of Lazarus, and joyfully accept evil things in this life.

Aug.
Quæst.
Ev. lib.
ii.qu.38.
AUG. All this then is said to Him because he chose the happiness of the world, and loved no other life but that in which he proudly boasted; but he says, *Lazarus received evil things*, because he knew that the perishableness of this life, its labours, sorrows, and sickness, are the penalty of sin, for we all die in Adam who by transgression was made liable to death.

Chrys.
Conc.
3. de
Lazaro.
CHRYS. He says, *Thou receivedst good things in thy life*, (as if thy due;) as though he said, If thou hast done any good thing for which a reward might be due, thou hast received all things in that world, living luxuriously, abounding in riches, enjoying the pleasure of prosperous undertakings; but he if he committed any evil has received all, afflicted with poverty, hunger, and the depths of wretchedness. And each of you came hither naked; Lazarus indeed of sin, wherefore he receives his consolation; thou of righteousness, wherefore thou endurest thy inconsolable punishment:

and hence it follows, *But now he is comforted, and thou art tormented.*

GREG. Whatsoever then ye have well in this world, when ye recollect to have done any thing good, be very fearful about it, lest the prosperity granted you be your recompense for the same good.   And when ye behold poor men doing any thing blameably, fear not, seeing that perhaps those whom the remains of the slightest iniquity defiles, the fire of honesty cleanses.   CHRYS. But you will say, Is there no one who shall enjoy pardon, both here and there?   This is indeed a hard thing, and among those which are impossible.   For should poverty press not, ambition urges ; if sickness provoke not, anger inflames ; if temptations assail not, corrupt thoughts often overwhelm.   It is no slight toil to bridle anger, to check unlawful desires, to subdue the swellings of vain-glory, to quell pride or haughtiness, to lead a severe life.   He that doeth not these things, can not be saved.

GREG. It may also be answered, that evil men receive in this life good things, because they place their whole joy in transitory happiness, but the righteous may indeed have good things here, yet not receive them for reward, because while they seek better things, that is, eternal, in their judgment whatever good things are present seem by no means good.

CHRYS. But after the mercy of God, we must seek in our own endeavours for hope of salvation, not in numbering fathers, or relations, or friends.   For brother does not deliver brother ; and therefore it is added, *And beside all this between us and you there is a great gulf fixed.*   THEOPHYL. The great gulf signifies the distance of the righteous from sinners. For as their affections were different, so also their abiding places do not slightly differ.   CHRYS. The gulf is said to be fixed, because it cannot be loosened, moved, or shaken.

AMBROSE ; Between the rich and the poor then there is a great gulf, because after death rewards cannot be changed. Hence it follows, *So that they who would pass from hence to you cannot, nor come thence to us.*   CHRYS. As if he says, We can see, we cannot pass ; and we see what we have escaped, you what you have lost ; our joys enhance your torments, your torments our joys.   GREG. For as the

*Greg.
in Hom.
40.*

*Chrys.
Conc.
3. de
Lazaro.*

*Greg.
ubi sup.*

*Chrys.
in Conc.
de Laz.*

*Greg.
ubi sup.*

wicked desire to pass over to the elect, that is, to depart from the pangs of their sufferings, so to the afflicted and tormented would the just pass in their mind by compassion, and wish to set them free. But the souls of the just, although in the goodness of their nature they feel compassion, after being united to the righteousness of their Author, are constrained by such great uprightness as not to be moved with compassion towards the reprobate. Neither then do the unrighteous pass over to the lot of the blessed, because they are bound in everlasting condemnation, nor can the righteous pass to the reprobate, because being now made upright by the righteousness of judgment, they in no way pity them from any compassion. THEOPHYL. You may from this derive an argument against the followers of Origen, who say, that since an end is to be placed to punishments, there will be a time when sinners shall be gathered to the righteous and to God. AUG. For it is shewn by the unchangeableness of the Divine sentence, that no aid of mercy can be rendered to men by the righteous, even though they should wish to give it; by which he reminds us, that in this life men should relieve those they can, since hereafter even if they be well received, they would not be able to give help to those they love. For that which was written, *that they may receive you into everlasting habitations*, was not said of the proud and unmerciful, but of those who have made to themselves friends by their works of mercy, whom the righteous receive, not as if by their own power benefitting them, but by Divine permission.

Aug.
Qu. Ev.
lib. ii.
qu. 88.

27. Then he said, I pray thee therefore, father, that thou wouldest send him to my father's house:

28. For I have five brethren; that he may testify unto them, lest they also come into this place of torment.

29. Abraham saith unto him, They have Moses and the prophets; let them hear them.

30. And he said, Nay, father Abraham: but if one went unto them from the dead, they will repent.

31. And he said unto him, If they hear not Moses and the prophets, neither will they be persuaded, though one rose from the dead.

GREG. When the rich man in flames found that all hope was Greg. Hom. 40. in Ev. taken away from him, his mind turns to those relations whom he had left behind, as it is said, *Then said he, I pray thee therefore, father Abraham, to send him to my father's house.* AUG. He asks that Lazarus should be sent, because he felt Aug. ubi sup. himself unworthy to offer testimony to the truth. And as he had not obtained even to be cooled for a little while, much less does he expect to be set free from hell for the preaching of the truth. CHRYS. Now mark his perverseness; not even in the midst of his torments does he keep to truth. If Abraham is thy father, how sayest thou, Send him to thy father's house? But thou hast not forgotten thy father, for he has been thy ruin.

GREG. The hearts of the wicked are sometimes by their Greg. ut sup. own punishment taught the exercise of charity, but in vain; so that they indeed have an especial love to their own, who while attached to their sins did not love themselves. Hence it follows, *For I have five brethren, that he may testify to them, lest they also come into this place of torment.*

AMBROSE; But it is too late for the rich man to begin to be master, when he has no longer time for learning or teaching. GREG. And here we must remark what fearful Greg. ut sup. sufferings are heaped upon the rich man in flames. For in addition to his punishment, his knowledge and memory are preserved. He knew Lazarus whom he despised, he remembered his brethren whom he left. For that sinners in punishment may be still more punished, they both see the glory of those whom they had despised, and are harassed about the punishment of those whom they have unprofitably loved. But to the rich man seeking Lazarus to be sent to them, Abraham immediately answers, as follows, *Abraham saith to him, They have Moses and the prophets, let them hear them.*

CHRYS. As if he said, Thy brethren are not so much thy Chrys. Conc. 4. de Lazaro. care as God's, who created them, and appointed them teachers to admonish and urge them. But by Moses and the Prophets, he here means the Mosaic and prophetic writings. AMBROSE; In this place our Lord most plainly declares the Old Testament to be the ground of faith, thwarting the treachery of the Jews, and precluding the iniquity of Heretics.

Greg. in Hom. 40. GREG. But he who had despised the words of God, supposed that his followers could not hear them. Hence it is added, *And he said, Nay, father Abraham, but if one went to them from the dead they would repent.* For when he heard the Scriptures he despised them, and thought them fables, and therefore according to what he felt himself, he judged the like of his brethren. GREG. NYSS. But we are also taught Greg. lib. de Anima. something besides, that the soul of Lazarus is neither anxious about present things, nor looks back to aught that it has left behind, but the rich man, (as it were caught by birdlime,) even after death is held down by his carnal life. For a man who becomes altogether carnal in his heart, not even after he has Greg. ubi sup. put off his body is out of the reach of his passions. GREG. But soon the rich man is answered in the words of truth; for it follows, *And he said unto him, If they hear not Moses and the prophets, neither will they believe though one rose from the dead.* For they who despise the words of the Law, will find the commands of their Redeemer who rose from the dead, as they are more sublime, so much the more difficult to fulfil.

Chrys. ut sup. CHRYS. But that it is true that he who hears not the Scriptures, takes no heed to the dead who rise again, the Jews have testified, who at one time indeed wished to kill Lazarus, but at another laid hands upon the Apostles, notwithstanding that some had risen from the dead at the hour of the Cross. Observe this also, that every dead man is a servant, but whatever the Scriptures say, the Lord says. Therefore let it be that dead men should rise again, and an angel descend from heaven, the Scriptures are more worthy of credit than all. For the Lord of Angels, the Lord as well of the living and the dead, is their author. But if God knew this that the dead rising again, profited the living, He would not have omitted it, seeing that He disposes all things for our advantage. Again, if the dead were often to rise again, this too would in time be disregarded. And the devil

also would easily insinuate perverse doctrines, devising resurrection also by means of his own instruments, not indeed
really raising up the deceased, but by certain delusions
deceiving the sight of the beholders, or contriving, that is,
setting up some to pretend death.

AUG. But some one may say, If the dead have no care for Aug.
the living, how did the rich man ask Abraham, that he should de cura
send Lazarus to his five brethren? But because he said this, tuis ha-
did the rich man therefore know what his brethren were benda.
doing, or what was their condition at that time? His care
about the living was such that he might yet be altogether
ignorant what they were doing, just as we care about the
dead, although we know nothing of what they do. But
again the question occurs, How did Abraham know that
Moses and the prophets are here in their books? whence
also had he known that the rich man had lived in luxury,
but Lazarus in affliction. Not surely when these things
were going on in their lifetime, but at their death he might
know through Lazarus' telling him, that in order that might not
be false which the prophet says; *Abraham heard us not.* The Isa. 63,
dead might also hear something from the angels who are 10.
ever present at the things which are done here. They might
also know some things which it was necessary for them to
have known, not only past, but also future, through the
revelation of the Church of God.

AUG. But these things may be so taken in allegory, that Aug.
by the rich man we understand the proud Jews ignorant of Quæst.
the righteousness of God, and going about to establish their qu. 38.
own. The purple and fine linen are the grandeur of the Rom.
kingdom. *And the kingdom of God* (he says) *shall be taken
away from you.* The sumptuous feasting is the boasting of
the Law, in which they gloried, rather abusing it to swell their
pride, than using it as the necessary means of salvation.
But the beggar, by name Lazarus, which is interpreted
" assisted," signifies want; as, for instance, some Gentile, or
Publican, who is all the more relieved, as he presumes
less on the abundance of his resources. GREG. Lazarus Greg.
then full of sores, figuratively represents the Gentile people, in Hom.
who when turned to God, were not ashamed to confess their Ev.
sins. Their wound was in the skin. For what is confession

of sins but a certain bursting forth of wounds. But Lazarus, full of wounds, *desired to be fed by the crumbs which fell from the rich man's table, and no one gave to him;* because that proud people disdained to admit any Gentile to the knowledge of the Law, and words flowed down to him from

Aug. ubi sup.

knowledge, as the crumbs fell from the table. AUG. But the dogs which licked the poor man's sores are those most wicked men who loved sin, who with a large tongue cease not to praise the evil works, which another loathes, groaning in himself, and confessing. GREG. Sometimes also in the holy Word by dogs are understood preachers; according to

Ps. 68, 23. Vulg.

that, *That the tongue of thy dogs may be red by the very blood of thy enemies;* for the tongue of dogs while it licks the wound heals it; for holy teachers, when they instruct us in confession of sin, touch as it were by the tongue the soul's wound. The rich man was buried in hell, but Lazarus was carried by angels into Abraham's bosom, that is, into that secret rest of which the truth says, *Many shall come from the east and the west, and shall lie down with Abraham, Isaac, and Jacob in the kingdom of heaven, but the children of the kingdom shall be cast into outer darkness.* But being afar off, the rich man lifted up his eyes to behold Lazarus, because the unbelievers while they suffer the sentence of their condemnation, lying in the deep, fix their eyes upon certain of the faithful, abiding before the day of the last Judgment in rest above them, whose bliss afterwards they would in no wise contemplate. But that which they behold is afar off, for thither they cannot attain by their merits. But he is described to burn chiefly in his tongue, because the unbelieving people held in their mouth the word of the Law, which in their deeds they despised to keep. In that part then a man will have most burning wherein he most of all shews he knew that which he refused to do. Now Abraham calls him his son, whom at the same time he delivers not from torments; because the fathers of this unbelieving people, observing that many have gone aside from their faith, are not moved with any compassion to rescue them from tor-

Aug. Quæst. Ev. lib. ii. qu.39.

ments, whom nevertheless they recognise as sons. AUG. By the five brothers whom he says he has in his father's house, he means the Jews who were called five, because

they were bound under the Law, which was given by Moses
who wrote five books.

CHRYS. Or he had five brothers, that is, the five senses, to
which he was before a slave, and therefore he could not love
Lazarus because his brethren loved not poverty. Those
brethren have sent thee into these torments, they cannot
be saved unless they die; otherwise it must needs be that
the brethren dwell with their brother. But why seekest thou
that I should send Lazarus? They have Moses and the
Prophets. Moses was the poor Lazarus who counted the
poverty of Christ greater than the riches of Pharaoh. Jeremiah, cast into the dungeon, was fed on the bread of
affliction; and all the prophets teach those brethren. But
those brethren cannot be saved unless some one rise from
the dead. For those brethren, before Christ was risen,
brought me to death; He is dead, but those brethren have
risen again. For my eye sees Christ, my ear hears Him,
my hands handle Him. From what we have said then, we
determine the fit place for Marcion and Manichæus, who
destroy the Old Testament. See what Abraham says, *If
they hear not Moses and the prophets.* As though he said,
Thou doest well by expecting Him who is to rise again;
but in them Christ speaks. If thou wilt hear them, thou wilt
hear Him also. GREG. But the Jewish people, because they
disdained to spiritually understand the words of Moses, did
not come to Him of whom Moses had spoken.

AMBROSE; Or else, Lazarus is poor in this world, but rich
to God; for not all poverty is holy, nor all riches vile,
but as luxury disgraces riches, so holiness commends
poverty. Or is there any Apostolical man, poor in speech,
but rich in faith, who keeps the true faith, requiring not the
appendage of words. To such a one I liken him who ofttimes beaten by the Jews offered the wounds of his body
to be licked as it were by certain dogs. Blessed dogs, unto
whom the dropping from such wounds so falls as to fill the
heart and mouth of those whose office it is to guard the
house, preserve the flock, keep off the wolf! And because
the word is bread, our faith is of the word; the crumbs are
as it were certain doctrines of the faith, that is to say, the
mysteries of the Scriptures. But the Arians, who court the

*Heb. 11,
26.
Jer. 38,
9.*

*Greg.
in Hom.
40.*

alliance of regal power that they may assail the truth of the Church, do not they seem to you to be in purple and fine linen? And these, when they defend the counterfeit instead of the truth, abound in flowing discourses. Rich heresy has composed many Gospels, and poor faith has kept this single Gospel, which it had received. Rich philosophy has made itself many gods, the poor Church has known only one. Do not those riches seem to you to be poor, and that poverty to be rich? AUG. Again also that story may be so under-stood, as that we should take Lazarus to mean our Lord; *lying at the gate of the rich man,* because he condescended to the proud ears of the Jews in the lowliness of His incarnation; *desiring to be fed from the crumbs which fell from the rich man's table,* that is, seeking from them even the least works of righteousness, which through pride they would not use for their own table, (that is, their own power,) which works, although very slight and without the discipline of perseverance in a good life, sometimes at least they might do by chance, as crumbs frequently fall from the table. The wounds are the sufferings of our Lord, the dogs who licked them are the Gentiles, whom the Jews called unclean, and yet, with the sweetest odour of devotion, they lick the sufferings of our Lord in the Sacraments of His Body and Blood throughout the whole world. Abraham's bosom is understood to be the hiding place of the Father, whither after His Passion our Lord rising again was taken up, whither He was said to be carried by the angels, as it seems to me, because that reception by which Christ reached the Father's secret place the angels announced to the disciples. The rest may be taken according to the former explanation, because that is well understood to be the Father's secret place, where even before the resurrection the souls of the righteous live with God.

Aug.
ubi sup.

1. Then said he unto the disciples, It is impossible
but that offences will come: but woe unto him,
through whom they come!

2. It were better for him that a millstone were
hanged about his neck, and he cast into the sea, than
that he should offend one of these little ones.

THEOPHYL. Because the Pharisees were covetous and
railed against Christ when He preached poverty, He put to
them the parable of the rich man and Lazarus. Afterwards,
in speaking with His disciples concerning the Pharisees, He
declares them to be men who caused division, and placed
obstacles in the divine way. As it follows; *Then said he
unto his disciples, It is impossible but that offences will
come*, that is, hindrances to a good life and which is
pleasing to God. CYRIL; Now there are two kinds of
offences, of which the one resist the glory of God, but
the other serve only to cause a stumbling-block to the
brethren. For the inventions of heresies, and every word
that is spoken against the truth, are obstructions to the glory
of God. Such offences however do not seem to be mentioned here, but rather those which occur between friends
and brethren, as strifes, slanders, and the like. Therefore
He adds afterwards, *If thy brother trespass against thee,
rebuke him.* THEOPHYL. Or, He says that there must arise
many obstacles to preaching and to the truth, as the Pharisees hindered the preaching of Christ. But some ask, If
it needs be that offences should come, why does our Lord
rebuke the author of the offences? for it follows, *But woe to
him through whom they come.* For whatsoever necessity

engenders is pardonable, or deserving of pardon. But observe, that necessity itself derives its birth from free-will. For our Lord, seeing how men cling to evil, and put forward nothing good, spoke with reference to the consequence of those things which are seen, that offences must needs come; just as if a physician, seeing a man using an unwholesome diet, should say, It is impossible but that such a one should be sick. And therefore to him that causes offences He denounces woe, and threatens punishment, saying, *It were better for him that a mill-stone were hanged about his neck, and he cast into the sea, &c.* BEDE; This is spoken according to the custom of the province of Palestine; for among the ancient Jews the punishment of those who were guilty of the greater crimes was that they should be sunk into the deep with a stone tied to them; and in truth it were better for a guilty man to finish his bodily life by a punishment however barbarous, yet temporal, than for his innocent brother to deserve the eternal death of his soul. Now he who can be offended is rightly called a little one; for he who is great, whatsoever he is witness of, and how great soever his sufferings, swerves not from the faith. As far then as we can without sin, we ought to avoid giving offence to our neighbours. But if an offence is taken at the truth, it is better to let the offence be, than that truth should be abandoned. CHRYS. But by the punishment of the man who offends, learn the reward of him who saves. For had not the salvation of one soul been of such exceeding care to Christ, He would not threaten with such a punishment the offender.

3. Take heed to yourselves: If thy brother trespass against thee, rebuke him; and if he repent, forgive him.

4. And if he trespass against thee seven times in a day, and seven times in a day turn again to thee, saying, I repent; thou shalt forgive him.

AMBROSE; After the parable of the rich man who is tormented in punishment, Christ added a commandment to give forgiveness to those who turn themselves from their trespasses, lest any one through despair should not be reclaimed from his fault; and hence it is said, *Take heed to yourselves.* THEOPHYL. As if He says, Offences must needs come; but it does not follow that you must perish, if only you be on your guard: as it need not that the sheep should perish when the wolf comes, if the shepherd is watching. And since there are great varieties of offenders, (for some are incurable, some are curable,) He therefore adds, *If thy brother trespass against thee, rebuke him.*

AMBROSE; That there might neither be hard-wrung pardon, nor a too easy forgiveness, neither a harsh upbraiding, to dishearten, nor an overlooking of faults, to invite to sin; therefore it is said in another place, *Tell him his fault* Mat. 18, *between him and thee alone.* For better is a friendly cor- 15. rection, than a quarrelsome accusation. The one strikes shame into a man, the other moves his indignation. He who is admonished will more likely be saved, because he fears to be destroyed. For it is well that he who is corrected should believe you to be rather his friend than his enemy. For we more readily give ear to counsel than yield to injury. Fear is a weak preserver of consistency, but shame is an excellent master of duty. For he who fears is restrained, not amended. But He has well said, *If he trespass against thee.* For it is not the same thing to sin against God and to sin against man. BEDE; But we must mark, that He does not bid us forgive every one who sins, but him only who repents of his sins. For by taking this course we may avoid offences, hurting no one, correcting the sinner with a righteous zeal, extending the bowels of mercy to the penitent. THEOPHYL. But some one may well ask, If when I have several times forgiven my brother he again trespass against me, what must I do with him? In answer therefore to this question He adds, *And if he trespass against thee seven times in a day, and seven times in a day turn again to thee, saying, I repent; forgive him.*

BEDE; By using the number seven He assigns no bound to the giving of pardon, but commands us either to forgive all sins, or always to forgive the penitent. For by seven

the whole of any thing or time is frequently represented.
AMBROSE; Or this number is used because God rested on the
seventh day from His works. After the seventh day of the
world everlasting rest is promised us, that as the evil works of
that world shall then cease, so also may the sharpness of
punishment be abated.

5. And the apostles said unto the Lord, Increase
our faith.

6. And the Lord said, If ye had faith as a grain
of mustard seed, ye might say unto this sycamine
tree, Be thou plucked up by the root, and be thou
planted in the sea; and it should obey you.

THEOPHYL. The disciples hearing our Lord discoursing of
certain arduous duties, such as poverty, and avoiding offences, entreat Him to increase their faith, that so they
might be able to follow poverty, (for nothing so prompts to
a life of poverty as faith and hope in the Lord,) and through
faith to guard against giving offences. Therefore it is said, *And
the Apostles said unto the Lord, Increase our faith.* GREG.
That is, that the faith which has already been received in its
beginning, might go on increasing more and more unto perfection. AUG. We may indeed understand that they asked for the
increase of that faith by which men believe in the things which
they see not; but there is further signified a faith in things,
whereby not with the words only, but the things themselves
present, we believe. And this shall be, when the Wisdom of
God, by whom all things were made, shall reveal Himself
openly to His saints face to face.

THEOPHYL. But our Lord told them that they asked well,
and that they ought to believe stedfastly, forasmuch as faith
could do many things; and hence it follows, *And the Lord
said, If ye had faith as a grain of mustard seed, &c.* Two
mighty acts are here brought together in the same sentence;
the transplanting of that which was rooted in the earth, and
the planting thereof in the sea, (for what is ever planted in the
waves?) by which two things He declares the power of faith.

CHRYS. He mentions the mustard seed, because, though
small in size, it is mightier in power than all the others.

Greg. 22. Mor. c. 21.

Aug. de Quæst. Ev.lib.2. qu. 39.

Chrys. Hom. 57. in Matt.

He implies then that the least part of faith can do great things. But though the Apostles did not transplant the mulberry tree, do not thou accuse them; for our Lord said not, You shall transplant, but, You shall be able to transplant. But they did not, because there was no need, seeing that they did greater things. But some one will ask, How does Christ say, that it is the least part of faith which can transplant a mulberry tree or a mountain, whereas Paul says that it is all faith which moves mountains? We must then answer, that the Apostle imputes the moving of mountains to all faith, not as though only the whole of faith could do this, but because this seemed a great thing to carnal men on account of the vastness of the body.

BEDE; Or our Lord here compares perfect faith to a grain of mustard seed, because it is lowly in appearance, but fervid in heart. But mystically by the mulberry tree, (whose fruit and branches are red with a blood-red colour,) is represented the Gospel of the cross, which, through the faith of the Apostles being uprooted by the word of preaching from the Jewish nation, in which it was kept as it were in the lineal stock, was removed and planted. in the sea of the Gentiles. AMBROSE; Or this is said because faith keeps out the unclean spirit, especially since the nature of the tree falls in with this meaning. For the fruit of the mulberry is at first white in the blossom, and being formed from thence grows red, and blackens as it gets ripe. The devil also having by transgression fallen from the white flower of the angelic nature and the bright beams of his power, grows terrible in the black odour of sin. CHRYS. The mulberry may be also compared to the devil, for as by the leaves of the mulberry tree certain worms are fed, so the devil, by the imaginations which proceed from him, is feeding for us a never dying worm; but this mulberry tree faith is able to pluck out of our souls, and plunge it into the deep.

7. But which of you, having a servant plowing or feeding cattle, will say unto him by and by, when he is come from the field, Go and sit down to meat?

8. And will not rather say unto him, Make ready

Hom. 32 in 1 ad Cor. c. 13. 2.

wherewith I may sup, and gird thyself, and serve me, till I have eaten and drunken ; and afterward thou shalt eat and drink ?

9. Doth he thank that servant because he did the things that were commanded him ?   I trow not.

10. So likewise ye, when ye shall have done all those things which are commanded you, say, We are unprofitable servants : we have done that which was our duty to do.

THEOPHYL. Because faith makes its possessor a keeper of God's commandments, and adorns him with wonderful works ; it would seem from thence that a man might thereby fall into the sin of pride.   Our Lord therefore forewarned His Apostles by a fit example, not to boast themselves in their virtues, saying, *But which of you having a servant plowing, &c.*

Aug. de Quæst. Ev. l. 2. qu. 39. AUG. Or else ; To the many who understand not this faith in the truth already present, our Lord might seem not to have answered the petitions of His disciples.   And there appears a difficulty in the connexion here, unless we suppose He meant the change from faith to faith, from that faith, namely, by which we serve God, to that whereby we enjoy Him.   For then will our faith be increased when we first believe the word preached, next the reality present.   But that joyful contemplation possesseth perfect peace, which is given unto us in the everlasting kingdom of God.   And that perfect peace is the reward of those righteous labours, which are performed in the administration of the Church.   Be then the servant in the field ploughing, or feeding, that is, in this life either following his worldly business, or serving foolish men, as it were cattle, he must after his labours return home, that is, be united to the Church.

BEDE ; Or the servant departs from the field when giving up for a time his work of preaching, the teacher retires into his own conscience, pondering his own words or deeds within himself.   To whom our Lord does not at once say, Go from this mortal life, and sit down to meat, that is, refresh thyself in the everlasting resting-place of a blessed life. AMBROSE; For we know that no one sits down before he has first passed over. Moses indeed also passed over, that he might see a great sight. Since then thou not only sayest to thy servant, *Sit down to meat*, but requirest from him another service, so in this life the Lord does not put up with the performance of one work and labour, because as long as we live we ought always to work. Therefore it follows, *And will not rather say, Make ready wherewith I may sup.* BEDE; He bids make ready wherewith he may sup, that is, after the labours of public discourse, He bids him humble himself in self-examination. With such a supper our Lord desires to be fed. But to gird one's self is to collect the mind which has been enfolded in the base coil of fluctuating thoughts, whereby its steps in the cause of good works are wont to be entangled. For he who girds up his garments does so, that in walking he may not be tripped up. But to minister unto God, is to acknowledge that we have no strength without the help of His grace.

AUG. While His servants also are ministering, that is, preaching the Gospel, our Lord is eating and drinking the faith and confession of the Gentiles. It follows, *And afterward thou shalt eat and drink.* As if He says, After that I have been delighted with the work of thy preaching, and refreshed myself with the choice food of thy compunction, then at length shalt thou go, and feast thyself everlastingly with the eternal banquet of wisdom. *Aug. de Quæst. Ev. ubi sup.*

CYRIL; Our Lord teaches us that it is no more than the just and proper right of a master to require, as their bounden duty, subjection from servants, adding, *Doth he thank that servant because he did the things that were commanded him? I trow not.* Here then is the disease of pride cut away. Why boastest thou thyself? Dost thou know that if thou payest not thy debt, danger is at hand, but if thou payest, thou doest nothing thankworthy? As St. Paul says, *For though I preach the Gospel I have nothing to glory of, for necessity is laid upon me, yea, woe is unto me if I preach not the Gospel.* *1 Cor. 9, 16.*

Observe then that they who have rule among us, do not thank their subjects, when they perform their appointed service, but by kindness gaining the affections of their people, breed in them a greater eagerness to serve them. So likewise

God requires from us that we should wait upon Him as
His servants, but because He is merciful, and of great
goodness, He promises reward to them that work, and the
greatness of His loving-kindness far exceeds the labours of
His servants.

AMBROSE; Boast not thyself then that thou hast been a
good servant. Thou hast done what thou oughtest to have
done. The sun obeys, the moon submits herself, the angels are
subject; let us not then seek praise from ourselves. Therefore
He adds in conclusion, *So likewise ye, when ye have done
all good things, say, We are unprofitable servants, we have
done that which it was our duty to do.* BEDE; Servants,
I say, because bought with a price; unprofitable, for the Lord
needeth not our good things, or because *the sufferings of
this present time are not worthy to be compared to the
glory which shall be revealed in us.* Herein then is the
perfect faith of men, when having done all things which
were commanded them, they acknowledge themselves to be
imperfect.

1 Cor.
6, 20.
Ps. 16,
2.
Rom. 8,
18.

11. And it came to pass, as he went to Jerusalem,
that he passed through the midst of Samaria and
Galilee.

12. And as he entered into a certain village,
there met him ten men that were lepers, which stood
afar off:

13. And they lifted up their voices, and said, Jesus,
Master, have mercy on us.

14. And when he saw them, he said unto them,
Go shew yourselves unto the priests. And it came
to pass, that, as they went, they were cleansed.

15. And one of them, when he saw that he was
healed, turned back, and with a loud voice glorified
God,

16. And fell down on his face at his feet, giving
him thanks: and he was a Samaritan.

17. And Jesus answering said, Were there not ten
cleansed? but where are the nine?

18. There are not found that returned to give glory to God, save this stranger.

19. And he said unto him, Arise, go thy way : thy faith hath made thee whole.

AMBROSE; After speaking the foregoing parable, our Lord censures the ungrateful; TIT. BOST. saying, *And it came to pass,* shewing that the Samaritans were indeed well disposed towards the mercies above mentioned, but the Jews not so. For there was enmity between the Jews and the Samaritans, and He to allay this, passed into the midst of both nations, that he might cement both into one new man.

CYRIL; The Saviour next manifests His glory by drawing over Israel to the faith. As it follows, *And as he entered into a certain village, there met him ten men that were lepers,* men who were banished from the towns and cities, and counted unclean, according to the rites of the Mosaic law.

TIT. BOST. They associated together from the sympathy they felt as partakers of the same calamity, and were waiting till Jesus passed, anxiously looking out to see Him approach. As it is said, *Which stood afar off,* for the Jewish law esteems leprosy unclean, whereas the law of the Gospel calls unclean not the outward, but the inward leprosy.

THEOPHYL. They therefore stand afar off as if ashamed of the uncleanness which was imputed to them, thinking that Christ would loathe them as others did. Thus they stood afar off, but were made nigh unto Him by their prayers. *For the Lord is nigh unto all them that call upon him in truth.* Therefore it follows, *And they lifted up their voices,* Ps. 145, 18. *and said, Jesus, Master, have mercy upon us.* TIT. BOST. They pronounce the name of Jesus, and gain to themselves the reality. For Jesus is by interpretation Saviour. They say, *Have mercy upon us,* because they were sensible of His power, and sought neither for gold and silver, but that their bodies might put on again a healthful appearance. THEO-PHYL. They do not merely supplicate or entreat Him as if He were a man, but they call Him Master or Lord, as if almost they looked upon Him as God. But He bids them shew themselves to the priests, as it follows, *And when he saw them, he said, Go, shew yourselves unto the priests.* For they were examined whether they were cleansed from their leprosy or not.

CYRIL; The law also ordered, that those who were cleansed from leprosy should offer sacrifice for the sake of their purification. THEOPHYL. Therefore in bidding them go to the priests, he meant nothing more than that they were just about to be healed; and so it follows, *And it came to pass that as they went they were healed.* CYRIL; Whereby the Jewish priests who were jealous of His glory might know that it was by Christ granting them health that they were suddenly and miraculously healed.

THEOPHYL. But out of the ten, the nine Israelites were ungrateful, whereas the Samaritan stranger returned and lifted up his voice in thanksgiving, as it follows, *And one of them turned back, and with a loud voice glorified God.* TIT. BOST. When he found that he was cleansed, he had boldness to draw near, as it follows, *And fell down on his face at his feet giving him thanks.* Thus by his prostration and prayers shewing at once both his faith and his gratitude.

It follows, *And he was a Samaritan.* THEOPHYL. We may gather from this that a man is not one whit hindered from pleasing God because he comes from a cursed race, only let him bear in his heart an honest purpose. Further, let not him that is born of saints boast himself, for the nine who were Israelites were ungrateful; and hence it follows, *And Jesus answering him said, Were there not ten cleansed?* TIT. BOST. Wherein it is shewn, that strangers were more ready to receive the faith, but Israel was slow to believe; and so it follows, *And he said unto him, Arise, go thy way, thy faith has made thee whole.*

Aug de
Quæst.
Ev. l. ii.
qu. 40.

AUG. The lepers may be taken mystically for those who, having no knowledge of the true faith, profess various erroneous doctrines. For they do not conceal their ignorance, but blazen it forth as the highest wisdom, making a vain show of it with boasting words. But since leprosy is a blemish in colour, when true things appear clumsily mixed up with false in a single discourse or narration, as in the colour of a single body, they represent a leprosy streaking and disfiguring as it were with true and false dyes the colour of the

human form.   Now these lepers must be so put away from the
Church, that being as far removed as possible, they may with
loud shouts call upon Christ.   But by their calling Him
Teacher, I think it is plainly implied that leprosy is truly
the false doctrine which the good teacher may wash away.
Now we find that of those upon whom our Lord bestowed
bodily mercies, not one did He send to the priests, save
the lepers, for the Jewish priesthood was a figure of that
priesthood which is in the Church.   All vices our Lord
corrects and heals by His own power working inwardly
in the conscience, but the teaching of infusion by means
of the Sacrament, or of catechizing by word of mouth, was
assigned to the Church. *And as they went, they were
cleansed;* just as the Gentiles to whom Peter came, having
not yet received the sacrament of Baptism, whereby we come
spiritually to the priests, are declared cleansed by the infusion of the Holy Spirit.   Whoever then follows true and
sound doctrine in the fellowship of the Church, pro-
claiming himself to be free from the confusion of lies, as it were
a leprosy, yet still ungrateful to his Cleanser does not prostrate himself with pious humility of thanksgiving, is like to
those of whom the Apostle says, *that when they knew* Rom. 1,
God, they glorified him not as God, nor were thankful. Such ²¹·
then will remain in the ninth number as imperfect.   For the
nine need one, that by a certain form of unity they may be
cemented together, in order to become ten.   But he who gave
thanks was approved of as a type of the one only Church.
And since these were Jews, they are declared to have lost
through pride the kingdom of heaven, wherein most of
all unity is preserved.   But the man who was a Samaritan,
which is by interpretation " guardian," giving back to Him
who gave it that which he had received, according to the
Psalm, *My strength will I preserve for thee,* has kept the Ps. 59,
unity of the kingdom with humble devotion.   BEDE; He ⁹·
fell upon his face, because he blushes with shame when
he remembers the evils he had committed.   And he is commanded to rise and walk, because he who, knowing his own
weakness, lies lowly on the ground, is led to advance by the
consolation of the divine word to mighty deeds.   But if
faith made him whole, who hurried himself back to give

thanks, therefore does unbelief destroy those who have neglected to give glory to God for mercies received. Wherefore that we ought to increase our faith by humility, as it is declared in the former parable, so in this is it exemplified in the actions themselves.

20. And when he was demanded of the Pharisees, when the kingdom of God should come, he answered them and said, The kingdom of God cometh not with observation :

21. Neither shall they say, Lo here! or, lo there! for, behold, the kingdom of God is within you.

CYRIL; Because our Saviour, in His discourses which He addressed to others, spake often of the kingdom of God, the Pharisees derided Him; hence it is said, *And when he was asked by the Pharisees when the kingdom of God should come.* As though they said tauntingly, " Before the kingdom of God come, which Thou speakest of, the death of the cross will be Thy lot." But our Lord testifying His patience, when reviled reviles not again, but the rather because they were evil, returns not a scornful answer; for it follows, *He answered and said, The kingdom cometh not with observation;* as if he says, " Seek not to know the time when the kingdom of heaven shall again be at hand. For that time can be observed neither by men nor angels, not as the time of the Incarnation which was proclaimed by the foretelling of Prophets and the heraldings of Angels." Wherefore He adds, *Neither shall they say, Lo here! or, Lo there!* Or else, They ask about the kingdom of God, because, as is said below, they thought that on our Lord's coming into Jerusalem, the kingdom of God would be immediately manifested. Therefore our Lord answers, that the kingdom of God will not come with observation. CYRIL; Now it is only for the benefit of each individual that He says that which follows, *For behold the kingdom of God is within you ;* that is, it rests with you and your own hearts to receive it. For every man who is justified by faith and the grace of God, and adorned with virtues, may obtain the kingdom of heaven. GREG. NYSS. Or, per-

Greg. lib. de prop. sec. Deum.

haps, the kingdom of God being within us, means that joy
that is implanted in our hearts by the Holy Spirit. For that
is, as it were, the image and pledge of the everlasting joy
with which in the world to come the souls of the Saints
rejoice. BEDE; Or the kingdom of God means that He
Himself is placed in the midst of them, that is, reigning in
their hearts by faith.

22. And he said unto the disciples, The days will
come, when ye shall desire to see one of the days of
the Son of man, and ye shall not see it.

23. And they shall say to you, See here; or, see
there: go not after them, nor follow them.

24. For as the lightning, that lighteneth out of
the one part under heaven, shineth unto the other
part under heaven; so shall also the Son of man be
in his day.

25. But first must he suffer many things, and be
rejected of this generation.

CYRIL; When our Lord said, *The kingdom of God is
within you*, He would fain prepare His disciples for suffering,
that being made strong they might be able to enter the
kingdom of God; He therefore foretells to them, that before
His coming from heaven at the end of the world, persecution
will break out upon them. Hence it follows, *And he said
unto the disciples, The days will come, &c.* meaning that so
terrible will be the persecution, that they would desire to see
one of His days, that is, of that time when they yet walked
with Christ. Truly the Jews ofttimes beset Christ with reproaches and insults, and sought to stone Him, and ofttimes
would have hurled Him down from the mountain; but even
these seem to be looked upon as slight in comparison
of greater evils that are to come. THEOPHYL. For their life
was then without trouble, for Christ took care of them and
protected them. But the time was coming when Christ
should be taken away, and they should be exposed to perils,
being brought before kings and princes, and then they

should long for the first time and its tranquillity. BEDE; Or, by the day of Christ He signifies His kingdom, which we hope will come, and He rightly says, *one day*, because there shall no darkness disturb the glory of that blessed time. It is right then to long for the day of Christ, yet from the earnestness of our longing, let us not vision to ourselves as though the day were at hand. Hence it follows, *And they shall say to you, Lo here! and, Lo there!* EUSEB. As if he said, If at the coming of Antichrist, his fame shall be spread abroad, as though Christ had appeared, go not out, nor follow him. For it cannot be that He who was once seen on earth, shall any more dwell in the corners of the earth. It will therefore be he of whom we speak, not the true Christ. For this is the clear sign of the second coming of our Saviour, that suddenly the lustre of His coming shall fill the whole world; and so it follows, *For as the lightning that lighteneth, &c.* For He will not appear walking upon the earth, as any common man, but will illuminate our whole universe, manifesting to all men the radiance of His divinity.

BEDE; And he well says, *that lighteneth out of the one part under heaven,* because the judgment will be given under the heaven, that is, in the midst of the air, as the Apostle says, *We shall be caught up together with them in the clouds.* But if the Lord shall appear at the Judgment like lightning, then shall no one remain hidden in the deep of his heart, for the very brightness of the Judge pierces through him; we may also take this answer of our Lord to refer to His coming, whereby He comes daily into His Church. For ofttimes have heretics so vexed the Church, by saying that the faith of Christ stands in their own dogma, that the faithful in those times longed that the Lord would if it were possible even for one day return to the earth, and Himself make known what was the true faith. *And you shall not see it,* because it need not that the Lord should again testify by a bodily presence that which has been spiritually declared by the light of the Gospel, once scattered and diffused throughout the whole world. CYRIL; Now His disciples supposed that He would go to Jerusalem, and would at once make a manifestation of the kingdom of God. To rid them therefore of this belief, He informs them that it became Him first to suffer the

1 Thess.
4, 17.

Life-giving Passion, then to ascend to the Father and shine forth from above, that He might judge the world in righteousness. Hence He adds, *But first must he suffer many things, and be rejected of this generation.*

BEDE; He means the generation not only of the Jews, but also of all wicked men, by whom even now in His own body, that is, His Church, the Son of man suffers many things, and is rejected. But while He spake many things of His coming in glory, He inserts something also concerning His Passion, that when men saw Him dying, whom they had heard would be glorified, they might both soothe their sorrow for His sufferings by the hope of the promised glory, and at the same time prepare themselves, if they love the glories of His kingdom, to look without alarm upon the horrors of death.

26. And as it was in the days of Noe, so shall it be also in the days of the Son of man.

27. They did eat, they drank, they married wives, they were given in marriage, until the day that Noe entered into the ark, and the flood came, and destroyed them all.

28. Likewise also as it was in the days of Lot; they did eat, they drank, they bought, they sold, they planted, they builded ;

29. But the same day that Lot went out of Sodom it rained fire and brimstone from heaven, and destroyed them all.

30. Even thus shall it be in the day when the Son of man is revealed.

BEDE; The coming of our Lord, which He had compared to lightning flying swiftly across the heavens, He now likens to the days of Noah and Lot, when a sudden destruction came upon mankind. CHRYS. For refusing to believe the words *Chrys.* of warning they were suddenly visited with a real punishment *Hom. 1.* from God; but their unbelief proceeded from self-indulgence, *1. ad* and softness of mind. For such as a man's wishes and *Thess.* inclinations are, will also be his expectations. Therefore it follows, *they eat and drank.*

AMBROSE; He rightly declares the deluge to have been caused by our sins, for God did not create evil, but our deservings found it out for themselves. Let it not however be supposed that marriages, or again meat and drink, are condemned, seeing that by the one succession is sustained, by the other nature, but moderation is to be sought for in all things. For whatsoever is more than this is of evil. BEDE; Now Noah builds the ark mystically. The Lord builds His Church of Christ's faithful servants, by uniting them together in one, as smooth pieces of wood; and when it is perfectly finished, He enters it: as at the day of Judgment, He who ever dwells within His Church enlightens it with His visible presence. But while the ark is in building, the wicked flourish, when it is entered, they perish; as they who revile the saints in their warfare here, shall when they are crowned hereafter be smitten with eternal condemnation.

EUSEB. Having used the example of the deluge, that no one might expect a future deluge by water, our Lord cites, secondly, the example of Lot, to shew the manner of the destruction of the wicked, namely, that the wrath of God would descend upon them by fire from heaven. BEDE; Passing by the unutterable wickedness of the Sodomites, He mentions only those which may be thought trifling offences, or none at all; that you may understand how fearfully unlawful pleasures are punished, when lawful pleasures taken to excess receive for their reward fire and brimstone.

EUSEB. He does not say that fire came down from heaven upon the wicked Sodomites before that Lot went out from them, just as the deluge did not swallow up the inhabitants of the earth before that Noah entered the ark; for as long as Noah and Lot dwelt with the wicked, God suspended His anger that they might not perish together with the sinners, but when He would destroy those, He withdrew the righteous. So also at the end of the world, the consummation shall not come before all the just are separated from the wicked. BEDE; For He who in the mean time though we see Him not yet sees all things, shall then appear to judge all things. And He shall come especially at that time, when He shall see all who are forgetful of His judgments in bondage to this

world. THEOPHYL. For when Antichrist has come, then
shall men become wanton, given up to abominable vices, as
the Apostle says, *Lovers of pleasure rather than lovers of* 2 Tim.
God. For if Antichrist is the dwelling-place of every sin, ³, ⁴·
what else will he then implant in the miserable race of men,
but what belongs to himself. And this our Lord implies by
the instances of the deluge and the people of Sodom.
BEDE; Now mystically, Lot, which is interpreted ' turning
aside,' is the people of the elect, who, while in Sodom, i. e.
among the wicked, live as strangers, to the utmost of
their power turning aside from all their wicked ways. But
when Lot went out, Sodom is destroyed, for at the end of
the world, the angels shall go forth and sever the wicked from Matt.
among the just, and cast them into a furnace of fire. The ¹³, ⁴⁹·
fire and brimstone, however, which He relates to have rained
from heaven, does not signify the flame itself of everlasting
punishment, but the sudden coming of that day.

31. In that day, he which shall be upon the housetop, and his stuff in the house, let him not come
down to take it away: and he that is in the field, let
him likewise not return back.

32. Remember Lot's wife.

33. Whosoever shall seek to save his life shall lose
it; and whosoever shall lose his life shall preserve it.

AMBROSE; Because good men must needs on account of
the wicked be sore vexed in this world, in order that they
may receive a more plentiful reward in the world to come,
they are here punished with certain remedies, as it is here
said, *In that day, &c.* that is, if a man goes up to the top of
his house and rises to the summit of the highest virtues, let
him not fall back to the grovelling business of this world.
AUG. For he is on the housetop who, departing from carnal
things, breathes as it were the free air of a spiritual life. But
the vessels in the house are the carnal senses, which many
using to discover truth which is only taken in by the intellect,
have entirely missed it. Let the spiritual man then beware,
lest in the day of tribulation he again take pleasure in the

carnal life which is fed by the bodily senses, and descend to take away this world's vessels. It follows, *And he that is in the field, let him not return back;* that is, He who labours in the Church, as Paul planting and Apollos watering, let him not look back upon the worldly prospects which he has renounced.

THEOPHYL. Matthew relates all these things to have been said by our Lord, with reference to the destruction of Jerusalem, that when the Romans came upon them, they who were on the housetop should not come down to take any thing, but fly at once, nor they that were in the field return home. And surely so it was at the taking of Jerusalem, and again will be at the coming of Antichrist, but much more at the completion of all things, when that intolerable destruction shall come.

EUSEB. He hereby implies that a persecution will come from the son of perdition upon Christ's faithful. By that day then He means the time previous to the end of the world, in which let not him who is flying return, nor care to lose his goods, lest he imitate Lot's wife, who when she fled out of the city of Sodom, turning back, died, and became a pillar of salt.

AMBROSE; Because thus she looked behind, she lost the gift of her nature. For Satan is behind, behind also Sodom. Wherefore flee from intemperance, turn away from lust, for recollect, that he who turned not back to his old pursuits escaped, because he reached the mount; whereas she looking back to what was left behind, could not even by the aid of her husband reach the mount, but remained fixed. AUG. Lot's wife represents those who in time of trouble look back and turn aside from the hope of the divine promise, and hence she was made a pillar of salt as a warning to men not to do likewise, and to season as it were their hearts, lest they become corrupt.

THEOPHYL. Next follows the promise, *Whosoever shall seek, &c.* as if he said, Let no man in the persecutions of Antichrist seek to secure his life, for he shall lose it, but whoso shall expose himself to trials and death shall be safe, never submitting himself to the tyrant from his love of life. CYRIL; How a man may lose his own life to save it,

St. Paul explains when he speaks of some who crucified Gal. 5, their flesh with the affections and lusts, that is, with per-[24.] severance and devotion engaging in the conflict.

34. I tell you, in that night there shall be two men in one bed ; the one shall be taken, and the other shall be left.

35. Two women shall be grinding together ; the one shall be taken, and the other left.

36. Two men shall be in the field ; the one shall be taken, and the other left.

37. And they answered and said unto him, Where, Lord ? And he said unto them, Wheresoever the body is, thither will the eagles be gathered together.

BEDE ; Our Lord had just before said, that he who is in the field must not return back ; and lest this should seem to have been spoken of those only who would openly return from the field, that is, who would publicly deny their Lord, He goes on to shew, that there are some who, while seeming to turn their face forward, are yet in their heart looking behind. AMBROSE ; He rightly says, *night*, for Antichrist is the hour of darkness, because he pours a dark cloud over the minds of men while he declares himself to be Christ. But Christ as lightning shines brightly, that we may be able to see in that night the glory of the resurrection. AUG. Or Aug. de He says, in that night, meaning in that tribulation. THEO- Qu. Ev. lib. ii. PHYL. Or He teaches us the suddenness of Christ's coming, qu. 41. which we are told will be in the night. And having said that the rich can scarcely be saved, He shews that not all the rich perish, nor all the poor are saved. CYRIL ; For by the two men in one bed, He seems to denote the rich who repose themselves in worldly pleasures, for a bed is a sign of rest. But not all who abound in riches are wicked, but if one is good and elect in the faith, he will be taken, but another who is not so will be left. For when our Lord descends to judgment, He will send His Angels, who while they leave behind on the earth the rest to suffer punishment, will bring the holy and righteous men to Him; according to the Apostle's words, *We shall be caught up together in the clouds to meet Christ in the air.* AMBROSE; Or out of the same bed of human infirmity, one is left, that is, rejected, another is taken up, that is, is caught to meet Christ in the air. By the two grinding together, he seems to imply the poor and the oppressed. To which belongs what follows. *Two men shall be in the field, &c.* For in these there is no slight difference. For some nobly bear up against the burden of poverty, leading a lowly but honest life, and these shall be taken up; but the others are very active in wickedness, and they shall be left. Or those grinding at the mill seem to represent such as seek nourishment from hidden sources, and from secret places draw forth things openly to view. And perhaps the world is a kind of corn mill, in which the soul is shut up as in a bodily prison. And in this corn mill either the synagogue or the soul exposed to sin, like the wheat, softened by grinding and spoilt by too great moisture, cannot separate the outward from the inner parts, and so is left because its flour dissatisfies. But the holy Church, or the soul which is not soiled by the stains of sin, which grinds such wheat as is ripened by the heat of the eternal sun, presents to God a good flour from the secret shrines of the heart. Who the two men in the field are we may discover if we consider, that there are two minds in us, one of the outer man which wasteth away, the other of the inner man which is renewed by the Sacrament. These are then the labourers in the field, the one of which by diligence brings forth good fruit, the other by idleness loses that which he has. Or those who are compared we may interpret to be two nations, one of which being faithful is taken, the other being unfaithful is left.

AUG. Or there are three classes of men here represented. The first is composed of those who prefer their ease and quiet, and busy not themselves in secular or ecclesiastical concerns. And this quiet life of theirs is signified by the bed. The next class embraces those who being placed among the people are governed by teachers. And such he has described by the name of women, because it is best for them to be ruled by the advice of those who are set over them; and he has described these as grinding at the mill, because in their hands revolves the wheel and circle of temporal concerns. And with reference to these matters he has represented them as grinding together, inasmuch as they give their services to the benefit of the Church. The third class are those who labour in the ministry of the Church as in the field of God. In each of these three classes then there are two sorts of men, of which the one abide in the Church and are taken up, the other fall away and are left. AMBROSE; For God is not unjust that He should separate in His reward of their deserts men of like pursuits in life, and not differing in the quality of their actions. But the habit of living together does not equalize the merits of men, for not all accomplish what they attempt, but he only who shall persevere to the end shall be saved. CYRIL; When He said that some should be taken up, the disciples not unprofitably inquire, ‘ Where, Lord ?’ BEDE; Our Lord was asked two questions, where the good should be taken up, and where the bad left; He gave only one answer, and left the other to be understood, saying, *Wheresoever the body is, thither will the eagles be gathered together.* CYRIL; As if He said, As when a dead body is thrown away, all the birds which feed on human flesh flock to it, so when the Son of man shall come, all the eagles, that is, the saints, shall haste to meet Him. AMBROSE; For the souls of the righteous are likened to eagles, because they soar high and forsake the lower parts, and are said to live to a great age. Now concerning the body, we can have no doubt, and above all if we remember that Joseph received the body from Pilate. And do not you see the eagles around Matt. the body are the women and Apostles gathered together 28. around our Lord's sepulchre? Do not you see them then, *when he shall come in the clouds, and every eye shall behold* Rev. 1, *him?* But the body is that of which it was said, *My* 7. *flesh is meat indeed;* and around this body are the eagles John 6, 55. which fly about on the wings of the Spirit, around it also eagles which believe that Christ has come in the flesh. And this body is the Church, in which by the grace of baptism we are renewed in the Spirit.

EUSEB. Or by the eagles feeding on the dead animals, he has here described the rulers of the world, and those who shall at that time persecute the saints of God, in whose power are left all those who are unworthy of being taken up, who are called the body or carcase. Or by the eagles are meant the avenging powers which shall fly about to torment the wicked. Aug. Now these things which Luke has given us in a different place from Matthew, he either relates by anticipation, so as to mention beforehand what was afterwards spoken by our Lord, or he means us to understand that they were twice uttered by Him.

Aug. de Con.Ev. l. ii. c. 7.

1. And he spake a parable unto them to this end, that men ought always to pray, and not to faint;

2. Saying, There was in a city a judge, which feared not God, neither regarded man:

3. And there was a widow in that city; and she came unto him, saying, Avenge me of mine adversary.

4. And he would not for a while: but afterwards he said within himself, Though I fear not God, nor regard man;

5. Yet because this widow troubleth me, I will avenge her, lest by her continual coming she weary me.

6. And the Lord said, Hear what the unjust judge saith.

7. And shall not God avenge his own elect, which cry day and night unto him, though he bear long with them?

8. I tell you that he will avenge them speedily. Nevertheless when the Son of man cometh, shall he find faith on the earth?

THEOPHYL. Our Lord having spoken of the trials and dangers which were coming, adds immediately afterward their remedy, namely, constant and earnest prayer. CHRYS. He who hath redeemed thee, hath shewn thee what He would have thee do. He would have thee be instant in prayer, He would have thee ponder in thy heart the blessings

thou art praying for, He would have thee ask and receive
what His goodness is longing to impart. He never refuses
His blessings to them that pray, but rather stirs men up by
His mercy not to faint in praying. Gladly accept the Lord's
encouragement: be willing to do what He commands, not to
do what He forbids. Lastly, consider what a blessed privilege is granted thee, to talk with God in thy prayers, and
make known to Him all thy wants, while He though not
in words, yet by His mercy, answers thee, for He despiseth
not petitions, He tires not but when thou art silent.
BEDE; We should say that he is always praying, and
faints not, who never fails to pray at the canonical hours.
Or all things which the righteous man does and says
towards God, are to be counted as praying. AUG. Our

Aug.
lib. ii.
qu. 45.

Lord utters His parables, either for the sake of the comparison, as in the instance of the creditor, who when forgiving
his two debtors all that they owed him was most loved by
him who owed him most; or on account of the contrast,
from which he draws his conclusion; as, for example, *if God
so clothe the grass of the field, which to-day is, and to-
morrow is cast into the oven, shall he not much more clothe
you, O ye of little faith.* So also here when he brings forward the case of the unjust judge. THEOPHYL. We may
observe, that irreverence towards man is a token of a greater
degree of wickedness. For as many as fear not God, yet are
restrained by their shame before men, are so far the less sinful; but when a man becomes reckless also of other men, the
burden of his sins is greatly increased.

It follows, *And there was a widow in that city.* AUG.
The widow may be said to resemble the Church, which
appears desolate until the Lord shall come, who now
secretly watches over her. But in the following words, *And
she came unto him, saying, Avenge me, &c.* we are told
the reason why the elect of God pray that they may be
avenged; which we find also said of the martyrs in the

Rev. 6,
10.

Revelations of St. John, though at the same time we are
very plainly reminded to pray for our enemies and persecutors. This avenging of the righteous then we must
understand to be, that the wicked may perish. And
they perish in two ways, either by conversion to righte-

ousness, or by punishment having lost the opportunity of
conversion. Although, if all men were converted to God,
there would still remain the devil to be condemned at the
end of the world. And since the righteous are longing for
this end to come, they are not unreasonably said to desire
vengeance. CYRIL; Or else; Whenever men inflict injury
upon us, we must then think it a noble thing to be forgetful
of the evil; but when they offend against the glory of God
by taking up arms against the ministers of God's ordinance,
we then approach God imploring His help, and loudly re-
buking them who impugn His glory.

AUG. If then with the most unjust judge, the perseverance
of the suppliant at length prevailed even to the fulfilment of ^{nt sup.}
her desire, how much more confident ought they to feel who
cease not to pray to God, the Fountain of justice and mercy?
And so it follows. *And the Lord said, Hear what, &c.*
THEOPHYL. As if He said, If perseverance could melt a judge
defiled with every sin, how much more shall our prayers
incline to mercy God the Father of all mercies! But some
have given a more subtle meaning to the parable, saying, that
the widow is a soul that has put off the old man, (that is, the
devil,) who is her adversary, because she approaches God,
the righteous Judge, who neither fears (because He is God
alone) nor regards man, for with God there is no respect of
persons. Upon the widow then, or soul ever supplicating Him
against the devil, God shews mercy, and is softened by her
importunity. After having taught us that we must in the
last days resort to prayer because of the dangers that are
coming, our Lord adds, *Nevertheless, when the Son of man
cometh, shall he find faith on the earth?* AUG. Our Lord
speaks this of perfect faith, which is seldom found on earth. <sup>Aug.
Serm.
115.</sup>
See how full the Church of God is; were there no faith, who
would enter it? Were there perfect faith, who would not
move mountains? BEDE; When the Almighty Creator shall
appear in the form of the Son of man, so scarce will the elect be,
that not so much the cries of the faithful as the torpor of the
others will hasten the world's fall. Our Lord speaks then as
it were doubtfully, not that He really is in doubt, but to reprove us; just as we sometimes, in a matter of certainty, might
use the words of doubt, as, for instance, in chiding a servant,

Aug.
ut sup. " Remember, am I not thy master?" Aug. Our Lord adds
this to shew, that when faith fails, prayer dies. In order to
pray then, we must have faith, and that our faith fail not, we
must pray. Faith pours forth prayer, and the pouring forth
of the heart in prayer gives stedfastness to faith.

9. And he spake this parable unto certain which
trusted in themselves that they were righteous, and
despised others :

10. Two men went up into the temple to pray;
the one a Pharisee, and the other a Publican.

11. The Pharisee stood and prayed thus with himself, God, I thank thee, that I am not as other men
are, extortioners, unjust, adulterers, or even as this
Publican.

12. I fast twice in the week, I give tithes of all
that I possess.

13. And the Publican, standing afar off, would not
lift up so much as his eyes unto heaven, but smote
upon his breast, saying, God be merciful to me a
sinner.

14. I tell you, this man went down to his house
justified rather than the other : for every one that
exalteth himself shall be abased ; and he that humbleth himself shall be exalted.

Aug.
Serm.
115. Aug. Since faith is not a gift of the proud but of the
humble, our Lord proceeds to add a parable concerning
humility and against pride. Theophyl. Pride also beyond
all other passions disturbs the mind of man. And hence
the very frequent warnings against it. It is moreover a contempt of God; for when a man ascribes the good he doth to
himself and not to God, what else is this but to deny God?
For the sake then of those that so trust in themselves, that
they will not ascribe the whole to God, and therefore
despise others, He puts forth a parable, to shew that righteousness, although it may bring man up to God, yet if he is

clothed with pride, casts him down to hell. GREEK EX. To be Aste-
diligent in prayer was the lesson taught by our Lord in the rius.
parable of the widow and the judge, He now instructs us
how we should direct our prayers to Him, in order that our
prayers may not be fruitless. The Pharisee was condemned
because he prayed heedlessly. As it follows, *The Pharisee
stood and prayed with himself.* THEOPHYL. It is said
" standing," to denote his haughty temper. For his very
posture betokens his extreme pride. BASIL; " He prayed Basil.
with himself," that is, not with God, his sin of pride sent him c. 2.
back into himself. It follows, *God, I thank thee.* AUG. Aug.
His fault was not that he gave God thanks, but that he 115.
asked for nothing further. Because thou art full and
aboundest, thou hast no need to say, *Forgive us our debts.*
What then must be his guilt who impiously fights against
grace, when he is condemned who proudly gives thanks?
Let those hear who say, " God has made me man, I made
myself righteous. O worse and more hateful than the
Pharisee, who proudly called himself righteous, yet gave
thanks to God that he was so.

THEOPHYL. Observe the order of the Pharisee's prayer.
He first speaks of that which he had not, and then of that
which he had. As it follows, *That I am not as other men
are.* AUG. He might at least have said, " as many men;" Aug.
for what does he mean by " other men," but all besides him- ut sup.
self? " I am righteous, he says, the rest are sinners."
GREG. There are different shapes in which the pride of Greg.
self-confident men presents itself; when they imagine that 23. Mor.
either the good in them is of themselves; or when believing it
is given them from above, that they have received it for their
own merits; or at any rate when they boast that they have that
which they have not. Or lastly, when despising others they
aim at appearing singular in the possession of that which
they have. And in this respect the Pharisee awards to himself
especially the merit of good works. AUG. See how he Aug.
derives from the Publican near him a fresh occasion for ut sup.
pride. It follows, *Or even as this Publican;* as if he says,
" I stand alone, he is one of the others."

CHRYS. To despise the whole race of man was not enough Chrys.
for him; he must yet attack the Publican. He would have Hom. 2.
de Pœn.

sinned, yet far less if he had spared the Publican, but now in
one word he both assails the absent, and inflicts a wound on
him who was present. To give thanks is not to heap reproaches on others. When thou returnest thanks to God,
let Him be all in all to thee. Turn not thy thoughts to
men, nor condemn thy neighbour. BASIL; The difference
between the proud man and the scorner is in the outward
form alone. The one is engaged in reviling others, the
other in presumptuously extolling himself. CHRYS. He who
rails at others does much harm both to himself and others.
First, those who hear him are rendered worse, for if sinners
they are made glad in finding one as guilty as themselves, if
righteous, they are exalted, being led by the sins of others to
think more highly of themselves. Secondly, the body of the
Church suffers; for those who hear him are not all content to
blame the guilty only, but to fasten the reproach also on the
Christian religion. Thirdly, the glory of God is evil spoken of;
for as our well-doing makes the name of God to be glorified,
so our sins cause it to be blasphemed. Fourthly, the object
of reproach is confounded and becomes more reckless and
immoveable. Fifthly, the ruler is himself made liable to
punishment for uttering things which are not seemly.

THEOPHYL. It becomes us not only to shun evil, but also
to do good; and so after having said, *I am not as other men
are, extortioners, unjust, adulterers,* he adds something by
way of contrast, *I fast twice in a week.* They called the week
the Sabbath, from the last day of rest. The Pharisees fasted
upon the second and fifth day. He therefore set fasting
against the passion of adultery, for lust is born of luxury; but
to the extortioners and usurists he opposed the payment of
tithes; as it follows, *I give tithes of all I possess;* as if he
says, So far am I from indulging in extortion or injuring, that
I even give up what is my own. GREG. So it was pride that
laid bare to his wily enemies the citadel of his heart, which
prayer and fasting had in vain kept closed. Of no use are
all the other fortifications, as long as there is one place which
the enemy has left defenceless.

AUG. If you look into his words, you will find that he asked
nothing of God. He goes up indeed to pray, but instead of
asking God, praises himself, and even insults him that asked.

Hom. 3.
in Matt.

Basil.
ubi sup.

Sabba-
tho.

Greg.
19. Mor.
c. 21.

The Publican, on the other hand, driven by his stricken conscience afar off, is by his piety brought near. THEOPHYL. Although reported to have stood, the Publican yet differed from the Pharisee, both in his manner and his words, as well as in his having a contrite heart. For he feared to lift up his eyes to heaven, thinking unworthy of the heavenly vision those which had loved to gaze upon and wander after earthly things. He also smote his breast, striking it as it were because of the evil thoughts, and moreover rousing it as if asleep. And thus he sought only that God would be reconciled to him, as it follows, saying, *God, be merciful.*

CHRYS. He heard the words, that I am not as the Publican. He was not angry, but pricked to the heart. The one uncovered the wound, the other seeks for its remedy. Let no one then ever put forth so cold an excuse as, I dare not, I am ashamed, I cannot open my mouth. The devils have that kind of fear. The devil would fain close against thee every door of access to God.

AUG. Why then marvel ye, whether God pardons, since He himself acknowledges it. The Publican stood afar off, yet drew near to God. And the Lord was nigh unto him, and heard him, *For the Lord is on high, yet hath he regard to the lowly.* He lifted not so much as his eyes to heaven; that he might be looked upon, he looked not himself. Conscience weighed him down, hope raised him up, he smote his own breast, he exacted judgment upon himself. Therefore did the Lord spare the penitent. Thou hast heard the accusation of the proud, thou hast heard the humble confession of the accused. Hear now the sentence of the Judge; *Verily I say unto you, this man went down to his house justified rather than the other.*

Aug.
Serm.
115.

CHRYS. This parable represents to us two chariots on the race course, each with two charioteers in it. In one of the chariots it places righteousness with pride, in the other sin and humility. You see the chariot of sin outstrip that of righteousness, not by its own strength but by the excellence of humility combined with it, but the other is defeated not by righteousness, but by the weight and swelling of pride. For as humility by its own elasticity rises above the weight of pride, and leaping up reaches to God, so pride by its

Chrys.
de Inc.
DeiNat.
Hom. 5.

great weight easily depresses righteousness. Although therefore thou art earnest and constant in well doing, yet thinkest
thou mayest boast thyself, thou art altogether devoid of the
fruits of prayer. But thou that bearest a thousand loads of
guilt on thy conscience, and only thinkest this thing of thyself
that thou art the lowest of all men, shalt gain much confidence
before God. And He then goes on to assign the reason of His
sentence. *For every one who exalteth himself shall be
abased, and he that humbleth himself shall be exalted.* The
word humility has various meanings. There is the humility
of virtue, as, *A humble and contrite heart, O God, thou wilt
not despise.* There is also a humility arising from sorrows, as,
He has humbled my life upon the earth. There is a humility
derived from sin, and the pride and insatiability of riches.
For can any thing be more low and debased than those who
grovel in riches and power, and count them great things?
BASIL ; In like manner it is possible to be honourably elated
when your thoughts indeed are not lowly, but your mind by
greatness of soul is lifted up towards virtue. This loftiness of
mind is seen in a cheerfulness amidst sorrow ; or a kind of
noble dauntlessness in trouble ; a contempt of earthly things,
and a conversation in heaven. And this loftiness of mind
seems to differ from that elevation which is engendered
of pride, just as the stoutness of a well-regulated body
differs from the swelling of the flesh which proceeds from
dropsy.

CHRYS. This inflation of pride can cast down even from
heaven the man that taketh not warning, but humility can raise
a man up from the lowest depth of guilt. The one saved the
Publican before the Pharisee, and brought the thief into Paradise before the Apostles ; the other entered even into the
spiritual powers. But if humility though added to sin
has made such rapid advances, as to pass by pride united to
righteousness, how much swifter will be its course when you
add to it righteousness ? It will stand by the judgment-seat
of God in the midst of the angels with great boldness. Moreover if pride joined to righteousness had power to depress it,
unto what a hell will it thrust men when added to sin? This
I say not that we should neglect righteousness, but that we
should avoid pride. THEOPHYL. But should any one per-

Chrys.
in Ps.
142.

Ps. 51,
17.

Ps. 142,
3.

Basil.
in Esai.
2. 12.

Chrys.
Hom. de
Prof.
Ev.

chance marvel that the Pharisee for uttering a few words in
his own praise is condemned, while Job, though he poured
forth many, is crowned, I answer, that the Pharisee spoke
these at the same time that he groundlessly accused others;
but Job was compelled by an urgent necessity to enumerate
his own virtues for the glory of God, that men might not
fall away from the path of virtue.

BEDE; Typically, the Pharisee is the Jewish people, who
boast of their ornaments because of the righteousness of the
law; but the Publican is the Gentiles, who being at a distance
from God confess their sins. Of whom the one for His pride
returned humbled, the other for his contrition was thought
worthy to draw near and be exalted.

15. And they brought unto him also infants, that
he would touch them: but when his disciples saw it,
they rebuked them.

16. But Jesus called them unto him, and said,
Suffer little children to come unto me, and forbid
them not: for of such is the kingdom of God.

17. Verily I say unto you, Whosoever shall not
receive the kingdom of God as a little child shall in
no wise enter therein.

THEOPHYL. After what He had said, our Lord teaches us
a lesson of humility by His own example; He does not turn
away the little children who are brought to Him, but graciously receives them. AUG. To whom are they brought to Aug.
be touched, but to the Saviour? And as being the Saviour Serm.
they are presented to Him to be saved, who came to save that 115.
which was lost. But with regard to these innocents, when
were they lost? The Apostle says, *By one man sin entered* Rom. 5,
into the world. Let then the little children come as the sick 12.
to a physician, the lost to their Redeemer.

AMBROSE; It may be thought strange by some that the disciples wished to prevent the little children from coming to our
Lord, as it is said, *when they saw it, they rebuked them.* But
we must understand in this either a mystery, or the effect of
their love to Him. For they did it not from envy or harsh

feeling towards the children, but they manifested a holy zeal
in their Lord's service, that he might not be pressed by the
crowds. Our own interest must be given up where an injury
is threatened to God. But we may understand the mystery
to be, that they desired the Jewish people to be first saved,
of whom they were according to the flesh.

They knew indeed the mystery, that to both nations the
call was to be made, (for they entreated for the Canaanitish
woman,) but perhaps they were still ignorant of the order.
It follows, *But Jesus called them unto him, and said, Suffer
little children, &c.* One age is not preferred to another, else
it were hurtful to grow up. But why does He say that
children are fitter for the kingdom of heaven ? It is because
they are ignorant of guile, are incapable of theft, dare not
return a blow, are unconscious of lust, have no desire for
wealth, honours, or ambition. But to be ignorant of these
things is not virtue, we must also despise them. For virtue
consists not in our inability to sin, but in our unwillingness.
Childhood then is not meant here, but that goodness which
rivals the simplicity of childhood. BEDE ; Hence our Lord
pointedly says, *of such*, not " of these," to shew that to
character, not to age, is the kingdom given, and to such as
have a childlike innocence and simplicity is the promise of
the reward. AMBROSE ; Lastly, our Saviour expressed this
when He said, *Verily I say unto you, Whosoever will not
receive the kingdom of God as a little child, &c.* What
child were Christ's Apostles to imitate but Him of whom
Esaias speaks, *Unto us a Child is given?* Who *when He
was reviled, reviled not again.* So that there is in childhood
a certain venerable antiquity, and in old age a childlike
innocence. BASIL ; We shall receive the kingdom of God
as a child if we are disposed towards our Lord's teaching as
a child under instruction, never contradicting nor disputing
with his masters, but trustfully and teachably imbibing learning. THEOPHYL. The wise men of the Gentiles therefore
who seek for wisdom in a mystery, which is the kingdom of
God, and will not receive this without the evidence of
logical proof, are rightly shut out from this kingdom.

Isai. 9, 6.
1 Pet. 2.

Basil.
in Reg.
Brev.
ad int.
217.

18. And a certain ruler asked him, saying, Good Master, what shall I do to inherit eternal life ?

19. And Jesus said unto him, Why callest thou me good ? none is good, save one, that is, God.

20. Thou knowest the commandments, Do not commit adultery, Do not kill, Do not steal, Do not bear false witness, Honour thy father and thy mother.

21. And he said, All these have I kept from my youth up.

22. Now when Jesus heard these things, he said unto him, Yet lackest thou one thing : sell all that thou hast, and distribute unto the poor, and thou shalt have treasure in heaven : and come, follow me.

23. And when he heard this, he was very sorrowful : for he was very rich.

BEDE ; A certain ruler having heard our Lord say, that only those who would be like little children should enter the kingdom of heaven, entreats Him to explain to him not by parable but openly by what works he may merit to obtain eternal life. AMBROSE ; That ruler tempting Him said, *Good Master*, he ought to have said, Good God. For although goodness exists in divinity and divinity in goodness, yet by adding *Good Master*, he uses good only in part, not in the whole. For God is good altogether, man partially. CYRIL ; Now he thought to detect Christ in blaming the law of Moses, while He introduced His own commands. He went then to the Master, and calling Him *good*, says that he wishes to be taught by Him, for he sought to tempt Him. But He who takes the wise in their craftiness answers him fitly as follows, *Why callest thou me good? there is none good, save God alone.* AMBROSE ; He does not deny that He is good, but points to God. None is good then except he be full of goodness. But should it strike any one that it is said, *none is good*, let this also strike him, *save God*, and if the Son is not excepted from God, surely neither is Christ excepted from good. For how is He not good who is born from good? *A good tree brings forth good fruits.* How is Matt. 7, 17.

He not good, seeing that the substance of His goodness which He took unto Him from the Father has not degenerated in the Son which did not degenerate in the Spirit. *Thy good spirit,* he says, *shall lead me into a land of uprightness.* But if the Spirit is good who received from the Son, verily He also is good who gave It. Because then it was a lawyer who tempted Him, as is plainly shewn in another book, He therefore well said, *None is good, save God,* that He might remind him that it was written, *Thou shalt not tempt the Lord thy God,* but he the rather *gives thanks to the Lord that He is good.*

Ps. 148, 10.

Deut. 6, 16. Ps.11,8.

Chrys. Hom. 63. in Matt.

CHRYS. Or else; I shall not hesitate to call this ruler covetous, for with this Christ reproaches him, but I say not that he was a tempter. TIT. BOST. When he says then, *Good Master, what shall I do to inherit eternal life?* it is the same as if he says, Thou art good; vouchsafe me then an answer to my question. I am learned in the Old Testament, but I see in Thee something far more excellent. For Thou makest no earthly promises, but preachest the kingdom of heaven. Tell me then, what shall I do to inherit eternal life? The Saviour then considering his meaning, because faith is the way to good works, passes over the question he asked, and leads him to the knowledge of faith; as if a man was to ask a physician, "What shall I eat?" and he was to shew him what ought to go before his food. And then He sends him to His Father, saying, *Why callest thou me good?* not that He was not good, for He was the good branch from the good tree, or the good Son of the good Father. AUG. It may seem that the account given in Matthew is different, where it is said, "Why askest thou me of good?" which might apply better to the question which he asked, *What good shall I do?* In this place he both calls Him good, and asks the question about good. It will be best then to understand both to have been said, *Why callest thou me good?* and, Why askest thou me of good? though the latter may rather be implied in the former.

Aug. de Quæst. Ev. lib. ii.qu 63. Matt. 10.

TIT. BOST. After instructing him in the knowledge of the faith, He adds, *Thou knowest the commandments.* As though He said, Know God first, and then will it be time to seek what thou askest. CYRIL; But the ruler expected to hear Christ say, Forsake the commandments of Moses, and listen to Mine.

Whereas He sends him to the former; as it follows, *Thou shalt not kill, Thou shalt not commit adultery.* THEOPHYL. The law first forbids those things to which we are most prone, as adultery for instance, the incitement to which is within us, and of our nature; and murder, because rage is a great and savage monster. But theft and bearing false witness are sins which men seldom fall into. And besides, the former also are the more grievous sins, therefore He places theft and bearing false witness in the second place, as both less common, and of less weight than the other. BASIL; Now we must not understand by thieves, only such as cut strips off hides, or commit robberies in the baths. But all such also as, when appointed leaders of legions, or installed governors of states or nations, are guilty of secret embezzlement, or violent and open exactions. TIT. BOST. But you may observe that these commandments consist in not doing certain things; that if thou hast not committed adultery, thou art chaste; if thou stealest not, honestly disposed; if thou bearest not false witness, truth-telling. Virtue then we see is rendered easy through the goodness of the Lawgiver. For He speaks of avoiding of evil, not practising of good. And any cessation from action is easier than any actual work.

THEOPHYL. Because sin against parents, although a great crime, very rarely happens, He places it last of all, *Honour thy father and mother.* AMBROSE; Honour is concerned not only with paying respect, but also with giving bountifully. For it is honouring to reward deserts. Feed thy father, feed thy mother, and when thou hast fed them thou hast not requited all the pangs and agony thy mother underwent for thee. To the one thou owest all thou hast, to the other all thou art. What a condemnation, should the Church feed those whom thou art able to feed! But it may be said, What I was going to bestow upon my parents, I prefer to give to the Church. God seeks not a gift which will starve thy parents, but the Scripture says as well that parents are to be fed, as that they are to be left for God's sake, should they check the love of a devout mind.

It follows, *And he said, All these things have I kept from my youth up.* JEROME; The young man speaks false, for if he had fulfilled that which was afterwards placed among the

Basil. in Esai. cap. 1. 23.

Hier. in Matt. 19, 19.

commandments, *Thou shalt love thy neighbour as thyself,* how was it that when he heard, *Go and sell all that thou hast, and give to the poor, he went away sorrowful?* BEDE; Or we must not think him to have lied, but to have avowed that he had lived honestly, that is, at least in outward things, else Mark could never have said, *And Jesus seeing him, loved him.*

Mark
10, 21.

TIT. BOST. Our Lord next declares, that though a man has kept the old covenant, he is not perfect, since he lacks to follow Christ. *Thou yet lackest one thing, Sell all that thou hast, &c.* As if He says, Thou askest how to possess eternal life; scatter thy goods among the poor, and thou shalt obtain it. A little thing is that thou spendest, thou receivest great things. ATHAN. For when we despise the world, we must not imagine we have resigned any thing great, for the whole earth in comparison of the heaven is but a span long; therefore even should they who renounce it be lords of the whole earth, yet still it would be nothing worth in comparison of the kingdom of heaven. BEDE; Whoever then wishes to be perfect must sell all that he hath, not a part only, as Ananias and Sapphira did, but the whole. THEOPHYL. Hence when he says, *All that thou hast,* He inculcates the most complete poverty. For if there is any thing left over or remaining to thee, thou art its slave. BASIL; He does not tell us to sell our goods, because they are by nature evil, for then they would not be God's creatures; He therefore does not bid us cast them away as if they were bad, but distribute them; nor is any one condemned for possessing them, but for abusing them. And thus it is, that to lay out our goods according to God's command both blots out sins, and bestows the kingdom. CHRYS. God might indeed feed the poor without our taking compassion upon them, but He wishes the givers to be bound by the ties of love to the receivers. BASIL; When our Lord says, *Give to the poor,* it becomes a man no longer to be careless, but diligently to dispose of all things, first of all by himself if in any measure he is able, if not, by those who are known to be faithful, and prudent in their management; for *cursed is he who doeth the work of the Lord negligently.* CHRYS. But it is asked, how does Christ acknowledge the giving all things to the poor to be

Athan.
ex Apol.
de sua
fuga.

Basil.
in Reg.
Brev.
int. 92.

Chrys.
Hom.
22. in 1.
ad Cor.

Basil.
in Reg.
fus.disp.
3. ad int.
9.

Jerem.
49, 10.
Chrys.
Hom.
32. in 1.
ad Cor.

perfection, whereas St. Paul declares this very thing without charity to be imperfect. Their harmony is shewn in the words which succeed, *And come, follow me*, which betokens it to be from love. *For herein shall all men know that ye are my disciples, if ye have love one toward another.* THEOPHYL. John 13, 35. Together with poverty must exist all the other virtues, therefore He says, *Come, follow me*, that is, In all other things be My disciples, be always following Me.

CYRIL; The ruler was not able to contain the new word, but being like an old bottle, burst with sorrow. BASIL; The merchant when he goes to the market, is not loth to part with all that he has, in order to obtain what he requires, but thou art grieved at giving mere dust and ashes that thou mayest gain everlasting bliss. Basil. Hom. de eleemos.

24. And when Jesus saw that he was very sorrowful, he said, How hardly shall they that have riches enter into the kingdom of God!

25. For it is easier for a camel to go through a needle's eye, than for a rich man to enter into the kingdom of God.

26. And they that heard it said, Who then can be saved?

27. And he said, The things which are impossible with men are possible with God.

28. Then Peter said, Lo, we have left all, and followed thee.

29. And he said unto them, Verily I say unto you, There is no man that hath left house, or parents, or brethren, or wife, or children, for the kingdom of God's sake,

30. Who shall not receive manifold more in this present time, and in the world to come life everlasting.

THEOPHYL. Our Lord, seeing that the rich man was sorrowful when it was told him to surrender his riches, marvelled, saying, *How hardly shall they that have riches enter into the kingdom of God!* He says not, It is impossible

for them to enter, but it is difficult. For they might through
their riches reap an heavenly reward, but it is a hard thing,
seeing that riches are more tenacious than birdlime, and
hardly is the soul ever plucked away, that is once seized by
them. But he next speaks of it as impossible. *It is easier
for a camel to go through a needle's eye.* The word in the
Greek answers equally to the animal called the camel, and
to a cable, or ship rope. However we may understand it,
impossibility is implied. What must we say then? First of all
that the thing is positively true, for we must remember that
the rich man differs from the steward, or dispenser of riches.
The rich man is he who reserves his riches to himself, the
steward or dispenser one who holds them entrusted to his

Chrys.
Hom.
24. in 1
ad Cor.

care for the benefit of others. CHRYS. Abraham indeed
possessed wealth for the poor. And all they who righteously
possess it, spend it as receiving it from God, according to
the divine command, while those who have acquired wealth
in an ungodly way, are ungodly in their use of it; whether
in squandering it on harlots or parasites, or hiding it in the

Hom.
18. in
Joan.

ground, but sparing nothing for the poor. He does not
then forbid men to be rich, but to be the slaves of their
riches. He would have us use them as necessary, not keep
guard over them. It is of a servant to guard, of a master
to dispense. Had he wished to preserve them, He would
never have given them to men, but left them to remain in
the earth.

THEOPHYL. Again, observe that He says, a rich man can
not possibly be saved, but one who possesses riches hardly;
as if he said, The rich man who has been taken captive by
his riches, and is a slave to them, shall not be saved; but
he who possesses or is the master of them shall with difficulty
be saved, because of human infirmity. For the devil is ever
trying to make our foot slip as long as we possess riches,
and it is a hard matter to escape his wiles. Poverty therefore

Chrys.
Hom.
80. in
Matt.

is a blessing, and as it were free from temptation. CHRYS.
There is no profit in riches while the soul suffers poverty,
no hurt in poverty, while the soul abounds in wealth. But
if the sign of a man waxing rich is to be in need of nothing,
and of becoming poor to be in want, it is plain that the poorer
a man is, the richer he grows. For it is far easier for one

in poverty to despise wealth, than for the rich.   Nor again
is avarice wont to be satisfied by having more, for thereby
are men only the more inflamed, just as a fire spreads,
the more it has to feed upon.   Those which seem to be
the evils of poverty, it has in common with riches, but the
evils of riches are peculiar to them.   AUG. The name of Aug. de
"rich" he here gives to one who covets temporal things, and Evang.
boasts himself in them.   To such rich men are opposed the lib. ii.
poor in spirit, of whom is the kingdom of heaven.   Now
mystically it is easier for Christ to suffer for the lovers of this
world, than for the lovers of this world to be converted to
Christ.   For by the name of a camel He would represent
Himself: for He voluntarily humbled Himself to bear the
burdens of our infirmity.   By the needle He signifies sharp
piercings, and thereby the pangs received in His Passion,
but by the form of the needle He describes the straitening of
the Passion.   CHRYS. These weighty words so far exceeded Chrys.
the capacity of the disciples, that when they heard them, 63. in
they asked, *Who then can be saved?* not that they feared for Matt.
themselves, but for the whole world.   AUG. Seeing that Aug.
there is an incomparably greater number of poor which ut sup.
might be saved by forsaking their riches, they understood that
all who love riches, even though they cannot obtain them,
were to be counted among the number of the rich.   It follows,
*And he said to them, The things which are impossible with
men are possible with God,* which must not be taken as if
a rich man with covetousness and pride might enter into the
kingdom of God, but that it is possible with God for a man
to be converted from covetousness and pride, to charity and
humility.   THEOPHYL. With men therefore whose thoughts
creep earthward, salvation is impossible, but with God it is
possible.   For when man shall have God for his counsellor,
and shall have received the righteousness of God and His
teaching concerning poverty, as well as have invoked His
aid, this shall be possible to him.

CYRIL; The rich man who has despised many things will
naturally expect a reward, but he who possessing little resigns
what he has, may fairly ask what there is in store for him; as
it follows, *Then Peter said, Lo, we have left all.*   Matthew
adds, *What shall we have therefore?*   BEDE; As if he says, Matt.
19, 27.

We have done what Thou commandedst us, what reward then wilt Thou give us? And because it is not enough to have left all things, he adds that which made it perfect, saying, *And have followed thee.* CYRIL; It was necessary to say this, because those who forsake a few things, as far as regards their motives and obedience, are weighed in the same balance with the rich, who have forsaken all, inasmuch as they act from the like affections, in voluntarily making a surrender of all that they possess. And therefore it follows, *Verily I say unto you, there is no man that hath left house, &c. who shall not receive manifold more, &c.* He inspires all who hear Him with the most joyful hopes, confirming His promises to them with an oath, beginning His declaration with *Verily.* For when the divine teaching invites the world to the faith of Christ, some perhaps regarding their unbelieving parents are unwilling to distress them by coming to the faith, and have the like respect of others of their relations; while some again forsake their father and mother, and hold lightly the love of their whole kindred in comparison of the love of Christ.

BEDE; The sense then is this; He who in seeking the kingdom of God has despised all earthly affections, has trampled under foot all riches, pleasures, and smiles of the world, shall receive far greater in the present time. Upon the ground of this declaration, some of the Jews build up the fable of a millennium after the resurrection of the just, when all things which we have given up for God's sake shall be restored with manifold interest, and eternal life be granted. Nor do they from their ignorance seem to be aware, that even if in other things there might be a fit promise of restoration, yet in the matter of wives, who might be according to some Evangelists an hundred fold, it would be manifestly shocking, especially since our Lord declares that in the resurrection there will be no marrying. And according to Mark, those things which have been given up, He declares shall be received at this time with persecutions, which these Jews assert will be absent for a thousand years.

CYRIL; This then we say, that he who gives up all worldly and carnal things will gain for himself far greater, inasmuch as the Apostles, after leaving a few things, obtained the manifold gifts of grace, and were accounted great every where. We

then shall be like to them. If a man has left his home, he
shall receive an abiding place above. If his father, he shall
have a Father in heaven. If he has forsaken his kindred,
Christ shall take him for a brother. If he has given up a
wife, he shall find divine wisdom, from which he shall beget
spiritual offspring. If a mother, he shall find the heavenly
Jerusalem, who is our mother. From brethren and sisters
also united together with him by the spiritual bond of his
will, he shall receive in this life far more kindly affections.

31. Then he took unto him the twelve, and said
unto them, Behold, we go up to Jerusalem, and all
things that are written by the prophets concerning the Son of man shall be accomplished.

32. For he shall be delivered unto the Gentiles,
and shall be mocked, and spitefully entreated, and
spitted on:

33. And they shall scourge him, and put him to
death : and the third day he shall rise again.

34. And they understood none of these things :
and this saying was hid from them, neither knew they
the things which were spoken.

GREG. The Saviour foreseeing that the hearts of His disci- Greg.
ples would be troubled at His Passion, tells them long before- Hom. 2.
hand both the suffering of His Passion and the glory of His in Ev.
Resurrection. BEDE; And knowing that there would arise
certain heretics, saying, that Christ taught things contrary to
the Law and the Prophets, He shews already that the voices
of the Prophets had proclaimed the accomplishment of His
Passion, and the glory which should follow.

CHRYS. He speaks with His disciples apart, concerning Chrys.
His Passion. For it was not fitting to publish this word to Hom.
the multitudes, lest they should be troubled, but to His disci- 65. in
ples He foretold it, that being habituated by expectation, they Matt.
might be the more able to bear it.

CYRIL; And to convince them that He foreknew His
Passion, and of His own accord came to it, that they might
not say, " How has He fallen into the hands of the enemy,

who promised us salvation?" He relates in order the successive events of the Passion; *He shall be delivered unto the
Gentiles, and shall be mocked, and scourged, and spitted on.*
Chrys. CHRYS. Esaias prophesied of this when he said, *I gave my
ubi sup. *back to the smiters, and my cheeks to them that plucked off
Isa. 50, *the hair: I hid not my face from shame and spitting.* The
5.
Isa. 53, Prophet also foretold the crucifixion, saying, *He hath poured
12. *out his soul unto death, and was numbered with the transgressors;* as it is said here, *And after they have scourged
him, they shall put him to death.* But David foretold Christ's
Ps. 16, resurrection, *For thou shalt not leave my soul in hell,* and so
10. it is here added, *And on the third day he shall rise again.*

Isid. ISIDORE; I marvel at the folly of those who ask how Christ
l. ii. Ep. rose again before the three days. If indeed He rose later than
212. he had foretold, it were a mark of weakness, but if sooner, a
token of the highest power. For when we see a man who
has promised his creditor that he will pay him his debt after
three days, fulfilling his promise on that very day, we are so far
from looking upon him as deceitful, that we admire his veracity.
I must add, however, that He said not that He should rise
again after three days, but on the third day. You have then
the preparation, the Sabbath until sun set, and the fact that
He rose after the Sabbath was over.

CYRIL; The disciples did not as yet know exactly
what the Prophets had foretold, but after He rose again,
Luke 24, He opened their understanding that they should under-
25. stand the Scriptures. BEDE; For because they desired
His life above all things, they could not hear of His death,
and as they knew him to be not only a spotless man,
but also very God, they thought He could in no wise
die. And whenever in the parables, which they frequently
heard Him utter, He said any thing concerning His Passion,
they believed it to be spoken allegorically, and referred to
something else. Hence it follows, *And this saying was hid
from them, neither knew they the things which were spoken.*
But the Jews, who conspired against His life, knew that He
spoke concerning His Passion, when he said, *The Son of man
must be lifted up;* therefore said they, *We have heard in our
law that Christ abideth for ever, and how sayest thou the
Son of man must be lifted up?*

35. And it came to pass, that as he was come nigh unto Jericho, a certain blind man sat by the way side begging:

36. And hearing the multitude pass by, he asked what it meant.

37. And they told him, that Jesus of Nazareth passeth by.

38. And he cried, saying, Jesus, thou Son of David, have mercy on me.

39. And they which went before rebuked him, that he should hold his peace: but he cried so much the more, Thou Son of David, have mercy on me.

40. And Jesus stood, and commanded him to be brought unto him: and when he was come near, he asked him,

41. Saying, What wilt thou that I shall do unto thee? And he said, Lord, that I may receive my sight.

42. And Jesus said unto him, Receive thy sight: thy faith hath saved thee.

43. And immediately he received his sight, and followed him, glorifying God: and all the people, when they saw it, gave praise unto God.

GREG. Because the disciples being yet carnal were unable to receive the words of mystery, they are brought to a miracle. Before their eyes a blind man receives his sight, that by a divine work their faith might be strengthened. THEOPHYL. And to shew that our Lord did not even walk without doing good, He performed a miracle on the way, giving His disciples this example, that we should be profitable in all things, and that nothing in us should be in vain. AUG. We might understand the expression of being nigh to Jericho, as if they had already gone out of it, but were still near. It might, though less common in this sense, be so taken here, since Matthew relates, that as they were going out of Jericho, two men received their sight who sat by the way side. There need be

*Greg.
Hom. 2.
in Ev.*

no question about the number, if we suppose that one of the Evangelists remembering only one was silent about the other. Mark also mentions only one, and he too says that he received his sight as they were going out of Jericho; he has given also the name of the man and of his father, to let us understand that this one was well known, but the other not so, so that it might come to pass that the one who was known would be naturally the only one mentioned. But seeing that what follows in St. Luke's Gospel most plainly proves the truth of his account, that while they were yet coming to Jericho, the miracle took place, we cannot but suppose that there were two such miracles, the first upon one blind man when our Lord was coming to that city, the second on two, when He was departing out of it; Luke relating the one, Matthew the other.

Hom. de cæco et Zacchæo. PSEUDO-CHRYS. There was a great multitude gathered round Christ, and the blind man indeed knew Him not, but felt a drawing towards Him, and grasped with his heart what his sight embraced not. As it follows, *And when he heard the multitude passing by, he asked what it was.* And those that saw spoke indeed according to their own opinion. *And they told him that Jesus of Nazareth passeth by.* But the blind man cried out. He is told one thing, he proclaims another; for it follows, *And he cried out, saying, Jesus, thou Son of David, have mercy on me.* Who taught thee this, O man? Hast thou that art deprived of sight read books? Whence then knowest thou the Light of the world? *Verily the Lord giveth sight to the blind.*

Ps. 146, 8.

CYRIL; Having been brought up a Jew, he was not ignorant that of the seed of David should God be born according to the flesh, and therefore he addresses Him as God, saying, *Have mercy upon me.* Would that those might imitate him who divide Christ into two. For he speaks of Christ as God, yet calls Him Son of David. But they marvel at the justice of his confession, and some even wished to prevent him from confessing his faith. But by checks of this kind his ardour was not damped. For faith is able to resist all, and to triumph over all. It is a good thing to lay aside shame in behalf of divine worship. For if for money's sake some are bold, is it not fitting when the soul is at stake, to put on a righteous boldness? As it follows, *But he cried*

out the more, Son of David, &c. The voice of one invoking
in faith stops Christ, for He looks back upon them who call
upon Him in faith. And accordingly He calls the blind man
to Him, and bids him draw nigh, that he in truth who had first
laid hold on Him in faith, might approach Him also in the
body. The Lord asks this blind man as he drew near,
What wilt thou that I shall do? He asks the question purposely, not as ignorant, but that those who stood by might
know that he sought not money, but divine power from God.
And thus it follows, *But he said, Lord, that I may receive
my sight.*

PSEUDO-CHRYS. Or because the Jews perverting the truth Chrys.
might say, as in the case of him who was born blind, *This is* $_{\text{John 9,}}^{\text{ut sup.}}$
not he, but one like unto him, He wished the blind first to make 8.
manifest the infirmity of his nature, that then he might fully
acknowledge the greatness of the grace bestowed upon him.
And as soon as the blind man explained the nature of his
request, with words of the highest authority He commanded
him to see. As it follows, *And Jesus said to him, Receive
thy sight.* This served only still more to increase the guilt
of unbelief in the Jews. For what prophet ever spoke in this
way? Observe moreover what the physician claims from
him whom he has restored to health. *Thy faith hath saved
thee.* For faith then mercies are sold. Where faith is
willing to accept, there grace abounds. And as from the
same fountain some in small vessels draw little water,
while others in large draw much, the fountain knowing no
difference in measure; and as according to the windows
which are opened, the sun sheds more or less of its brightness within; so according to the measure of a man's
motives does he draw down supplies of grace. The voice of
Christ is changed into the light of the afflicted. For He was
the Word of true light. And thus it follows, *And immediately he said.* But the blind man as before his restoration
he shewed an earnest faith, so afterwards did he give plain
tokens of his gratitude; *And he followed him, glorifying
God.* CYRIL; From which it is clear, that he was released
from a double blindness, both bodily and intellectual.
For he would not have glorified Him as God, had he not
truly seen Him as He is. But he also gave occasion to others

to glorify God; as it follows, *And all the people, when they saw it, gave praise unto God.* BEDE; Not only for the gift of light obtained, but for the merit of the faith which obtained it. PSEUDO-CHRYS. We may here well inquire, why Christ forbids the healed demoniac who wished to follow Him, but permits the blind man who had received his sight. There seems to be a good reason for both the one case and the other. He sends away the former as a kind of herald, to proclaim aloud by the evidence of his own state his benefactor, for it was indeed a notable miracle to see a raving madman brought to a sound mind. But the blind man He allows to follow Him, since He was going up to Jerusalem about to accomplish the high mystery of the Cross, that men having a recent report of a miracle might not suppose that He suffered so much from helplessness as from compassion.

AMBROSE; In the blind man we have a type of the Gentile people, who have received by the Sacrament of our Lord the brightness of the light which they had lost. And it matters not whether the cure is conveyed in the case of one or two blind men, inasmuch as deriving their origin from Ham and Japhet, the sons of Noah, in the two blind men they put forward two authors of their race. GREG. Or, blindness is a symbol of the human race, which in our first parent knowing not the brightness of heavenly light, now suffers the darkness of his condemnation. Jericho is interpreted ' the moon,' whose monthly wanings represent the feebleness of our mortality. While then our Creator is drawing nigh to Jericho, the blind is restored to sight, because when God took upon Him the weakness of our flesh, the human race received back the light which it had lost. He then who is ignorant of this brightness of the everlasting light, is blind. But if he does no more than believe in the Redeemer who said, *I am the way, the truth, and the life;* he sits by the way side. If he both believes and prays that he may receive the everlasting light, he sits by the way side and begs. Those that went before Jesus, as He was coming, represent the multitude of carnal desires, and the busy crowd of vices which before that Jesus comes to our heart, scatter our thoughts, and disturb us even in our prayers. But the blind man cried out the more; for the more violently we are assailed by our

Chrys. ubi sup.

Greg. Hom. 2. in Ev.

John 13, 6.

restless thoughts, the more fervently ought we to give ourselves to prayer. As long as we still suffer our manifold fancies
to trouble us in our prayers, we feel in some measure Jesus
passing by. But when we are very stedfast in prayer, God
is fixed in our heart, and the lost light is restored. Or to
pass by is of man, to stand is of God. The Lord then
passing by heard the blind man crying, standing still restored
him to sight, for by His humanity in compassion to our
blindness He has pity upon our cries, by the power of His
divinity He pours upon us the light of His grace.

Now for this reason He asks what the blind man wished,
that He might stir up his heart to prayer, for He wishes that to
be sought in prayer, which He knows beforehand both that
we seek and He grants. AMBROSE; Or, He asked the blind
man to the end that we might believe, that without confession no man can be saved. GREG. The blind man seeks Greg.
from the Lord not gold, but light. Let us then seek not for ^{ubi sup.}
false riches, but for that light which together with the Angels
alone we may see, the way whereunto is faith. Well then was
it said to the blind, *Receive thy sight; thy faith hath saved
thee.* He who sees, also follows, because the good which
he understands he practises.

AUG. If we interpret Jericho to mean the moon, and there- Aug. de
fore death, our Lord when approaching His death commanded Quæst.
the light of the Gospel to be preached to the Jews only, who Ev. 1. ii.
are signified by that one blind man whom Luke speaks of, qu. 48.
but rising again from the dead and ascending to heaven, to
both Jews and Gentiles; and these two nations seem to be
denoted by the two blind men whom Matthew mentions.

1. And Jesus entered and passed through Jericho.

2. And, behold, there was a man named Zacchæus, which was the chief among the Publicans, and he was rich.

3. And he sought to see Jesus who he was; and could not for the press, because he was little of stature.

4. And he ran before, and climbed up into a sycomore tree to see him : for he was to pass that way.

5. And when Jesus came to the place, he looked up, and saw him, and said unto him, Zacchæus, make haste, and come down; for to day I must abide at thy house.

6. And he made haste, and came down, and received him joyfully.

7. And when they saw it, they all murmured, saying, That he was gone to be guest with a man that is a sinner.

8. And Zacchæus stood, and said unto the Lord ; Behold, Lord, the half of my goods I give to the poor; and if I have taken any thing from any man by false accusation, I restore him fourfold.

9. And Jesus said unto him, This day is salvation come to this house, forsomuch as he also is a son of Abraham.

10. For the Son of man is come to seek and to save that which was lost.

AMBROSE; Zacchæus in the sycamore, the blind man by the way side: upon the one our Lord waits to shew mercy, upon the other He confers the great glory of abiding in his house. The chief among the Publicans is here fitly introduced. For who will hereafter despair of himself, now that he attains to grace who gained his living by fraud. And he too moreover a rich man, that we may know that not all rich men are covetous.   CYRIL; But Zacchæus made no delay in what he did, and so was accounted worthy of the favour of God, which gives sight to the blind, and calls them who are afar off.

TIT. BOST. The seed of salvation had begun to spring up in him, for he desired to see Jesus, having never seen Him. For if he had seen Him, he would long since have given up the Publican's wicked life. No one that sees Jesus can remain any longer in wickedness. But there were two obstacles to his seeing Him. The multitude not so much of men as of his sins prevented him, for he was little of stature. AMBROSE; What means the Evangelist by describing his stature, and that of none other? It is perhaps because he was young in wickedness, or as yet weak in the faith. For he was not yet prostrate in sin who could climb up. He had not yet seen Christ. TIT. BOST. But he discovered a good device; running before he climbed up into a sycamore, and saw Him whom he had long wished for, i.e. Jesus, passing by. Now Zacchæus desired no more than to see, but He who is able to do more than we ask for, granted to Him far above what he expected; as it follows, *And when Jesus came to the place, he looked up, and saw him.* He saw the soul of the man striving earnestly to live a holy life, and converts him to godliness. AMBROSE; Uninvited he invites Himself to his house; as it follows, *Zacchæus, make haste, and come down, &c.* for He knew how richly He would reward his hospitality. And though He had not yet heard the word of invitation, He had already seen the will.

BEDE; See here, the camel disencumbered of his hunch passes through the eye of a needle, that is, the rich man and the publican abandoning his love of riches, and loathing his dishonest gains, receives the blessing of his Lord's company. It follows, *And he made haste, and came down, and received him joyfully.* AMBROSE; Let the rich learn that guilt

attaches not to the goods themselves, but to those who know
not how to use them.   For riches, as they are hindrances to
virtue in the unworthy, so are they means of advancing it in
the good.

Hom.
de cæc.
et Zacc. PSEUDO-CHRYS. Observe the gracious kindness of the
Saviour. The innocent associates with the guilty, the fountain
of justice with covetousness, which is the source of injustice.
Having entered the publican's house, He suffers no stain from
the mists of avarice, but disperses them by the bright beam
of His righteousness.   But those who deal with biting words
and reproaches, try to cast a slur upon the things which were
done by Him ; for it follows, *And when they saw it, they all
murmured, saying, That he was gone to be guest with a
man that is a sinner*. But He, though accused of being a
wine-bibber and a friend of publicans, regarded it not, so long
as He could accomplish His end.   As a physician sometimes
can not save his patients from their diseases without the
defilement of blood.   And so it happened here, for the publican was converted, and lived a better life. *Zacchæus stood,
and said unto the Lord, Behold, Lord, the half of my goods
I give to the poor; and if I have defrauded any man, I
restore him fourfold*. Behold here is a marvel : without
learning he obeys.   And as the sun pouring its rays into a
house enlightens it not by word, but by work, so the Saviour
by the rays of righteousness put to flight the darkness of sin ;
for the light shineth in darkness.   Now every thing united
is strong, but divided, weak ; therefore Zacchæus divides
into two parts his substance.   But we must be careful to
observe, that his wealth was not made up from unjust gains,
but from his patrimony, else how could he restore fourfold
what he had unjustly extorted.   He knew that the law ordered
what was wrongly taken away to be restored fourfold, that
if the law deterred not, a man's losses might soften him.
Zacchæus waits not for the judgment of the law, but makes
himself his own judge.

THEOPHYL. If we examine more closely, we shall see that
nothing was left of his own property.   For having given
half of his goods to the poor, out of the remainder he restored
fourfold to those whom he had injured.   He not only
promised this, but did it.   For he says not, " I will give the

half, and I will restore fourfold, but, *I give*, and *I restore.*
To such Christ announces salvation; *Jesus saith unto him,*
This day is salvation come to this house, signifying that
Zacchæus had attained to salvation, meaning by the house
the inhabitant thereof. And it follows, *forasmuch as he also*
is a son of Abraham. For He would not have given the
name of a son of Abraham to a lifeless building. BEDE;
Zacchæus is called the son of Abraham, not because he was
born of Abraham's seed, but because he imitates his faith,
that as Abraham left his country and his father's house, so he
abandoned all his goods in giving them to the poor. And He
well says, " He also," to declare that not only those who had
lived justly, but those who are raised up from a life of
injustice, belong to the sons of promise. THEOPHYL. He
said not that he " was" a son of Abraham, but that he now is.
For before when he was the chief among the publicans, and
bore no likeness to the righteous Abraham, he was not his
son. But because some murmured that he tarried with
a man who was a sinner, he adds in order to restrain them,
For the Son of man came to seek and to save that which was
lost. PSEUDO-CHRYS. Why do ye accuse me if I bring sinners ubi sup.
to righteousness? So far am I from hating them, that for their
sakes I came. For I came to heal, not to judge, therefore
am I the constant guest of those that are sick, and I suffer
their noisomeness that I may supply remedies. But some
one may ask, how does Paul bid us, *If we have a brother* 1 Cor.
that is a fornicator or covetous man, with such not even 5, 11.
to take food; whereas Christ was the guest of publicans?
They were not as yet so far advanced as to be brethren,
and besides, St. Paul bids us avoid our brethren only when
they persist in evil, but these were converted. BEDE;
Mystically, Zacchæus, which is by interpretation " justified,"
signifies the Gentile believers, who were depressed and
brought very low by their worldly occupations, but sanctified
by God. And he was desirous to see our Saviour entering
Jericho, inasmuch as he sought to share in that faith which
Christ brought into the world. CYRIL; The crowd is the
tumultuous state of an ignorant multitude, which cannot see
the lofty top of wisdom. Zacchæus therefore, while he was in
the crowd, saw not Christ, but having advanced beyond the

2 s 2

vulgar ignorance, was thought worthy to entertain Him,
whom he desired to look upon.   BEDE; Or the crowd,
that is, the general habit of vice, which rebuked the blind
man crying out, lest he should seek the light, also impedes
Zacchæus looking up, that he might not see Jesus; that as by
crying out the more the blind man overcame the crowd, so
the man weak in the faith by forsaking earthly things, and
climbing the tree of the Cross, surmounts the opposing multi-
titude. The sycamore, which is a tree resembling the mulberry
in foliage, but exceeding it in height, whence by the Latins
it is called " lofty," is called the " foolish fig-tree;" and so the
Cross of our Lord sustains believers, as the fig-tree figs, and is
mocked by unbelievers as foolishness.   This tree Zacchæus,
who was little in stature, climbed up, that he might be raised
together with Christ; for every one who is humble, and
conscious of his own weakness, cries out, *God forbid that*
I should glory, save in the cross of our Lord Jesus Christ.
AMBROSE; He has well added, that our Lord was to pass
that way, either where the sycamore-tree was, or where he
was who was about to believe, that so He might preserve the
mystery, and sow the seeds of grace.   For He had so come
as that through the Jews He came to the Gentiles.   He sees
then Zacchæus above, for already the excellence of his faith
shone forth amidst the fruits of good works, and the loftiness
of the fruitful tree; but Zacchæus stands out above the tree, as
one who is above the law.   BEDE; The Lord as He journeyed
came to the place where Zacchæus had climbed the sycamore,
for having sent His preachers throughout the world in whom
He Himself spoke and went, He comes to the Gentile
people, who were already raised up on high through faith in
His Passion, and whom when He looked up He saw, for He
chose them through grace.   Now our Lord once abode in
the house of the chief of the Pharisees, but when He did
works such as none but God could do, they railed at Him.
Wherefore hating their deeds He departed, saying, *Your*
house shall be left unto you desolate; but now He must
needs stay at the house of the weak Zacchæus, that is, by the
grace of the new law brightly shining, He must take rest in
the hearts of the lowly nations. But that Zacchæus is bid to
come down from the sycamore tree, and prepare an abode for

Gal. 6,
14.

Matt.
23, 38.

Christ, this is what the Apostle says, *Yea, though we have* 2 Cor. 5, *known Christ after the flesh, yet now henceforth know we* 16. *Him no more.* And again elsewhere, *For though he was* 2 Cor. *crucified through weakness, yet he liveth by the power of* 13, 4. *God.* It is plain that the Jews always hated the salvation of the Gentiles; but salvation, which formerly filled the houses of the Jews, has this day shone upon the Gentiles, forasmuch as this people also by believing on God is a son of Abraham.

THEOPHYL. It is easy to turn this to a moral use. For whoever surpasses many in wickedness is small in spiritual growth, and cannot see Jesus for the crowd. For disturbed by passion and worldly things, he beholds not Jesus walking, that is, working in us, not recognising His operation. But he climbs up to the top of a sycamore-tree, in that he rises above the sweetness of pleasure, which is signified by a fig, and subduing it, and so becoming more exalted, he sees and is seen by Christ. GREG. Or because the sycamore is from Greg. its name called the foolish fig, the little Zacchæus gets up into Mor. 27. the sycamore and sees the Lord, for they who humbly choose c. 46. the foolish things of this world are those who contemplate most closely the wisdom of God. For what is more foolish in this world than not to seek for what is lost, to give our possessions to robbers, to return not injury for injury? However, by this wise foolishness, the wisdom of God is seen, not yet really as it is, but by the light of contemplation.

THEOPHYL. The Lord said to him, *Make haste and come down*, that is, " Thou hast ascended by penitence to a place too high for thee, come down by humility, lest thy exaltation cause thee to slip. I must abide in the house of a humble man. We have two kinds of goods in us, bodily, and spiritual; the just man gives up all his bodily goods to the poor, but he forsakes not his spiritual goods, but if he has extorted any thing from any one, he restores to him fourfold; signifying thereby that if a man by repentance walks in the opposite path to his former perverseness, he by the manifold practice of virtue heals all his old offences, and so merits salvation, and is called the son of Abraham, because he went out from his own kindred, that is, from his ancient wickedness.

11. And as they heard these things, he added and spake a parable, because he was nigh to Jerusalem, and because they thought that the kingdom of God should immediately appear.

12. He said therefore, A certain nobleman went into a far country to receive for himself a kingdom, and to return.

13. And he called his ten servants, and delivered them ten pounds, and said unto them, Occupy till I come.

14. But his citizens hated him, and sent a message after him, saying, We will not have this man to reign over us.

15. And it came to pass, that when he was returned, having received the kingdom, then he commanded these servants to be called unto him, to whom he had given the money, that he might know how much every man had gained by trading.

16. Then came the first, saying, Lord, thy pound hath gained ten pounds.

17. And he said unto him, Well, thou good servant: because thou hast been faithful in a very little, have thou authority over ten cities.

18. And the second came, saying, Lord, thy pound hath gained five pounds.

19. And he said likewise to him, Be thou also over five cities.

20. And another came, saying, Lord, behold, here is thy pound, which I have kept laid up in a napkin:

21. For I feared thee, because thou art an austere

man: thou takest up that thou layedst not down, and reapest that thou didst not sow.

22. And he saith unto him, Out of thine own mouth will I judge thee, thou wicked servant. Thou knewest that I was an austere man, taking up that I laid not down, and reaping that I did not sow:

23. Wherefore then gavest not thou my money into the bank, that at my coming I might have required mine own with usury?

24. And he said unto them that stood by, Take from him the pound, and give it to him that hath ten pounds.

25. (And they said unto him, Lord, he hath ten pounds.)

26. For I say unto you, That unto every one which hath shall be given; and from him that hath not, even that he hath shall be taken away from him.

27. But those mine enemies, which would not that I should reign over them, bring hither, and slay them before me.

EUSEBIUS; There were some who thought that our Saviour's kingdom would commence at His first coming, and they were expecting it shortly to appear when He was preparing to go up to Jerusalem; so astonished were they by the divine miracles which He did. He therefore informs them, that He should not receive the kingdom from His Father until He had left mankind to go to His Father. THEOPHYL. The Lord points out the vanity of their imaginations, for the senses cannot embrace the kingdom of God; He also plainly shews to them, that as God He knew their thoughts, putting to them the following parable, *A certain nobleman, &c.*

CYRIL; This parable is intended to set before us the mysteries of Christ from the first to the last. For God was made man, who was the Word from the beginning; and

though He became a servant, yet was He noble because of
His unspeakable birth from the Father. BASIL; Noble, not

Basil. in
Esai. c.
13. 13.

only in respect of His Godhead, but of His manhood, being
sprung from the seed of David according to the flesh. He
went into a far country, separated not so much by distance of
place as by actual condition. For God Himself is nigh to
every one of us, when our good works bind us to Him.
And He is afar off, as often as by cleaving to destruction, we
remove ourselves away from Him. To this earthly country
then He came at a distance from God, that He might
receive the kingdom of the Gentiles, according to the Psalm,

Ps. 2, 8. *Ask of me, and I will give thee the heathen for thine in-*

Aug. de
Qu. Ev.
lib. ii.
qu. 40.

heritance. AUG. Or the far country is the Gentile Church,
extending to the uttermost parts of the earth. For He went
that the fulness of the Gentiles might come in; He will
return that all Israel may be saved.

EUSEB. Or by His setting out into a far country, He
denotes His own ascension from earth to heaven. But when
He adds, *To receive for himself a kingdom, and to
return;* He points out His second appearance, when He
shall come as a King and in great glory. He first of all
calls Himself a man, because of His nativity in the flesh,
then noble; not yet a King, because as yet at His first
appearance He exercised no kingly power. It is also well
said to obtain for Himself a kingdom, according to Daniel,

Dan. 7,
13.

Behold one like the Son of man came with the clouds of

Heb. 1,
3.

heaven, and a kingdom was given to him. CYRIL; *For
ascending up to heaven, He sits on the right hand of the
Majesty on high.* But being ascended, He hath dispensed
to those that believe on Him different divine graces, as unto
the servants were committed their Lord's goods, that gaining
something they might bring him token of their service. As it
follows, *And he called his ten servants, and delivered them
ten pounds.* CHRYS. Holy Scripture is accustomed to use the
number ten as a sign of perfection, for if any one wishes to
count beyond it, he has again to begin from unity, having in
ten as it were arrived at a goal. And so in the giving of the
talents, the one who reaches the goal of divine obedience

Aug.
ut sup.

is said to have received ten pounds. AUG. Or by the ten
pounds he signifies the law, because of the ten command-

ments, and by the ten servants, those to whom while under
the law grace was preached. For so we must interpret
the ten pounds given them for trading, seeing that they understood the law, when its veil was removed, to belong to the
Gospel. BEDE; A pound which the Greeks call μνᾶ is equal
in weight to a hundred drachmas, and every word of Scripture,
as suggesting to us the perfection of the heavenly life, shines
as it were with the greatness of the hundredth number.

EUSEB. By those then who receive the pounds, He means
His disciples, giving a pound to each, since He entrusts to all
an equal stewardship; He bade them put it out to use, as it
follows, *Occupy till I come.* Now there was no other employ-
ment but to preach the doctrine of His kingdom to those who
would hear it. But there is one and the same doctrine for
all, one faith, one baptism. And therefore is one pound
given to each. CYRIL; But greatly indeed do these differ
from those who denied the kingdom of God, of whom it is
added, *But his citizens hated him.* And this it is for which
Christ upbraided the Jews, when He said, *But now have they* John 15,
both seen and hated me and my Father. But they re- 24.
jected His kingdom, saying to Pilate, *We have no king but* John 19,
Cæsar. EUSEB. By *citizens* He signifies the Jews, who were 15.
sprung from the same lineage according to the flesh, and
with whom He joined in the customs of the law. AUG. Aug. de
And they sent a message after Him, because after His resur- Quæst.
Ev. ut
rection also, they persecuted His Apostles, and refused the sup.
preaching of the Gospel.

EUSEB. After our Saviour had instructed them in the
things belonging to His first coming, He proceeds to set forth
His second coming with majesty and great glory, saying, *And*
it came to pass, that when he was returned, having received
the kingdom. CHRYS. Holy Scripture notes two kingdoms Chrys.
Hom.
of God, one indeed by creation, since by right of creation He 39. in I.
is King over all men; the other by justification, since He reigns ad Cor.
over the just, of their own will made subject to Him. And
this is the kingdom which He is here said to have received.

AUG. He also returns after having received His kingdom, Aug. de
Quæst.
because in all glory will He come who appeared lowly to Ev. ut
them to whom He said, *My kingdom is not of this world.* sup.
John 18,
CYRIL; But when Christ returns, having taken unto Him- 36.

self His kingdom, the ministers of the word will receive their deserved praises and delight in heavenly rewards, because they multiplied their talent by acquiring more talents, as it is added, *Then came the first, saying, Lord, thy pound has gained ten pounds.* BEDE; The first servant is the order of teachers sent to the circumcision, who received one pound to put out to use, inasmuch as it was ordered to preach one faith. But this one pound gained ten pounds, because by its teaching it united to itself the people who were subject to the law. It follows, *And he said unto him, Well done, thou good servant: because thou hast been faithful in a very little, &c.* The servant is faithful in a very little who does not adulterate the word of God. For all the gifts we receive now are but small in comparison of what we shall have. GREEK Ex. Because he receives the reward of his own good works, he is said to be set over ten cities. And some conceiving unworthily of these promises imagine that they themselves are preferred to magistracies and chief places in the earthly Jerusalem, which is built with precious stones, because they have had their conversation honest in Christ; so little do they purge their soul of all hankering after power and authority among men. AMBROSE; But the ten cities are the souls over whom he is rightly placed who has deposited in the minds of men his Lord's money and the holy words, which are tried as silver is tried in the fire. For as Jerusalem is said to be built as a city, so are peace-making souls. And as angels have rule, so have they who have acquired the life of angels.

Eva-grius.

Ps. 121, 3.

It follows, *And the second came, saying, Lord, thy pound has gained five pounds.* BEDE; That servant is the assembly of those who were sent to preach the Gospel to the uncircumcision, whose pound, that is the faith of the Gospel, gained five pounds, because it converted to the grace of Evangelical faith, the nations before enslaved to the five senses of the body. *And he said likewise to him, Be thou also over five cities;* that is, be exalted to shine through the faith and conversation of those souls which thou hast enlightened.

AMBROSE; Or perhaps differently; he who gained five pounds has all the moral virtues, for there are five senses of the body. He who gained ten has so much more, that is to say, the mysteries of the law as well as the moral virtues.

The ten pounds may also here be taken to mean the ten words, that is, the teaching of the law; the five pounds, the ordering of discipline. *But the scribe must be perfect in all things.* And rightly, since He is speaking of the Jews, are there two only who bring their pounds multiplied, not indeed by a gainful interest of money, but a profitable stewardship of the Gospel. For there is one kind of usury in money lent on interest, another in heavenly teaching. CHRYS. For in earthly wealth it does not belong to one man to be made rich without another being made poor, but in spiritual riches, without his making another rich also. For in earthly matters participation lessens, in spiritual it increases wealth.

AUG. Or else; That one of those who well employed their money gained ten pounds, another five, signifies that they acquired them for the flock of God, by whom the law was now understood through grace, either because of the ten commandments of the law, or because he, through whom the law was given, wrote five books; and to this belong the ten and five cities over which He appoints them to preside. For the manifold meanings or interpretations which spring up concerning some individual precept or book, when reduced and brought together in one, make as it were a city of living eternal reasons. Hence a city is not a multitude of living creatures, but of reasonable beings bound together by the fellowship of one law. The servants then who bring an account of that which they had received, and are praised for having gained more, represent those giving in their account who have well employed what they had received, to increase their Lord's riches by those who believe on Him, while they who are unwilling to do this are signified by that servant who kept his pound laid up in a napkin; of whom it follows, *And the third came, saying, Lord, behold, here is thy pound, which I have kept laid up in a napkin, &c.* For there are some who flatter themselves with this delusion, saying, It is enough for each individual to answer concerning himself, what need then of others to preach and minister, in order that every one should be compelled also to give an account of himself, seeing that in the Lord's sight even they are without excuse to whom the law was not given, and who were not asleep

Aug. de Quæst. Evan. lib. ii. qu. 46.

at the time of the preaching of the Gospel, for they might have
known the Creator through the creature; and then it follows,
For I feared thee, because thou art an austere man, &c. For
this is, as it were, to reap when he did not sow, that is, to hold
those guilty of ungodliness to whom this word of the law or
the Gospel was not preached, and avoiding as it were this
peril of judgment, with slothful toil they rest from the min-
istration of the word. And this it is to tie up in a napkin
what they had received. THEOPHYL. For with a napkin the
face of the dead is covered; well then is this idler said to
have wrapped up his pound in a napkin, because leaving it
dead and unprofitable he neither touched nor increased it.

BEDE; Or to tie up money in a napkin is to hide the gifts
we have received under the indolence of a sluggish body.
But that which he thought to have used as an excuse is
turned to his own blame, as it follows, *He says unto him,
Out of thy own mouth will I judge thee, thou wicked servant.*
He is called a wicked servant, as being slothful in business,
and proud in questioning his Lord's judgment. *Thou knewest that I was an austere man, taking up that I laid not
down, and reaping that I did not sow: wherefore then gavest
thou not my money into the bank?* As though he said, If
thou knewest me to be a hard man, and a seeker of what is
not mine own, why did not the thought of this strike thee
with terror, that thou mightest be sure that I would require
mine own with strictness?

But money or silver is the preaching of the Gospel and
the word of God, for the words of the Lord are pure words
Ps.12,6. *as silver tried in the fire.* And this word of the Lord ought
to be given to the bank, that is, put into hearts meet and
Aug. de ready to receive it. AUG. Or the bank into which the money
Quæst.
Ev. ubi was to be given, we take to be the very profession of religion
sup. which is publicly put forth as a means necessary to salvation.

CHRYS. In the payment of earthly riches the debtors are
obliged only to strictness. Whatever they receive, so much
must they return, nothing more is required of them. But
with regard to the words of God, we are not only bound diligently to keep, but we are commanded to increase; and hence
it follows, *that at my coming I might have required the same*

with usury.　BEDE; For they who by faith receive the riches
of the word from a teacher, must by their works pay it back
with usury, or be earnestly desirous to know something more
than what they have as yet learnt from the mouth of their
preachers. CYRIL; It is the work of teachers to engraft in their
hearers' minds wholesome and profitable words, but of divine
power to win the hearers to obedience, and render their understanding fruitful. Now this servant, so far from being commended or thought worthy of honour, was condemned as slothful, as it follows, *And he said unto them that stood by, Take
from him the pound, and give to him that hath ten pounds.*
AUG. Signifying thereby that both he will lose the gift of God, Aug. de
who having, hath not, that is, useth it not, and that he will Ev. 1. ii.
have it increased, who having, hath, that is, rightly useth it. qu. 46.

BEDE; The mystical meaning I suppose is this, that at the
coming in of the Gentiles all Israel shall be saved, and that Rom. 11,
then the abundant grace of the Spirit will be poured out 26.
upon the teachers. CHRYS. He says then to them that stood Chrys.
by, *Take from him the pound*, because it is not the part of a 43. in
wise man to punish, but he needs some one else as the minister Act.
of the judge in executing punishment. For even God does
not Himself inflict punishment, but through the ministry
of His angels. AMBROSE; Nothing is said of the other servants, who like wasteful debtors lost all that they had received. By those two servants who gained by trading, are
signified that small number, who in two companies were sent
as dressers of the vineyard; by the remainder all the Jews.
It follows, *And they said unto him, Lord, he has ten pounds.*
And lest this should seem unjust, it is added, *For to every
one that hath, it shall be given.* THEOPHYL. For seeing that
he gained ten, by multiplying his pound tenfold, it is plain
that by having more to multiply, he would be an occasion of
greater gain to his Lord. But from the slothful and idle,
who stirs not himself to increase what he has received, shall
be taken away even that which he possesses, that there may
be no gap in the Lord's account when it is given to others
and multiplied. But this is not to be applied only to the
words of God and teaching, but also to the moral virtues;
for in respect of these also, God sends us His gracious gifts,
endowing one man with fasting, another with prayer, another

with mildness or humility; but all these so long as we watch strictly over ourselves we shall multiply, but if we grow cold we shall extinguish. He adds of His adversaries, *But those mine enemies who would not that I should reign over them,* *bring them hither, and slay them before me.* AUG. Whereby He describes the ungodliness of the Jews who refused to be converted to Him. THEOPHYL. Whom he will deliver to death, casting them into the outer fire. But even in this world they were most miserably slain by the Roman army.

CHRYS. These things are of force against the Marcionists. For Christ also says, *Bring hither my enemies, and slay* *them before me.* Whereas they say Christ indeed is good, but the God of the Old Testament evil. Now it is plain that both the Father and the Son do the same things. For the Father sends His army to the vineyard, and the Son causes His enemies to be slain before Him. CHRYS. This parable as it is related in Luke is different from that given in Matthew concerning the talents. For in the former indeed out of one and the same principal there were different sums produced, seeing that from the profits of one pound received, one servant brought five, another ten pounds. But with Matthew it is very different. For he who received two pounds, thereto added two more. He who received five, gained as much again. So the rewards given are unlike also.

Margin notes: Aug. ubi sup. | Mat. 21, 41. | Chrys. Hom. 78. in Matt. | Mat. 25.

28. And when he had thus spoken, he went before, ascending up to Jerusalem.

29. And it came to pass, when he was come nigh to Bethphage and Bethany, at the mount called the mount of Olives, he sent two of his disciples,

30. Saying, Go ye into the village over against you; in the which at your entering ye shall find a colt tied, whereon yet never man sat: loose him, and bring him hither.

31. And if any man ask you, Why do ye loose him? thus shall ye say unto him, Because the Lord hath need of him.

32. And they that were sent went their way, and found even as he had said unto them.

33. And as they were loosing the colt, the owners thereof said unto them, Why loose ye the colt?

34. And they said, The Lord hath need of him.

35. And they brought him to Jesus: and they cast their garments upon the colt, and they set Jesus thereon.

36. And as he went, they spread their clothes in the way.

TIT. BOST. Because the Lord had said, *The kingdom of heaven is at hand,* they that saw Him going up to Jerusalem thought that He was going then to commence the kingdom of God. When then the parable was finished in which He reproved the error above mentioned, and shewed plainly that He had not yet vanquished that death which was plotting against him, he proceeded forth to His passion, going up to Jerusalem. BEDE; Proving at the same time that the parable had been pronounced concerning the end of that city which was about both to slay Him, and to perish itself by the scourge of the enemy. It follows, *And it came to pass, when he was come nigh to Bethphage, &c.* Bethphage was a small village belonging to the priests on Mount Olivet. Bethany was also a little town or hamlet on the side of the same mountain, about fifteen stades from Jerusalem.

CHRYS. At the beginning of His ministry our Lord shewed Himself indifferent to the Jews, but when He had given sufficient token of His power, He transacts every thing with the highest authority. Many are the miracles which then took place. He foretold to them, ye shall find an unbroken colt. He foretels also that no one should hinder them, but as soon as they heard it, should hold their peace. TIT. BOST. Here it was evident that there would be a divine summons. For no one can resist God calling for what is His own. But the disciples when ordered to fetch the colt refused not the office as a slight one, but went to bring him. BASIL; So likewise should we set about even the low-

Chrys. Hom. 66. in Matt.

est works with the greatest zeal and affection, knowing that whatever is done with God before our eyes is not slight, but meet for the kingdom of heaven.

TITUS; They who had tied the ass are struck dumb, because of the greatness of His mighty power, and are unable to resist the words of the Saviour; for " the Lord" is a name of majesty, and as a King was He about to come in the sight of all the people.

Aug. de con. Ev. lib. ii. cap. 66. AUG. Nor matters it that Matthew speaks of an ass and its foal, while the others say nothing of the ass; for when both may be conceived, there is no variance even though one relate one thing, and another another, much less where one relates one thing, another both.

non occ. GLOSS. The disciples waited upon Christ not only in bringing the colt of another, but also with their own garments, some of which they placed upon the ass, others they strewed in the way. BEDE; According to the other Evangelists, not the disciples only, but very many also out of the crowds scattered their garments in the way.

AMBROSE; Mystically, our Lord came to Mount Olivet, that he might plant new olive trees on the heights of virtue. And perhaps the mountain itself is Christ, for who else could bear such fruit of olives abounding in the fulness of the Spirit? BEDE; Rightly are the towns described as placed on Mount Olivet, that is, on the Lord Himself, who rekindles the unction of spiritual graces with the light of knowledge and piety.

ORIGEN; Bethany is interpreted, the house of obedience, but Bethphage the house of cheek bones, being a place belonging to the priests, for cheek bones in the sacrifices were the right of the priests, as it is commanded in the law. To that place then where obedience is, and where the priests have the possession, our Saviour sends His disciples to loose the ass's colt. AMBROSE; For they were in the village, and the colt was tied with its mother, nor could it be loosed except by the command of the Lord. The apostle's hand looses it. Such was the act, such the life, such the grace. Be such, that thou mayest be able to loose those that are bound. In the ass indeed Matthew represented the mother of error, but in the colt Luke has described the general character of the Gentile people. And rightly, *whereon yet*

never man sat, for none before Christ called the nations of the
Gentiles into the Church. But this people was tied and bound
by the chains of iniquity, being subject to an unjust master,
the servant of error, and could not claim to itself authority
whom not nature but crime had made guilty. Since *the
Lord* is spoken of, one master is recognised. O wretched
bondage under a doubtful mastery! For he has many masters
who has not one. Others bind that they may possess, Christ
looses that he may keep, for He knew that gifts are more powerful than chains. ORIGEN; There were then many masters of
this colt, before that the Saviour had need of him. But as
soon as He began to be the master, there ceased to be any other.
For no one can serve God and mammon. When we are the Matt. 6,
servants of wickedness we are subject to many vices and 24.
passions, but the Lord has need of the colt, because He would
have us loosed from the chain of our sins.

ORIGEN; Now I think this place is not without reason Orig.
said to be a small village. For as if it were a village without Joan.
any further name, in comparison of the whole earth the tom. ii.
whole heavenly country is despised.

AMBROSE; Nor is it for nothing that two disciples are
directed thither; Peter to Cornelius, Paul to the rest. And
therefore He did not mark out the persons, but determined
the number. Still should any one require the persons, he
may believe it to be spoken of Philip, whom the Holy Spirit
sent to Gaza, when he baptized the eunuch of Queen Acts 8,
Candace. THEOPHYL. Or the two sent imply this, that 38.
the Prophets and Apostles make up the two steps to the
bringing in of the Gentiles, and their subjection to Christ.
But they bring the colt from a certain village, that it may be
known to us that this people was rude and unlearned.
CYRIL; Those men who were directed, when they were
loosing the colt, did not use their own words, but spoke as
Jesus had told them, that you may know that not by their
own words, but the word of God, not in their own name
but in Christ's, they implanted the faith among the Gentile
nations; and by the command of God the hostile powers
ceased, which claimed to themselves the obedience of the
Gentiles. ORIGEN; The disciples next place their garments Orig.
upon the ass, and cause the Saviour to sit thereon, inasmuch in Luc.
37.

as they take upon themselves the word of God, and make it
to rest upon the souls of their hearers. They divest themselves of their garments, and strew them in the way, for the
clothing of the Apostles is their good works. And truly does
the ass loosened by the disciples and carrying Jesus, walk
upon the garments of the Apostles, when it imitates their
doctrine. Which of us is so blessed, that Jesus should rest
upon him? AMBROSE; For it pleased not the Lord of the
world to be borne upon the ass's back, save that in a hidden
mystery by a more inward sitting, the mystical Ruler might
take His seat in the secret depths of men's souls, guiding
the footsteps of the mind, bridling the wantonness of the
heart. His word is a rein, His word is a goad.

37. And when he was come nigh, even now at
the descent of the mount of Olives, the whole multitude of the disciples began to rejoice and praise
God with a loud voice for all the mighty works that
they had seen;

38. Saying, Blessed be the King that cometh in
the name of the Lord : peace in heaven, and glory in
the highest.

39. And some of the Pharisees from among the
multitude said unto him, Master, rebuke thy disciples.

40. And he answered and said unto them, I tell
you that, if these should hold their peace, the stones
would immediately cry out.

ORIGEN; As long as our Lord was in the mount His
Apostles only were with Him, but when He began to be
near the descent, then there came to Him a multitude of the
people. THEOPHYL. He calls by the name of disciples not
only the twelve, or the seventy-two, but all who followed
Christ, whether for the sake of the miracles, or from a
certain charm in His teaching, and to them may be added
the children, as the other Evangelists relate. Hence it
follows, *For all the mighty works which they had seen.*

BEDE; They beheld indeed many of our Lord's miracles, but marvelled most at the resurrection of Lazarus. For as John says, *For this cause the people also met him, for that they heard that he had done this miracle.* For it must be observed that this was not the first time of our Lord's coming to Jerusalem, but He came often before, as John relates. AMBROSE; The multitude then acknowledging God, proclaims Him King, repeats the prophecy, and declares that the expected Son of David according to the flesh had come, saying, *Blessed be the King that cometh in the name of the Lord.* BEDE; That is, in the name of God the Father, although it might be taken " in His own name," since He Himself is the Lord. But His own words are better guides to the meaning when He says, *I am come in my Father's name.* For Christ is the Master of humility. Christ is not called King as one who exacts tribute, or arms His forces with the sword, or visibly crushes His enemies, but because He rules men's minds, and brings them believing, hoping, and loving into the kingdom of heaven. For He was willing to be King of Israel, to shew His compassion, not to increase His power. But because Christ appeared in the flesh, as the redemption and light of the whole world, well do both the heaven and earth, each in their turn, chaunt His praises. When He is born into the world, the heavenly hosts sing; when He is about to return to heaven, men send back their note of praise. As it follows, *Peace in heaven.* THEOPHYL. That is, the ancient warfare, wherein we were at enmity against God, has ceased. *And glory in the highest,* inasmuch as Angels are glorifying God for such a reconciliation. For this very thing, that God visibly walks in the land of His enemies, shews that He has peace with us. But the Pharisees when they heard that the crowd called Him King, and praised Him as God, murmured, imputing the name of King to sedition, the name of God to blasphemy. *And some of the Pharisees said, Master, rebuke thy disciples.* BEDE; O the strange folly of the envious; they scruple not to call Him Master, because they knew He taught the truth, but His disciples, as though themselves were better taught, they deem worthy of rebuke.

CYRIL; But the Lord forbade not them that glorified Him

as God, but rather forbade those that blamed them, so bearing witness to Himself concerning the glory of the Godhead. Hence it follows, *He answered and said unto them, I tell you, if these should hold their peace, the stones would immediately cry out.* THEOPHYL. As if He said, Not without cause do men praise me thus, but being constrained by the mighty works which they have seen. BEDE; And so at the crucifixion of our Lord, when His kinsfolk were silent from fear, the stones and rocks sang forth, while after that He gave up the ghost, the earth was moved, and the rocks were rent, and the graves opened. AMBROSE; Nor is it wonderful that the stones against their nature should chaunt forth the praises of the Lord, whom His murderers, harder than the rocks, proclaim aloud, that is, the multitude, in a little while about to crucify their God, denying Him in their hearts, whom with their mouths they confess. Or perhaps it is said, because, when the Jews were struck silent after the Lord's Passion, the living stones, as Peter calls them, were about to cry out. ORIGEN; When we also are silent, (that is, when the love of many waxeth cold,) the stones cry out, for God can from stones raise up children to Abraham. AMBROSE; Rightly we read that the crowds praising God met Him at the descent of the mountain, that they might signify that the works of the heavenly mystery had come to them from heaven. BEDE; Again, when our Lord descends from the mount of Olives, the multitude descend also, because since the Author of mercy has suffered humiliation, it is necessary that all those who need His mercy should follow His footsteps.

1 Pet. 2, 5.

41. And when he was come near, he beheld the city, and wept over it,

42. Saying, If thou hadst known, even thou, at least in this thy day, the things which belong unto thy peace! but now they are hid from thine eyes.

43. For the days shall come upon thee, that thine enemies shall cast a trench about thee, and compass thee round, and keep thee in on every side,

44. And shall lay thee even with the ground, and thy children within thee; and they shall not leave in thee one stone upon another; because thou knewest not the time of thy visitation.

ORIGEN; All the blessings which Jesus pronounced in His Gospel He confirms by His own example, as having declared, *Blessed are the meek;* He afterwards sanctions it by saying, *Learn of me, for I am meek;* and because He had said, *Blessed are they that weep,* He Himself also wept over the city. CYRIL; For Christ had compassion upon the Jews, who wills that all men should be saved. Which had not been plain to us, were it not revealed by a certain mark of His humanity. For tears poured forth are the tokens of sorrow.

GREG. The merciful Redeemer wept then over the fall of the false city, which that city itself knew not was about to come upon it. As it is added, *saying, If thou hadst known,* *even thou* (we may here understand) *wouldest weep.* Thou who now rejoicest, for thou knowest not what is at hand. It follows, *at least in this thy day.* For when she gave herself up to carnal pleasures, she had the things which in her day might be her peace. But why she had present goods for her peace, is explained by what follows, *But now they are hidden from thy eyes.* For if the eyes of her heart had not been hidden from the future evils which were hanging over her, she would not have been joyful in the prosperity of the present. Therefore He shortly added the punishment which was near at hand, saying, *For the days shall come upon thee.* {Greg. Hom. 39. in Ev.}

CYRIL; *If thou hadst known, even thou.* The Jews were not worthy to receive the divinely inspired Scriptures, which relate the mystery of Christ. For as often as Moses is read, a veil overshadows their heart that they should not see what has been accomplished in Christ, who being the truth puts to flight the shadow. And because they regarded not the truth, they rendered themselves unworthy of the salvation which flows from Christ. EUSEBIUS; He here declares that His coming was to bring peace to the whole world. For unto this He came, that He should preach both to them that were near, and those that were afar off. But as they did not wish to receive the peace that was announced to them, it was hid from them. And therefore the siege which was shortly to come upon them He most expressly foretells, adding, *For the days shall come* Greg. *upon thee, &c.* GREG. By these words the Roman leaders nt sup. are pointed out. For that overthrow of Jerusalem is described, which was made by the Roman emperors Vespasian and Titus.

EUSEBIUS; But how these things were fulfilled we may gather from what is delivered to us by Josephus, who though he was a Jew, related each event as it took place, in exact accordance with Christ's prophecies. GREG. This too which is added, namely, *They shall not leave in thee one stone upon another*, is now witnessed in the altered situation of the same city, which is now built in that place where Christ was crucified without the gate, whereas the former Jerusalem, as it is called, was rooted up from the very foundation. And the crime for which this punishment of overthrow was inflicted is added, *Because thou knewest not the time of thy visitation.* THEOPHYL. That is, *of my coming.* For I came to visit and to save thee, which if thou hadst known and believed on Me, thou mightest have been reconciled to the Romans, and exempted from all danger, as did those who believed on Christ.

ORIGEN; I do not deny then that the former Jerusalem was destroyed because of the wickedness of its inhabitants, but I ask whether the weeping might not perhaps concern this your spiritual Jerusalem. For if a man has sinned after receiving the mysteries of truth, he will be wept over. Moreover, no Gentile is wept over, but he only who was of Greg. Jerusalem, and has ceased to be. GREG. For our Redeemer nt sup. does not cease to weep through His elect whenever he perceives any to have departed from a good life to follow evil ways. Who if they had known their own damnation, hanging over them, would together with the elect shed tears over themselves. But the corrupt soul here has its day, rejoicing in the passing time; to whom things present are its peace, seeing that it takes delight in that which is temporal. It shuns the foresight of the future which may disturb its present mirth; and hence it follows, *But now are they hid from thine eyes.* ORIGEN; But our Jerusalem is also wept over, because after sin enemies surround it, (that is, wicked spirits,) and cast a trench round it to besiege it, and leave not a stone behind; especially when a man after long continency, after years of chastity, is overcome, and enticed by the blandishments of the flesh, has lost his fortitude and his modesty, and has committed fornication, they will not leave on him one stone upon another, according to Ezekiel, *His former righteousness I will not remember.* Ezek. 18, 24.

GREG. Or else; The evil spirits lay siege to the soul, as it goes forth from the body, for being seized with the love of the flesh, they caress it with delusive pleasures. They surround it with a trench, because bringing all its wickedness which it has committed before the eyes of its mind, they close confine it to the company of its own damnation, that being caught in the very extremity of life, it may see by what enemies it is blockaded, yet be unable to find any way of escape, because it can no longer do good works, since those which it might once have done it despised. On every side also they inclose the soul when its iniquities rise up before it, not only in deed but also in word and thought, that she who before in many ways greatly enlarged herself in wickedness, should now at the end be straitened every way in judgment. Then indeed the soul by the very condition of its guilt is laid prostrate on the ground, while its flesh which it believed to be its life is bid to return to dust. Then its children fall in death, when all unlawful thoughts which only proceed from it, are in the last punishment of life scattered abroad. These may also be signified by the stones. For the corrupt mind when to a corrupt thought it adds one more corrupt, places one stone upon another. But when the soul is led to its doom, the whole structure of its thoughts is rent asunder. But the wicked soul God ceases not to visit with His teaching, sometimes with the scourge and sometimes with a miracle; that the truth which it knew not it may hear, and though still despising it, may return pricked to the heart in sorrow, or overcome with mercies may be ashamed at the evil which it has done. But because it knows not the time of its visitation, at the end of life it is given over to its Greg. Hom. 39. in Ev.

enemies, that with them it may be joined together in the bond of everlasting damnation.

45. And he went into the temple, and began to cast out them that sold therein, and them that bought;

46. Saying unto them, It is written, My house is the house of prayer: but ye have made it a den of thieves.

47. And he taught daily in the temple. But the Chief Priests and the Scribes and the chief of the people sought to destroy him,

48. And could not find what they might do: for all the people were very attentive to hear him.

Greg.
ut sup.

GREG. When He had related the evils that were to come upon the city, He straightway entered the temple, that He might cast out them that bought and sold in it. Shewing that the destruction of the people arose chiefly from the guilt of the priests. AMBROSE; For God wishes not His temple to be a house of traffic, but the dwelling-place of holiness, nor does He fix the priestly service in a saleable performance of religion, but in a free and willing obedience.

CYRIL; Now there were in the temple a number of sellers who sold animals, by the custom of the law, for the sacrificial victims, but the time was now come for the shadows to pass away, and the truth of Christ to shine forth. Therefore Christ, who together with the Father was worshipped in the temple, commanded the customs of the law to be reformed, but the temple to become a house of prayer; as it is added, *My house, &c.* GREG. For they who sat in the temple to receive money would doubtless sometimes make exaction to the injury of those who gave them none.

THEOPHYL. The same thing our Lord did also at the beginning of His preaching, as John relates; and now He did it a second time, because the crime of the Jews was much increased by their not having been chastened by the former warning.

Aug. Now mystically, you must understand by the temple Aug. de
Qu. Ev.
lib. ii. Christ Himself, as man in His human nature, or with His body united to Him, that is, the Church. But inasmuch as He is qu. 48. the Head of the Church, it was said, *Destroy this temple,* John 2,
19. *and I will raise it up in three days.* Inasmuch as the Church is joined to Him, is the temple understood, of which He seems to have spoken in the same place, *Take these away from hence;* signifying that there would be those in the Church who would rather be pursuing their own interest, or find a shelter therein to conceal their wickedness, than follow after the love of Christ, and by confession of their sins receiving pardon be restored.

Greg. But our Redeemer does not withdraw His word Greg.
Hom.
39. ut
sup. of preaching even from the unworthy and ungrateful. Accordingly after having by the ejection of the corrupt maintained the strictness of discipline, He now pours forth the gifts of grace. For it follows, *And he was teaching daily in the temple.* Cyril; Now from what Christ had said and done it was meet that men should worship Him as God, but far from doing this, they sought to slay Him; as it follows, *But the chief priests and scribes and the chief of the people sought to destroy him.* Bede; Either because He daily taught in the temple, or because He had cast the thieves therefrom, or that coming thereto as King and Lord, He was greeted with the honour of a heavenly hymn of praise. Cyril; But the people held Christ in far higher estimation than the Scribes and Pharisees, and chiefs of the Jews, who not receiving the faith of Christ themselves, rebuked others. Hence it follows, *And they could not find what they might do: for all the people were very attentive to hear him.* Bede; This may be taken in two ways; either that fearing a tumult of the people they knew not what they should do with Jesus, whom they had settled to destroy; or they sought to destroy Him because they perceived their own authority set aside, and multitudes flocking to hear Him. Greg. Greg.
ut sup. Mystically, such as the temple of God is in a city, such is the life of the religious in a faithful people. And there are frequently some who take upon themselves the religious habit, and while they are receiving the privilege of Holy Orders, are sinking the sacred office of religion into a bargain

of worldly traffic. For the sellers in the temple are those
who give at a certain price that which is the rightful possession of others. For to sell justice is to observe it on condition of receiving a reward. But the buyers in the temple
are those, who whilst unwilling to discharge what is just to
their neighbour, and disdaining to do what they are in duty
bound to, by paying a price to their patrons, purchase sin.

ORIGEN; If any then sells, let him be cast out, and especially if he sells doves. For of those things which have been
revealed and committed to me by the Holy Spirit, I either
sell for money to the people, or do not teach without hire,
what else do I but sell a dove, that is, the Holy Spirit?
AMBROSE; Therefore our Lord teaches generally that all
worldly bargains should be far removed from the temple of
God; but spiritually He drove away the money-changers,
who seek gain from the Lord's money, that is, the divine
Scripture, lest they should discern good and evil. GREG.
And these make the house of God a den of thieves, because
when corrupt men hold religious offices, they slay with the
sword of their wickedness their neighbours, whom they
ought to raise to life by the intercession of their prayers.
The temple also is the soul of the faithful, which if it put
forth corrupt thoughts to the injury of a neighbour, then is it
become as it were a lurking place of thieves. But when the
soul of the faithful is wisely instructed to shun evil, truth
teaches daily in the temple.

Greg.
ut sup.

CHAP. XX.

1. And it came to pass, that on one of those days, as he taught the people in the temple, and preached the Gospel, the Chief Priests and the Scribes came upon him with the elders,

2. And spake unto him, saying, Tell us, by what authority doest thou these things? or who is he that gave thee this authority?

3. And he answered and said unto them, I will also ask you one thing; and answer me:

4. The baptism of John, was it from heaven, or of men?

5. And they reasoned with themselves, saying, If we shall say, From heaven; he will say, Why then believed ye him not?

6. But and if we say, Of men; all the people will stone us: for they be persuaded that John was a prophet.

7. And they answered, that they could not tell whence it was.

8. And Jesus said unto them, Neither tell I you by what authority I do these things.

AUG. Having related the casting out of those that bought and sold in the temple, Luke omits Christ's going to Bethany and His return again to the city, and the circumstances of the fig-tree, and the answer which was made to the astonished disciples, concerning the power of faith. And having omitted all these, as he does not, like Mark, pursue the events of each day in order, he commences with these words, ^{Aug. de con. Ev. l.ii.c.69.}

And it came to pass, that on one of those days; by which we may understand that day on which Matthew and Mark related that event to have taken place. EUSEB. But the rulers who should have been struck with wonder at one who taught such heavenly doctrines, and have been convinced by His words and deeds that this was the same Christ whom the Prophets had foretold, came to hinder Him, so helping onward the destruction of the people. For it follows, *And spake unto him, saying, Tell us, by what authority doest thou these things? &c.* As if he said; By the law of Moses, those only who are sprung from the blood of Levi have authority to teach, and power over the sacred buildings. But Thou who art of the line of Judah usurpest the offices assigned to us. Whereas, O Pharisee, if thou hadst known the Scriptures, thou wouldest have called to mind that this is the Priest after the order of Melchisedec, who offers to God them that believe on Him by that worship which is above the law. Why then art thou troubled. He cast out of the sacred house things which seemed necessary for the sacrifices of the law, because He calls us by faith to the true righteousness.

BEDE; Or when they say, *By what authority doest thou these things?* they doubt concerning the power of God, and wish it to be understood that of the devil He doeth this. Adding moreover, *And who is he that gave thee this authority?* Most plainly do they deny the Son of God when they think that not by His own power but another's He doeth miracles. Now our Lord by a simple answer might have refuted such a calumny; but He wisely asks a question, that by their silence or their words they might condemn themselves. *And he answered and said unto them, I also will ask, &c.* THEOPHYL. For that He might shew that they had always rebelled against the Holy Spirit, and that besides Isaiah, whom they remembered not, they had refused to believe John whom they had lately seen; He now in his turn puts the question to them, proving that if so great a Prophet as John who was accounted greatest among them had been disbelieved when he testified of Him, they would in no wise believe Him, answering by what authority He did this.

EUSEB. His question concerning John the Baptist is not from whence was he sprung, but whence received he his law of baptism. But they feared not to shun the truth. For God sent John as a voice, crying, *Prepare ye the way of the Lord.* But they dreaded to speak the truth, lest it should be said, *Why did ye not believe?* and they scruple to blame the forerunner, not from fear of God, but of the people; as it follows, *And they reasoned within themselves, saying, If we shall say, From heaven; he will say, Why then believed ye him not.* BEDE; As if He should say, He whom you confess had his gift of prophecy from heaven, and gave testimony to Me. And ye heard from him by what power I should do these things. It follows, *But if we shall say, Of men; the whole people will stone us: for they be persuaded that John was a prophet.* Therefore perceived they in whatever way they should answer they would fall into a trap, fearing the stoning, but much more the confession of the truth. And then it follows, *And they answered, that they could not tell whence it was.* Because they will not confess that which they knew, they were baffled, and the Lord would not tell them what He knew; as it follows, *And Jesus said unto them, Neither will I tell you by what authority I do these things.* For there are two reasons especially why we should conceal the truth from those that ask; for example, when the questioner is incapable of understanding what he asks, or when from hatred or contempt he is unworthy to have his questions answered.

9. Then began he to speak to the people this parable; A certain man planted a vineyard, and let it forth to husbandmen, and went into a far country for a long time.

10. And at the season he sent a servant to the husbandmen, that they should give him of the fruit of the vineyard : but the husbandmen beat him, and sent him away empty.

11. And again he sent another servant : and they beat him also, and entreated him shamefully, and sent him away empty.

12. And again he sent a third: and they wounded him also, and cast him out.

13. Then said the lord of the vineyard, What shall I do? I will send my beloved son: it may be they will reverence him when they see him.

14. But when the husbandmen saw him, they reasoned among themselves, saying, This is the heir: come, let us kill him, that the inheritance may be our's.

15. So they cast him out of the vineyard, and killed him. What therefore shall the lord of the vineyard do unto them?

16. He shall come and destroy these husbandmen, and shall give the vineyard to others. And when they heard it, they said, God forbid.

17. And he beheld them, and said, What is this then that is written, The stone which the builders rejected, the same is become the head of the corner?

18. Whosoever shall fall upon that stone shall be broken; but on whomsoever it shall fall, it will grind him to powder.

EUSEB. The rulers of the Jewish people being now assembled together in the temple, Christ put forth a parable, foretelling by a figure the things they were about to do to Him, and the rejection that was in store for them. AUG. Matthew has omitted for brevity's sake what Luke has not, namely, that the parable was spoken not to the rulers only who asked concerning His authority, but also to the people.

AMBROSE; Now many derive different meanings from the name vineyard, but Esaias clearly relates the vineyard of the Lord of Sabaoth to be the house of Israel. This vineyard who else but God planted? BEDE; The man then who plants the vineyard is the same who, according to another parable, hired labourers into his vineyard. EUSEB. But the parable which Esaias gives denounces the vineyard, whereas our Saviour's parable is not directed against the vineyard, but

(margin notes) Aug. de con. Ev. l. ii. c. 70.   Isa. 5.

the cultivators of it; of whom it is added, *And he let it out to husbandmen*, that is, to the elders of the people, and the chief priests, and the doctors, and all the nobles. THEOPHYL. Or each one of the people is the vineyard, each likewise is the husbandman, for every one of us takes care of himself. Having committed then the vineyard to the husbandmen, he went away, that is, he left them to the guidance of their own judgment. Hence it follows, *And went into a far country for a long time.* AMBROSE; Not that our Lord journeys from place to place, seeing that He is ever present in every place, but that He is more present to those who love Him, while He removes Himself from those who regard Him not. But He was absent for a long time, lest His coming to require His fruit might seem too early. For the more indulgent it is, it renders obstinacy the less excusable.

CYRIL; Or God took Himself away from the vineyard for the course of many years, for since the time that He was seen to descend in the likeness of fire upon Mount Sinai, He no longer vouchsafed to them His visible presence; though no change took place, in which He sent not His prophets and righteous men to give warning thereof; as it follows, *And at the time of the vintage he sent a servant to the husbandmen, that they should give him of the fruit of the vineyard.* THEOPHYL. He says of the fruit of the vineyard, because not the whole fruit, but part only, He wished to receive. For what does God gain from us, but His own knowledge, which is also our profit. BEDE; But it is rightly written fruit, not increase. For there was no increase in this vineyard. The first servant sent was Moses, who for forty years sought of the husbandmen the fruit of the law which he had given, but he was wroth against them, for they provoked his spirit. Hence it follows, *But they beat him, and sent him away empty.*

AMBROSE; And it came to pass that He ordained many others, whom the Jews sent back to him disgraced and empty, for they could reap nothing from them; as it follows, *And again he sent another servant.* BEDE; By the other servant is meant David, who was sent after the commandment of the law, that he by the music of his psalmody might stir up the husbandmen to the exercise of good works. But they on the

Exod. 19.

1 Sam.
20, 1.
1 Kings
12, 16. contrary declared, *What portion have we in David, neither have we inheritance in the son of Jesse.* Hence it follows, *And they beat him also, and entreated him shamefully, and sent him away empty.* But He does not stop here, for it follows, *And again he sent a third:* whereby we must understand the company of prophets who constantly visited the people with their testimony. But which of the Prophets did they not persecute; as it follows, *And they wounded him also, and cast him out.* Now these three successions of servants, our Lord elsewhere shews to comprehend under a figure all the teachers under the law, when He says, *For all those things must be fulfilled which were written in the law of Moses, and the Prophets, and the Psalms, concerning me.*

THEOPHYL. After the prophets then had suffered all these things, the Son is delegated; for it follows, *Then said the Lord of the vineyard, What shall I do?* That the Lord of the vineyard speaks doubtingly, arises not from ignorance, for what is there that the Lord knows not? but He is said to hesitate, that the free will of man may be preserved. CYRIL; The Lord of the vineyard also ponders what He should do, not that He is in need of ministers, but that having thoroughly tried every device of human aid, yet His people being in no wise healed, He may add something greater; as He goes on to say, *I will send my beloved son: it may be they will reverence him when they see him.* THEOPHYL. Now He said this, not as ignorant that they would treat Him worse than they did the prophets, but because the Son ought to be reverenced by them. But if they should still be rebellious and slay Him, this would crown their iniquity. Lest therefore any should say that the Divine Presence has necessarily been the cause of their disobedience, He uses purposely this doubtful mode of speech.

AMBROSE; When then the only-begotten Son was sent to them, the unbelieving Jews, wishing to be rid of the Heir, put Him to death by crucifying Him, and rejected Him by denying Him. Christ is the Heir and the Testator likewise. The Heir, because He survives His own death; and of the testament which He Himself bequeathed, He reaps as it were the hereditary profits in our advances. BEDE; But our Lord most clearly proves that the Jewish rulers crucified the Son of God not from ignorance but for envy. For they knew it was He to whom it was said, *I will give thee the* Ps. 2, 8. *heathen for thine inheritance. And they cast him out of the vineyard, and slew him.* Because Jesus, that He might Heb. 13, sanctify the people by His blood, suffered without the gate. ^12.

THEOPHYL. Since we have already assumed the people, not Jerusalem, to be the vineyard, it may perhaps be more properly said that the people indeed slew Him without the vineyard; that is, our Lord suffered without the hands of the people, because in truth the people did not with their own hands inflict death upon Him, but delivered Him up to Pilate and the Gentiles. But some by the vineyard have understood the Scripture, which not believing they slew the Lord. And so without the vineyard, that is, without Scripture, our Lord is said to have suffered.

BEDE; Or was He cast out of the vineyard and slain, because He was first driven out of the hearts of the unbelievers, and then fastened to the cross?

CHRYS. Now it was not accidentally but part of the purpose of the divine dispensation that Christ came after the prophets. For God does not pursue all things at once, but accommodates Himself to mankind through His great mercy; for if they despised His Son coming after His servants, much less would they have heard Him before. For they who listened not to the inferior commands, how would they have heard the greater?

AMBROSE; He rightly puts a question to them, that they may condemn themselves by their own words, as it follows, *What then will the Lord of the vineyard do to them?* BASIL; And this happens as it were to men who are condemned, having nothing to answer to the plain evidence of justice. But it is the property of Divine mercy not to inflict punishment in secret, but to foretell it with threatenings, that so it might recall men to repentance; and thus it follows here, *He shall come and destroy those husbandmen.* AMBROSE; He says, the Lord of the vineyard will come, because in the Son is present also the Father's majesty; or because in the last times He will be more graciously present by His Spirit in the hearts of men.

CYRIL; The Jewish rulers were shut out then, because they resisted their Lord's will, and made the vineyard barren which was entrusted to them. But the cultivation of the vineyard was given to the Priests of the New Testament, upon which the Scribes and Pharisees, as soon as they perceived the force of the parable, refuse to permit it, saying as follows, *God forbid.* They did not however escape any whit the more, because of their obstinacy and disobedience to the faith of Christ.

THEOPHYL. Now Matthew seems to relate the parable differently; that when our Saviour asked indeed, *What will he do then to the husbandmen?* the Jews answered, *he will miserably destroy them.* But there is no difference between the two circumstances. The Jews at first pronounced that opinion, then perceiving the point of the parable said, *God forbid,* as Luke here relates. AUG. Or else, in the multitude of which we are speaking there were those who craftily asked our Lord by what authority He acted; there were those also who not craftily, but faithfully, cried aloud, *Blessed is he who cometh in the name of the Lord.* And so there would be some who would say, *He will miserably destroy those husbandmen, and let out his vineyard to others.* Which are rightly said to have been the words of our Lord Himself, either on account of their truth, or because of the unity of the members with the head; while there would be others also who would say to those who made this answer, God forbid, inasmuch as they understood the parable was spoken against themselves. It follows, *And he beheld them, and said, What is this then that is written, The stone which the builders rejected, the same is become the head of the corner?* BEDE; As if He said, How shall the prophecy be fulfilled, except that Christ, being rejected and slain by you, is to be preached to the Gentiles, who will believe on Him, that as the corner stone He may thus from both nations build up one temple to Himself? EUSEB. Christ is called *a stone* on account of His earthly body, *cut out without hands,* as in the vision of Daniel, because of His birth of the Virgin. But the stone is neither of silver nor gold, because He is not any glorious King, but a man lowly and despised, wherefore the builders rejected Him. THEOPHYL. For the

Aug. de con. Ev. lib. iv. cap. 70.

Dan. 2, 34.

rulers of the people rejected Him, when they said, *This man* John 9, *is not of God.* But He was so useful and so precious, that ^{16.} He was placed as the head stone of the corner. CYRIL; But holy Scripture compares to a corner the meeting together 1 Pet. 2, of the two nations, the Jew and the Gentile, into one faith. 7. Eph. 2, For the Saviour has compacted both peoples into one new 20. man, reconciling them in one body to the Father. Of saving help then is that stone to the corner made by it, but to the Jews who resist this spiritual union, it bringeth destruction.

THEOPHYL. He mentions two condemnations or destructions of them, one indeed of their souls, which they suffered being offended in Christ. And He touches this when He says, *Whosoever shall fall upon that stone shall be shaken to pieces.* But the other of their captivity and extermination, which the Stone that was despised by them brought upon them. And He points to this when He says, *But upon whomsoever it shall fall, it shall grind him to powder,* or winnow him. For so were the Jews winnowed through the whole world, as the straw from the threshing floor. And mark the order of things; for first comes the wickedness committed against Him, then follows the just vengeance of God. BEDE; Or else, He who is a sinner, yet believes on Christ, falls indeed upon the stone and is shaken, for he is preserved by penitence unto salvation. But upon whomsoever it shall fall, that is, upon whom the stone itself has come down because he denied it, it shall grind him to powder, so that not even a broken piece of a vessel shall be left, in which may be drunk a little water. Or, He means by those who fall upon Him, such as only despise Him, and therefore do not yet utterly perish, but are shaken violently so that they cannot walk upright. But upon whom it falls, upon them shall He come in judgment with everlasting punishment, therefore shall it grind them to powder, that they may be as *the dust* Ps. 1, 4. *which the wind scatters from the face of the earth.*

AMBROSE; The vineyard is also our type. For the husbandman is the Almighty Father, the vine is Christ, but we John 15, are the branches. Rightly are the people of Christ called a ^{5.} vine, either because it carries on its front the sign of the cross, or because its fruits are gathered in the latter time of the year, or because to all men, as to the equal rows of vines, poor as

well as rich, servants as well as masters, there is an equal
allotment in the Church without distinction of persons. And
as the vine is married to the trees, so is the body to the soul.
Loving this vineyard, the husbandman is wont to dig it and
prune it, lest it grow too luxuriant in the shade of its foliage,
and check by unfruitful boastfulness of words the ripening
of its natural character. Here must be the vintage of the
whole world, for here is the vineyard of the whole world.

Bede. in   BEDE; Or understanding it morally; to every one of the
Marc. faithful is let out a vineyard to cultivate, in that the mystery
12. of baptism is entrusted to him to work out. One servant is
sent, a second and a third, when the Law, the Psalms, and
the Prophets are read. But the servant who is sent is said
to be treated despitefully or beaten, when the word heard is
despised or blasphemed. The heir who is sent that man kills
Heb. 6, as far as he can, who by sin tramples under foot the Son of
6. God. The wicked husbandman being destroyed, the vineyard
is given to another, when with the gift of grace, which the
proud man spurned, the humble are enriched.

19. And the Chief Priests and the Scribes the
same hour sought to lay hands on him; and they
feared the people: for they perceived that he had
spoken this parable against them.

20. And they watched him, and sent forth spies,
which should feign themselves just men, that they
might take hold of his words, that so they might
deliver him unto the power and authority of the
governor.

21. And they asked him, saying, Master, we know
that thou sayest and teachest rightly, neither acceptest thou the person of any, but teachest the way
of God truly:

22. Is it lawful for us to give tribute unto Cæsar,
or no?

23. But he perceived their craftiness, and said unto
them, Why tempt ye me?

24. Shew me a penny. Whose image and super-scription hath it ? They answered and said, Cæsar's.

25. And he said unto them, Render therefore unto Cæsar the things which be Cæsar's, and unto God the things which be God's.

26. And they could not take hold of his words before the people : and they marvelled at his answer, and held their peace.

CYRIL; It became indeed the rulers of the Jews, per-ceiving that the parable was spoken of them, to depart from evil, having been thus as it were warned concern-ing the future. But little mindful of this, they rather gather a fresh occasion for their crimes. The commandment of the Law restrained them not, which says, *The innocent and righ-* Exod. *teous men thou shalt not slay,* but the fear of the people [23, 7.] checked their wicked purpose. For they set the fear of man before the reverence of God. The reason of this purpose is given, *for they perceived that he spoke this parable against them.* BEDE; And so by seeking to slay Him, they proved the truth of what He had said in the parable. For He Him-self is the Heir, whose unjust death He said was to be pu-nished. They are the wicked husbandmen who sought to kill the Son of God. This also is daily committed in the Church when any one, only in name a brother, is ashamed or afraid, because of the many good men with whom he lives, to break into that unity of the Church's faith and peace which he abhors. And because the chief priests sought to lay hold of our Lord but could not by themselves, they tried to accomplish it by the hands of the governor; as it follows, *And they watched him, &c.* CYRIL; For they seemed to be trifling, yet were in earnest, forgetful of God, who says, *Who is this that hideth his counsel from me?* For Job 42, they come to Christ the Saviour of all, as though He were [3.] a common man, as it follows, *that they might take him in his speech.*

THEOPHYL. They laid snares for our Lord, but got their own feet entangled in them. Listen to their cunning, *And they asked Him, saying, Master, we know that thou sayest and teachest rightly.* BEDE; This smooth and artful question was to entice the answerer to say that he fears God rather than Cæsar, for it follows, *Neither acceptest thou the person of any, but teachest the way of God truly.* This they say, to entice Him to tell them that they ought not to pay tribute, in order that the servants of the guard, (who according to the other Evangelists are said to have been present,) might immediately upon hearing it seize Him as the leader of a sedition against the Romans. And so they proceed to ask, *Is it lawful to give tribute to Cæsar, or not?* For there was a great division among the people, some saying that for the sake of security and quiet, seeing that the Romans fought for all, they ought to pay tribute; while the Pharisees, on the contrary, declared, that the people of God who gave tithes and first fruits, ought not to be subject to the law of man. THEOPHYL. Therefore it was intended, in case He said they ought to give tribute to Cæsar, that He should be accused by the people, as placing the nation under the yoke of slavery, but if He forbade them to pay the tax, that they should denounce Him as a stirrer up of divisions to the governor. But He escapes their snares, as it follows, *Perceiving their craftiness, he said unto them, Why tempt ye me? Shew me a penny. Whose image and superscription has it?* AMBROSE; Our Lord here teaches us, how cautious we ought to be in our answers to heretics or Jews; as He has said elsewhere, *Be ye wise as serpents.*

Mat. 10, 16.

BEDE; Let those who impute the question of our Saviour to ignorance, learn from this place that Jesus was well able to know whose image was on the money; but He asks the question, that He might give a fitting answer to their words; for it follows, *They answered and said, Cæsar's.* We must not suppose Augustus is thereby meant, but Tiberius, for all the Roman kings were called Cæsar, from the first Caius Cæsar. But from their answer our Lord easily solves the question, for it follows, *And he said unto them, Render unto Cæsar the things which be Cæsar's, and unto God the things which be God's.* TITUS; As if He said, With your words ye tempt me, obey me in works. Ye have indeed Cæsar's image, ye have undertaken his offices, to him therefore give tribute, to God fear. For God requireth not money, but faith. BEDE; Render also to God the things which be God's, that is to say, tithes, first fruits, offerings, and sacrifices. THEOPHYL. And observe that He said not, give, but return. For it is a debt. Thy prince protects thee from enemies, renders thy life tranquil. Surely then thou art bound to pay him tribute. Nay, this very piece of money which thou bringest thou hast from him. Return then to the king the king's money. God also has given thee understanding and reason, make then a return of these to Him, that thou mayest not be compared to the beasts, but in all things mayest walk wisely. AMBROSE; Be unwilling then, if thou wouldest not offend Cæsar, to possess worldly goods. And thou rightly teachest, first to render the things which be Cæsar's. For no one can be the Lord's unless he has first renounced the world. Oh most galling chain! To promise to God, and pay not. Far greater is the contract of faith than that of money.

ORIGEN; Now this place contains a mystery. For there are two images in man, one which he received from God, as it is written, *Let us make man in our own image:* another from the enemy, which he has contracted through dis- Gen. 1, 26. obedience and sin, allured and won by the enticing baits of the prince of this world. For as the penny has the image of the emperor of the world, so he who does the works of the power of darkness, bears the image of Him whose works he doth. He says then, *Render unto Cæsar the things which be Cæsar's,* that is, cast away the earthly image, that ye may be able, by putting on the heavenly image, to render unto God the things which be God's, namely, to love God. Which things Moses says God requires of us. But God makes this demand of us, not because He has need that we should Deut. give Him any thing, but that, when we have given, He might 10, 12. grant us this very same gift for our salvation.

BEDE; Now they who ought rather to have believed such great wisdom, marvelled that in all their cunning they had found no opportunity of catching Him. As it follows, *And they could not take hold of his words before the people: and they marvelled at his answer, and held their peace.* THEOPHYL. This was their main object, to rebuke Him

before the people, which they were unable to do because of
the wonderful wisdom of His answer.

27. Then came to him certain of the Sadducces,
which deny that there is any resurrection; and they
asked him,

28. Saying, Master, Moses wrote unto us, If any
man's brother die, having a wife, and he die without
children, that his brother should take his wife, and
raise up seed unto his brother.

29. There were therefore seven brethren: and the
first took a wife, and died without children.

30. And the second took her to wife, and he died
childless.

31. And the third took her; and in like manner
the seven also: and they left no children, and died.

32. Last of all the woman died also.

33. Therefore in the resurrection whose wife of
them is she? for seven had her to wife.

34. And Jesus answering said unto them, The
children of this world marry, and are given in
marriage:

35. But they which shall be accounted worthy to
obtain that world, and the resurrection from the
dead, neither marry, nor are given in marriage:

36. Neither can they die any more: for they are
equal unto the angels; and are the children of God,
being the children of the resurrection.

37. Now that the dead are raised, even Moses
shewed at the bush, when he calleth the Lord the
God of Abraham, and the God of Isaac, and the God
of Jacob.

38. For he is not a God of the dead, but of the
living: for all live unto him.

39. Then certain of the Scribes answering said, Master, thou hast well said.

40. And after that they durst not ask him any question at all.

BEDE; There were two heresies among the Jews, one of the Pharisees, who boasted in the righteousness of their traditions, and hence they were called by the people, " separated;" the other of the Sadducees, whose name signified " righteous," claiming to themselves that which they were not. When the former went away, the latter came to tempt Him. ORIGEN; The heresy of the Sadducees not only denies the resurrection of the dead, but also believes the soul to die with the body. Watching then to entrap our Saviour in His words, they proposed a question just at the time when they observed Him teaching His disciples concerning the resurrection ; as it follows, *And they asked him, saying, Master, Moses wrote to us, If a brother, &c.* AMBROSE; According to the letter of the law, a woman is compelled to marry, however unwilling, in order that a brother may raise up seed to his brother who is dead. The letter therefore killeth, but the Spirit is the master of charity. THEOPHYL. Now the Sadducees resting upon a weak foundation, did not believe in the doctrine of the resurrection. For imagining the future life in the resurrection to be carnal, they were justly misled, and hence reviling the doctrine of the resurrection as a thing impossible they invent the story, *There were seven brothers, &c.* BEDE; They devise this story in order to convict those of folly, who assert the resurrection of the dead. Hence they object a base fable, that they may deny the truth of the resurrection. Bede.
ut sup.

AMBROSE; Mystically, this woman is the synagogue, which had seven husbands, as it is said to the Samaritan, *Thou hadst five husbands,* because the Samaritan follows only the five books of Moses, the synagogue for the most part seven. And from none of them has she received the seed of an hereditary offspring, and so can have no part with her husbands in the resurrection, because she perverts the spiritual meaning of the precept into a carnal. For not any carnal brother is pointed at, who should raise seed to his John 4,
18.

deceased brother, but that brother who from the dead people of the Jews should claim unto himself for wife the wisdom of the divine worship, and from it should raise up seed in the Apostles, who being left as it were unformed in the womb of the synagogue, have according to the election of grace been thought worthy to be preserved by the admixture of a new seed.   BEDE; Or these seven brothers answer to the reprobate, who throughout the whole life of the world, which revolves in seven days, are fruitless in good works, and these being carried away by death one after another, at length the course of the evil world, as the barren woman, itself also passes away.   THEOPHYL. But our Lord shews that in the resurrection there will be no fleshly conversation, thereby overthrowing their doctrine together with its slender foundation; as it follows, *And Jesus said unto them, The*

Aug de *children of this world marry, &c.*   AUG. For marriages are
Quæst.
Ev. l. ii. for the sake of children, children for succession, succession
cap. 49. because of death.   Where then there is no death, there are no marriages; and hence it follows, *But they which shall be accounted worthy, &c.*   BEDE; Which must not be taken as if only they who are worthy were either to rise again or be without marriage, but all sinners also shall rise again, and abide without marriage in that new world.   But our Lord wished to mention only the elect, that He might incite the minds of His hearers to search into the glory of the resurrection.

Aug. de   AUG. As our discourse is made up and completed by
Quæst.
Ev. ubi departing and succeeding syllables, so also men themselves
sup. whose faculty discourse is, by departure and succession make up and complete the order of this world, which is built up with the mere temporal beauty of things.   But in the future life, seeing that the Word which we shall enjoy is formed by no departure and succession of syllables, but all things which it has it has everlastingly and at once, so those who partake of it, to whom it alone will be life, shall neither depart by death, nor succeed by birth, even as it now is with the angels; as it follows, *For they are equal to the angels.*   CYRIL; For as the multitude of the angels is indeed very great, yet they are not propagated by generation, but have their being from creation, so also to those who rise

again, there is no more necessity for marriage; as it follows, *And are the children of God.* THEOPHYL. As if He said, Because it is God who worketh in the resurrection, rightly are they called the sons of God, who are regenerated by the resurrection. For there is nothing carnal seen in the regeneration of them that rise again, there is neither coming together, nor the womb, nor birth. BEDE; Or they are equal to the angels, and the children of God, because made new by the glory of the resurrection, with no fear of death, with no spot of corruption, with no quality of an earthly condition, they rejoice in the perpetual beholding of God's presence.

ORIGEN; But because the Lord says in Matthew, which is here omitted, *Ye do err, not knowing the Scriptures,* I ask the question, where is it so written, *They shall neither marry, nor be given in marriage?* for as I conceive there is no such thing to be found either in the Old or New Testament, but the whole of their error had crept in from the reading of the Scriptures without understanding; for it is said in Esaias, *My elect shall not have children for a curse.* Whence they suppose that the like will happen in the resurrection. But Paul interpreting all these blessings as spiritual, knowing them not to be carnal, says to the Ephesians, *Ye have blessed us in all spiritual blessings.* THEOPHYL. Or to the reason above given the Lord added the testimony of Scripture, *Now that the dead are raised, Moses also shewed at the bush,* as the Lord saith, *I am the God of Abraham, the God of Isaac, and the God of Jacob.* As if he said, If the patriarchs have once returned to nothing so as not to live with God in the hope of a resurrection, He would not have said, *I am,* but, I was, for we are accustomed to speak of things dead and gone thus, I was the Lord or Master of such a thing; but now that He said, *I am,* He shews that He is the God and Lord of the living. This is what follows, *But he is not a God of the dead, but of the living: for all live unto him.* For though they have departed from life, yet live they with Him in the hope of a resurrection. BEDE; Or He says this, that after having proved that the souls abide after death, (which the Sadducees denied,) He might next introduce the resurrection also of the bodies, which together

Mat. 22, 29.

Isai. 65, 23.

Eph. 1, 3.

Exod. 3, 6.

with the souls have done good or evil. But that is a true life which the just live unto God, even though they are dead in the body. Now to prove the truth of the resurrection, He might have brought much more obvious examples from the Prophets, but the Sadducees received only the five books of Moses, rejecting the oracles of the Prophets.

Chrys. CHRYS. As the saints claim as their own the common
deAnna, Lord of the world, not as derogating from His dominion, but
Serm. 4. testifying their affection after the manner of lovers, who do not brook to love with many, but desire to express a certain peculiar and especial attachment; so likewise does God call Himself especially the God of these, not thereby narrowing but enlarging His dominion; for it is not so much the multitude of His subjects that manifests His power, as the virtue of His servants. Therefore He does not so delight in the name of the God of heaven and earth, as in that of the God of Abraham, Isaac, and Jacob. Now among men servants are thus denominated by their masters; for we say, ' The steward *of* such a man,' but on the contrary God is called the God *of* Abraham.

THEOPHYL. But when the Sadducees were silenced, the Scribes commend Jesus, for they were opposed to them, saying to Him, *Master, thou hast well said.* BEDE; And since they had been defeated in argument, they ask Him no further questions, but seize Him, and deliver Him up to the Roman power. From which we may learn, that the poison of envy may indeed be subdued, but it is a hard thing to keep it at rest.

41. And he said unto them, How say they that Christ is David's son?

42. And David himself saith in the book of Psalms, The LORD said unto my Lord, Sit thou on my right hand,

43. Till I make thine enemies thy footstool.

44. David therefore calleth him Lord, how is he then his son?

THEOPHYL. Although our Lord was shortly about to enter on His Passion, He proclaims His own Godhead, and that

too neither incautiously nor boastfully, but with modesty.
For He puts a question to them, and having thrown them
into perplexity, leaves them to reason out the conclusion;
as it follows, *And he said unto them, How say they that
Christ is David's son?* AMBROSE; They are not blamed here
because they acknowledge Him to be David's Son, for the Luke
blind man for so doing was thought worthy to be healed. 18, 42.
And the children saying, *Hosanna to the Son of David*, 21, 9.
rendered to God the glory of the highest praise; but they
are blamed because they believe Him not to be the Son of
God. Hence it is added, *And David himself saith in the
book of Psalms, The Lord said unto my Lord.* Both the Ps. 110,
Father is Lord and the Son is Lord, but there are not two 1.
Lords, but one Lord, for the Father is in the Son, and the
Son is in the Father. He Himself sits at the right hand of
the Father, for He is coequal with the Father, inferior to
none; for it follows, *Sit thou at my right hand.* He is not
honoured by sitting at the right hand, nor is He degraded
by being sent. Degrees of dignity are not sought for, where
is the fulness of divinity.

AUG. By the sitting we must not conceive a posture of the Aug. de
human limbs, as if the Father sat on the left and the Son on Symbo-
lo. ad
the right, but the right hand itself we must interpret to be Catech.
the power which that Man received who was taken up into l. ii. c. 7.
Himself by God, that He should come to judge, who at first
came to be judged. CYRIL; Or, that He sits on the Father's
right hand proves His heavenly glory. For whose throne is
equal, their Majesty is equal. But sitting when it is said of
God signifies a universal kingdom and power. Therefore
He sitteth at the right hand of the Father, because the Word
proceeding from the substance of the Father, being made
flesh, putteth not off His divine glory.

THEOPHYL. He manifests then that He is not opposed to
the Father, but agrees with Him, since the Father resists the
Son's enemies, *Until I make thine enemies thy footstool.*
AMBROSE; We must believe then that Christ is both God
and man, and that His enemies are made subject to Him by
the Father, not through the weakness of His power, but
through the unity of their nature, since in the one the other
works. For the Son also subjects enemies to the Father, in

John 17, 6. that He glorifies the Father upon earth. THEOPHYL. Therefore He asks the question, and having excited their doubts, leaves them to deduce the consequence; as it follows, *David therefore calleth him Lord, how is he then his son?* CHRYS. David in truth was both the Father and the servant of Christ, the former indeed according to the flesh, the latter in the Spirit.

CYRIL; We then likewise in answer to the new Pharisees, who neither confess the Son of the holy Virgin to be the true Son of God, nor to be God, but divide one son into two, put the like objections: How then is the Son of David David's Lord, and that not by human lordship, but divine?

45. Then in the audience of all the people he said unto his disciples,

46. Beware of the Scribes, which desire to walk in long robes, and love greetings in the markets, and the highest seats in the synagogues, and the chief rooms at feasts;

47. Which devour widows' houses, and for a shew make long prayers: the same shall receive greater damnation.

Chrys. Hom. 19. in Joann. CHRYS. Now nothing is more powerful than to argue from the Prophets. For this is even of more weight than miracles themselves. For when Christ worked miracles, He was often gainsayed. But when He cited the Prophets, men were at once silent, because they had nothing to say. But when they were silent, He warns against them; as it is said, *Then in the audience of all the people he said to his disciples.* THEOPHYL. For as He was sending them to teach the world, He rightly warns them not to imitate the pride of the Pharisees. *Beware of the Scribes, who desire to walk in long robes*, that is, to go forth into public, dressed in fine Luke 16, 19. clothes, which was one of the sins remarked in the rich man.

CYRIL; The passions of the Scribes were the love of vainglory and the love of gain. That the disciples should avoid these hateful crimes, He gives them this warning, and adds, *And love greetings in the markets.* THEOPHYL. Which is the way of those who court and hunt after a good reputation, or they do it for the sake of collecting money.

It follows, *And the chief seats in synagogues.* BEDE; He does not forbid those to sit first in the synagogue, or at the feast, to whom this dignity belongs by right, but He tells them to beware of those who love this unduly; denouncing not the distinction, but the love of it. Though the other also would not be free from blame, when the same men who wish to take part in the disputes in the market, desire also to be called masters in the synagogue. For two reasons we are bid to beware of those who seek after vain-glory, either lest we be led away by their pretences, supposing those things to be good which they do, or be inflamed with jealousy, desiring in vain to be praised for the good deeds which they pretend to. But they seek not only for praise from men, but money; for it follows, *Who devour widows' houses, and for a shew make long prayers.* For pretending to be righteous and of great merit before God, they do not fail to receive large sums of money from the sick and those whose consciences are disturbed with their sins, as though they would be their protectors in the judgment. CHRYS. Thrusting themselves also into the possessions of widows, they grind down their poverty, not content to eat as it may be afforded them, but greedily devouring; using prayer also to an evil end, they thus expose themselves to a heavier condemnation; as it follows, *These shall receive the greater damnation.* THEOPHYL. Because they not only do what is evil, but make a pretence of prayer, so making virtue an excuse for their sin. They also impoverish widows whom they were bound to pity, by their presence driving them to great expenses. BEDE; Or because they seek from men praise and money, they are punished with the greater damnation.

1. And he looked up, and saw the rich men casting their gifts into the treasury.

2. And he saw also a certain poor widow casting in thither two mites.

3. And he said, Of a truth I say unto you, that this poor widow hath cast in more than they all :

4. For all these have of their abundance cast in unto the offerings of God : but she of her penury hath cast in all the living that she had.

Gloss. non occ. GLOSS. Our Lord having rebuked the covetousness of the Scribes who devoured widows' houses, commends the almsgiving of a widow ; as it is said, *And he looked up, and saw the rich men casting into the treasury, &c.*

BEDE; In the Greek language, φυλάξαι signifies to keep, and *gaza* in Persian means riches, hence gazophylacium is used for the name of the place in which money is kept. Now there was a chest with an opening at the top placed near the altar, on the right hand of those entering the house of God, into which the Priests cast all the money, which was given for the Lord's temple. But our Lord as He overthrows those who trade in His house, so also He remarks those who bring gifts, giving praise to the deserving, but condemning the bad. Hence it follows, *And he saw also a certain poor widow casting in thither two mites.* CYRIL; She offered two *oboli*, which with the sweat of her brow she had earned for her daily living, or what she daily begs for at the hands of others she gives to God, shewing that her poverty is fruitful to her. Therefore does she surpass the others, and by a just award receives a crown from God; as it follows, *Of a truth I say unto you, that this poor widow hath cast in more, &c.* BEDE; For whatever we offer with an honest heart is well pleasing to God, who hath respect unto the heart, not the substance, nor does He weigh the amount of that which is given in sacrifice, but of that from which it is taken; as it follows, *For all these have cast in of their abundance, but she all that she had.* CHRYS. For God regarded not the scantiness of the offering, but the overflowing of the affection. Almsgiving is not the bestowing a few things out of many, but it is that of the widow emptying herself of her whole substance. But if you cannot offer as much as the widow, at least give all that remains over.

BEDE; Now mystically, the rich men who cast their gifts into the treasury signify the Jews puffed up with the righteousness of the law; the poor widow, the simplicity of the Church which is called poor, because it has either cast away the spirit of pride, or its sins, as if they were worldly riches. But the Church is a widow, because her Husband endured death for her. She cast two mites into the treasury, because in God's sight, in whose keeping are all the offerings of our works, she presents her gifts, whether of love to God and her neighbour, or of faith and prayer. And these excel all the works of the proud Jews, for they of their abundance cast into the offerings of God, in that they presume on their righteousness, but the Church casts in all her living, for every thing that hath life she believes to be the gift of God. THEOPHYL. Or the widow may be taken to mean any soul bereft as it were of her first husband, the ancient law, and not worthy to be united to the Word of God. Who brings to God instead of a dowry faith and a good conscience, and so seems to offer more than those who are rich in words, and abound in the moral virtues of the Gentiles.

5. And as some spake of the temple, how it was adorned with goodly stones and gifts, he said,

6. As for these things which ye behold, the days will come, in the which there shall not be left one stone upon another, that shall not be thrown down.

7. And they asked him, saying, Master, but when shall these things be? and what sign will there be when these things shall come to pass?

8. And he said, Take heed that ye be not deceived: for many shall come in my name, saying, I am Christ; and the time draweth near: go ye not therefore after them.

Euseb. How beautiful was every thing relating to the structure of the temple, history informs us, and there are yet preserved remains of it, enough to instruct us in what was once the character of the buildings. But our Lord proclaimed to those that were wondering at the building of the temple, that there should not be left in it one stone upon another. For it was meet that that place, because of the presumption of its worshippers, should suffer every kind of desolation. BEDE; For it was ordained by the dispensation of God that the city itself and the temple should be overthrown, lest perhaps some one yet a child in the faith, while wrapt in astonishment at the rites of the sacrifices, should be carried away by the mere sight of the various beauties. AMBROSE; It was spoken then of the temple made with hands, that it should be overthrown. For there is nothing made with hands which age does not impair, or violence throw down, or fire burn. Yet there is also another temple, that is, the synagogue, whose ancient building falls to pieces as the Church rises. There is also a temple in every one, which falls when faith is lacking, and above all when any one falsely shields himself under the name of Christ, that so he may rebel against his inward inclinations.

CYRIL; Now His disciples did not at all perceive the force of His words, but supposed they were spoken of the end of the world. Therefore asked they Him, saying, *Master, but when shall these things be? and what sign, &c.*

AMBROSE; Matthew adds a third question, that both the time of the destruction of the temple, and the sign of His coming, and the end of the world, might be inquired into by the disciples. But our Lord being asked when the destruction of the temple should be, and what the sign of His

coming, instructs them as to the signs, but does not mind to
inform them as to the time. It follows, *Take heed that ye
be not deceived.* ATHAN. For since we have received, Athan.
delivered unto us by God, graces and doctrines which are cont.
above man, (as, for example, the rule of a heavenly life, Arian.
power against evil spirits, the adoption and the knowledge of
the Father and the Word, the gift of the Holy Spirit,) our
adversary the devil goeth about seeking to steal from us the
seed of the word which has been sown. But the Lord, shutting
up in us His teaching as His own precious gift, warns us, lest we
be deceived. And one very great gift He gives us, the word
of God, that not only we be not led away by what appears,
but even if there is ought lying concealed, by the grace of
God we may discern it. For seeing that the devil is the
hateful inventor of evil, what he himself is he conceals,
but craftily assumes a name desirable to all; just as if a man
wishing to get into his power some children not His own,
should in the absence of the parents counterfeit their looks,
and lead away the children who were longing for them. In
every heresy then the devil says in disguise, "I am Christ,
and with me there is truth." And so it follows, *For many
shall come in my name, saying, I am Christ; and the time
draweth near.* CYRIL; For before His descent from heaven,
there shall come some to whom we must not give place.
For the Only-begotten Son of God, when He came to save
the world, wished to be in secret, that He might bear the
cross for us. But His second coming shall not be in secret,
but terrible and open. For He shall descend in the glory of
God the Father, with the Angels attending Him, to judge the
world in righteousness. Therefore He concludes, *Go ye not
therefore after them.* TIT. BOST. Or perhaps He does not
speak of false Christs coming before the end of the world,
but of those who existed in the Apostles' time. BEDE; For
there were many leaders when the destruction of Jerusalem
was at hand, who declared themselves to be Christ, and that
the time of deliverance was drawing nigh. Many heresiarchs
also in the Church have preached that the day of the Lord
is at hand, whom the Apostles condemn. Many Anti- 2 Thess.
christs also came in Christ's name, of whom the first was 2, 2.
Simon Magus, who said, *This man is the great power of God.* Acts 8,
10.

2 x 2

9. But when ye shall hear of wars and commotions, be not terrified: for these things must
first come to pass; but the end is not by and by.

10. Then said he unto them, Nation shall rise
against nation, and kingdom against kingdom:

11. And great earthquakes shall be in divers
places, and famines, and pestilences; and fearful
sights and great signs shall there be from heaven.

Greg. GREG. God denounces the woes that shall forerun the
in Hom.
35. in destruction of the world, that so they may the less disturb
Evang. when they come, as having been foreknown. For darts
strike the less which are foreseen. And so He says, *But
when ye shall hear of wars and commotions, &c.* Wars refer
to the enemy, commotions to citizens. To shew us then
that we shall be troubled from within and without, He asserts
that the one we suffer from the enemy, the other from our own
brethren. AMBROSE; But of the heavenly words none are
greater witnesses than we, upon whom the ends of the world
have come. What wars and what rumours of wars have we
received!

GREG. But that the end will not immediately follow these
evils which come first, it is added, *These things must first
come to pass; but the end is not yet, &c.* For the last
tribulation is preceded by many tribulations, because many
evils must come first, that they may await that evil which has
no end. It follows, *Then said he unto them, Nation shall
rise against nation, &c.* For it must needs be that we
should suffer some things from heaven, some from earth,
some from the elements, and some from men. Here then
are signified the confusions of men. It follows, *And great
earthquakes shall be in divers places.* This relates to the
Chrys. wrath from above. CHRYS. For an earthquake is at one time a
Hom.
11. in sign of wrath, as when our Lord was crucified the earth shook;
Acta. but at another time it is a token of God's providence, as
when the Apostles were praying, the place was moved where
Greg. they were assembled. It follows, *and pestilence.* GREG.
in Hom.
35. Look at the vicissitudes of bodies. *And famine.* Observe
the barrenness of the ground. *And fearful sights and great*

signs there shall be from heaven. Behold the variableness
of the climate, which must be ascribed to those storms which
by no means regard the order of the seasons. For the things
which come in fixed order are not signs. For every thing
that we receive for the use of life we pervert to the service of
sin, but all those things which we have bent to a wicked use,
are turned to the instruments of our punishment. AMBROSE;
The ruin of the world then is preceded by certain of the
world's calamities, such as famine, pestilence, and persecution. THEOPHYL. Now some have wished to place the
fulfilment of these things not only at the future consummation of all things, but at the time also of the taking of
Jerusalem. For when the Author of peace was killed, then
justly arose among the Jews wars and sedition. But from wars
proceed pestilence and famine, the former indeed produced
by the air infected with dead bodies, the latter through the
lands remaining uncultivated. Josephus also relates the
most intolerable distresses to have occurred from famine;
and at the time of Claudius Cæsar there was a severe famine,
as we read in the Acts, and many terrible events happened, Acts 11,
forboding, as Josephus says, the destruction of Jerusalem. 28.

CHRYS. But He says, that the end of the city shall not
come immediately, that is, the taking of Jerusalem, but there
shall be many battles first. BEDE; The Apostles are also
exhorted not to be alarmed by these forerunners, nor to
desert Jerusalem and Judæa. But the kingdom against
kingdom, and the pestilence of those whose word creepeth as
a cancer, and the famine of hearing the word of God, and
the shaking of the whole earth, and the separation from the
true faith, may be explained also in the heretics, who contending one with another bring victory to the Church.
AMBROSE; There are also other wars which the Christian
wages, the struggles of different lusts, and the conflicts of
the will; and domestic foes are far more dangerous than
foreign.

12. But before all these, they shall lay their hands
on you, and persecute you, delivering you up to the
synagogues, and into prisons, being brought before
kings and rulers for my name's sake.

13. And it shall turn to you for a testimony.

14. Settle it therefore in your hearts, not to meditate before what ye shall answer :

15. For I will give you a mouth and wisdom, which all your adversaries shall not be able to gainsay nor resist.

16. And ye shall be betrayed both by parents, and brethren, and kinsfolks, and friends ; and some of you shall they cause to be put to death.

17. And ye shall be hated of all men for my name's sake.

18. But there shall not an hair of your head perish.

19. In your patience possess ye your souls.

Greg. Hom. 35. in Evang. GREG. Because the things which have been prophesied of arise not from the injustice of the inflictor of them, but from the deserts of the world which suffers them, the deeds or wicked men are foretold; as it is said, *But before all these things, they shall lay their hands upon you:* as if He says, First the hearts of men, afterwards the elements, shall be disturbed, that when the order of things is thrown into confusion, it may be plain from what retribution it arises. For although the end of the world depends upon its own appointed course, yet finding some more corrupt than others who shall rightly be overwhelmed in its fall, our Lord makes them known. CYRIL; Or He says this, because before that Jerusalem should be taken by the Romans, the disciples, having suffered persecution from the Jews, were imprisoned and brought before rulers; Paul was sent to Rome to Cæsar, and stood before Festus and Agrippa.

It follows, *And it shall turn to you for a testimony.* In the Greg. ut sup. Greek it is εἰς μαρτύριον, that is, for the glory of martyrdom. GREG. Or, for a testimony, that is, against those who by persecuting you bring death upon themselves, or living do not imitate you, or themselves becoming hardened perish without excuse, from whom the elect take example that they may live. But as hearing so many terrible things the hearts of men may be troubled, He therefore adds for their consolation, *Settle it therefore in your hearts, &c.* THEOPHYL. For because they were foolish and inexperienced, the Lord tells them this, that they might not be confounded when about to give account to the wise. And He adds the cause, *For I will give you a mouth and wisdom, which all your adversaries shall not be able to gainsay or resist.* As if He said, Ye shall forthwith receive of me eloquence and wisdom, so that all your adversaries, were they gathered together in one, shall not be able to resist you, neither in wisdom, that is, the power of the understanding, nor in eloquence, that is, excellence of speech, for many men have often wisdom in their mind, but being easily provoked to their great disturbance, mar the whole when their time of speaking comes. But not such were the Apostles, for in both these gifts they were highly favoured. GREG. As if the Lord said to His disciples, " Be not afraid, go forward to the battle, it is I that fight; you utter the words, I am He that speaketh." AMBROSE; Now in one place Christ speaks in His disciples, as here; in another, the Father; in another the Spirit of the Father speaketh. These do not differ but agree together. In that one speaketh, three speak, for the voice of the Trinity is one.

THEOPHYL. Having in what has gone before dispelled the fear of inexperience, He goes on to warn them of another very certain event, which might agitate their minds, lest falling suddenly upon them, it should dismay them; for it follows, *And ye shall be betrayed both by parents, and brethren, and kinsfolk, and some of you shall they cause to be put to death.* GREG. We are the more galled by the persecutions we suffer from those of whose dispositions we made sure, because together with the bodily pain, we are tormented by the bitter pangs of lost affection. GREG. NYSS. But let us consider the state of things at that time. While all men were suspected, kinsfolk were divided against one another, each differing from the other in religion; the gentile son stood up the betrayer of his believing parents, and of his believing son the unbelieving father became the determined accuser; no age was spared in the persecution of the faith; women were unprotected even by the natural weakness of their sex.

THEOPHYL. To all this He adds the hatred which they
shall meet with from all men. GREG. But because of the
hard things foretold concerning the affliction of death, there
immediately follows a consolation, concerning the joy of the
resurrection, when it is said, *But there shall not an hair
of your head perish.* As though He said to the martyrs,
Why fear ye for the perishing of that which when cut, pains,
when that can not perish in you, which when cut gives no
pain? BEDE; Or else, There shall not perish a hair of the
head of our Lord's Apostles, because not only the noble
deeds and words of the Saints, but even the slightest thought
shall meet with its deserving reward.

GREG. He who preserves patience in adversity, is thereby
rendered proof against all affliction, and so by conquering
himself, he gains the government of himself; as it follows, *In
your patience shall ye possess your souls.* For what is it to
possess your souls, but to live perfectly in all things, and
sitting as it were upon the citadel of virtue to hold in subjection every motion of the mind? GREG. By patience then
we possess our souls, because when we are said to govern
ourselves, we begin to possess that very thing which we are.
But for this reason, the possession of the soul is laid in the
virtue of patience, because patience is the root and guardian
of all virtues. Now patience is to endure calmly the evils
which are inflicted by others, and also to have no feeling of
indignation against him who inflicts them.

Marginal notes: Greg. ut sup. / Greg. Mor. 5. c. 16. / Greg. Hom. 35. in Ev.

20. And when ye shall see Jerusalem compassed
with armies, then know that the desolation thereof is
nigh.

21. Then let them which are in Judæa flee to the
mountains; and let them which are in the midst of it
depart out; and let not them that are in the countries
enter thereinto.

22. For these be the days of vengeance, that all
things which are written may be fulfilled.

23. But woe unto them that are with child, and to
them that give suck, in those days! for there shall be
great distress in the land, and wrath upon this people.

24. And they shall fall by the edge of the sword, and shall be led away captive into all nations: and Jerusalem shall be trodden down of the Gentiles, until the times of the Gentiles be fulfilled.

BEDE; Hitherto our Lord had been speaking of those things which were to come to pass for forty years, the end not yet coming. He now describes the very end itself of the desolation, which was accomplished by the Roman army; as it is said, *And when ye shall see Jerusalem compassed, &c.* EUSEB. By the desolation of Jerusalem, He means that it was never again to be set up, or its legal rites to be reestablished, so that no one should expect, after the coming siege and desolation, any restoration to take place, as there was in the time of the Persian king, Antiochus the Great, and Pompey. AUG. Aug. ad Hesych. Ep. 199. These words of our Lord, Luke has here related to shew, that the abomination of desolation which was prophesied by Daniel, and of which Matthew and Mark had spoken, was Mat. 24. fulfilled at the siege of Jerusalem. AMBROSE; For the Jews Mark 13. thought that the abomination of desolation took place when the Romans, in mockery of a Jewish observance, cast a pig's head into the temple. EUSEB. Now our Lord, foreseeing that there would be a famine in the city, warned His disciples in the siege that was coming, not to betake themselves to the city as a place of refuge, and under God's protection, but rather to depart from thence, and flee to the mountains. BEDE; The ecclesiastical history relates, that all the Christians who were in Ecc. Hist. lib. iii. Judæa, when the destruction of Jerusalem was approaching, being warned of the Lord, departed from that place, and c. 5. dwelt beyond the Jordan in a city called Pella, until the desolation of Judæa was ended.

AUG. And before this, Matthew and Mark said, *And let* Aug. ut sup. *him that is on the housetop not come down into his house;* and Mark added, *neither enter therein to take any thing out of his house;* in place of which Luke subjoins, *And let them which are in the midst of it depart out.*

BEDE; But how, while the city was already compassed with an army, were they to depart out? except that the preceding word " then" is to be referred, not to the actual time of the siege, but the period just before, when first the armed soldiers began to disperse themselves through the parts of Galilee and Samaria.

Aug. uti sup. AUG. But where Matthew and Mark have written, *Neither let him which is in the field return back to take his clothes*, Luke adds more clearly, *And let not them that are in the countries enter thereinto, for these be the days of vengeance, that all the things which are written may be fulfilled.* BEDE; And these are the days of vengeance, that is, the days exacting vengeance for our Lord's blood. AUG. Then Luke follows Aug. ubi sup. in words similar to those of the other two; *But woe to them that are with child, and them that give suck in those days;* and thus has made plain what might otherwise have been doubtful, namely, that what was said of the abomination of desolation belonged not to the end of the world, but the taking of Jerusalem. BEDE; He says then, *Woe to them that nurse*, or *give suck*, as some interpret it, whose womb or arms now heavy with the burden of children, cause no slight obstacle to the speed of flight. THEOPHYL. But some say that the Lord hereby signified the devouring of children, which Josephus also relates.

Chrys. adv. oppug. mon. vit. CHRYS. He next assigns the cause of what he had just now said, *For there shall be great distress in the land, and wrath upon this people.* For the miseries that took hold of them were such as, in the words of Josephus, no calamity can henceforth compare to them. EUSEB. For so in truth it was, that when the Romans came and were taking the city, many multitudes of the Jewish people perished in the mouth of the sword; as it follows, *And they shall fall by the edge of the sword.* But still more were cut off by famine. And these things happened at first indeed under Titus and Vespasian, but after them in the time of Hadrian the Roman general, when the land of their birth was forbidden to the Jews. Hence it follows, *And they shall be led away captive into all nations.* For the Jews filled the whole land, reaching even to the ends of the earth, and when their land was inhabited by strangers, they alone could not enter it; as it follows, *And Jerusalem shall be trodden down of the Gentiles, until the times of the Gentiles be fulfilled.* BEDE; Which indeed Rom. 11, 25. the Apostle makes mention of when he says, *Blindness in*

part is happened to Israel, and so all Israel shall be saved.
Which when it shall have gained the promised salvation,
hopes not rashly to return to the land of its fathers. AM-
BROSE; Now mystically, the abomination of desolation is the
coming of Antichrist, for with ill-omened sacrilege he pollutes
the innermost recesses of the heart, sitting as it is literally in
the temple, that he may claim to himself the throne of divine
power. But according to the spiritual meaning, he is well
brought in, because he desires to impress firmly on the affections the footstep of his unbelief, disputing from the Scriptures
that he is Christ. Then shall come desolation, for very many
falling away shall depart from the true religion. Then shall
be the day of the Lord, since as His first coming was to redeem sin, so also His second shall be to subdue iniquity, lest
more should be carried away by the error of unbelief. There
is also another Antichrist, that is, the Devil, who is trying to
besiege Jerusalem, i. e. the peaceful soul, with the hosts of his
law. When then the Devil is in the midst of the temple,
there is the desolation of abomination. But when upon any
one in trouble the spiritual presence of Christ has shone,
the unjust one is cast out, and righteousness begins her reign.
There is also a third Antichrist, as Arius and Sabellius and
all who with evil purpose lead us astray. But these are they
who are with child, to whom woe is denounced, who enlarge
the size of their flesh, and the step of whose inmost soul
waxes slow, as those who are worn out in virtue, pregnant
with vice. But neither do those with child escape condemnation, who though firm in the resolution of good acts, have
not yet yielded any fruits of the work undertaken. These are
those which conceive from fear of God, but do not all bring
forth. For there are some which thrust forth the word abor-
tive before their delivery. There are others too which have
Christ in the womb, but have not yet formed Him. Therefore she who brings forth righteousness, brings forth Christ.
Let us also hasten to nourish our children, lest the day of
judgment or death find us as it were the parents of an imperfect offspring. And this you will do if you keep all the words
of righteousness in your heart, and wait not the time of old
age, but in your earliest years, without corruption of your
body, quickly conceive wisdom, quickly nourish it. But at

the end shall all Judæa be made subject to the nations which
Rev. 1, 16; 19, 15. shall believe, by the mouth of the spiritual sword, which is
the two-edged word.

25. And there shall be signs in the sun, and in
the moon, and in the stars ; and upon the earth distress of nations, with perplexity ; the sea and the
waves roaring ;

26. Men's hearts failing them for fear, and for
looking after those things which are coming on
the earth : for the powers of heaven shall be shaken.

27. And then shall they see the Son of man coming
in a cloud with power and great glory.

BEDE; The events which were to follow the fulfilment of
the times of the Gentiles He explains in regular order, saying,
There shall be signs in the sun, and in the moon, and in the stars.
AMBROSE; All which signs are more clearly described in Matthew, *Then shall the sun be darkened, and the moon shall
not give her light, and the stars shall fall from heaven.*
EUSEB. For at that time when the end of this perishing life
1 Cor. 7, 13. shall be accomplished, and, as the Apostle says, *The fashion
of this world passeth away*, then shall succeed a new world,
in which instead of sensible light, Christ Himself shall shine
as a sunbeam, and as the King of the new world, and so
mighty and glorious will be His light, that the sun which
now dazzles so brightly, and the moon and all the stars, shall
be hidden by the coming of a far greater light. CHRYS. For
as in this world the moon and the stars are soon dimmed by
the rising of the sun, so at the glorious appearance of Christ
shall the sun become dark, and the moon not shed her ray,
and the stars shall fall from heaven, stripped of their former
attire, that they may put on the robe of a better light. EUSEB.
What things shall befall the world after the darkening of
the orbs of light, and whence shall arise the straitening of
nations, He next explains as follows, *And on the earth distress
of nations, by reason of the confusion of the roaring of the*

sea. Wherein He seems to teach, that the beginning of the
universal change will be owing to the failing of the watery
substance. For this being first absorbed or congealed, so
that no longer is heard the roaring of the sea, nor do the waves
reach the shore because of the exceeding drought, the other
parts of the world, ceasing to obtain the usual vapour which
came forth from the watery matter, shall undergo a revolution.
Accordingly since the appearance of Christ must put down
the prodigies which resist God, namely, those of Antichrist,
the beginnings of wrath shall take their rise from droughts,
such as that neither storm nor roaring of the sea be any more
heard. And this event shall be succeeded by the distress of
the men who survive; as it follows, *Men's hearts being dried
up for fear, and looking after those things which shall come
upon the whole world.* But the things that shall then come
upon the world He proceeds to declare, adding, *For the
powers of heaven shall be shaken.*

THEOPHYL. Or else, When the higher world shall be
changed, then also the lower elements shall suffer loss;
whence it follows, *And on the earth distress of nations, &c.*
As if He said, the sea shall roar terribly, and its shores shall
be shaken with the tempest, so that of the people and nations
of the earth there shall be distress, that is, a universal misery,
so that they shall pine away from fear and expectation of
the evils which are coming upon the world.

AUG. But you will say, your punishment compels you to Aug.
confess that the end is now approaching, seeing the fulfil- ad Hes.
Ep. 199.
ment of that which was foretold. For it is certain there is no
country, no place in our time, which is not affected or
troubled. But if those evils which mankind now suffer are
sure signs that our Lord is now about to come, what meaneth
that which the Apostle says, *For when they shall say peace* 1 Thess.
and safety. Let us see then if it be not perhaps better to 5, 3.
understand the words of prophecy to be not so fulfilled, but
rather that they will come to pass when the tribulation of the
whole world shall be such that it shall belong to the Church,
which shall be troubled by the whole world, not to those who
shall trouble it. For they are those who shall say, *Peace and
safety.* But now these evils which are counted the greatest
and most immoderate, we see to be common to both the king-

doms of Christ and the Devil. For the good and the evil are alike afflicted with them, and among these great evils is the yet universal resort to licentious feasts. Is not this the being dried up from fear, or rather the being burnt up from lust?

THEOPHYL. But not only shall men be tossed about when the world shall be changed, but angels even shall stand amazed at the terrible revolutions of the universe. Hence it follows, *And the powers of heaven shall be shaken.* GREG. For whom does He call the powers of heaven, but the angels, dominions, principalities, and powers? which at the coming of the strict Judge shall then appear visibly to our eyes, that they may strictly exact judgment of us, seeing that now our invisible Creator patiently bears with us. EUSEB. When also the Son of God shall come in glory, and shall crush the proud empire of the son of sin, the angels of heaven attending Him, the doors of heaven which have been shut from the foundation of the world shall be opened, that the things that are on high may be witnessed. CHRYS. Or the heavenly powers shall be shaken, although themselves know it not. For when they see the innumerable multitudes condemned, they shall not stand there without trembling. BEDE; Thus it is said in Job, *the pillars of heaven tremble and are afraid at his reproof.* What then do the boards do, when the pillars tremble? what does the shrub of the desert suffer, when the cedar of Paradise is shaken? EUSEB. Or the powers of heaven are those which preside over the sensible parts of the universe, which indeed shall then be shaken that they may attain to a better state. For they shall be discharged from the ministry with which they serve God toward the sensible bodies in their perishing condition. AUG. But that the Lord may not seem to have foretold as extraordinary those things concerning His second coming, which were wont to happen to this world even before His first coming, and that we may not be laughed at by those who have read more and greater events than these in the history of nations, I think what has been said may be better understood to apply to the Church. For the Church is the sun, the moon, and the stars, to whom it was said, *Fair as the moon, elect as the sun.* And she will then not be seen for the unbounded rage of the

Greg. Hom. 1. in Ev.

Chrys. ad Olymp. Ep. 2.

Job 26, 11.

Aug. ad Hes. ut sup.

Cant. 6, 10.

persecutors. AMBROSE; While many also fall away from religion, clear faith will be obscured by the cloud of unbelief, for to me that Sun of righteousness is either diminished or increased according to my faith; and as the moon in its monthly wanings, or when it is opposite the sun by the interposition of the earth, suffers eclipse, so also the holy Church when the sins of the flesh oppose the heavenly light, cannot borrow the brightness of divine light from Christ's rays. For in persecutions, the love of this world generally shuts out the light of the divine Sun; the stars also fall, that is, men who shine in glory fall when the bitterness of persecution waxes sharp and prevails. And this must be until the multitude of the Church be gathered in, for thus are the good tried and the weak made manifest. AUG. But in the words, Aug. *And upon the earth distress of nations*, He would understand ut sup. by *nations*, not those which shall be blessed in the seed of Abraham, but those which shall stand on the left hand.

AMBROSE; So severe then will be the manifold fires of our souls, that with consciences depraved through the multitude of crimes, by reason of our fear of the coming judgment, the dew of the sacred fountain will be dried upon us. But as the Lord's coming is looked for, in order that His presence may dwell in the whole circle of mankind or the world, which now dwells in each individual who has embraced Christ with his whole heart, so the powers of heaven shall at our Lord's coming obtain an increase of grace, and shall be moved by the fulness of the Divine nature more closely infusing itself. There are also heavenly powers which proclaim the glory of God, which shall be stirred by a fuller infusion of Christ, that they may see Christ. AUG. Or the powers of Aug. heaven shall be stirred, because when the ungodly persecute, ut sup. some of the most stout-hearted believers shall be troubled.

THEOPHYL. It follows, *And then shall they see the Son of* Theoph. *man coming in the clouds*. Both the believers and unbe- ut sup. lievers shall see Him, for He Himself as well as His cross shall glisten brighter than the sun, and so shall be observed of all. AUG. But the words, *coming in the clouds*, may be Aug. taken in two ways. Either coming in His Church as it were ut sup. in a cloud, as He now ceases not to come. But then it shall be with great power and majesty, for far greater will His power and might appear to His saints, to whom He will give great virtue, that they may not be overcome in such a fearful persecution.   Or in His body in which He sits at His Father's right hand He must rightly be supposed to come, and not only in His body, but also in a cloud, for He will come even as He went away, *And a cloud received him out of their sight.*   CHRYS. For God ever appears in a cloud, according to the Psalms, *clouds and darkness are round about him.* Therefore shall the Son of man come in the clouds as God, and the Lord, not secretly, but in glory worthy of God.   Therefore He adds, *with great power and majesty.*   CYRIL; *Great* must be understood in like manner.   For His first appearance He made in our weakness and lowliness, the second He shall celebrate in all His own power.   GREG. For in power and majesty will men see Him, whom in lowly stations they refused to hear, that so much the more acutely they may feel His power, as they are now the less willing to bow the necks of their hearts to His sufferings.

Ps. 17, 11.

Greg. ut sup.

28. And when these things begin to come to pass, then look up, and lift up your heads; for your redemption draweth nigh.

29. And he spake to them a parable; Behold the fig tree, and all the trees;

30. When they now shoot forth, ye see and know of your own selves that summer is now nigh at hand.

31. So likewise ye, when ye see these things come to pass, know ye that the kingdom of God is nigh at hand.

32. Verily I say unto you, This generation shall not pass away, till all be fulfilled.

33. Heaven and earth shall pass away: but my words shall not pass away.

Greg. Hom. 1. in Ev.

GREG. Having in what has gone before spoken against the reprobate, He now turns His words to the consolation of the elect; for it is added, *When these things begin to be, look up, and lift up your heads, for your redemption draweth*

nigh; as if he says, When the buffettings of the world multiply, lift up your heads, that is, rejoice your hearts, for when
the world closes whose friends ye are not, the redemption is
near which ye seek.   For in holy Scripture the head is often
put for the mind, for as the members are ruled by the head,
so are the thoughts regulated by the mind.   To lift up our
heads then, is to raise up our minds to the joys of the heavenly country.   EUSEB. Or else, To those that have passed
through the body and bodily things, shall be present spiritual and heavenly bodies : that is, they will have no more to
pass the kingdom of the world, and then to those that are
worthy shall be given the promises of salvation.   For having
received the promises of God which we look for, we who
before were crooked shall be made upright, and we shall lift up
our heads who were before bent low ; because the redemption
which we hoped for is at hand ; that namely for which the
whole creation waiteth.   THEOPHYL. That is, perfect liberty
of body and soul.   For as the first coming of our Lord was
for the restoration of our souls, so will the second be manifested unto the restoration of our bodies.

EUSEB. He speaks these things to His disciples, not as to
those who would continue in this life to the end of the world,
but as if uniting in one body of believers in Christ both
themselves and us and our posterity, even to the end of the
world.   .

GREG. That the world ought to be trampled upon and
despised, He proves by a wise comparison, adding, *Behold*
the fig tree and all the trees, when they now put forth fruit,
ye know that summer is near.   As if He says, As from the
fruit of the tree the summer is perceived to be near, so from
the fall of the world the kingdom of God is known to be at
hand.   Hereby is it manifested that the world's fall is our fruit.
For hereunto it puts forth buds, that whomsoever it has fos-
tered in the bud it may consume in slaughter.   But well is
the kingdom of God compared to summer ; for then the
clouds of our sorrow flee away, and the days of life brighten
up under the clear light of the Eternal Sun.   AMBROSE ; Matthew speaks of the fig-tree only, Luke of all the trees.   But
the fig-tree shadows forth two things, either the ripening of
what is hard, or the luxuriance of sin ; that is, either that, when

Greg.
ut sup.

the fruit bursts forth in all trees and the fruitful fig-tree abounds, (that is, when every tongue confesses God, even the Jewish people confessing Him,) we ought to hope for our Lord's coming, in which shall be gathered in as at summer the fruits of the resurrection. Or, when the man of sin shall clothe himself in his light and fickle boasting as it were the leaves of the synagogue, we must then suppose the judgment to be drawing near. For the Lord hastens to reward faith, and to bring an end of sinning.

Aug.
ut sup.

AUG. But when He says, *When ye shall see these things to come to pass*, what can we understand but those things which were mentioned above. But among them we read, *And then shall they see the Son of man coming.* When therefore this is seen, the kingdom of God is not yet, but nigh at hand. Or must we say that we are not to understand all the things before mentioned, when He says, *When ye shall see these things, &c.* but only some of them; this for example being excepted, *And then shall they see the Son of man.* But Matthew would plainly have it taken with no exception, for he says, *And so ye, when ye see all these things,* among which is the seeing the coming of the Son of man; in order that it may be understood of that coming whereby He now comes in His members as in clouds, or in the Church as in a great cloud. TIT. BOST. Or else, He says, *the kingdom of God is at hand*, meaning that when these things shall be, not yet shall all things come to their last end, but they shall be already tending towards it. For the very coming of our Lord itself, casting out every principality and power, is the preparation for the kingdom of God. EUSEB. For as in this life, when winter dies away, and spring succeeds, the sun sending forth its warm rays cherishes and quickens the seeds hid in the ground, just laying aside their first form, and the young plants sprout forth, having put on different shades of green; so also the glorious coming of the Only-begotten of God, illuminating the new world with His quickening rays, shall bring forth into light from more excellent bodies than before the seeds that have long been hidden in the whole world, i. e. those who sleep in the dust of the earth. And having vanquished death, He shall reign from henceforth the life of the new world.

GREG. But all the things before mentioned are confirmed with great certainty, when He adds, *Verily I say unto you, &c.* BEDE; He strongly commends that which he thus foretels. And, if one may so speak, his oath is this, *Amen, I say unto you.* Amen is by interpretation " true." Therefore the truth says, *I tell you the truth,* and though He spoke not thus, He could by no means lie. But by generation he means either the whole human race, or especially the Jews. EUSEB. Or by generation He means the new generation of His holy Church, shewing that the generation of the faithful would last up to that time, when it would see all things, and embrace with its eyes the fulfilment of our Saviour's words. THEOPHYL. For because He had foretold that there should be commotions, and wars, and changes, both of the elements and in other things, lest any one might suspect that Christianity itself also would perish, He adds, *Heaven and earth shall pass away, but my words shall not pass away:* as if He said, *Though all things should be shaken, yet shall my faith fail not.* Whereby He implies that He sets the Church before the whole creation. The creation shall suffer change, but the Church of the faithful and the words of the Gospel shall abide for ever. GREG. Or else, *The heaven and earth* *shall pass away, &c.* As if He says, All that with us seems lasting, does not abide to eternity without change, and all that with Me seems to pass away is held fixed and immoveable, for My word which passeth away utters sentences which remain unchangeable, and abide for ever.

BEDE; But by the heaven which shall pass away we must understand not the æthereal or the starry heaven, but the air from which the birds are named " of heaven." But if the earth shall pass away, how does Ecclesiastes say, *The earth standeth* *for ever?* Plainly then the heaven and earth in the fashion which they now have shall pass away, but in essence subsist eternally.

34. And take heed to yourselves, lest at any time your hearts be overcharged with surfeiting, and drunkenness, and cares of this life, and so that day come upon you unawares.

35. For as a snare shall it come on all them that dwell on the face of the whole earth.

36. Watch ye therefore, and pray always, that ye may be accounted worthy to escape all these things that shall come to pass, and to stand before the Son of man.

THEOPHYL. Our Lord declared above the fearful and sensible signs of the evils which should overtake sinners, against which the only remedy is watching and prayer, as it is said, *And take heed to yourselves, lest at any time, &c.*

Basil. BASIL; Every animal has within itself certain instincts which Hom. 1. it has received from God, for the preservation of its own in illud Attende being. Wherefore Christ has also given us this warning, that tibi. what comes to them by nature, may be ours by the aid of reason and prudence: that we may flee from sin as the brute creatures shun deadly food, but that we seek after righteousness, as they wholesome herbs. Therefore saith He, *Take heed to yourselves*, that is, that you may distinguish the noxious from the wholesome. But since there are two ways of taking heed to ourselves, the one with the bodily eyes, the other by the faculties of the soul, and the bodily eye does not reach to virtue; it remains that we speak of the operations of the soul. *Take heed*, that is, Look around you on all sides, keeping an ever watchful eye to the guardianship of your soul. He says not, Take heed to your own or to the things around, but *to yourselves*. For ye are mind and spirit, your body is only of sense. Around you are riches, arts, and all the appendages of life, you must not mind these, but your soul, of which you must take especial care. The same admonition tends both to the healing of the sick, and the perfecting of those that are well, namely, such as are the guardians of the present, the providers of the future, not judging the actions of others, but strictly searching their own, not suffering the mind to be the slave of their passions, but subduing the irrational part of the soul to the rational. But the reason why we should take heed He adds as follows, *Lest at any time your hearts be overcharged, &c.* TIT. BOST. As if He says, Beware lest the eyes of your mind wax heavy. For the cares of this life, and surfeiting, and drunkenness, scare away prudence, shatter and make shipwreck of faith.

CLEM. ALEX. Drunkenness is an excessive use of wine; crapula [1] is the uneasiness, and nausea attendant on drunkenness, a Greek word so called from the motion of the head. And a little below. As then we must partake of food lest we suffer hunger, so also of drink lest we thirst, but with still greater care to avoid falling into excess. For the indulgence of wine is deceitful, and the soul when free from wine will be the wisest and best, but steeped in the fumes of wine is lost as in a cloud. BASIL; But carefulness, or the care of this life, although it seems to have nothing unlawful in it, nevertheless if it conduce not to religion, must be avoided. And the reason why He said this He shews by what comes next, *And so that day come upon you unawares.* THEOPHYL. For that day will not come when men are expecting it, but unlooked for and by stealth, taking as a snare those who are unwary. *For as a snare shall it come upon all them that sit upon the face of the earth.* But this we may diligently keep far from us. For that day will take those that sit on the face of the earth, as the unthinking and slothful. But as many as are prompt and active in the way of good, not sitting and loitering on the ground, but rising from it, saying to themselves, Rise up, begone, for here there is no rest for thee. To such that day is not as a perilous snare, but a day of rejoicing.

EUSEB. He taught them therefore to take heed unto the things we have just before mentioned, lest they fall into the indolence resulting therefrom. Hence it follows, *Watch ye therefore, and pray always, that ye may be accounted worthy to escape all those things that shall come to pass.* THEOPHYL. Namely, hunger, pestilence, and such like, which for a time only threaten the elect and others, and those things also which are hereafter the lot of the guilty for ever. For these we can in no wise escape, save by watching and prayer.

AUG. This is supposed to be that flight which Matthew mentions; which must not be in the winter or on the sabbath day. To the winter belong the cares of this life, which are mournful as the winter, but to the sabbath surfeiting and

Clem. Al.
lib. ii.
Pædag.
c. 2.
[1] κραι-
παλη

Basil.
in Reg.
Brev. ad
int. 88.

Aug. de
Con.Ev.
l. ii. c.
77.

drunkenness, which drowns and buries the heart in carnal luxury and delight, since on that day the Jews are immersed in worldly pleasure, while they are lost to a spiritual sabbath. THEOPHYL. And because a Christian needs not only to flee evil, but to strive to obtain glory, He adds, *And to stand before the Son of man.* For this is the glory of angels, to stand before the Son of man, our God, and always to behold His face. BEDE; Now supposing a physician should bid us beware of the juice of a certain herb, lest a sudden death overtake us, we should most earnestly attend to his command; but when our Saviour warns us to shun drunkenness and surfeiting, and the cares of this world, men have no fear of being wounded and destroyed by them; for the faith which they put in the caution of the physician, they disdain to give to the words of God.

37. And in the day time he was teaching in the temple; and at night he went out, and abode in the mount that is called the mount of Olives.

38. And all the people came early in the morning to him in the temple, for to hear him.

BEDE; What our Lord commanded in word, He confirms by His example. For He who bid us watch and pray before the coming of the Judge, and the uncertain end of each of us, as the time of His Passion drew near, is Himself instant in teaching, watching, and prayer. As it is said, *And in the day time he was teaching in the temple*, whereby He conveys by His own example, that it is a thing worthy of God, to watch, or by word and deed to point out the way of truth to our neighbour. CYRIL; But what were the things He taught, unless such as transcended the worship of the law? THEOPHYL. Now the Evangelists are silent as to the greater part of Christ's teaching; for whereas He preached for the space nearly of three years, all the teaching which they have written down would scarcely, one might say, suffice for the discourse of a single day. For out of a great many things extracting a few, they have given only a taste as it were of the sweetness of His teaching. But our Lord here instructs us, that we ought to address God at night and in silence, but in day time to be doing good to men; and to gather indeed at night, but in the day distribute what we have gathered. As it is added, *And at night he went out and abode in the mount that is called Olivet.* Not that He had need of prayer, but He did this for our example.

CYRIL; But because His speech was with power, and with authority He applied to spiritual worship the things which had been delivered in figures by Moses and the Prophets, the people heard Him gladly. As it follows, *And the whole people made haste to come early to hear him in the temple.* But the people who came to Him before light might with fitness say, *O God my God, early do I wait upon thee.*

BEDE; Now mystically, we also when amid our prosperity we behave ourselves soberly, piously, and honestly, teach by day time in the temple, for we hold up to the faithful the model of a good work; but at night we abide on mount Olivet, when in the darkness of anguish we are refreshed with spiritual consolation; and to us also the people come early in the morning, when either having shaken off the works of darkness, or scattered all the clouds of sorrow, they follow our example.

1. Now the feast of unleavened bread drew nigh, which is called the Passover.

2. And the Chief Priests and Scribes sought how they might kill him ; for they feared the people.

CHRYS. The actions of the Jews were a shadow of our own. Accordingly if you ask of a Jew concerning the Passover, and the feast of unleavened bread, he will tell you nothing momentous, mentioning the deliverance from Egypt; whereas should a man inquire of me he would not hear of Egypt or Pharaoh, but of freedom from sin and the darkness of Satan, not by Moses, but by the Son of God; GLOSS. Whose Passion the Evangelist being about to relate, introduces the figure of it, saying, *Now the feast of unleavened bread drew nigh, which is called the Passover.* BEDE; Now the Passover, which is called in Hebrew " Phase," is not so named from the Passion, but from the passing over, because the destroying angel, seeing the blood on the doors of the Israelites, passed over them, and touched not their first-born. Or the Lord Himself, giving assistance to His people, walked over them. But herein is the difference between the Passover and the feast of unleavened bread, that by the Passover is meant that day alone on which the lamb was slain towards the evening, that is, on the fourteenth day of the first month, but on the fifteenth, when the Israelites went out of Egypt, followed the feast of unleavened bread for seven days, up to the twenty-first of the same month. Hence the writers of the Gospel substitute one indifferently for the other. As here it is said, *The day of unleavened bread, which is called the Passover.* But it is signified by a mystery, that Christ having suffered once for us, has commanded us through

*Gloss.
non occ.*

the whole time of this world which is passed in seven days, to live in the unleavened bread of sincerity and truth. CHRYS. The Chief Priests set about their impious deed on the feast, as it follows, *And the Chief Priests and Scribes, &c.* Moses ordained only one Priest, at whose death another was to be appointed. But at that time, when the Jewish customs had begun to fall away, there were many made every year. These then wishing to kill Jesus, are not afraid of God, lest in truth the holy time should aggravate the pollution of their sin, but every where fear man. Hence it follows, *For they feared the people.* BEDE; Not indeed that they apprehended sedition, but were afraid lest by the interference of the people He should be taken out of their hands. And these things Matthew reports to have taken place two days before the Passover, when they were assembled in the judgment hall of Caiaphas.

Chrys. Hom. 79. in Matt.

3. Then entered Satan into Judas surnamed Iscariot, being of the number of the twelve.

4. And he went his way, and communed with the Chief Priests and captains, how he might betray him unto them.

5. And they were glad, and covenanted to give him money.

6. And he promised, and sought opportunity to betray him unto them in the absence of the multitude.

THEOPHYL. Having already said that the Chief Priests sought means how they might slay Jesus without incurring any danger, he next goes on to relate the means which occurred to them, as it is said, *Then entered Satan into Judas.* TIT. BOST. Satan entered into Judas not by force, but finding the door open. For forgetful of all that he had seen, Judas now turned his thoughts solely to covetousness. CHRYS. St. Luke gives his surname, because there was another Judas. TIT. BOST. And he adds, *one of the twelve,* since he made up the number, though he did not truly discharge the Apostolic office. Or the Evangelist adds this, as it were for

Chrys. Hom. 80. in Matt.

contrast sake. As if he said, " He was of the first band of those who were especially chosen."

BEDE; There is nothing contrary to this in what John says, that after the sop Satan entered into Judas; seeing he now entered into him as a stranger, but then as his own, whom *Chrys. ut sup.* he might lead after him to do whatsoever he willed. CHRYS. Observe the exceeding iniquity of Judas, that he both sets out by himself, and that he does this for gain. It follows, *And he went his way, and communed with the chief priests and captains.* THEOPHYL. The magistrates here mentioned were those appointed to take care of the buildings of the temple, or it may be those whom the Romans had set over the people to keep them from breaking forth into tumult; *Chrys. ut sup.* for they were seditious. CHRYS. By covetousness then Judas became what he was, for it follows, *And they covenanted to give him money.* Such are the evil passions which covetousness engenders, it makes men irreligious, and compels them to lose all knowledge of God, though they have received a thousand benefits from Him, nay, even to injure Him, as it follows, *And he contracted with them.* THEOPHYL. That is, he bargained and promised. *And sought opportunity to betray him unto them,* without the crowds, that is, when he saw Him standing by Himself apart, in the absence of the multitude. BEDE; Now many shudder at the wickedness of Judas, yet do not guard against it. For whosoever despises the laws of truth and love, betrays Christ who is truth and love. Above all, when he sins not from infirmity or ignorance, but after the likeness of Judas seeks opportunity, when no one is present, to change truth for a lie, virtue for crime.

7. Then came the day of unleavened bread, when the Passover must be killed.

8. And he sent Peter and John, saying, Go and prepare us the Passover, that we may eat.

9. And they said unto him, Where wilt thou that we prepare?

10. And he said unto them, Behold, when ye are entered into the city, there shall a man meet you,

bearing a pitcher of water; follow him into the house where he entereth in.

11. And ye shall say unto the goodman of the house, The Master saith unto thee, Where is the guestchamber, where I shall eat the Passover with my disciples?

12. And he shall shew you a large upper room furnished : there make ready.

13. And they went, and found as he had said unto them : and they made ready the Passover.

TIT. BOST. Our Lord, in order to leave us a heavenly Passover, ate a typical one, removing the figure, that the truth might take its place. BEDE; By the day of unleavened bread of the Passover, He means the fourteenth day of the first month, the day on which, having put away the leaven, they were accustomed to hold the Passover, that is, the lamb, towards evening. EUSEB. But should any one say, " If on the first day of unleavened bread the disciples of our Saviour prepare the Passover, on that day then should we also celebrate the Passover;" we answer, that this was not an admonition, but a history of the fact. It is what took place at the time of the saving Passion ; but it is one thing to relate past events, another to sanction and leave them an ordinance to posterity. Moreover, the Saviour did not keep His Passover with the Jews at the time that they sacrificed the lamb. For they did this on the Preparation, when our Lord suffered. Therefore they entered not into the hall of Pilate, that they might John18, not be defiled, but might eat the Passover. For from the 28. time that they conspired against the truth, they drove far from them the Word of truth. Nor on the first day of unleavened bread, on which the Passover ought to be sacrificed, did they eat their accustomed Passover, for they were intent upon something else, but on the day after, which was the second of unleavened bread. But our Lord on the first day of unleavened bread, that is, on the fifth day of the week, kept the Passover with His disciples.

THEOPHYL. Now on the same fifth day He sends two of

His disciples to prepare the Passover, namely, Peter and John, the one in truth as loving, the other as loved. In all things shewing, that even to the end of His life He opposed not the law. And He sends them to a strange house; for He and His disciples had no house, else would He have kept the Passover in one of them. So it is added, *And they said, Where wilt thou that we prepare?* BEDE; As if to say, We have no abode, we have no place of shelter. Let those hear this, who busy themselves in building houses. Let them know that Christ, the Lord of all places, had not where to lay His head. CHRYS. But as they knew not to whom they were sent, He gave them a sign, as Samuel to Saul, as it follows, *And he said unto them, Behold, when ye are entered into the city, there shall a man meet you bearing a pitcher of water; follow him into the house where he entereth in.*

Chrys.
Hom.
81. in
Matt.
1 Sam.
10, 3.

AMBROSE; First observe the greatness of His divine power. He is talking with His disciples, yet knows what will happen in another place. Next behold His condescension, in that He chooses not the person of the rich or powerful, but seeks after the poor, and prefers a mean inn to the spacious palaces of nobles. Now the Lord was not ignorant of the name of the man whose mystery He knew, and that he would meet the disciples, but he is mentioned without a name, that he may be counted as ignoble. THEOPHYL. He sends them for this reason to an unknown man: to shew them that He voluntarily underwent His Passion, since He who so swayed the mind of one unknown to Him, that He should receive them, was able to deal with the Jews just as He wished. But some say that He gave not the name of the man, lest the traitor knowing his name might open the house to the Pharisees, and they should have come and taken Him before that the supper was eaten, and He had delivered the spiritual mysteries to His disciples. But He directs them by particular signs to a certain house; whence it follows, *And ye shall say to the goodman of the house, The Master saith, Where is the guestchamber, &c. And he will shew you an upper room, &c.* GLOSS. And perceiving these signs, the disciples zealously fulfilled all that had been commanded them; as it follows, *And they went, and found as he had said unto them, and made ready the Passover.* BEDE; To explain this Passover, the Apostle says, *Christ our*

Gloss.
non occ.

1 Cor. 5,
7.

Passover is sacrificed for us. Which Passover in truth must needs have been slain there, as it was so ordained by the Father's counsel and determination. And thus although on the next day, that is, the fifteenth, He was crucified, yet, on this night on which the lamb was slain by the Jews, being seized and bound, He consecrated the beginning of His sacrifice, that is, of His Passion.

THEOPHYL. By the day of unleavened bread, we must understand that conversation which is wholly in the light of the Spirit, having lost all trace of the old corruption of Adam's first transgression. And living in this conversation, it becomes us to rejoice in the mysteries of Christ. Now these mysteries Peter and John prepare, that is, action and contemplation, fervid zeal and peaceful meekness. And these preparers a certain man meets, because in what we have just mentioned, lies the condition of man who was created after the image of God. And he carries a pitcher of water, which signifies the grace of the Holy Spirit. But the pitcher is humbleness of heart; for He giveth grace to the humble, who know themselves to be but earth and dust. AMBROSE; Or the pitcher is a more perfect measure, but the water is that which was thought meet to be a sacrament of Christ; to wash, not to be washed.

BEDE; They prepare the Passover in that house, whither the pitcher of water is carried, for the time is at hand in which to the keepers of the true Passover, the typical blood is taken away from the lintel, and the baptism of the lifegiving fountain is consecrated to take away sin. ORIGEN; But I think Orig. that the man who meets the disciples as they enter into the city, in Matt. carrying a pitcher of water, was some servant of a master of 26. 18. a house, carrying water in an earthen vessel either for washing or for drinking. And this I think is Moses conveying the spiritual doctrine in fleshly histories. But they who follow him not, do not celebrate the Passover with Jesus. Let us then ascend with the Lord united to us, to the upper part in which is the guestchamber, which is shewn by the understanding, that is, the goodman of the house, to every one of the disciples of Christ. But this upper room of our house must be large enough to receive Jesus the Word of God, who is not comprehended but by those who are greater in comprehension. And this chamber must be made ready by the goodman of the house, (that is, the understanding,) for the Son of God, and it must be cleaned, wholly purged of the filth of malice. The master of the house also must not be any common person having a known name. Hence He says mystically in Matthew, *Go ye to such a one.* AMBROSE; Now in the upper parts he has a large room furnished, that you may consider how great were his merits in whom the Lord could sit down with His disciples, rejoicing in His exalted virtues.

Orig.
ut sup. ORIGEN; But we should know that they who are taken up with banquetings and worldly cares do not ascend into that upper part of the house, and therefore do not keep the Passover with Jesus. For after the words of the disciples wherewith they questioned the goodman of the house, (that is, the understanding,) the Divine Person came into that house to feast there with His disciples.

14. And when the hour was come, he sat down, and the twelve apostles with him.

15. And he said unto them, With desire I have desired to eat this Passover with you before I suffer:

16. For I say unto you, I will not any more eat thereof, until it be fulfilled in the kingdom of God.

17. And he took the cup, and gave thanks, and said, Take this, and divide it among yourselves:

18. For I say unto you, I will not drink of the fruit of the vine, until the kingdom of God shall come.

CYRIL; As soon as the disciples had prepared the Passover, they proceed to eat it; as it is said, *And when the hour was come, &c.* BEDE; By the hour of eating the Passover, He signifies the fourteenth day of the first month, far gone towards evening, the fifteenth moon just appearing on the earth. THEOPHYL. But how is our Lord said to sit down, whereas the Jews eat the Passover standing? They say, that when they had eaten the legal Passover, they sat down, according to the common custom, to eat their other food.

It follows, *And he said unto them, With desire have I desired to eat this Passover with you, &c.* CYRIL; He says this, because the covetous disciple was looking out for the time for betraying Him; but that he might not betray Him before the feast of the Passover, our Lord had not divulged either the house, or the man with whom He should keep the Passover. That this was the cause is very evident from these words. THEOPHYL. Or He says, *With desire have I desired;* as if to say, This is My last supper with you, therefore it is most precious and welcome to Me; just as those who are going away to a distance, utter the last words to their friends most affectionately. CHRYS. Or He says this, because after that Passover the Cross was at hand. But we find Him frequently prophesying of His own Passion, and desiring it to take place. BEDE; He first then desires to eat the typical Passover, and so to declare the mysteries of His Passion to the world. EUSEB. Or else; When our Lord was celebrating the new Passover, He fitly said, *With desire have I desired this Passover,* that is, the new mystery of the New Testament which He gave to His disciples, and which many prophets and righteous men desired before Him. He then also Himself thirsting for the common salvation, delivered this mystery, to suffice for the whole world. But the Passover was ordained by Moses to be celebrated in one place, that is, in Jerusalem. Therefore it was not adapted for the whole world, and so was not desired. EPIPH. Hereby we may refute the folly of the Ebionites concerning the eating of flesh, seeing that our Lord eats the Passover of the Jews. Therefore He pointedly said, " This Passover," that no one might transfer it to mean another. Epiph. adv. Hær.30. 22.

BEDE; Thus then was our Lord the approver of the legal Passover; and as He taught that it related to the figure of His own dispensation, He forbids it henceforth to be represented in the flesh. Therefore He adds, *For I say unto you, I will not any more eat thereof, until it be fulfilled in the kingdom of God.* That is, I will no more celebrate the Mosaic Passover, until, being spiritually understood, it is fulfilled in the Church. For the Church is the kingdom of God; as in Luke, *The kingdom of God is within you.* Again, the ancient Passover, which He desired to bring to an Luke 17, 21.

end, is also alluded to in what follows; *And he took the cup, and gave thanks, and said, Take ye, &c.* For this gave He thanks, that the old things were about to pass away, and Chrys. all things to become new. CHRYS. Remember then when conc. de Laz. thou sittest down to meat that after the meal thou must pray; therefore satisfy thy hunger, but with moderation, lest being overcharged thou shouldest not be able to bend thy knees in supplication and prayer to God. Let us not then after our meals turn to sleep, but to prayer. For Christ plainly signifies this, that the partaking of food should not be followed by sleep or rest, but by prayer and reading the holy Scripture. It follows, *For I say unto you, I will not drink of the fruit of the vine, until the kingdom of God come.* BEDE; This may be also taken literally, for from the hour of supper up to the time of resurrection He was about to drink no wine. Afterwards He partook both of meat and Acts 10, drink, as Peter testifies, *Who did eat and drink with him* 41. *after he rose from the dead.* THEOPHYL. The resurrection is called the kingdom of God, because it has destroyed death. Ps.93,1. Therefore David also says, *The Lord reigneth: He hath put* Isa. 63, *on beauty,* that is, a beautiful robe, *having put off the* 1. *corruption of the flesh.* But when the resurrection comes, He again drinks with His disciples; to prove that the resurrection was not a shadow only. BEDE; But it is far more natural, that as before of the typical lamb, so now also of the drink of the Passover, He should say that He would no more taste, until the glory of the kingdom of God being made manifest, the faith of the whole world should appear; that so by means of the spiritual changing of the two greatest commands of the law, namely, the eating and drinking of the Passover, you might learn that all the Sacraments of the law were to be transferred to a spiritual observance.

19. And he took bread, and gave thanks, and brake it, and gave unto them, saying, This is my body which is given for you: this do in remembrance of me.

20. Likewise also the cup after supper, saying,

This cup is the new testament in my blood, which is
shed for you.

BEDE; Having finished the rites of the old Passover, He
passes on to the new, which He desires the Church to celebrate
in memory of His redemption, substituting for the flesh and
blood of the lamb, the Sacrament of His own Flesh and Blood
in the figure of the bread and wine, *being made a Priest* Ps. 110,
for ever after the order of Melchisedech. Hence it is said, 4.
And he took bread, and gave thanks, as also He had given Heb. 7,
21.
thanks upon finishing the old feast, leaving us an example to
glorify God at the beginning and end of every good work.
It follows, *And brake it.* He Himself breaks the bread which
He holds forth, to shew that the breaking of His Body, that
is, His Passion, will not be without His will. *And gave unto
them, saying, This is my body which is given for you.* GREG. Greg.
NYSS. For the bread before the consecration is common bread, Orat. de
Bapt.
but when the mystery has consecrated it, it is, and it is called, Christ.
the Body of Christ. CYRIL; Nor doubt that this is true; for Cyril.
He plainly says, *This is my body;* but rather receive the in Luc.
words of thy Saviour in faith. For since He is the Truth,
He lies not. [a]They rave foolishly then who say that the mys- Ep. ad
tical blessing loses its power of sanctifying, if any remains are Calosyr.
left till the following day. For the most holy Body of Christ
will not be changed, but the power of blessing and the life-
giving grace is ever abiding in it. For the life-giving power in Luc.
of God the Father is the only-begotten Word, which was made ut sup.
flesh not ceasing to be the Word, but making the flesh life-
giving. What then? since we have in us the life of God, the
Word of God dwelling in us, will our body be life-giving?
But it is one thing for us by the habit of participation to
have in ourselves the Son of God, another for Himself to
have been made flesh, that is, to have made the body which
He took from the pure Virgin His own Body. He must needs
then be in a certain manner united to our bodies by His
holy Body and precious Blood, which we have received for a
life-giving blessing in the bread and wine. For lest we

[a] This passage is found in a page of   contains St. Cyril on Luke. See Maii
the same MS. in the Vatican which   Cl. Auct. vol. x. p. 375.

should be shocked, seeing the Flesh and Blood placed on the holy altars, God, in compassion to our infirmities, pours into the offerings the power of life, changing them into the reality of His own flesh, that the body of life may be found in us, as it were a certain life-giving seed. He adds, *Do this in comme-*

Chrys. Hom. 46. in Joan.

moration of me. CHRYS. Christ did this to bring us to a closer bond of friendship, and to betoken His love toward us, giving Himself to those who desire Him, not only to behold Him, but also to handle Him, to eat Him, to embrace Him with the fulness of their whole heart. Therefore as lions breathing fire do we depart from that table, rendered

Basil. Moral. Reg.21. c.3.Reg. Brev.ad int. 172. 2 Cor. 5, 25.

objects of terror to the devil. BASIL ; Learn then in what manner you ought to eat the Body of Christ, namely, in remembrance of Christ's obedience even unto death, that they who live may no more live in themselves, but in Him who died for them, and rose again.

THEOPHYL. Now Luke mentions two cups; of the one we spoke above, *Take this, and divide it among yourselves,* which we may say is a type of the Old Testament; but the other after the breaking and giving of bread, He Himself imparts to His disciples. Hence it is added, *Likewise also the cup after supper.* BEDE ; *He gave to them,* is here understood to

Aug.de Con.Ev. lib. iii. c. 1.

complete the sentence. AUG. Or because Luke has twice mentioned the cup, first before Christ gave the bread, then after He had given it, on the first occasion he has anticipated, as he frequently does, but on the second that which he has placed in its natural order, he had made no mention of before. But both joined together make the same sense which we find in the others, that is, Matthew and Mark. THEOPHYL. Our Lord calls the cup the New Testament, as it follows, *This cup is the New Testament in my blood, which shall be shed for you,* signifying that the New Testament has its beginning in His blood. For in the Old Testament the blood of animals was present when the law was given, but now the blood of the Word of God signifies to us the New Testament. But when He says, *for you,* He does not mean that for the Apostles only was His Body given, and His Blood poured out, but for the sake of all mankind. And the old Passover was ordained to remove the slavery of Egypt; but the blood of the lamb to protect the first-born. The new Passover was ordained to the remission of sins; but the Blood of Christ to preserve those who are dedicated to God.

CHRYS. For this Blood moulds in us a royal image, it suffers not our nobleness of soul to waste away, moreover it refreshes the soul, and inspires it with great virtue. This Blood puts to flight the devils, summons angels, and the Lord of angels. This Blood poured forth washed the world, and made heaven open. They that partake of it are built up with heavenly virtues, and arrayed in the royal robes of Christ; yea rather clothed upon by the King Himself. And since if thou comest clean, thou comest healthfully; so if polluted by an evil conscience, thou comest to thy own destruction, to pain and torment. For if they who defile the imperial purple are smitten with the same punishment as those who tear it asunder, it is not unreasonable that they who with an unclean heart receive Christ should be beaten with the same stripes as they were who pierced Him with nails. BEDE; Because the bread strengthens, and the wine produces blood in the flesh, the former is ascribed to the Body of Christ, the latter to His Blood. But because both we ought to abide in Christ, and Christ in us, the wine of the Lord's cup is mixed with water, for John bears witness, *The people are many waters.* THEOPHYL. But first the bread is given, next the cup. For in spiritual things labour and action come first, that is, the bread, not only because it is toiled for by the sweat of the brow, but also because while being eaten it is not easy to swallow. Then after labour follows the rejoicing of Divine grace, which is the cup. BEDE; For this reason then the Apostles communicated after supper, because it was necessary that the typical passover should be first completed, and then they should pass on to the Sacrament of the true Passover. But now in honour of so great a Sacrament, the masters of the Church think right that we should first be refreshed with the spiritual banquet, and afterward with the earthly. GREEK Ex. He that communicates receives the whole Body and Blood of our Lord, even though he receive but a part of the Mysteries. For as one seal imparts the whole of its device to different substances, and yet remains entire after distribution, and as one word penetrates to the hearing of many, so there is no doubt that

Marginal notes: Chrys. Hom. 46. in Joan. — Rev. 17, 15. — Euty-chius Patri-arch.

the Body and Blood of our Lord is received whole in all. But the breaking of the sacred bread signifies the Passion.

21. But, behold, the hand of him that betrayeth me is with me on the table.

22. And truly the Son of man goeth, as it was determined : but woe unto that man by whom he is betrayed.

23. And they began to enquire among themselves, which of them it was that should do this thing.

Aug. de Con.Ev. l.iii.c.1.

AUG. When our Lord had given the cup to His disciples, He again spoke of His betrayer, saying, *But, behold, the hand of him that betrayeth me, &c.* THEOPHYL. And this He said not only to shew that He knew all things, but also to declare unto us His own especial goodness, in that He left nothing undone of those things which belonged to Him to do; (for He gives us an example, that even unto the end we should be employed in reclaiming sinners;) and moreover to point out the baseness of the traitor who blushed not to be His guest. CHRYS. Yet though partaking of the mystery, he was not converted. Nay, his wickedness is made only the more awful, as well because under the pollution of such a design, he came to the mystery, as that coming he was not made better, either by fear, gratitude, or respect. BEDE; And yet our Lord does not especially point him out, lest being so plainly detected, he might only become the more shameless. But He throws the charge on the whole twelve, that the guilty one might be turned to repentance. He also proclaims his punishment, that the man whom shame had not prevailed upon, might by the sentence denounced against him be brought to amendment. Hence it follows, *And truly the Son of man goeth, &c.* THEOPHYL. Not as if unable to preserve Himself, but as determining for Himself to suffer death for the salvation of man.

Chrys. Hom. 82. in Matt.

Chrys. Hom. 81. in Matt.

CHRYS. Because then Judas in the things which are written of him acted with an evil purpose, in order that no one might deem him guiltless, as being the minister of the dispensation, Christ adds, *Woe unto that man by whom he is betrayed.*

BEDE; But woe also to that man, who coming unworthily to the Table of our Lord, after the example of Judas, betrays the Son, not indeed to Jews, but to sinners, that is, to his own sinful members. Although the eleven Apostles knew that they were meditating nothing against their Lord, yet notwithstanding because they trust more to their Master than themselves, fearing their own infirmities, they ask concerning a sin of which they had no consciousness. BASIL; For as in Basil. bodily diseases there are many of which the affected are not in Reg. Brev. ad sensible, but they rather put faith in the opinion of their int. 301. physicians, than trust their own insensibility; so also in the diseases of the soul, though a man is not conscious of sin in himself, yet ought he to trust to those who are able to have more knowledge of their own sins.

24. And there was also a strife among them, which of them should be accounted the greatest.

25. And he said unto them, The kings of the Gentiles exercise lordship over them; and they that exercise authority upon them are called benefactors.

26. But ye shall not be so : but he that is greatest among you, let him be as the younger; and he that is chief, as he that doth serve.

27 For whether is greater, he that sitteth at meat, or he that serveth? is not he that sitteth at meat? but I am among you as he that serveth.

THEOPHYL. While they were enquiring among themselves who should betray the Lord, they would naturally go on to say to one another, " Thou art the traitor," and so become impelled to say, " I am the best, I am the greatest." Hence it is said, *And there was also a strife among them which should be accounted the greatest.* GREEK EX. Or the strife Apolli- seems to have arisen from this, that when our Lord was de- narius in loc. parting from the world, it was thought that some one must become their head, as taking our Lord's place. BEDE; As good men seek in the Scriptures the examples of their fathers, that they may thereby gain profit and be humbled, so the

bad, if by chance they have discovered any thing blameable
in the elect, most gladly seize upon it, to shelter their own
iniquities thereby. Many therefore most eagerly read, that a
strife arose among the disciples of Christ. AMBROSE; If the
disciples did contend, it is not alleged as any excuse, but
held out as a warning. Let us then beware lest any con-
tentions among us for precedence be our ruin. BEDE; Rather
let us look not what carnal disciples did, but ·what their
spiritual Master commanded; for it follows, *And he said unto*
Chrys. *them, The kings of the Gentiles, &c.* CHRYS. He mentions
Hom.
65. in the Gentiles, to shew thereby how faulty it was. For it is
Matt. of the Gentiles to seek after precedence. CYRIL; Soft words
are also given them by their subjects, as it follows, *And they*
that exercise authority upon them are called benefactors.
Now they truly as alien from the sacred law are subject to
these evils, but your preeminence is in humility, as it follows,
Basil. *But ye shall not be so.* BASIL; Let not him that is chief be
in Reg.
fus. dis. puffed up by his dignity, lest he fall away from the blessed-
int. 30. ness of humility, but let him know that true humility is the
ministering unto many. As then he who attends many
wounded and wipes away the blood from their wounds, least
of all men enters upon the service for his own exaltation,
much more ought he to whom is committed the care of
his sick brethren as the minister of all, about to render an
account of all, to be thoughtful and anxious. And so let
ad int. him that is greatest be as the younger. Again, it is meet
31. that those who are in the chief places should be ready to offer
also bodily service, after our Lord's example, who washed
His disciples' feet. Hence it follows, *And he that is chief, as*
he that doth serve. But we need not fear that the spirit
of humility will be weakened in the inferior, while he is
being served by his superior, for by imitation humility is
extended.

AMBROSE; But it must be observed, that not every kind of
respect and deference to others betokens humility, for you
may defer to a person for the world's sake, for fear of his
power, or regard to your own interest. In that case you
seek to edify yourself, not to honour another. Therefore
there is one form of the precept given to all men, namely,
that they boast not about precedence, but strive earnestly

for humility. BEDE; In this rule however, given by our Lord, the great have need of no little judgment, that they do not indeed like the kings of the Gentiles delight to tyrannize over their subjects, and be puffed up with their praises, yet notwithstanding that they be provoked with a righteous zeal against the wickedness of offenders.

But to the words of the exhortation He subjoins His own example, as it follows, *For which is greater, he who sitteth at meat, or he that serveth? But I am among you, &c.* CHRYS. As if He says, Think not that thy disciple needs you, but that you do not need him. For I who need no one whom all things in heaven and earth need, have condescended to the degree of a servant. THEOPHYL. He shews Himself to be their servant, when He distributes the bread and the cup, of which service He makes mention, reminding them that if they have eaten of the same bread, and drunk of the same cup, if Christ Himself served all, they ought all to think the same things. BEDE; Or He speaks of that service wherewith, according to John, He their Lord and Master John 13, washed their feet. Although by the word itself *serving*, [5.] all that He did in the flesh may be implied, but by serving He also signifies that He poureth forth His blood for us.

28. Ye are they which have continued with me in my temptations.

29. And I appoint unto you a kingdom, as my Father hath appointed unto me ;

30. That ye may eat and drink at my table in my kingdom, and sit on thrones judging the twelve tribes of Israel.

THEOPHYL. As the Lord had denounced woe to the traitor, so on the other hand to the rest of the disciples He promises blessings, saying, *Ye are they which have continued with me, &c.* BEDE; For not the first effort of patience, but long-continued perseverance, is rewarded with the glory of the heavenly kingdom, for perseverance, (which is called constancy or fortitude of mind,) is, so to say, the pillar and prop of all virtues. The Son of God then conducts those who abide with Him in His temptations to the everlasting kingdom.

Rom. 6, 5. *For if we have been planted together in the likeness of his death, we shall be also in the likeness of his resurrection.* Hence it follows, *And I give to you a kingdom, &c.*

AMBROSE; The kingdom of God is not of this world. But it is not equality with God, but likeness to Him, unto which man must aspire. For Christ alone is the full image of God, on account of the unity of His Father's glory expressed in Him. But the righteous man is after the image of God, if for the sake of imitating the likeness of the Divine conversation, He through the knowledge of God despises the world. Therefore also we eat the Body and Blood of Christ, that we may be partakers of eternal life. Whence it follows, *That ye may eat and drink at my table in my kingdom.* For the reward promised to us is not food and drink, but the communication of heavenly grace and life. BEDE; Or the table offered to all saints richly to enjoy is the glory of a heavenly life, wherewith they who hunger and thirst after righteousness

Matt. 5, 6. shall be filled, resting in the long-desired enjoyment of the true God. THEOPHYL. He said this not as if they would have there bodily food, or as if His kingdom were to be a

Mat. 22, 30. Luke 20, 36. Rom. 14, 17. sensible one. For their life then shall be the life of angels, as He before told the Sadducees. But Paul also says that the kingdom of God is not meat and drink.

CYRIL; By means of the things of our present life He describes spiritual things. For they exercise a high privilege with earthly kings, who sit at their table as guests. So then by man's estimation He shews who shall be rewarded by Him with the greatest honours. BEDE; This then is the

Ps. 118, 16. exchange to the right hand of the Most High, that those who now in lowliness rejoice to minister to their fellow-servants, shall then at our Lord's table on high be fed with the banquet of everlasting life, and they who here in temptations abide with the Lord being unjustly judged, shall then come with Him as just judges upon their tempters. Hence it follows, *And sit on thrones judging the twelve tribes of Israel.* THEOPHYL. That is, the unbelievers condemned out of the twelve tribes. AMBROSE; But the twelve thrones are not as it were any resting-places for the bodily posture, but because since Christ judges after the Divine likeness by knowledge of the hearts, not by examination of the actions, rewarding virtue, condemning iniquity; so the Apostles are appointed to a spiritual judgment, for the rewarding of faith, the condemnation of unbelief, repelling error with virtue, inflicting vengeance on the sacrilegious. CHRYS. What then will Judas also sit there? Observe what the law was which God gave by Jeremiah, *If I have promised any good, and thou art counted unworthy of it, I will punish you.* Therefore speaking to His disciples He did not make a general promise, but added, *Ye who have continued with me in my temptations.* BEDE; From the high excellence of this promise Judas is excluded. For before the Lord said this, Judas must be supposed to have gone out. They also are excluded whoever having heard the words of the incomprehensible Sacrament, have gone backwards.

Chrys. Hom. 64. in Matt.

Jerem. 18, 10.

John 6, 67.

31. And the Lord said, Simon, Simon, behold, Satan hath desired to have you, that he may sift you as wheat :

32. But I have prayed for thee, that thy faith fail not : and when thou art converted, strengthen thy brethren.

33. And he said unto him, Lord, I am ready to go with thee, both into prison, and to death.

34. And he said, I tell thee, Peter, the cock shall not crow this day, before that thou shalt thrice deny that thou knowest me.

BEDE; Lest the eleven should be boastful, and impute it to their own strength, that they almost alone among so many thousands of the Jews were said to have continued with our Lord in His temptations, He shews them, that if they had not been protected by the aid of their Master succouring them, they would have been beaten down by the same storm as the rest. Hence it follows, *And the Lord said unto Simon, Simon, behold, Satan hath desired thee, that he may sift thee as wheat.* That is, he hath longed to tempt you and to shake you, as he who cleanses wheat by winnowing. Wherein He teaches that no man's faith is tried unless God permits it. THEOPHYL. Now this was said to Peter, because he was bolder than the rest, and might feel proud because of the things which Christ had promised. CYRIL; Or to shew that men being as nought, (as regards human nature, and the proneness of our minds to fall,) it is not meet that they should wish to be above their brethren. Therefore passing by all the others, He comes to Peter, who was the chief of them, saying, *But I have prayed for thee, that thy faith fail not.*

Chrys. Hom. 82. in Matt. CHRYS. Now He said not, ' I have granted,' but *I have prayed.* For He speaks humbly as approaching unto His Passion, and that He may manifest His human nature. For He who had spoken not in supplication, but by authority, Matt. 16, 18. *Upon this rock I will build my Church, and I will give thee the keys of the kingdom of heaven,* how should He have need of prayer that He might stay one agitated soul? He does not say, " I have prayed that thou deny not," but that thou do not abandon thy faith. THEOPHYL. For albeit thou art for a time shaken, yet thou holdest stored up, a seed of faith; though the spirit has shed its leaves in temptation, yet the root is firm. Satan then seeks to harm thee, because he is envious of my love for thee, but notwithstanding that I have prayed for thee, thou shalt fall. Hence it follows, *And when thou art converted, strengthen thy brethren.* As if He says, After that thou hast wept and repented thy denial of Me, strengthen thy brethren, for I have deputed thee to be the head of the Apostles. For this befits thee who art with Me, the strength and rock of the Church. And this must be understood not only of the Apostles who then were, but of all the faithful who were about to be, even to the end of the world; that none of the believers might despair, seeing that Peter though an Apostle denied his Lord, yet afterwards by ἱπιστά- τηι penitence obtained the high privilege of being the Ruler of the world. CYRIL; Marvel then at the superabundance of the Divine forbearance: lest He should cause a disciple to despair, before the crime was committed, He granted pardon, and again restored him to his Apostolic rank, saying, *Strengthen thy brethren.* BEDE; As if to say, As I by prayer protected your faith that it should not fail, so do you remember to sustain the weaker brethren, that they despair not of pardon. AMBROSE; Beware then of boasting, beware of the world; he is commanded to strengthen his own brethren, who said, *Master, we have left all, and followed thee.* Matt. 19, 27.

BEDE; Because the Lord said He had prayed for Peter's faith, Peter conscious of present affection and fervent faith, but unconscious of his coming fall, does not believe he could in any way fall from Christ. As it follows, *And he said unto him, Lord, I am ready to go with thee to prison and to death.* THEOPHYL. He burns forth indeed with too much love, and promises what is impossible to him. But it behoved him as soon as he heard from the Truth that he was to be tempted, to be no longer confident. Now the Lord, seeing that Peter spoke boastfully, reveals the nature of his temptation, namely, that he would deny Him; *I tell thee, Peter, the cock shall not crow this day, before that thou thrice deny, &c.* AMBROSE; Now Peter although earnest in spirit, yet still weak in bodily inclination, is declared about to deny his Lord; for he could not equal the constancy of the Divine will. Our Lord's Passion has rivals, but no equal. THEOPHYL. From hence we draw a great doctrine, that human resolve is not sufficient without the Divine support. For Peter with all his zeal, nevertheless when forsaken of God was overthrown by the enemy.

BASIL; We must know then, that God sometimes allows Basil. the rash to receive a fall, as a remedy to previous self-con- in Reg. fidence. But although the rash man seems to have committed int. 8. the same offence with other men, there is no slight difference. For the one has sinned by reason of certain secret assaults and almost against his will, but the others, having no care either for themselves or God, knowing no distinction between sin and virtuous actions. For the rash needing some assistance, in regard to this very thing in which he has sinned ought to suffer reproof. But the others, having destroyed all the good of their soul, must be afflicted, warned, rebuked, or made subject to punishment, until they acknowledge that God is a just Judge, and tremble.

AUG. Now what is here said concerning the foregoing Aug. denial of Peter is contained in all the Evangelists, but they de Con. do not all happen to relate it upon the same occasion in the c. 2. discourse. Matthew and Mark subjoin it after our Lord had departed from the house where He had eaten the Passover, but Luke and John before He went out from thence. But we may easily understand either that the two former used these words, recapitulating them, or the two others anticipating them: only it rather moves us, that not only the words but even the sentences of our Lord, in which Peter being troubled used that boast of dying either for or with our Lord, are given so differently, as rather to compel us to believe that he thrice uttered his boast at different parts of our Lord's discourse, and that he was thrice answered by our Lord, that before the cock crowed he should deny Him thrice.

35. And he said unto them, When I sent you without purse, and scrip, and shoes, lacked ye any thing? And they said, Nothing.

36. Then said he unto them, But now, he that hath a purse, let him take it, and likewise his scrip: and he that hath no sword, let him sell his garment, and buy one.

37. For I say unto you, that this that is written must yet be accomplished in me, And he was reckoned among the transgressors: for the things concerning me have an end.

38. And they said, Lord, behold, here are two swords. And he said unto them, It is enough.

CYRIL; Our Lord had foretold to Peter that he should deny Him; namely, at the time of His being taken. But having once made mention of His being taken captive, He next announces the struggle that would ensue against the Jews. Hence it is said, *And he said unto them, When I sent you without purse, &c.* For the Saviour had sent the holy Apostles to preach in the cities and towns the kingdom of heaven, bidding them to take no thought of the things of the body, but to place their whole hope of salvation in Him. CHRYS. Now as one who teaches to swim, at first indeed placing his

Chrys. in illud ad Rom. 16. Salutate Priscillam.

hands under his pupils, carefully supports them, but afterward
frequently withdrawing his hand, bids them help themselves,
nay even lets them sink a little; so likewise did Christ deal
with His disciples. At the beginning truly He was present to
them, giving them most richly abundance of all things; as it
follows, *And they said unto them, Nothing.* But when it
was necessary for them to shew their own strength, He withdrew from them for a little His grace, bidding them do something of themselves; as it follows, *But now he that hath a purse,*
that is, wherein to carry money, *let him take it, and likewise
his scrip,* that is, to carry provisions in. And truly when they
had neither shoes, nor girdle, nor staff, nor money, they never
suffered the want of any thing. But when He allowed them
purse and scrip, they seem to suffer hunger, and thirst, and
nakedness. As if He said to them, Hitherto all things have
been most richly supplied to you, but now I would have you
also experience poverty, therefore I hold you no longer to
the former rule, but I command you to get purse and scrip.
Now God might even to the end have kept them in plenty,
but for many reasons He was unwilling to do so. First
that they might impute nothing to themselves, but acknowledge that every thing flowed from God; secondly, that they
might learn moderation; thirdly, that they might not think
too highly of themselves. For this cause while He permitted
them to fall into many unlooked for evils, He relaxed the
rigour of the former law, lest it should become grievous and
intolerable.

BEDE; For He does not train His disciples in the same rule
of life, in time of persecution, as in the time of peace. When
He sent them to preach, He ordered them to take nothing in
the way, ordaining in truth, that He who preaches the Gospel
should live by the Gospel. But when the crisis of death was
at hand, and the whole nation persecuted both the shepherd
and the flock, He proposes a law adapted to the time, allowing
them to take the necessaries of life, until the rage of the
persecutors was abated, and the time of preaching the Gospel
had returned. Herein He leaves us also an example, that at
times when a just reason urges, we may intermit without blame Aug.
somewhat of the strictness of our determination. AUG. By cont.
Faust.
no inconsistency then of Him who commands, but by the lib.xxii.
c. 77.

reason of the dispensation, according to the diversity of times are commandments, counsels, or permissions changed.

AMBROSE; But He who forbids to strike, why does He order them to buy a sword? unless perchance that there may be a defence prepared, but no necessary retaliation; a seeming ability to be revenged, without the will. Hence it follows, *And he who has not,* (that is, a purse,) *let him sell his garment, and buy a sword.* CHRYS. What is this? He who said, *If any one strike you on the right cheek, turn unto him the other also,* now arms His disciples, and with a sword only. For if it were fitting to be completely armed, not only must a man possess a sword, but shield and helmet. But even though a thousand had arms of this kind, how could the eleven be prepared for all the attacks and lying in wait of people, tyrants, allies, and nations, and how should they not quake at the mere sight of armed men, who had been brought up near lakes and rivers? We must not then suppose that He ordered them to possess swords, but by the swords He points at the secret attack of the Jews. And hence it follows, *For I say unto you, that this that is written must be accomplished in me: And he was numbered with the transgressors.* THEOPHYL. While they were contending among themselves above concerning priority, He saith, It is not a time of dignities, but rather of danger and slaughter. Behold I even your Master am led to a disgraceful death, to be reckoned with the transgressors. For these things which are prophesied of Me have an end, that is, a fulfilment. Wishing then to hint at a violent attack, He made mention of a sword, not altogether revealing it, lest they should be seized with dismay, nor did He entirely provide that they should not be shaken by these sudden attacks, but that afterwards recovering, they might marvel how He gave Himself up to the Passion, a ransom for the salvation of men. BASIL; Or the Lord does not bid them carry purse and scrip and buy a sword, but predicts that it should come to pass, that in truth the Apostles, forgetful of the time of the Passion, of the gifts and law of their Lord, would dare to take up the sword. For often does the Scripture make use of the imperative form of speech in the place of prophecy. Still in many books we do not find, *Let him take, or buy,* but, he will take, he will buy. THEOPHYL. Or

Matt. 5, 39.

Isa. 53, 12.

Basil. Reg. Brev. int. 31.

He hereby foretels to them that they would incur hunger and thirst, which He implies by the scrip, and sundry kinds of misery, which he intends by the sword.

CYRIL; Or else; When our Lord says, *He who hath a purse, let him take it, likewise a scrip,* His discourse He addressed to His disciples, but in reality He regards every individual Jew; as if He says, If any Jew is rich in resources, let him collect them together and fly. But if any one oppressed with extreme poverty applies himself to religion, let him also sell his cloak and buy a sword. For the terrible attack of battle shall overtake them, so that nothing shall suffice to resist it. He next lays open the cause of these evils, namely, that He suffered the penalty due to the wicked, being crucified with thieves. And when it shall have come at last to this, the word of dispensation will receive its end. But to the persecutors shall happen all that has been foretold by the Prophets. These things then God prophesied concerning what should befall the country of the Jews, but the disciples understood not the depth of His words, thinking they had need of swords against the coming attack of the traitor. Whence it follows; *But they said, Lord, behold, here are two swords.* CHRYS. And in truth, if He wished them to use human aid, not a hundred swords would have sufficed; but if He willed not the assistance of man, even two are superfluous. THEOPHYL. Our Lord then was unwilling to blame them as not understanding Him, but saying, *It is enough,* He dismissed them; as when we are addressing any one, and see that he does not understand what is said, we say, Well, let us leave him, lest we trouble him. But some say, that our Lord said, *It is enough,* ironically; as if He said, Since there are two swords, they will amply suffice against so large a multitude as is about to attack us. BEDE; Or the two swords suffice for a testimony that Jesus suffered voluntarily. The one indeed was to teach the Apostles the presumption of their contending for their Lord, and His inherent virtue of healing; the other never taken out of its sheath, to shew that they were not even permitted to do all that they could for His defence. AMBROSE; Or, because the law does not forbid to return a blow, perhaps He says to Peter, as he is offering the two swords, *It is enough,* as though it were lawful until

the Gospel; in order that there may be in the law, the knowledge of justice; in the Gospel, perfection of goodness. There
is also a spiritual sword, that you may sell your patrimony,
and buy the word, by which the nakedness of the soul is
clothed. There is also a sword of suffering, so that you may
strip your body, and with the spoils of your sacrificed flesh
purchase for yourself the sacred crown of martyrdom. Again
it moves, seeing that the disciples put forward two swords,
whether perhaps one is not of the Old Testament, the other
of the New, whereby we are armed against the wiles of the
devil. Therefore the Lord says, *It is enough*, because he
wanted nothing who is fortified by the teaching of both
Testaments.

39. And he came out, and went, as he was wont,
to the mount of Olives; and his disciples also followed
him.

40. And when he was at the place, he said unto
them, Pray that ye enter not into temptation.

41. And he was withdrawn from them about a
stone's cast, and kneeled down, and prayed,

42. Saying, Father, if thou be willing, remove this
cup from me : nevertheless not my will, but thine, be
done.

BEDE; As He was to be betrayed by His disciple, our
Lord goes to the place of His wonted retirement, where He
might most easily be found; as it follows, *And he came
out, and went, as he was wont, to the mount of Olives.*
CYRIL; By day He was in Jerusalem, but when the darkness of night came on He held converse with His disciples
on the mount of Olives; as it is added, *And his disciples
followed.*   BEDE; Rightly does He lead the disciples, about to
be instructed in the mysteries of His Body, to the mount of
Olives, that He might signify that all who are baptized in
His death should be comforted with the anointing of the
Holy Spirit.

THEOPHYL. Now after supper our Lord betakes Himself
not to idleness or sleep, but to prayer and teaching. Hence

it follows, *And when he was at the place, he said unto them,*
Pray, &c. BEDE; It is indeed impossible for the soul of
man not to be tempted. Therefore he says not, Pray that
ye be not tempted, but, *Pray that ye enter not into tempt-*
ation, that is, that the temptation do not at last overcome
you.

CYRIL; But not to do good by words only, He went forward a little and prayed; as it follows, *And he was with-*
drawn from them about a stone's cast. You will every where
find Him praying apart, to teach you that with a devout
mind and quiet heart we should speak with the most high
God. He did not betake Himself to prayer, as if He was in
want of another's help, who is the Almighty power of the
Father, but that we may learn not to slumber in temptation,
but rather to be instant in prayer. BEDE; He also alone
prays for all, who was to suffer alone for all, signifying that
His prayer is as far distant from ours as His Passion. AUG.
He was torn from them about a stone's cast, as though He
would typically remind them that to Him they should point
the stone, that is, up to Him bring the intention of the law
which was written on stone. ^{Aug. de Qu. Evang. lib. ii. qu. 50.}

GREG. NYSS. But what meaneth His bending of knees? of
which it is said, *And he kneeled down, and prayed.* It is
the way of men to pray to their superiors with their faces on
the ground, testifying by the action that the greater of the
two are those who are asked. Now it is plain that human
nature contains nothing worthy of God's imitation. Accordingly the tokens of respect which we evince to one another,
confessing ourselves to be inferior to our neighbours, we have
transferred to the humiliation of the Incomparable Nature.
And thus He who bore our sicknesses and interceded for us,
bent His knee in prayer, by reason of the man which He
assumed, giving us an example, that we ought not to exalt
ourselves at the time of prayer, but in all things be conformed
to humility; *for God resisteth the proud, but giveth grace to*
the humble. ^{James 4, 6. 1 Pet. 5, 5.}

CHRYS. Now every art is set forth by the words and works
of him who teacheth it. Because then our Lord had come
to teach no ordinary virtue, therefore He speaks and does
the same things. And so having in words commanded to

pray, lest they enter into temptation, He does the same likewise in work, *saying, Father, if thou be willing, remove
this cup from me.* He saith not the words, *If thou wilt,* as
if ignorant whether it was pleasing to the Father. For such
knowledge was not more difficult than the knowledge of His
Father's substance, which He alone clearly knew, according
to John, *As the Father knoweth me, even so have I known
the Father.* Nor says He this, as refusing His Passion. For
He who rebuked a disciple, who wished to prevent His
Passion, so as even after many commendations, to call him
Satan, how should He be unwilling to be crucified? Consider
then why it was so said. How great a thing was it to hear
that the unspeakable God, who passes all understanding, was
content to enter the virgin's womb, to suck her milk, and to
undergo every thing human. Since then that was almost
incredible which was about to happen, He sent first indeed
Prophets to announce it, afterwards He Himself comes
clothed in the flesh, so that you could not suppose Him to
be a phantom. He permits His flesh to endure all natural
infirmities, to hunger, to thirst, to sleep, to labour, to be
afflicted, to be tormented; on this account likewise He refuses
not death, that He might manifest thereby His true humanity.

AMBROSE; He says then, *If thou will, remove this cup
from me,* as man refusing death, as God maintaining His
own decree. BEDE; Or He begs the cup to be removed
from Him, not indeed from fear of suffering, but from His
compassion for the first people, lest they should have to
drink the cup first drunk by Him. Therefore He says expressly, not, Remove from Me the cup, but *this cup,* that is,
the cup of the Jewish people, who can have no excuse for
their ignorance in slaying Me, having the Law and the
Prophets daily prophesying of Me.

DION. ALEX. Or when He says, *Let this cup pass from me,*
it is not, let it not come to Me, for unless it had come it
could not pass away. It was therefore when He perceived
it already present that He began to be afflicted and sorrowful, and as it was close at hand, He says, *Let this cup pass;*
for as that which has passed can neither be said not to have
come nor yet to remain, so also the Saviour asks first that
the temptation slightly assailing Him may pass away. And

margin notes:
John 10, 15.

Matt. 16, 23.

Dion. de Martyr. c. 7.

this is the not entering into temptation which He counsels to pray for. But the most perfect way of avoiding temptation is manifested, when he says, *Nevertheless, not my will, but thine be done.* For God is not a tempter to evil, but He wishes to grant us good things above what we either desire or understand. Therefore He seeks that the perfect will of His Father which He Himself had known, should dispose of the event, which is the same will as His own, as respects the Divine nature. But He shrinks to fulfil the human will, which He calls His own, and which is inferior to His Father's will. ATHAN. For here He manifests a double will. One indeed human, which is of the flesh, the other divine. For our human nature, because of the weakness of the flesh, refuses the Passion, but His divine will eagerly embraced it, for that it was not possible that He should be holden of death. GREG. NYSS. Now Apollinaris asserts that Christ had not His own will according to His earthly nature, but that in Christ exists only the will of God who descends from heaven. Let him then say what will is it which God would have by no means to be fulfilled? And the Divine nature does not remove His own will. BEDE; When He drew near His Passion, the Saviour also took upon Him the words of weak man; as when something threatens us which we do not wish to come to pass, we then through weakness seek that it may not be, to the end that we also may be prepared by fortitude to find the will of our Creator contrary to our own will.

Athan. de In- carn. et cont.Ar.

Greg. non occ.

43. And there appeared an angel unto him from heaven, strengthening him.

44. And being in an agony he prayed more earnestly: and his sweat was as it were great drops of blood falling down to the ground.

45. And when he rose up from prayer, and was come to his disciples, he found them sleeping for sorrow.

46. And said unto them, Why sleep ye? rise and pray, lest ye enter into temptation.

THEOPHYL. To make known unto us the power of prayer

that we may exercise it in adversity, our Lord when praying is comforted by an Angel. BEDE; In another place we read that Angels came and ministered unto Him. In testimony then of each nature, Angels are said both to have ministered to Him and comforted Him. For the Creator needed not the protection of His creature, but being made man as for our sakes He is sad, so for our sakes He is comforted. THEOPHYL. But some say that the Angel appeared, glorifying Him, saying, O Lord, Thine is the power, for Thou art able to vanquish death, and to deliver weak mankind. CHRYS. And because not in appearance but in reality He took upon Himself our flesh, in order to confirm the truth of the dispensation He submits to bear human suffering; for it follows, *And being in an agony he prayed more earnestly.* AMBROSE; Many are shocked at this place who turn the sorrows of the Saviour to an argument of inherent weakness from the beginning, rather than taken upon Him for the time. But I am so far from considering it a thing to be excused, that I never more admire His mercy and majesty; for He would have conferred less upon me had He not taken upon Him my feelings. For He took upon Him my sorrow, that upon me He might bestow His joy. With confidence therefore I name His sadness, because I preach His cross. He must needs then have undergone affliction, that He might conquer. For they have no praise of fortitude whose wounds have produced stupor rather than pain. He wished therefore to instruct us how we should conquer death, and what is far greater, the anguish of coming death. Thou smartedst then, O Lord, not from thy own but my wounds; *for he was wounded for our transgressions.* And perhaps He is sad, because that after Adam's fall the passage by which we must depart from this world was such that death was necessary. Nor is it far from the truth that He was sad for His persecutors, who He knew would suffer punishment for their wicked sacrilege.

Greg. Mor. 24. c. 17. GREG. He has expressed also the conflict of our mind in itself, as death approaches, for we suffer a certain thrill of terror and dread, when by the dissolution of the flesh we draw near to the eternal judgment; and with good reason, for the soul finds in a moment that which can never be changed.

Matt. 4, 11.

THEOPHYL. Now that the preceding prayer was of His human nature, not His divine, as the Arians say, is argued from what is said of His sweat, which follows, *And his sweat was as it were great drops of blood falling down to the ground.* BEDE; Let no one ascribe this sweat to natural weakness, nay, it is contrary to nature to sweat blood, but rather let him derive therefrom a declaration to us, that He was now obtaining the accomplishment of His prayer, namely, that He might purge by His blood the faith of His disciples, still convicted of human frailty.

AUG. Our Lord praying with a bloody sweat represented the martyrdoms which should flow from His whole body, which is the Church. THEOPHYL. Or this is proverbially said of one who has sweated intensely, that He sweated blood; the Evangelist then wishing to shew that He was moistened with large drops of sweat, takes drops of blood for an example. But afterwards finding His disciples asleep for sorrow, He upbraids them, at the same time reminding them to pray; for it follows, *And when he rose from prayer and was come to his disciples, he found them sleeping.* CHRYS. For it was midnight, and the disciples' eyes were heavy from grief, and their sleep was not that of drowsiness but sorrow. AUG. Now Luke has not stated after which prayer He came to His disciples, still in nothing does he disagree with Matthew and Mark.

Prosp. ex Aug. Sent. 68.

Aug. de Con. Ev. lib. iii. c. 4.

BEDE; Our Lord proves by what comes after, that He prayed for His disciples whom He exhorts by watching and prayer to be partakers of His prayer; for it follows, *And he saith unto them, Why sleep ye? Rise and pray, lest ye enter into temptation.* THEOPHYL. That is, that they should not be overcome by temptation, for not to be led into temptation is not to be overwhelmed by it. Or He simply bids us pray that our life may be quiet, and we be not cast into trouble of any kind. For it is of the devil and presumptuous, for a man to throw himself into temptation. Therefore James said not, " Cast yourselves into temptation," but, *When ye are fallen, count it all joy,* making a voluntary act out of an involuntary.

Jam. 1, 2.

47. And while he yet spake, behold a multitude,

and he that was called Judas, one of the twelve, went before them, and drew near unto Jesus to kiss him.

48. But Jesus said unto him, Judas, betrayest thou the Son of man with a kiss?

49. When they which were about him saw what would follow, they said unto him, Lord, shall we smite with the sword?

50. And one of them smote the servant of the high priest, and cut off his right ear.

51. And Jesus answered and said, Suffer ye thus far. And he touched his ear, and healed him.

52. Then Jesus said unto the chief priests, and captains of the temple, and the elders, which were come to him, Be ye come out, as against a thief, with swords and staves?

53. When I was daily with you in the temple, ye stretched forth no hands against me: but this is your hour, and the power of darkness.

Gloss.
non occ.

GLOSS. After first mentioning the prayer of Christ, St. Luke goes on to speak of His betrayal wherein He is betrayed by His disciple, saying, *And while he yet spake, behold a multitude, and he that was called Judas.* CYRIL; He says, *he that was called Judas,* holding his name as it were in abhorrence; but adds, *one of the twelve,* to signify the enormity of the traitor. For he who had been honoured as an apostle became the cause of the murder of Christ. CHRYS. For just as incurable wounds yield neither to severe nor soothing remedies, so the soul when once it is taken captive, and has sold itself to any particular sin, will reap no benefit from admonition. And so it was with Judas, who desisted not from His betrayal, though deterred by Christ by every manner of warning. Hence it follows, *And drew near unto Jesus to kiss him.* CYRIL; Unmindful of the glory of Christ, he thought to be able to act secretly, daring to make an especial token of love the instrument of his treachery.

CHRYS. Now we must not depart from admonishing our brethren, albeit nothing comes of our words. For even the streams though no one drink therefrom still flow on, and him whom thou hast not persuaded to-day, peradventure thou mayest to-morrow. For the fisherman after drawing empty nets the whole day, when it was now late takes a fish. And thus our Lord, though He knew that Judas was not to be converted, yet ceased not to do such things as had reference to him. It follows, *But Jesus said unto him, Judas, betrayest thou the Son of man with a kiss?* AMBROSE; It must be used I think by way of question, as if he arrests the traitor with a lover's affection. CHRYS. And He gives him his proper name, which was rather like one lamenting and recalling him, than one provoked to anger. AMBROSE; He says, *Betrayest thou with a kiss?* that is, dost thou inflict a wound with the pledge of love? with the instruments of peace dost thou impose death? a slave, dost thou betray thy Lord; a disciple, thy master; one chosen, Him who chose thee? CHRYS. But He said not, " Betrayest thou thy Master, thy Lord, thy Benefactor," but *the Son of man*, that is, the humble and meek, who though He were not thy Master and Lord, forasmuch as He has borne himself so gently toward thee, should have never been betrayed by thee.

AMBROSE; O great manifestation of Divine power, great discipline of virtue! Both the design of thy traitor is detected, and yet forbearance is not withheld. He shews whom it is Judas betrays, by manifesting things hidden; He declares whom he delivers up, by saying, *the Son of man*, for the human flesh, not the Divine nature, is seized. That however which most confounds the ungrateful, is the thought that he had delivered up Him, who though He was the Son of God, yet for our sakes wished to be the Son of man; as if He said, " For thee did I undertake, O ungrateful man, that which thou betrayest in hypocrisy. AUG. The Lord when He was betrayed first said this which Luke mentions, *Betrayest thou the Son of man with a kiss?* next, what Matthew says, *Friend, wherefore art thou come?* and lastly, what John records, *Whom seek ye?* AMBROSE; Our Lord

Chrys.
Conc. 1.
de Laz.

kissed him, not that He would teach us to dissemble, but both that He might not seem to shrink from the traitor, and that He might the more move him by not denying him the offices of love.

THEOPHYL. The disciples are inflamed with zeal, and unsheath their swords. But whence have they swords? Because they had slain the lamb, and had departed from the feast. Now the other disciples ask whether they should strike; but Peter, always fervent in defence of his Master, waits not for permission, but straightway strikes the servant of the High Priest; as it follows, *And one of them smote, &c.* AUG. He who struck, according to John, was Peter, but he whom he struck was called Malchus. AMBROSE; For Peter being well versed in the law, and full of ardent affection, knowing that it was counted righteousness in Phineas that he had killed the sacrilegious persons, struck the High Priest's servant.

Aug. de
Con. Ev.
lib. iii.
c. 5. AUG. Now Luke says, *But Jesus answered and said, Suffer ye thus far;* which is what Matthew records, *Put thy sword up into its sheath.* Nor will it move you as contrary thereto, that Luke says here that our Lord answered, *Suffer ye thus far,* as if He had so spoken after the blow to shew that what was done had pleased Him so far, but He did not wish it to proceed farther, seeing that in these words which Matthew has given, it may rather be implied that the whole circumstance in which Peter used the sword was displeasing to our Lord. For the truth is, that upon their asking, *Lord, shall we strike with the sword?* He then answered, *Suffer ye thus far,* that is, be not troubled with what is about to happen. They must be permitted to advance so far, that is, to take Me, and so to fulfil the things which were written of Me. For he would not say, *And Jesus answering,* unless He answered this question, not Peter's deed. But between the delay of their words of question to our Lord and His answer, Peter in the eagerness of defence struck the blow. And two things cannot be said, though one may be said and another may be done, at the same time. Then, as Luke says, He healed him who was struck, as it follows, *And he touched his ear, and healed him.* BEDE; For the Lord is never forgetful of His lovingkindness. While they are bringing death upon the righteous, He heals the wounds of His persecutors. AMBROSE; The Lord in wiping away the bloody wounds, conveyed thereby a divine mystery, namely, that the servant of the prince of this world, not by the condition of His nature but by guilt, should receive a wound on the ear, for that he had not heard the words of wisdom. Or, by Peter so willingly striking the ear, he taught that he ought not to have a ear outwardly, who had not one in a mystery. But why did Peter do this? Because he especially obtained the power of binding and loosing; therefore by his spiritual sword he takes away the interior ear of him who understandeth not. But the Lord Himself restores the hearing, shewing that even they, if they would turn, might be saved, who inflicted the wounds in our Lord's Passion; for that all sin may be washed away in the mysteries of faith. BEDE; Or that servant is the Jewish people sold by the High Priests to an unlawful obligation, who, by the Passion of our Lord, lost their right ear; that is, the spiritual understanding of the law. And this ear indeed is cut off by Peter's sword, not that he takes away the sense of understanding from those that hear, but manifests it withdrawn by the judgment of God from the careless. But the same right ear in those who among the same people have believed, is restored by the Divine condescension to its former office.

It follows, *Then said Jesus unto them, Are ye come out as against a thief with swords and staves? &c.* CHRYS. For they had come at night fearing an outbreak of the multitude, therefore He says, " What need was there of these arms against one who was always with you?" as it follows, *When I was daily with you.* CYRIL; Whereby He does not blame the chiefs of the Jews that they had not sooner prepared their murderous designs against Him, but convicts them of having presumptuously supposed they had attacked Him against His will; as if He says, " Ye did not take Me then, because I willed it not, but neither could ye now, did I not of My own accord surrender Myself into your hands." Hence it follows, *But this is your hour,* that is, a short time is permitted you to exercise your vengeance against Me, but the Father's will agrees with Mine. He also says, that this power is given to darkness, i. e. the Devil and the Jews, of rising in rebellion against Christ. And then is added, *And the power of darkness.* BEDE; As if He says, Therefore are ye assembled against Me in darkness, because your power, wherewith ye are thus armed against the light of the world, is in darkness. But it is asked, how Jesus is said to be addressing the chief priests, the officers of the temple, and the elders, who came to Him, whereas they are reported not to have gone of themselves, but to have sent their servants while they waited in the hall of Caiaphas? The answer then to this contradiction is, that they came not by themselves, but by those whom they sent to take Christ in the power of their command.

54. Then took they him, and led him, and brought him into the high priest's house. And Peter followed afar off.

55. And when they had kindled a fire in the midst of the hall, and were set down together, Peter sat down among them.

56. But a certain maid beheld him as he sat by the fire, and earnestly looked upon him, and said, This man was also with him.

57. And he denied him, saying, Woman, I know him not.

58. And after a little while another saw him, and said, Thou art also of them. And Peter said, Man, I am not.

59. And about the space of one hour after another confidently affirmed, saying, Of a truth this fellow also was with him: for he is a Galilæan.

60. And Peter said, Man, I know not what thou sayest. And immediately, while he yet spake, the cock crew.

61. And the Lord turned, and looked upon Peter. And Peter remembered the word of the Lord, how he had said unto him, Before the cock crow, thou shalt deny me thrice.

62. And Peter went out, and wept bitterly.

AMBROSE; The wretched men understood not the mystery,

nor had reverence unto an outpouring of compassion so merciful, that even His enemies He suffered not to be wounded.
For it is said, *Then took they him, &c.* When we read of
Jesus being holden, let us guard against thinking that He is
holden with respect to His divine nature, and unwilling
through weakness, for He is held captive and bound according to the truth of His bodily nature. BEDE; Now the Chief
Priest means Caiaphas, who according to John was High
Priest that year. AUG. But first He was led to Annas, the
father-in-law of Caiaphas, as John says, then to Caiaphas, as
Matthew says, but Mark and Luke do not give the name of
the High Priest. CHRYS. It is therefore said, *to the house* Chrys.
of the High Priest, that nothing whatever might be done Hom.
83. in
without the consent of the chief of the Priests. For thither Matt.
had they all assembled waiting for Christ. Now the great
zeal of Peter is manifested in his not flying when he saw
all the others doing so; for it follows, *But Peter followed
afar off.* AMBROSE; Rightly he followed afar off, soon
about to deny, for he could never have denied if he
had clung close to Christ. But herein must he be revered,
that he forsook not our Lord, even though he was afraid. Fear
is the effect of nature, solicitude of tender affection. BEDE;
But that when our Lord was going to His Passion, Peter followed afar off represents the Church about to follow indeed,
that is, to imitate our Lord's Passion, but in a far different
manner, for the Church suffers for herself, our Lord suffered
for the Church.

AMBROSE; And by this time there was a fire burning in the
house of the High Priest; as it follows, *And when they had
kindled a fire, &c.* Peter came to warm himself, because his
Lord being taken prisoner, the heart of his soul had been chilled
in him. PSEUDO-AUG. For to Peter were delivered the keys Pseudo-
of the kingdom of heaven, to him were entrusted an innume- Aug.
App.
rable multitude of people, who were wrapped up in sin. But Serm.
79.
Peter was somewhat too vehement, as the cutting off the ear
of the High Priest's servant betokens. If he then who was so
stern and so severe had obtained the gift of not sinning, what
pardon would he have given to the people committed to
him? Therefore Divine Providence suffers him first to be
holden of sin, that by the consciousness of his own fall he

might soften his too harsh judgment towards sinners. When
he wished to warm himself at the fire, a maid came to him, of
whom it follows, *But a certain maid beheld him, &c.* AM-
BROSE; What meaneth it, that a maid is the first to betray
Peter, whereas surely men ought the more easily to have recognised him, save that that sex should be plainly implicated in
our Lord's murder, in order that it might also be redeemed
by His Passion? But Peter when discovered denies, for
better that Peter should have denied, than our Lord's word
should have failed. Hence it follows, *And he denied, saying,*

Aug.
ut sup.
Woman, I know him not. AUG. What ails thee, Peter, thy
voice is suddenly changed? That mouth full of faith and
love, is turned to hatred and unbelief. Not yet awhile is the
scourge applied, not yet the instruments of torture. Thy in-
terrogator is no one of authority, who might cause alarm to
the confessor. The mere voice of a woman asks the question,
and she perhaps not about to divulge thy confession, nor
yet a woman, but a door-keeper, a mean slave.

AMBROSE; Peter denied, because he promised rashly. He
does not deny on the mount, nor in the temple, nor in his
own house, but in the judgment-hall of the Jews. There he
denies where Jesus was bound, where truth is not. And denying Him he says, *I know him not.* It were presumptuous to
say that he knew Him whom the human mind can not grasp.

Matt.
11, 17.
For *no one knoweth the Son but the Father.* Again, a
second time he denies Christ; for it follows, *And after a
little while another saw him, and said, Thou wert also one
of them.*

Aug.
de Con.
Ev. lib.
iii. c. 6.
AUG. And it is supposed that in the second denial
he was addressed by two persons, namely, by the maid whom
Matthew and Mark mention, and by another whom Luke
speaks of. With respect then to what Luke here relates,
And after a little while, &c. Peter had already gone out of
the gate, and the cock had crowed the first time, as Mark
says; and now he had returned, that, as John says, he might
again deny standing by the fire. Of which denial it follows,
And Peter said, Man, I am not. AMBROSE; For he preferred to deny himself rather than Christ, or because he
seemed to deny being of the company of Christ, he truly
denied himself. BEDE; In this denial then of Peter we affirm
that not only is Christ denied by him who says that He is

not Christ, but by him also, who, being a Christian, says he
is not.

AMBROSE; He is also asked a third time; for it follows,
*And about the space of one hour after, another confidently
affirmed, saying, Of a truth this fellow also was with him.*
AUG. What Matthew and Mark call *after a little while,* Aug.
Luke explains by saying, *about the space of one hour after;* de Con.
Ev. ut
but with regard to the space of time, John says nothing. sup.
Likewise when Matthew and Mark record not in the singular
but in the plural number those who conversed with Peter,
while Luke and John speak of one, we may easily suppose
either that Matthew and Mark used the plural for the singular
by a common form of speech, or that one person in particular
addressed Peter, as being the one who had seen him, and
that others trusting to his credit joined in pressing him.
But now as to the words which Matthew asserts were said to
Peter himself, *Truly thou art one of them, for thy speech
bewrayeth thee;* as also those which to the same Peter John
declared to have been said, *Did not I see thee in the garden?*
whereas Mark and Luke state that they spoke to one another
concerning Peter; we either believe that they held the right
opinion who say that they were really addressed to Peter;
(for what was said concerning him in his presence amounts
to the same as if it had been said to him;) or that they were
said in both ways, and that some of the Evangelists related
them one way, some the other. BEDE; But he adds, *For
he is a Galilæan;* not that the Galilæans spoke a different
language from the inhabitants of Jerusalem, who indeed were
Hebrews, but that each separate province and country having
its own peculiarities could not avoid a vernacular tone of
speech. It follows, *And Peter said, Man, I know not what
thou sayest.* AMBROSE; That is, I know not your blasphemies. But we make excuse for him. He did not excuse
himself. For an involved answer is not sufficient for our
confessing Jesus, but an open confession is required. And
therefore Peter is not represented to have answered this
deliberately, for he afterwards recollected himself, and wept.

BEDE; Holy Scripture is often wont to mark the character
of certain events by the nature of the times in which they
take place. Hence Peter who sinned at midnight repented

at cock-crow; for it follows, *And immediately, while he yet spake, the cock crew.* The error he committed in the darkness of forgetfulness, he corrected by the remembrance of

Aug. ut sup.
the true light. AUG. The cock-crow we understand to have been after the third denial of Peter, as Mark has expressed it. BEDE; This cock must, I think, be understood mystically as some great Teacher, who rouses the listless and sleepy, saying, *Awake, ye righteous, and sin not.*

Chrys. Hom. 83. in Joan.
CHRYS. Marvel now at the case of the Master, who though He was a prisoner, had exercised much forethought for His disciple, whom by a look He brought to Himself, and provoked to tears; for it follows, *And the Lord turned, and looked upon Peter.*

Aug. ut sup.
AUG. How we should understand this, requires some careful consideration; for Matthew says, *Peter was sitting without in the hall,* which he would not have said unless the transaction relating to our Lord were passing within. Likewise also, where Mark said, *And as Peter was beneath in the hall,* he shews that the things he had been speaking of took place not only within but in the upper part. How then did our Lord look upon Peter? not with His bodily face, since Peter was without in the hall among those who were warming themselves, while these things were going on in the inner part of the house. Wherefore, that looking upon Peter seems to me to have been done in a divine

Ps.13,3.
manner. And as it was said, *Look thou, and hear me,* and,

Ps. 6, 4.
Turn and deliver my soul, so I think the expression here used, *The Lord turned and looked upon Peter.* BEDE; For to look upon him is to have compassion, seeing that not only while penance is being practised, but that it may be practised, the mercy of God is necessary.

AMBROSE; Lastly, those whom Jesus looks upon weep for their sins. Hence it follows, *And Peter remembered the word of the Lord, how he had said to him, Before the cock crow, thou shalt deny me thrice. And he went out, and wept bitterly.* Why did he weep? Because he sinned as man. I read of his tears, I do not read of his confession. Tears wash away an offence which it is shame to confess in words. The first and second time he denied and wept not, for as yet our Lord had not looked upon him. He denied the third time, Jesus looked upon him, and he wept bitterly. So then

if thou wilt obtain pardon, wash away thy guilt in tears.
CYRIL; Now Peter did not dare to weep openly, lest he
should be detected by his tears, but he went out and wept.
He wept not because of punishment, but because he denied
his beloved Lord, which was more galling than any punishment.

63. And the men that held Jesus mocked him, and
smote him.

64. And when they had blindfolded him, they
struck him on the face, and asked him, saying, Prophesy, who is it that smote thee?

65. And many other things blasphemously spake
they against him.

66. And as soon as it was day, the elders of the
people and the chief priests and the scribes came
together, and led him into their council, saying,

67. Art thou the Christ? tell us. And he said
unto them, If I tell you, ye will not believe:

68. And if I also ask you, ye will not answer me,
nor let me go.

69. Hereafter shall the Son of man sit on the right
hand of the power of God.

70. Then said they all, Art thou then the Son of
God? And he said unto them, Ye say that I am.

71. And they said, What need we any further
witness? for we ourselves have heard of his own
mouth.

AUG. The temptation of Peter which took place between Aug.
the mockings of our Lord is not related by all the Evangelists de Con.
Ev. lib.
in the same order. For Matthew and Mark first mention iii. c. 7.
those, then Peter's temptation; but Luke has first described
the temptations of Peter, then the mockings of our Lord,
saying, *And the men that held Jesus mocked him, &c.*
CHRYS. Jesus, the Lord of heaven and earth, sustains and

patience. THEOPHYL. Likewise the Lord of prophets is derided as a false prophet. It follows, *And they blindfolded him.* This they did as a dishonour to Him who wished to be accounted by the people as a prophet. But He who was struck with the blows of the Jews, is struck also now by the blasphemies of false Christians. And they blindfolded Him, not that He should not see their wickedness, but that they might hide His face from them. But heretics, and Jews, and wicked Catholics, provoke Him with their vile actions, as it were mocking Him, saying, *Who smote thee?* while they flatter themselves that their evil thoughts and works of dark-

Aug. de Con. Ev. ut sup. ness are not known by Him. AUG. Now our Lord is supposed to have suffered these things until morning in the house of the High Priest, to which He was first led. Hence it follows, *And as soon as it was day, the elders of the people and the chief priests and the scribes came together, and led him into their council, saying, Art thou the Christ? &c.* BEDE; They wished not for truth, but were contriving calumny. Because they expected that Christ would come only as man, of the root of David, they sought this of Him, that if He should say, " I am the Christ," they might falsely accuse Him of claiming to Himself the kingly power.

THEOPHYL. He knew the secrets of their hearts, that they who had not believed His works would much less believe His words. Hence it follows, *And he said unto them, If I tell you, ye will not believe, &c.* BEDE; For He had often

John 10, 30. declared Himself to be the Christ; as when he said, *I and my Father are one,* and other such like things. *And if I also ask you, ye will not answer me.* For He had asked them how they said Christ was the Son of David, whereas David in the Spirit called Him his Lord. But they wished neither to believe His words nor to answer His questions. However, because they sought to accuse falsely the seed of David, they hear something still farther; as it follows, *Hereafter shall the Son of man sit on the right hand of the power of God.* THEOPHYL. As if he said, There is no time left to you any longer for discourses and teaching, but hereafter shall be the time of judgment, when ye shall see Me, the Son of man, sitting on the right hand of the power of God. CYRIL; Whenever sitting and a throne are spoken

of God, His kingly and supreme majesty is signified. For
we do not imagine any judgment-seat to be placed, on which
we believe the Lord of all takes His seat; nor again, that
in any wise right hand or left hand appertain to the Divine
nature; for figure, and place, and sitting, are the properties
of bodies. But how shall the Son be seen to be of equal
honour and to sit together on the same throne, if He is not
the Son according to nature, having in Himself the natural
property of the Father? THEOPHYL. When then they heard
this, they ought to have been afraid, but after these words
they are the more frantic; as it follows, *All said, &c.* BEDE;
They understood that He called Himself the Son of God in
these words, *The Son of man shall sit on the right hand
of the power of God.* AMBROSE; The Lord had rather
prove Himself a King than call Himself one, that they might
have no excuse for condemning Him, when they confess the
truth of that which they lay against Him. It follows, *And
he said, Ye say that I am.* CYRIL; When Christ spoke
this, the company of the Pharisees were very wroth, uttering
shameful words; as it follows, *Then said they, What need we
any further witness? &c.* THEOPHYL. Whereby it is manifest, that the disobedient reap no advantage, when the more
secret mysteries are revealed to them, but rather incur the
heavier punishment. Wherefore such things ought to be
concealed from them.

CHAP. XXIII.

1. And the whole multitude of them arose, and led him unto Pilate.

2. And they began to accuse him, saying, We found this fellow perverting the nation, and forbidding to give tribute to Cæsar, saying that he himself is Christ a King.

3. And Pilate asked him, saying, Art thou the King of the Jews? And he answered him and said, Thou sayest it.

4. Then said Pilate to the chief priests and to the people, I find no fault in this man.

5. And they were the more fierce, saying, He stirreth up the people, teaching throughout all Jewry, beginning from Galilee to this place.

Aug. de Con.Ev. lib. iii. c. 7. AUG. Luke, after he had finished relating the denial of Peter, recapitulated all that took place concerning our Lord during the morning, mentioning some particulars which the others omitted; and so he has composed his narrative, giving a similar account with the rest, when he says, *And the whole multitude of them arose, and led him to Pilate, &c.* BEDE; That the word of Jesus might be fulfilled which He prophesied of His own death, *He shall be delivered to the Gentiles,* that is, to the Romans. For Pilate was a Roman, and the Romans had sent him as governor to Judæa. AUG. He next relates what happens before Pilate, as follows, *And they began to accuse him, saying, We found this fellow perverting our nation, &c.* Matthew and Mark do not give this, though affirming that they accused Him, but Luke has laid open the very charges which they falsely brought against Him.

Aug. lib. iii. c. 8.

THEOPHYL. Most plainly are they opposed to the truth. For our Lord was so far from forbidding to give tribute, that He commanded it to be given. How then did He pervert the people? Was it that He might take possession of the kingdom? But this is incredible to all, for when the whole multitude wished to choose Him for their king, He was aware of it, and fled. BEDE; Now two charges having been brought against our Lord, namely, that He forbade to pay tribute to Cæsar, and called Himself Christ the King, it may be that Pilate had chanced to hear that which our Lord spake, *Render unto Cæsar the things which be Cæsar's;* and therefore setting aside this accusation as a palpable lie of the Jews, he thought fit to ask concerning that alone of which he knew nothing, the saying about *the kingdom;* for it follows, *Pilate asked him, saying, Art thou the King of the Jews, &c.* THEOPHYL. It seems to me that he asked this question of Christ by way of deriding the wantonness or hypocrisy of the alleged charge. As if he said, Thou a poor humble naked man, with none to help Thee, art accused of seeking a kingdom, for which Thou wouldest need many to help Thee, and much money. BEDE; He answers the governor in the same words which He used to the Chief Priests, that Pilate might be condemned by his own voice; for it follows, *And he answering said, Thou sayest.*

THEOPHYL. Now they finding nothing else to support their calumny, have resort to the aid of clamour, for it follows, *And they were the more fierce, saying, He stirreth up the people, teaching throughout all Jewry, beginning from Galilee to this place.* As if they said, He perverts the people, not in one part only, but beginning from Galilee He arrives at this place, having passed through Judæa. I think then that they purposely made mention of Galilee, as desirous to alarm Pilate, for the Galilæans were of a different sect and given to sedition, as, for example, Judas of Galilee who is mentioned in the Acts of the Apostles. BEDE; But with these words they accuse not Him, but themselves. For to have taught the people, and by teaching to have roused them from their former idleness, and doing this to have passed through the whole land of promise, was an evidence not of sin, but of virtue. AMBROSE; Our Lord is accused

and is silent, for He needs no defence.   Let them cast about
for defence who fear to be conquered.   He does not then
confirm the accusation by His silence, but He despises it
by not refuting it.   Why then should He fear who does not
court safety? The Safety of all men forfeits His own, that He
may gain that of all.

6. When Pilate heard of Galilee, he asked whether
the man were a Galilæan.

7. And as soon as he knew that he belonged
unto Herod's jurisdiction, he sent him to Herod, who
himself also was at Jerusalem at that time.

8. And when Herod saw Jesus, he was exceeding
glad : for he was desirous to see him of a long season,
because he had heard many things of him ; and he
hoped to have seen some miracle done by him.

9. Then he questioned with him in many words ;
but he answered him nothing.

10. And the chief priests and scribes stood and
vehemently accused him.

11. And Herod with his men of war set him at
nought, and mocked him, and arrayed him in a
gorgeous robe, and sent him again to Pilate.

12. And the same day Pilate and Herod were
made friends together : for before they were at enmity
between themselves.

BEDE; Pilate having determined not to question our Lord
concerning the above-mentioned accusation, is the rather
glad now that an opportunity offers to escape from passing
judgment upon Him.   Hence it is said, *When Pilate heard
of Galilee, he asked whether the man were a Galilæan.*
And lest he should be compelled to pass sentence against
one whom he knew to be innocent, and delivered for envy,
sends Him to be heard by Herod, preferring that he who
was the Tetrarch of our Lord's country might be the person
either to acquit or punish Him; for it follows, *And as soon
as he knew that he belonged to Herod's jurisdiction.*

THEOPHYL. Wherein he follows the Roman law, which provided that every man should be judged by the governor of his own jurisdiction.

GREG. Now Herod wished to make proof of Christ's fame, desiring to witness His miracles; for it follows, *And when Herod saw Jesus, he was glad, &c.* THEOPHYL. Not as though he was about to gain any benefit from the sight, but seized with curiosity he thought he should see that extraordinary man, of whose wisdom and wonderful works he had heard so much. He also wished to hear from His mouth what He could say. Accordingly he asks Him questions, making a sport of Him, and ridiculing Him. But Jesus, who performed all things prudently, and who, as David testifies, *ordereth His words with discretion,* thought it right in such a case to be silent. For a word uttered to one whom it profiteth nothing becomes the cause of his condemnation. Therefore it follows, *But he answered him nothing.* AMBROSE; He was silent and did nothing, for Herod's unbelief deserved not to see Him, and the Lord shunned display. And perhaps typically in Herod are represented all the ungodly, who if they have not believed the Law and the Prophets, cannot see Christ's wonderful works in the Gospel.

GREG. From these words we ought to derive a lesson, that whenever our hearers wish as if by praising us to gain knowledge from us, but not to change their own wicked course, we must be altogether silent, lest if from love of ostentation we speak God's word, both they who were guilty cease not to be so, and we who were not become so. And there are many things which betray the motive of a hearer, but one in particular, when they always praise what they hear, yet never follow what they praise. GREG. The Redeemer therefore though questioned held His peace, though expected disdained to work miracles. And keeping Himself secretly within Himself, left those who were satisfied to seek for outward things, to remain thankless without, preferring to be openly set at nought by the proud, than be praised by the hollow voices of unbelievers. Hence it follows, *And the chief priests and scribes stood and vehemently accused him. And Herod with his men of war set him at nought, and mocked him, and arrayed him in a white robe.* AMBROSE; It is not

Marginal notes:
Greg. Mor. 10. c. 31.
Ps. 112, 5.
Greg. Mor. 22. c. 16.
Greg. Mor. 10. c. 31.

without reason that He is arrayed by Herod in a white robe, as bearing a sign of His immaculate Passion, that the Lamb of God without spot would take upon Himself the sins of the world. THEOPHYL. Nevertheless, observe how the Devil is thwarted by the thing which He does. He heaps up scorn and reproaches against Christ, whereby it is made manifest that the Lord is not seditious. Otherwise He would not have been derided, when so great a danger was afloat, and that too from a people who were held in suspicion, and so given to change. But the sending of Christ by Pilate to Herod, becomes the commencement of a mutual friendship, Pilate not receiving those who were subject to Herod's authority, as it is added, *And they were made friends, &c.* Observe the Devil every where uniting together things separate, that he may compass the death of Christ. Let us blush then, if for the sake of our salvation we keep not even our friends in union with us.

AMBROSE; Under the type also of Herod and Pilate, who from enemies were made friends by Jesus Christ, is preserved the figure of the people of Israel and the Gentile nation; that through our Lord's Passion should come to pass the future concord of both, yet so that the people of the Gentiles should receive the word of God first, and then transmit it by the devotion of their faith to the Jewish people; that they too may with the glory of their majesty clothe the body of Christ, which before they had despised. BEDE; Or this alliance between Herod and Pilate signifies that the Gentiles and Jews, though differing in race, religion, and character, agree together in persecuting Christians.

13. And Pilate, when he had called together the chief priests and the rulers and the people,

14. Said unto them, Ye have brought this man unto me, as one that perverteth the people: and, behold, I, having examined him before you, have found no fault in this man touching those things whereof ye accuse him:

15. No, nor yet Herod: for I sent you to him; and, lo, nothing worthy of death is done unto him.

16. I will therefore chastise him, and release him.

17. (For of necessity he must release one unto them at the feast.)

18. And they cried out all at once, saying, Away with this man, and release unto us Barabbas:

19. (Who for a certain sedition made in the city, and for murder, was cast into prison.)

20. Pilate therefore, willing to release Jesus, spake again to them.

21. But they cried, saying, Crucify him, crucify him.

22. And he said unto them the third time, Why, what evil hath he done? I have found no cause of death in him: I will therefore chastise him, and let him go.

23. And they were instant with loud voices, requiring that he might be crucified. And the voices of them and of the chief priests prevailed.

24. And Pilate gave sentence that it should be as they required.

25. And he released unto them him that for sedition and murder was cast into prison, whom they had desired; but he delivered Jesus to their will.

AUG. Luke returns to those things which were going on before the governor, from which he had digressed in order to relate what took place with Herod; saying as follows, *And Pilate, when he had called, &c.* from which we infer, that he has omitted the part wherein Pilate questioned our Lord what He had to answer to His accusers.

AMBROSE; Here Pilate, who as a judge acquits Christ, is made the minister of His crucifixion. He is sent to Herod, sent back to Pilate, as it follows, *Nor yet Herod, for I sent you to him, and behold nothing worthy of death is done unto him.* They both refuse to pronounce Him guilty, yet for fear's sake, Pilate gratifies the cruel desires of the Jews. THEO-

PHYL. Wherefore by the testimony of two men, Jesus is declared innocent, but the Jews His accusers brought forward no witness whom they could believe. See then how truth triumphs. Jesus is silent, and His enemies witness for Him; the Jews make loud cries, and not one of them corroborates their clamour. BEDE; Perish then those writings, which, composed so long a time after Christ, convict not the accused of magical arts against Pilate, but the writers themselves of treachery and lying against Christ.

THEOPHYL. Pilate therefore lenient and easy, yet wanting in firmness for the truth, because afraid of being accused, adds, *I will therefore chastise him and release him.* BEDE; As if he said, I will subject Him to all the scourgings and mockings you desire, but do not thirst after the innocent blood. It follows, *For of necessity he must release one unto them, &c.* an obligation not imposed by a decree of the imperial law, but binding by the annual custom of the nation, whom in such things he was glad to please. THEOPHYL. For the Romans permitted the Jews to live according to their own laws and customs. And it was a natural custom of the Jews to seek pardon of the prince for those who were condemned, as they asked Jonathan of Saul. And hence it is now added, with respect to their petition, *And they cried all at once,* *Away with this man, and release unto us Barabbas, &c.* AM-BROSE; Not unreasonably do they seek the pardon of a murderer, who were themselves demanding the death of the innocent. Such are the laws of iniquity, that what innocence hates, guilt loves. And here the interpretation of the name affords a figurative resemblance, for Barabbas is in Latin, the son of a father. Those then to whom it is said, *Ye are of your father the Devil,* are represented as about to prefer to the true Son of God the son of their father, that is, Anti-christ. BEDE; Even to this day their request still clings to the Jews. For since when they had the choice given to them, they chose a robber for Jesus, a murderer for a Saviour; rightly lost they both life and salvation, and became subject to such robberies and seditions among themselves as to forfeit both their country and kingdom. THEOPHYL. Thus it came to pass, the once holy nation rages to slay, the Gentile Pilate forbids slaughter; as it follows, *Pilate therefore spoke*

1 Sam. 14, 45.

again unto them, but they cried out, Crucify, &c. BEDE;
With the worst kind of death, that is, crucifixion, they long
to murder the innocent. For they who hung on the cross,
with their hands and feet fixed by nails to the wood, suffered
a prolonged death, that their agony might not quickly cease;
but the death of the cross was chosen by our Lord, as
that which having overcome the Devil, He was about to
place as a trophy on the brows of the faithful. THEOPHYL.
Three times did Pilate acquit Christ, for it follows, *And
he said unto them the third time, Why, what evil hath
he done? I will chastise him, and let him go.* BEDE;
This chastisement wherewith Pilate sought to satisfy the
people, lest their rage should go even so far as to crucify
Jesus, John's words bear testimony that he not only threatened
but performed together with mockings and scourgings. But
when they saw all their charges which they brought against
the Lord baffled by Pilate's diligent questioning, they resort
at last to prayers only; entreating that He might be crucified.
THEOPHYL. They cry out the third time against Christ,
that by this third voice, they may approve the murder to be
their own, which by their entreaties they extorted; for it
follows, *And Pilate gave sentence that it should be as they
required. And he released him that for sedition and murder
was cast into prison, but delivered Jesus to their will.* CHRYS.
For they thought they could add this, namely, that Jesus was
worse than a robber, and so wicked, that neither for mercy's
sake, or by the privilege of the feast, ought He to be let free.

26. And as they led him away, they laid hold upon
one Simon, a Cyrenian, coming out of the country,
and on him they laid the cross, that he might bear it
after Jesus.

27. And there followed him a great company of
people, and of women, which also bewailed and
lamented him.

28. But Jesus turning unto them said, Daughters
of Jerusalem, weep not for me, but weep for yourselves, and for your children.

29. For, behold, the days are coming, in the which they shall say, Blessed are the barren, and the wombs that never bare, and the paps which never gave suck.

30. Then shall they begin to say to the mountains, Fall on us; and to the hills, Cover us.

31. For if they do these things in a green tree, what shall be done in the dry?

32. And there were also two other, malefactors, led with him to be put to death.

Gloss.
non occ.
GLOSS. Having related the condemnation of Christ, Luke naturally goes on to speak of His crucifixion; as it is said, *And as they led him away, they laid hold upon one Simon,*

Aug. de
Con.Ev.
lib. iii.
c. 10.
&c. AUG. But John relates that Jesus bore His own cross, from which is understood that He was Himself carrying His cross, when He went forth to that place which is called Calvary; but as they journeyed Simon was forced into the service on the road, and the cross was given him to carry as far as that place. THEOPHYL. For no one else accepted to bear the cross, because the wood was counted an abomination. Accordingly upon Simon the Cyrenian they imposed as it were to his dishonour the bearing of the cross, which others refused. Here is fulfilled that prophecy of Isaiah,

Isa.9,6.
Whose government shall be upon his shoulder. For the government of Christ is His cross; for which the Apostle

Phil. 2,
9.
says, *God hath exalted him.* And as for a mark of dignity, some wear a belt, others a head dress, so our Lord the cross. And if thou seekest, thou wilt find that Christ does not reign in us save by hardships, whence it comes that the luxurious are the enemies of the cross of Christ. AMBROSE; Christ therefore bearing His cross, already as a conqueror carried His trophies. The cross is laid upon His shoulders, because, whether Simon or Himself bore it, both Christ bore it in the man, and the man in Christ. Nor do the accounts of the Evangelists differ, since the mystery reconciles them. And it is the rightful order of our advance that Christ should first Himself erect the trophy of His cross, then hand it down to be raised by His martyrs. He is not a Jew who bears the

cross, but an alien and a foreigner, nor does he precede but follow, according as it is written, *Let him take up his cross, and follow me.*

BEDE; Simon is by interpretation " obedient," Cyrene " an heir." By this man therefore the people of the Gentiles are denoted, who formerly foreigners and aliens to the covenant, have now by obedience been made heirs of God. But Simon coming out of a village, bears the cross after Jesus, because forsaking the pagan rites, he obediently embraces the footsteps of our Lord's Passion. For a village is in Greek called πάγος, from whence Pagans derive their name. THEOPHYL. Or he takes up the cross of Christ, who comes from the village; that is, he leaves this world and its labours, going forward to Jerusalem, that is, heavenly liberty. Hereby also we receive no slight instruction. For to be a master after the example of Christ, a man must himself first take up his cross, and in the fear of God crucify his own flesh, that he may so lay it upon those that are subject and obedient to him.

But there followed Christ a great company of people, and of women. BEDE; A large multitude indeed followed the cross of Christ, but with very different feelings. For the people who had demanded His death were rejoicing that they should see Him dying, the women weeping that He was about to die. But He was followed by the weeping only of women, not because that vast crowd of men was not also sorrowful at His Passion, but because the less esteemed female sex could more freely give utterance to what they thought. CYRIL; Women also are ever prone to tears, and have hearts easily disposed to pity.

THEOPHYL. He bids those who weep for Him cast their eyes forward to the evils that were coming, and weep for themselves. CYRIL; Signifying that in the time to come women would be bereft of their children. For when war breaks out upon the land of the Jews, all shall perish, both small and great. Hence it follows, *For, behold, the days are coming, in the which they shall say, Blessed are the barren, &c.* THEOPHYL. Seeing indeed that women shall cruelly roast their children, and the belly which had produced shall miserably again receive that which it bore. BEDE; By these days He signifies the time of the siege and captivity which was coming upon them from the Romans, of which He had said before, *Woe to them that are with child, and give suck in those days.* It is natural, when captivity by an enemy is threatening, to seek for refuge in fastnesses or hidden places, where men may lie concealed. And so it follows, *Then shall they begin to say to the mountains, Fall on us; and to the hills, Cover us.* For Josephus relates, that when the Romans pressed hard upon them, the Jews sought hastily the caverns of the mountains, and the lurking places in the hills. It may be also that the words, *Blessed are the barren,* are to be understood of those of both sexes, who have made themselves eunuchs for the kingdom of heaven's sake, and that it is said to the mountains and hills, *Fall upon us,* and *Cover us,* because all who are mindful of their own weakness, when the crisis of their temptations breaks upon them, have sought to be protected by the example, precepts, and prayers, of certain high and saintly men.

It follows, *But if they do these things in a green tree, what shall be done in the dry?* GREG. He has called Himself the green wood and us the dry, for He has in Himself the life and strength of the Divine nature; but we who are mere men are called the dry wood. THEOPHYL. As though He said to the Jews, If then the Romans have so raged against Me, a fruit-bearing and ever flourishing tree, what will they not attempt against you the people, who are a dry tree, destitute of every lifegiving virtue, and bearing no fruit? BEDE; Or as if He spake to all: If I who have done no sin being called the tree of life, do not depart from the world without suffering the fire of my Passion, what torment think ye awaits those who are barren of all fruits?

THEOPHYL. But the Devil, desiring to engender an evil opinion of our Lord, caused robbers also to be crucified with Him; whence it follows, *And there were two other malefactors led with him to be put to death.*

33. And when they were come to the place, which is called Calvary, there they crucified him, and the malefactors, one on the right hand, and the other on the left.

ATHAN. When mankind became corrupted, then Christ ^{Athan.} manifested His own body, that where corruption has been ^{Hom. in Pass.} seen, there might spring up incorruption. Wherefore He is ^{Dom.} crucified in the place of Calvary; which place the Jewish doctors say was the burial-place of Adam. BEDE; Or else, without the gate were the places where the heads of condemned criminals were cut off, and they received the name of Calvary, that is, beheaded. Thus for the salvation of all men the innocent is crucified among the guilty, that where sin abounded, there grace might much more abound.

CYRIL; The only-begotten Son of God did not Himself in His own nature in which He is God suffer the things which belong to the body, but rather in His earthly nature. For of one and the same Son both may be affirmed, namely, that He doth not suffer in His divine nature, and that He suffered in His human. EUSEB. But if, on the contrary, after His intercourse with men, He suddenly disappeared, flying away to avoid death, He might be likened by man to a phantom. And just as if any one wished to exhibit some incombustible vessel, which triumphed over the nature of fire, he would put it into the flame, and then directly draw it out from the flame unharmed; so the Word of God, wishing to shew that the instrument which He used for the salvation of men was superior to death, exposed His mortal body to death to manifest His nature, then after a little rescued it from death by the force of His divine power. This is indeed the first cause of Christ's death. But the second is the manifestation of the divine power of Christ inhabiting a body. For seeing that men of old deified those who were destined to a like end with themselves, and whom they called Heroes and Gods, He taught that He alone of the dead must be acknowledged the true God, who having vanquished death is adorned with the rewards of victory, having trodden death under His feet. The third reason is, that a victim must be slain for the whole race of mankind, which being offered, the whole power of the evil spirits was destroyed, and every error put to silence. There is also another cause of the healthgiving death, that the disciples with secret faith might behold the resurrection after death. Whereunto they were taught to lift up their own hopes, that despising death they might embark cheerfully in the conflict with error.

Athan.
de Inc.
Verb.
Dei.

ATHAN. Now our Saviour came to accomplish not His own death, but that of man, for He experienced not death who is Life. Therefore not by His own death did He put off the body, but He endured that which was inflicted by men. But although His body had been afflicted, and was loosed in the sight of all men, yet was it not fitting that He who should heal the sicknesses of others should have His own body visited with sickness. But yet if without any disease He had put off His body apart in some remote place, He would not be believed when speaking of His resurrection. For death must precede resurrection; why then should He openly proclaim His resurrection, but die in secret? Surely if these things had happened secretly, what calumnies would unbelieving men have invented? How would the victory of Christ over death appear, unless undergoing it in the sight of all men He had proved it to be swallowed up by the incorruption of His body? But you will say, At least He ought to have devised for Himself a glorious death, to have avoided the death of the cross. But if He had done this, He would have made Himself suspected of not having power over every kind of death As then the champion by laying prostrate whomsoever the enemy has opposed to him is shewn to be superior to all, so the Life of all men took upon Him that death which His enemies inflicted, because it was the most dreadful and shameful, the abominable death upon the cross, that having destroyed it, the dominion of death might be entirely overthrown. Wherefore His head is not cut off as John's was; He was not sawn asunder as Isaiah, that He might preserve His body entire, and indivisible to death, and not become an excuse to those who would divide the Church. For He wished to bear the curse of sin which we had incurred, by taking upon Him the accursed death of the cross, as it is said, *Cursed is he that hangeth upon a tree.* He dies also on the cross with outstretched hands, that with one indeed He may draw to Him the ancient people, with the other the Gentiles, joining both to Himself. Dying also on the cross He purges the air of evil spirits, and prepares for us an ascent into hea--

ven. THEOPHYL. Because also by a tree death had entered, it must needs be that by a tree it should be abolished, and that the Lord passing unconquered through the pains of a tree should subdue the pleasures which flow from a tree.

GREG. NYSS. But the figure of the cross from one centre of contact branching out into four separate terminations, signifies the power and providence of Him who hung upon it extending every where. AUG. For not without reason did He choose this kind of death, in order that He might be the master of breadth and length, and heighth and depth. For breadth lies in that cross piece of wood which is fastened from above. This belongs to good works, because on it the hands are outstretched. Length lies in that which is seen reaching from the former piece to the ground, for there in a certain manner we stand, that is, abide firm or persevere. And this is applied to longsuffering. Heighth is in that piece of wood which is left reaching upwards from that which is fixed across, that is, to the head of the Crucified; for the expectation of those who hope for better things is upward. Again, that part of the wood which is fixed hidden in the ground, signifies the depth of unrestrained grace. CHRYS. Two thieves also they crucified on the two sides, that He might be a partaker of their reproach; as it follows, *And the thieves one on his right hand, the other on his left.* But it did not so turn out. For of them nothing is said, but His cross is every where honoured. Kings, laying aside their crowns, assume the cross on their purple, on their diadems, on their arms. On the consecrated table, throughout the whole earth, the cross glitters. Such things are not of men. For even in their lifetime those who have acted nobly are mocked by their own actions, and when they perish their actions perish also. But in Christ it is quite different. For before the cross all things were gloomy, after it all things are joyful and glorious, that you may know that not a mere man was crucified. BEDE; But the two robbers crucified with Christ signify those who under the faith of Christ undergo either the pains of martyrdom, or the rules of a still stricter continence. But they do this for eternal glory, who imitate the actions of the thief on the right hand; while they who do it to gain the praise of men, imitate the thief on the left hand.

Greg.
Nyss.
Orat. 1.
de Res.
Christ.
Aug. de
Gr. Nov.
Test.
Ep. 140.

Chrys.
Hom.
87. in
Matt.

34. Then said Jesus, Father, forgive them ; for they know not what they do. And they parted his raiment, and cast lots.

35. And the people stood beholding. And the rulers also with them derided him, saying, He saved others ; let him save himself, if he be Christ, the chosen of God.

36. And the soldiers also mocked him, coming to him, and offering him vinegar,

37. And saying, If thou be the king of the Jews, save thyself.

CHRYS. Because the Lord had said, *Pray for them that persecute you*, this likewise He did, when He ascended the cross, as it follows, *Then said Jesus, Father, forgive them*, not that He was not able Himself to pardon them, but that He might teach us to pray for our persecutors, not only in word, but in deed also. But He says, *Forgive them*, if they should repent. For He is gracious to the penitent, if they are willing after so great wickedness to wash away their guilt by faith. BEDE ; Nor must we imagine here that He prayed in vain, but that in those who believed after His passion He obtained the fruit of His prayers? It must be remarked, however, that He prayed not for those who chose rather to crucify, rather than to confess Him whom they knew to be the Son of God, but for such as were ignorant what they did, having a zeal for God, but not according to knowledge, as He adds, *For they know not what they do*. GREEK Ex. But for those who after the crucifixion remain in unbelief, no one can suppose that they are excused by ignorance, because of the notable miracles that with a loud voice proclaimed Him to be the Son of God.

AMBROSE ; It is important then to consider, in what condition He ascends the cross ; for I see Him naked. Let him then who prepares to overcome the world, so ascend that he seek not the appliances of the world. Now Adam was overcome who sought for a covering. He overcame who laid aside His covering. He ascends such as nature formed us, God being our Creator. Such as the first man had dwelt in paradise, such did

Matt. 5, 44.

the second man enter paradise. But about to ascend the cross rightly, did He lay aside His royal garments, that you may know that He suffered not as God, but as man, though Christ is both. ATHAN. He also who for our sakes took upon Him all our conditions, put on our garments, the signs of Adam's death, that He might put them off, and in their stead clothe us with life and incorruption. ^{Athan. Hom. in Pass. Dom.}

It follows, *And they parted his raiment among them, and cast lots.* THEOPHYL. For perhaps many of them were in want. Or perhaps rather they did this as a reproach, and from a kind of wantonness. For what treasure did they find in His garments? BEDE; But in the lot the grace of God seems to be commended; for when the lot is cast, we yield not to the merits of any person, but to the secret judgment of God. AUG. This matter indeed was briefly related by the three first Evangelists, but John more distinctly explains how it was done. ^{Aug. de Con. Ev. lib. iii. c. 12.}

THEOPHYL. They did it then mockingly. For when the rulers scoffed, what can we say of the crowd? for it follows, *And the people stood,* who in truth had entreated that He should be crucified, *waiting,* namely, for the end. *And the rulers also with them derided.* AUG. Having mentioned the rulers, and said nothing of the priests, St. Luke comprehended under a general name all the chief men, so that hereby may be understood both the scribes and the elders. BEDE; And these also unwillingly confess that He saved others, for it follows, *Saying, He saved others, let him save himself, &c.* ATHAN. Now our Lord being truly the Saviour, wished not by saving Himself, but by saving His creatures, to be acknowledged the Saviour. For neither is a physician by healing himself known to be a physician, unless he also gives proof of his skill towards the sick. So the Lord being the Saviour had no need of salvation, nor by descending from the cross did He wish to be acknowledged the Saviour, but by dying. For truly a much greater salvation does the death of the Saviour bring to men, than the descent from the cross. GREEK EX. Now the Devil, seeing that there was no protection for him, was at a loss, and as having no other resource, tried at last to offer Him vinegar to drink. But he knew not that he was doing this against himself; for the ^{Aug. ubi sup.} ^{Athan. ubi sup.}

bitterness of wrath caused by the transgression of the law, in which he kept all men bound, he now surrendered to the Saviour, who took it and consumed it, in order that in the place of vinegar, He might give us wine to drink, which Prov. 9, 5. wisdom had mingled. THEOPHYL. But the soldiers offered Christ vinegar, as it were ministering unto a king, for it follows, *saying, If thou art the king of the Jews, save thyself.* BEDE; And it is worthy of remark, that the Jews blaspheme and mock the name of Christ, which was delivered to them by the authority of Scripture; whereas the soldiers, as being ignorant of the Scriptures, insult not Christ the chosen of God, but the King of the Jews.

38. And a superscription also was written over him in letters of Greek, and Latin, and Hebrew, THIS IS THE KING OF THE JEWS.

39. And one of the malefactors which were hanged railed on him, saying, If thou be Christ, save thyself and us.

40. But the other answering rebuked him, saying, Dost not thou fear God, seeing thou art in the same condemnation ?

41. And we indeed justly ; for we receive the due reward of our deeds : but this man hath done nothing amiss.

42. And he said unto Jesus, Lord, remember me when thou comest into thy kingdom.

43. And Jesus said unto him, Verily I say unto thee, To day shalt thou be with me in paradise.

THEOPHYL. Observe a second time the device of the devil turned against himself. For in letters of three different characters he published the accusation of Jesus, that in truth it might not escape one of the passers by, that He was crucified because He made Himself King. For it is said, *In Greek, Latin, and Hebrew,* by which it was signified, that the most powerful of the nations, (as the Romans,) the wisest, (as the Greeks,) those who most worshipped God,(as the Jewish nation,)

must be made subject to the dominion of Christ. AMBROSE;
And rightly is the title placed above the cross, because
Christ's kingdom is not of the human body, but of the power
of God. I read the title of the King of the Jews, when
I read, *My kingdom is not of this world.* I read the cause of Christ written above His head, when I read, *And the Word was God.* For *the head of Christ is God.* CYRIL;
Now one of the thieves uttered the same revilings as the Jews,
but the other tried to check his words, while he confessed his
own guilt, adding, *We indeed justly, for we receive the due
reward of our deeds.* CHRYS. Here the condemned performs
the office of judge, and he begins to decide concerning truth
who before Pilate confessed his crime only after many
tortures. For the judgment of man from whom secret things
are hid is of one kind; the judgment of God who searches
the heart of another. And in the former case punishment
follows after confession, but here confession is made unto
salvation. But he also pronounces Christ innocent, adding,
But this man hath done nothing wrong : as if to say, Behold
a new injury, that innocence should be condemned with
crime. We kill the living, He raised the dead. We have
stolen from others, He bids us give up even what is our own.
The blessed thief thus taught those that stood by, uttering
the words by which he rebuked the other. But when he
saw that the ears of those who stood by were stopped up,
he turns to Him who knoweth the hearts; for it follows,
*And he said to Jesus, Lord, remember me when thou comest
into thy kingdom.* Thou beholdest the Crucified, and thou
acknowledgest Him to be thy Lord. Thou seest the form of
a condemned criminal, and thou proclaimest the dignity of a
king. Stained with a thousand crimes, thou askest the Fountain
of righteousness to remember thy wickedness, saying, But I
discover thy hidden kingdom; and thou turnest away my
public iniquities, and acceptest the faith of a secret intention.
Wickedness usurped the disciple of truth, truth did not change
the disciple of wickedness.

GREG. On the cross nails had fastened his hands and
feet, and nothing remained free from torture, but his heart and
tongue. By the inspiration of God, the thief offered to Him
the whole which he found free, that as it is written, *With*

Margin notes: John 18, 36. John 1, 1. 1 Cor. 11, 3. Greg. Mor. 18. c. 40. Rom. 10, 10.

1 Cor.
13, 13. *the heart he might believe unto righteousness, with the mouth he might confess unto salvation.* But the three virtues which the Apostle speaks of, the thief suddenly filled with grace both received and preserved on the cross. He had faith, for example, who believed that God would reign whom he saw dying equally with himself. He had hope who asked for an entrance into His kingdom. He preserved charity also zealously in his death, who for his iniquity reproved his brother and fellow-thief, dying for a like crime to his own.

AMBROSE; A most remarkable example is here given of seeking after conversion, seeing that pardon is so speedily granted to the thief. The Lord quickly pardons, because the thief is quickly converted. And grace is more abundant than prayer; for the Lord ever gives more than He is asked for. The thief asked that He should remember him, but our Lord answers, *Verily I say unto thee, This day shalt thou be with me in Paradise.* To be with Christ is life, and where Christ is, there is His kingdom. THEOPHYL. And as every king who returns victorious carries in triumph the best of his spoils, so the Lord having despoiled the devil of a portion of his plunder, carries it with Him into Paradise.

CHRYS. Here then might one see the Saviour between the thieves weighing in the scales of justice faith, and unbelief. The devil cast Adam out of Paradise. Christ brought the thief into Paradise before the whole world, before the Apostles. By a mere word and by faith alone he entered into Paradise, that no one after his sins might despair of entrance. Mark the rapid change, from the cross to heaven, from condemnation to Paradise, that you may know that the Lord did it all, not with regard to the thief's good intention, but His own mercy.

But if the reward of the good has already taken place, surely a resurrection will be superfluous. For if He introduced the thief into Paradise while his body remained in corruption without, it is clear there is no resurrection of the body. Such are the words of some, But shall the flesh which has partaken of the toil be deprived of the reward? Hear Paul 1 Cor.
15, 53. speaking, *Then must this corruptible put on incorruption.* But if the Lord promised the kingdom of heaven, but introduced the thief into Paradise, He does not yet recompense

him the reward. But they say, Under the name of Paradise
He signified the kingdom of heaven, using a well-known
name in addressing a thief who knew nothing of difficult
teaching. Now some do not read it, *This day shalt thou be
with me in Paradise*, but thus, *I say unto thee on this day*,
and then follows, *thou shalt be with me in Paradise*. But we
will add a still more obvious solution. For physicians when
they see a man in a desperate state, say, He is already dead.
So also the thief, since he no longer fears his falling back to
perdition, is said to have entered Paradise. THEOPHYL. This
however is more true than all, that although they have not
obtained all the promises, I mean, the thief and the other saints
in order that without us they might not be made perfect, they Heb. 11,
are notwithstanding in the kingdom of heaven and Paradise. 40.

GREG. NYSS. Here again, we must examine how the thief
should be thought worthy of Paradise, seeing that a flaming
sword prevents the entrance of the saints. But observe that
the word of God describes it as turning about, so as it
should obstruct the unworthy, but open a free entrance to
life to the worthy. GREG. Or that flaming sword is said Greg.
to be *turning*, because that He knew the time would come Mor. 12.
when it must be removed; when He in truth should come, c. 9.
who by the mystery of His incarnation was to open to us the
way of Paradise. AMBROSE; But it must also be explained
how the others, that is, Matthew and Mark, introduced two
thieves reviling, while Luke, one reviling, the other resisting
him. Perhaps this other at first reviled, but was suddenly
converted. It may also have been spoken of one, but in
the plural number; as in the Hebrews, *They wandered in* Heb. 11,
goat-skins, and they were sawn asunder; whereas Elijah 37.
alone is related to have had a goat-skin, and Isaiah to have
been sawn asunder. But mystically, the two thieves represent
the two sinful people who were to be crucified by baptism with
Christ, whose disagreement likewise represents the difference
of believers. BEDE; For as many of us as were baptized in Rom. 6,
Christ Jesus, were baptized in His death; but we are washed 3.
by baptism, seeing we were sinners. But some, in that they
praise God suffering in the flesh, are crowned; others, in that
they refuse to have the faith or works of baptism, are deprived
of the gift which they have received.

44. And it was about the sixth hour, and there was a darkness over all the earth until the ninth hour.

45. And the sun was darkened, and the veil of the temple was rent in the midst.

46. And when Jesus had cried with a loud voice, he said, Father, into thy hands I commend my spirit: and having said thus, he gave up the ghost.

CYRIL; As soon as the Lord of all had been given up to be crucified, the whole framework of the world bewailed its rightful Master, and the light was darkened at mid-day, which was a manifest token that the souls of those who crucified Him would suffer darkness. AUG. What is here said of the darkness, the other two Evangelists, Matthew and Mark, confirm, but St. Luke adds the cause whence the darkness arose, saying, *And the sun was darkened.* AUG. This darkening of the sun it is quite plain did not happen in the regular and fixed course of the heavenly bodies, because it was then the Passover, which is always celebrated at the full moon. But a regular eclipse of the sun does not take place except at new moon. DIONYS. When we were both at Heliopolis together, we both saw at the same time in a marvellous manner the moon meeting the sun, (for it was not then the time of new moon,) and then again, from the ninth hour until evening supernaturally brought back to the edge of the sun's diameter. Besides, we observed that this obscuration began from the east, and having reached as far as the sun's western border at length returned, and that the loss and restoration of light took place not from the same side, but from opposite sides of the diameter. Such were the miraculous events of that time, and possible to Christ alone who is the cause of all things. GREEK EX. This miracle then took place that it might be made known, that He who had undergone death was the Ruler of the whole creation. AMBROSE; The sun also is eclipsed to the sacrilegious, that it may overshadow the scene of their awful wickedness; darkness was spread over the eyes of the unbelieving, that the light of faith might rise again. BEDE; But Luke, wish-

Margin notes: Amos 8, 9. Aug. de Con.Ev. lib. iii. c. 17. Aug. de Civ.Dei, l.iii.c.15. Dion. Areop. ad Polyc. ad diametrum solis.

ing to join miracle to miracle, adds, *And the veil of the temple was rent in twain.* This took place when our Lord expired, as Matthew and Mark bear witness, but Luke related it by anticipation.

THEOPHYL. By this then our Lord shewed that the Holy of Holies should be no longer inaccessible, but being given over into the hands of the Romans, should be defiled, and its entrance laid open. AMBROSE; The veil also is rent, by which is declared the division of the two people, and the profanation of the synagogue. The old veil is rent that the Church may hang up the new veils of faith. The covering of the synagogue is drawn up, that we may behold with the eyes of the mind the inward mysteries of religion now revealed to us. THEOPHYL. Whereby it is signified that the veil which kept us asunder from the holy things which are in heaven, is broken through, namely, enmity and sin. AMBROSE; It took place also at that time when every mystery of Christ's assumed mortality was fulfilled, and His immortality alone remained; as it follows, *And when Jesus had cried with a loud voice, he said.*

BEDE; By invoking the Father He declares Himself to be the Son of God, but by commending His Spirit, He signifies not the weakness of His strength, but His confidence in the same power with the Father. AMBROSE; The flesh dies that the Spirit may rise again. The Spirit is commended to the Father, that heavenly things also may be loosed from the chain of iniquity, and peace be made in heaven, which earthly things should follow.

CHRYS. Now this voice teaches us, that the souls of the saints are not henceforth shut up in hell as before, but are with God, Christ being made the beginning of this change. ATHAN. For He commends to His Father through Himself all mankind quickened in Him; for we are His members; as the Apostle says, *Ye are all one in Christ.* GREG. NYSS. But it becomes us to enquire how our Lord distributes Himself into three parts at once; into the bowels of the earth, as He told the Pharisees; into the Paradise of God, as He told the thief; into the hands of the Father, as it is said here. To those however who rightly consider, it is scarcely worthy of question, for He who by His divine power is in every

Athan. de Incar. et cont. Ar. Gal. 3, 28. Greg. Orat. i. de Res.

place, is present in any particular place. AMBROSE; His spirit then is commended to God, but though He is above He yet gives light to the parts below the earth, that all things may be redeemed. For Christ is all things, and in Christ are all things. GREG. NYSS. There is another explanation, that at the time of His Passion, His Divinity being once united to His humanity, left neither part of His humanity, but of its own accord separated the soul from the body, yet shewed itself abiding in each. For through the body in which He suffered death He vanquished the power of death, but through the soul He prepared for the thief an entrance into Paradise. Now Isaiah says of the heavenly Jerusalem, which is no other than Paradise, *Upon my hands I have painted thy walls;* whence it is clear, that he who is in Paradise dwelleth in the hands of the Father. DAMASC. Or to speak more expressly, In respect of His body, He was in the grave, in respect of His soul, He was in hell, and with the thief in Paradise; but as God, on the throne with His Father and the Holy Spirit. THEOPHYL. But crying with a loud voice He gives up the ghost, because He had in Himself the power of laying down His life and taking it up again. AMBROSE; He gave up His Spirit, because He did not lose it as one unwilling; for what a man sends forth is voluntary, what he loses, compulsory.

Greg. ut sup.

Is. 49, 16. ap. LXX.

Damasc. Hom. de Sabb. San.

47. Now when the centurion saw what was done, he glorified God, saying, Certainly this was a righteous man.

48. And all the people that came together to that sight, beholding the things which were done, smote their breasts, and returned.

49. And all his acquaintance, and the women that followed him from Galilee, stood afar off, beholding these things.

Aug. iv. de Trin. c. 13.

AUG. When after uttering that voice He immediately gave up the ghost, those who were present greatly marvelled. For those who hung upon the cross were generally tortured by a prolonged death. Hence it is said, *Now when the centurion saw, &c.* AUG. There is no contradiction in that Aug. Matthew says, that the centurion seeing the earthquake mar-de Con. velled, whereas Luke says that he marvelled, that Jesus while iii. c. 20. uttering the loud voice expired, shewing what power He had when He was dying. But in that Matthew not only says, *at the sight of the earthquake,* but added, *and at the things that were done,* he has made it clear that there was ample room for Luke to say, that the centurion marvelled at the death of the Lord. But because Luke also himself said, *Now when the centurion saw what was done,* he has included in that general expression all the marvellous things which took place at that hour, as if relating one marvellous event of which all those miracles were the parts and members. Again, because one Evangelist stated that the centurion said, *Truly this man was the Son of God,* but Luke gives the words, *was a just man,* they might be supposed to differ. But either we ought to understand that both these were said by the centurion, and that one Evangelist related one, another another. Or perhaps, that Luke expresses the opinion of the centurion, in what respect he called Him the Son of God. For perhaps the centurion did not know Him to be the Only-begotten, equal to the Father, but called Him the Son of God, because he believed Him to be just, as many just persons are called the sons of God. But again, because Gen. 6, Matthew added, *those who were with the centurion,* while 24. Luke omits this, there is no contradiction, since one says what another is silent about. And Matthew said, *They were greatly afraid;* but Luke does not say that *he feared,* but that *he glorified God.* Who then does not see that by fearing he glorified God?

THEOPHYL. The words of our Lord seem now to be fulfilled, wherein He said, *When I shall be lifted up I will draw all men unto me.* For when lifted upon the cross He drew to Him the thief and the centurion, besides some of the Jews also, of whom it follows, *And all the people that came together smote their breasts.* BEDE; By their smiting their breasts as if betokening a penitential sorrow, two things may be understood; either that they bewailed Him unjustly slain whose life they loved, or that remembering that they had demanded His death, they trembled to see Him in death still farther glorified. But we may observe, that the Gentiles fearing God glorify Him with works of public confession; the Jews only striking their breasts returned silent home.

AMBROSE; O the breasts of the Jews, harder than the rocks! The judge acquits, the officer believes, the traitor by his death condemns his own crime, the elements flee away, the earth quakes, the graves are opened; the hardness of the Jews still remains immoveable, though the whole world is shaken. BEDE; Rightly then by the centurion is the faith of the Church signified, which in the silence of the synagogue bears witness to the Son of God. And now is fulfilled that com-
Ps. 88,
18. plaint which the Lord makes to His Father, *neighbour and friend hast thou put far from me, and mine acquaintance because of misery.* Hence it follows, *And all his acquaintance stood afar off.* THEOPHYL. But the race of women formerly cursed remains and sees all these things; for it follows, *And the women which followed him from Galilee, seeing these things.* And thus they are the first to be renewed by justification, or by the blessing which flows from His passion, as also from His resurrection.

50. And, behold, there was a man named Joseph, a counsellor; and he was a good man, and a just:

51. (The same had not consented to the counsel and deed of them;) he was of Arimathæa, a city of the Jews: who also himself waited for the kingdom of God.

52. This man went unto Pilate, and begged the body of Jesus.

53. And he took it down, and wrapped it in linen, and laid it in a sepulchre that was hewn in stone, wherein never man before was laid.

54. And that day was the preparation, and the sabbath drew on.

55. And the women also, which came with him from Galilee, followed after, and beheld the sepulchre, and how his body was laid.

56. And they returned, and prepared spices and

ointments; and rested the sabbath day according to the commandment.

GREEK Ex. Joseph had been at one time a secret disciple Photius. of Christ, but at length bursting through the bonds of fear, and become very zealous, he took down the body of our Lord, basely hanging on the cross; thus gaining a precious jewel by the meekness of His words. Hence it follows, *And, behold, there was a man named Joseph, a counsellor.* BEDE; A counsellor, or decurio, is so called because he is of the order of the curia or council, and administers the office of the curia. He is also wont to be called curialis, from his management of civil duties. Joseph then is said to have been of high rank in the world, but of still higher estimation before God; as it follows, *A good man, and a just, of Arimathæa, a city of the Jews, &c.* Arimathæa is the same as Ramatha, the city of Helcanah and Samuel.

AUG. Now John says, that Joseph was a disciple of Jesus. Aug. Hence it is also here added, *Who also himself waited for the* de Con. *kingdom of God.* But it naturally causes surprise how he iii. c. 22. who for fear was a secret disciple should have dared to beg our Lord's body, which none of those who openly followed Him dared to do; for it is said, *This man went unto Pilate, and begged the body of Jesus.* We must understand then, that he did this from confidence in his rank, by which he might be privileged to enter familiarly into Pilate's presence. But in performing that last funeral rite, he seems to have cared less for the Jews, although it was his custom in hearing our Lord to avoid their hostility.

BEDE; So then being fitted by the righteousness of his works for the burial of our Lord's body, he was worthy by the dignity of his secular power to obtain it. Hence it follows, *And he took it down, and wrapped it in linen.* By the simple burial of our Lord, the pride of the rich is condemned, who not even in their graves can be without their wealth. ATHAN. They also act absurdly who embalm the Athan. bodies of their dead, and do not bury them, even supposing in Vit. Ant. 90. them to be holy. For what can be more holy or greater than our Lord's body? And yet this was placed in a tomb until it rose again the third day. For it follows, *And he laid it in a hewn sepulchre.* BEDE; That is, hewn out of a rock, lest if it had been built of many stones, and the foundations of the tomb being dug up after the resurrection, the body should be said to have been stolen away. It is laid also in a new tomb, *wherein never man before was laid,* lest when the rest of the bodies remained after the resurrection, it might be suspected that some other had risen again. But because man was created on the sixth day, rightly being crucified on the sixth day our Lord fulfilled the secret of man's restitution. It follows, *And it was the day of the παρασκευή,* which means the preparation, the name by which they called the sixth day, because on that day they prepared the things which were necessary for the Sabbath. But because on the seventh day the Creator rested from His work, the Lord on the Sabbath rested in the grave. Hence it follows, *And the Sabbath was dawning.* Now we said above, that all His acquaintance stood afar off, and the women which followed Him. These then of His acquaintance, after His body was taken down, returned to their homes, but the women who more tenderly loved Him, following His funeral, desired to see the place where He was laid. For it follows, *And the women also, which came with him from Galilee, followed after, and beheld the sepulchre, and how his body was laid,* that in truth they might make the offerings of their devotion at the proper time.

THEOPHYL. For they had not yet sufficient faith, but prepared as if for a mere man spices and ointments, after the manner of the Jews, who performed such duties to their dead. Hence it follows, *And they returned, and prepared spices.* For our Lord being buried, they were occupied as long as it was lawful to work, (that is, until sun-set,) in preparing ointments. But it was commanded to keep silence on the Sabbath, that is, rest from evening to evening. For it follows, *And rested the sabbath day according to the commandment.*

AMBROSE; Now mystically, the just man buries the body of Christ. For the burial of Christ is such as to have no guile or wickedness in it. But rightly did Matthew call the man rich, for by carrying Him that was rich he knew not the poverty of faith. The just man covers the body of Christ

with linen. Do thou also clothe the body of Christ with
His own glory, that thou mayest be thyself just. And if thou
believest it to be dead, still cover it with the fulness of His
own divinity. But the Church also is clothed with the grace
of innocence.

BEDE; He also wraps Jesus in clean linen, who has
received Him with a pure mind. AMBROSE; Nor without
meaning has one Evangelist spoken of a new tomb, another
of the tomb of Joseph. For the grave is prepared by those
who are under the law of death; the Conqueror of death has
no grave of His own. For what fellowship hath God with
the grave. He alone is enclosed in this tomb, because the
death of Christ, although it was common according to the
nature of the body, yet was it peculiar in respect of power.
But Christ is rightly buried in the tomb of the just, that He
may rest in the habitation of justice. For this monument
the just man hews out with the piercing word in the hearts
of Gentile hardness, that the power of Christ might extend
over the nations. And very rightly is there a stone rolled
against the tomb; for whoever has in himself truly buried
Christ, must diligently guard, lest he lose Him, or lest there
be an entrance for unbelief.

BEDE; Now that the Lord is crucified on the sixth day
and rests on the seventh, signifies that in the sixth age of
the world we must of necessity suffer for Christ, and as it
were be crucified to the world. But in the seventh age, that Gal. 6,
is, after death, our bodies indeed rest in the tombs, but our 14.
souls with the Lord. But even at the present time also holy
women, (that is, humble souls,) fervent in love, diligently
wait upon the Passion of Christ, and if perchance they may
be able to imitate Him, with anxious carefulness ponder
each step in order, by which this Passion is fulfilled. And
having read, heard, and called to mind all these, they next
apply themselves to make ready the works of virtue, by which
Christ may be pleased, in order that having finished the
preparation of this present life, in a blessed rest they may
at the time of the resurrection meet Christ with the frankin-
cence of spiritual actions.

1. Now upon the first day of the week, very early in the morning, they came unto the sepulchre, bringing the spices which they had prepared, and certain others with them.

2. And they found the stone rolled away from the sepulchre.

3. And they entered in, and found not the body of the Lord Jesus.

4. And it came to pass, as they were much perplexed thereabout, behold, two men stood by them in shining garments :

5. And as they were afraid, and bowed down their faces to the earth, they said unto them, Why seek ye the living among the dead ?

6. He is not here, but is risen : remember how he spake unto you when he was yet in Galilee,

7. Saying, The Son of man must be delivered into the hands of sinful men, and be crucified, and the third day rise again.

8. And they remembered his words,

9. And returned from the sepulchre, and told all these things unto the eleven, and to all the rest.

10. It was Mary Magdalene, and Joanna, and Mary the mother of James, and other women that were with them, which told these things unto the apostles.

11. And their words seemed to them as idle tales, and they believed them not.

12. Then arose Peter, and ran unto the sepulchre; and stooping down, he beheld the linen clothes laid by themselves, and departed, wondering in himself at that which was come to pass.

BEDE; Devout women not only on the day of preparation, but also when the sabbath was passed, that is, at sun-set, as soon as the liberty of working returned, bought spices that they might come and anoint the body of Jesus, as Mark testi-Mark fies. Still as long as night time restrained them, they came 16, 1. not to the sepulchre. And therefore it is said, *On the first day of the week, very early in the morning, &c.* One of the unaSab-Sabbath, or the first of the Sabbath, is the first day from the bathi. Sabbath; which Christians are wont to call "the Lord's day," because of our Lord's resurrection. But by the women coming to the sepulchre very early in the morning, is manifested their great zeal and fervent love of seeking and finding the Lord. AMBROSE; Now this place has caused great perplexity to many, because while St. Luke says, *Very early in the morning,* Matthew says that it was in the evening of the sabbath that the women came to the sepulchre. But you may suppose that the Evangelists spoke of different occasions, so as to understand both different parties of women, and different appearances. Because however it was written, that *in the* Matt. *evening of the sabbath, as it began to dawn towards the* 28, 1. *first day of the week,* our Lord rose, we must so take it, as that neither on the morning of the Lord's day, which is the first after the sabbath, nor on the sabbath, the resurrection should be thought to have taken place. For how are the three days fulfilled? Not then as the day grew towards evening, but in the evening of the night He rose. Lastly, in the Greek it is " late;" but late signifies both the hour at ὀψὲ the end of the day, and the slowness of any thing; as we say, " I have been lately told." Late then is also the dead of the night. And thus also the women had the opportunity of coming to the sepulchre when the guards were asleep. And that you may know it was in the night time, some of the women are ignorant of it. They know who watch night and day, they know not who have gone back. According to John, one Mary

Magdalene knows not, for the same person could not first
know and then afterwards be ignorant. Therefore if there
are several Maries, perhaps also there are several Mary
Magdalenes, since the former is the name of a person, the

Aug. de
Con. Ev.
lib. iii.
c. 24.
second is derived from a place. AUG. Or Matthew by the
first part of the night, which is the evening, wished to represent
the night itself, at the end of which night they came to the
sepulchre, and for this reason, because they had been now
preparing since the evening, and it was lawful to bring spices
because the sabbath was over. EUSEB. The Instrument of
the Word lay dead, but a great stone enclosed the sepulchre,
as if death had led Him captive. But three days had not
yet elapsed, when life again puts itself forth after a sufficient
proof of death, as it follows, *And they found the stone rolled
away.* THEOPHYL. An angel had rolled it away, as Matthew

Chrys.
Hom.
90. in
Matt.
declares. CHRYS. But the stone was rolled away after the
resurrection, on account of the women, that they might
believe that the Lord had risen again, seeing indeed the
grave without the body. Hence it follows, *And they entered
in, and found not the body of the Lord Jesus.* CYRIL; When
then they found not the body of Christ which was risen, they
were distracted by various thoughts, and for their love of
Christ and the tender care they had shewn Him, were thought
worthy of the vision of angels. For it follows, *And it came
to pass as they were much perplexed thereabout, behold,
two men stood by them in shining garments.* EUSEB. The
messengers of the health-bearing resurrection and their
shining garments stand for tokens of pleasantness and rejoicing. For Moses preparing plagues against the Egyptians,
perceived an angel in the flame of fire. But not such were
those who appeared to the women at the sepulchre, but
calm and joyful as became them to be seen in the kingdom
and joy of the Lord. And as at the Passion the sun was
darkened, holding forth signs of sorrow and woe to the
crucifiers of our Lord, so the angels, heralds of life and
resurrection, marked by their white garments the character
of the health-bearing feast day.

AMBROSE; But how is it that Mark has mentioned one
young man sitting in white garments, and Matthew one, but
John and Luke relate that there were seen two angels sitting

in white garments. AUG. We may understand that one Aug. de Con. Ev. ut sup. Angel was seen by the women, as both Mark and Matthew say, so as supposing them to have entered into the sepulchre, that is, into a certain space which was fenced off by a kind of wall in front of the stone sepulchre; and that there they saw an Angel sitting on the right hand, which Mark says, but that afterwards when they looked into the place where our Lord was lying, they saw within two other Angels standing, (as Luke says,) who spoke to encourage their minds, and build up their faith. Hence it follows, *And as they were afraid.* BEDE; The holy women, when the Angels stood beside them, are reported not to have fallen to the ground, but to have bowed their faces to the earth; nor do we read that any of the saints, at the time of our Lord's resurrection, worshipped with prostration to the ground either our Lord Himself, or the Angels who appeared to them. Hence has arisen the ecclesiastical custom, either in memory of our Lord's resurrection, or in the hope of our own, of praying on every Lord's day, and through the whole season of Pentecost, not with bended knees, but with our faces bowed to the earth. But not in the sepulchre, which is the place of the dead, was He to be sought, who rose from the dead to life. And therefore it is added, *They said to them,* that is, the Angels to the women, *Why seek ye the living among the dead? He is not here, but is risen.* On the third day then, as He Himself foretold to the women, together with the rest of His disciples, He celebrated the triumph of His resurrection. Hence it follows, *Remember how he spake unto you when he was yet in Galilee, saying, The Son of man must be delivered into the hands of sinful men, and be crucified, and on the third day rise again, &c.* For on the day of the preparation at the ninth hour giving up the ghost, buried in the evening, early on the morning of the first day of the week He rose again. ATHAN. He might indeed at once have raised Athan. Lib. de Inc. Fil. Dei. His body from the dead. But some one would have said that He was never dead, or that death plainly had never existed in Him. And perhaps if the resurrection of our Lord had been delayed beyond the third day, the glory of incorruption had been concealed. In order therefore to shew His body to be dead, He suffered the interval of one day, and on the third day manifested His body to be without corruption. BEDE; One day and two nights also He lay in the sepulchre, because He joined the light of His single death to the darkness of our double death.

CYRIL; Now the women, when they had received the sayings of the Angels, hastened to tell them to the disciples; as it follows, *And they remembered his words, and returned from the sepulchre, and told all these things to the eleven, and to all the rest.* For woman who was once the minister of death, is now the first to receive and tell the awful mystery of the resurrection. The female race has obtained therefore both deliverance from reproach, and the withdrawal of the curse. AMBROSE; It is not allowed to women to teach in the church, but they shall ask their husbands at home. To those then who are at home is the woman sent. But who these women were he explains, adding, *It was Mary Magdalene,* BEDE; (who was also the sister of Lazarus,) *and Joanna,* (the wife of Chuza, Herod's steward,) *and Mary the mother of James,* (that is, the mother of James the less, and Joseph.) And it is added generally of the others, *and other women that were with them, which told these things to the Apostles.* BEDE; For that the woman might not endure the everlasting reproach of guilt from men, she who had transfused sin into the man, now also transfuses grace. THEOPHYL. Now the miracle of the resurrection is naturally incredible to mankind. Hence it follows, *And their words seemed to them as idle tales.* BEDE; Which was not so much their weakness, as so to speak our strength. For the resurrection itself was demonstrated to those who doubted by many proofs, which while we read and acknowledge we are through their doubts confirmed in the truth.

THEOPHYL. Peter, as soon as he heard this, delays not, but runs to the sepulchre; for fire when applied to matter knows no delay; as it follows, *Then arose Peter, and ran to the sepulchre.*

EUSEB. For he alone believed the women saying that they had seen Angels; and as he was of more ardent feelings than the rest, he anxiously put himself foremost, looking every where for the Lord; as it follows, *And stooping down, he beheld the linen clothes laid by themselves.* THEOPHYL. But

1 Tim. 2, 12. 1 Cor. 14, 35.

Bede. ex Amb.

Bede. ex Greg.

now when he was at the tomb, he first of all obtained that he
should marvel at those things which had before been derided
by himself or the others ; as it is said, *And departed, wondering in himself at that which was come to pass;* that is, wondering in himself at the way in which it had happened, how the
linen clothes had been left behind, since the body was anointed
with myrrh ; or what opportunity the thief had obtained,
that putting away the clothes wrapped up by themselves, he
should take away the body with the soldiers standing round.
Aug. Luke is supposed to have mentioned this concerning
Peter, recapitulating.   For Peter ran to the sepulchre at the
same time that John also went, as soon as it had been told to
them alone by the women, (especially Mary Magdalene,) that
the body was taken away.   But the vision of Angels took
place afterwards.   Luke therefore mentioned Peter only,
because to him Mary first told it.   It may also strike one,
that Luke says that Peter, not entering but stooping down,
saw the linen clothes by themselves, and departed wondering,
whereas John says, that he himself saw the linen clothes in
the same position, and that he entered after Peter.   We must
understand then that Peter first saw them stooping down,
which Luke mentions, John omits, but that he afterwards
entered before John came in.

Bede; According to the mystical meaning, by the women
coming early in the morning to the sepulchre, we have an
example given us, that having cast away the darkness of our
vices, we should come to the Body of the Lord.   For that
sepulchre also bore the figure of the Altar of the Lord, wherein
the mysteries of Christ's Body, not in silk or purple cloth, but
in pure white linen, like that in which Joseph wrapped it,
ought to be consecrated, that as He offered up to death for
us the true substance of His earthly nature, so we also in
commemoration of Him should place on the Altar the flax,
pure from the plant of the earth, and white, and in many ways
refined by a kind of crushing to death.   But the spices which
the women bring, signify the odour of virtue, and the sweetness of prayers by which we ought to approach the Altar.
The rolling back of the stone alludes to the unclosing of the
Sacraments which were concealed by the veil of the letter of
the law which was written on stone, the covering of which

being taken away, the dead body of the Lord is not found, but the living body is preached; for although we have known Christ according to the flesh, yet now henceforth know we Him no more. But as when the Body of our Lord lay in the sepulchre, Angels are said to have stood by, so also at the time of consecration are they to be believed to stand by the mysteries of Christ. Let us then after the example of the devout women, whenever we approach the heavenly mysteries, because of the presence of the Angels, or from reverence to the Sacred Offering, with all humility, bow our faces to the earth, recollecting that we are but dust and ashes.

2 Cor. 5, 16.

13. And, behold, two of them went that same day to a village called Emmaus, which was from Jerusalem about threescore furlongs.

14. And they talked together of all these things which had happened.

15. And it came to pass, that, while they communed together and reasoned, Jesus himself drew near, and went with them.

16. But their eyes were holden that they should not know him.

17. And he said unto them, What manner of communications are these that ye have one to another, as ye walk, and are sad?

18. And the one of them, whose name was Cleopas, answering said unto him, Art thou only a stranger in Jerusalem, and hast not known the things which are come to pass there in these days?

19. And he said unto them, What things? And they said unto him, Concerning Jesus of Nazareth, which was a prophet mighty in deed and word before God and all the people:

20. And how the chief priests and our rulers delivered him to be condemned to death, and have crucified him.

21. But we trusted that it had been he which should

have redeemed Israel: and beside all this, to day is
the third day since these things were done.

22. Yea, and certain women also of our company
made us astonished, which were early at the sepulchre ;

23. And when they found not his body, they came,
saying, that they had also seen a vision of angels,
which said that he was alive.

24. And certain of them which were with us went
to the sepulchre, and found it even so as the women
had said: but him they saw not.

GLOSS. After the manifestation of Christ's resurrection non occ.
made by the Angels to the women, the same resurrection is
further manifested by an appearance of Christ Himself to His
disciples; as it is said, *And behold two of them.* THEOPHYL.
Some say that Luke was one of these two, and for this reason
concealed his name. AMBROSE; Or to two of the disciples
by themselves our Lord shewed Himself in the evening,
namely, Ammaon and Cleophas. AUG. The fortress men- Aug. de
tioned here we may not unreasonably take to have been also lib. iii.
called according to Mark, a village. He next describes the c. 25.
fortress, saying, *which was from Jerusalem about the space
of sixty stades, called Emmaus.* BEDE; It is the same as
Nicopolis, a remarkable town in Palestine, which after the
taking of Judæa under the Emperor Marcus Aurelius Anto-
nius, changed together with its condition its name also. But
the stadium which, as the Greeks say, was invented by Her-
cules to measure the distances of roads, is the eighth part of a
mile ; therefore sixty stades are equal to seven miles and fifty
paces. And this was the length of journey which they were
walking, who were certain about our Lord's death and burial,
but doubtful concerning His resurrection. For the resurrection which took place after the seventh day of the week, no
one doubts is implied in the number eight. The disciples
therefore as they walk and converse about the Lord had completed the sixth mile of their journey, for they were grieving that
He who had lived without blame, had come at length even to

death, which He underwent on the sixth day. They had completed also the seventh mile, for they doubted not that He
rested in the grave. But of the eighth mile they had only
accomplished half; for the glory of His already triumphant
resurrection, they did not believe perfectly.

THEOPHYL. But the disciples above mentioned talked to
one another of the things which had happened, not as believing them, but as bewildered at events so extraordinary.
BEDE; And as they spoke of Him, the Lord comes near and
joins them, that He may both influence their minds with faith
Mat.18, in His resurrection, and fulfil that which He had promised,
20. *Where two or three are gathered together in my name, there
am I in the midst of them;* as it follows, *And it came to
pass while they communed together and reasoned, Jesus himself drew near and went with them.* THEOPHYL. For having
now obtained a spiritual body, distance of place is no obstacle
to His being present to whom He wished, nor did He any
further govern His body by natural laws, but spiritually and
supernaturally. Hence as Mark says, He appeared to them
in a different form, in which they were not permitted to know
Him; for it follows, *And their eyes were holden that they
should not know him;* in order truly that they may reveal
their entirely doubtful conceptions, and uncovering their
wound may receive a cure; and that they might know that
although the same body which suffered, rose again, yet it was
no longer such as to be visible to all, but only to those by
whom He willed it to be seen; and that they should not
wonder why henceforth He walks not among the people,
seeing that His conversation was not fit for mankind, but
rather divine; which is also the character of the resurrection
to come, in which we shall walk as the Angels and the sons
of God.

Greg. GREG. Rightly also He refrained from manifesting to them a
23. in form which they might recognise, doing that outwardly in the
Ev. eyes of the body, which was done by themselves inwardly in the
eyes of the mind. For they in themselves inwardly both loved
and doubted. Therefore to them as they talked of Him He
exhibited His presence, but as they doubted of Him He concealed the appearance which they knew. He indeed conversed with them, for it follows, *And he said to them, What*

manner of communications, &c. GREEK Ex. They were in Anonm.
truth discoursing among themselves, no longer expecting to _{in Cat.} see Christ alive, but sorrowing as concerning their Saviour Gr.
slain. Hence it follows, *And one of them whose name was Cleophas, answering him said, Art thou only a stranger?* THEOPHYL. As if he said, " Art thou a mere stranger, and one dwelling beyond the confines of Jerusalem, and therefore unacquainted with what has happened in the midst of it, that thou knowest not these things?* BEDE; Or he says this, because they thought Him a stranger, whose countenance they did not recognise. But in reality He was a stranger to them, from the infirmity of whose natures, now that He had obtained the glory of the resurrection, He was far removed, and to whose faith, as yet ignorant of His resurrection, He remained foreign. But again the Lord asks; for it follows, *And he said unto them, What things?* And their answer is given, *Concerning Jesus of Nazareth, who was a Prophet.* They confess Him to be a Prophet, but say nothing of the Son of God; either not yet perfectly believing, or fearful of falling into the hands of the persecuting Jews; either knowing not who He was, or concealing the truth which they believed. They add in praise of Him, *mighty in deed and word.* THEOPHYL. First comes deed, then word; for no word of teaching is approved unless first he who teaches shews himself to be a doer thereof. For acting goes before sight; for unless by thy works thou hast cleansed the glass of the understanding, the desired brightness does not appear. But still further it is added, *Before God and all the people.* For first of all we must please God, and then have regard as far as we can to honesty before men, that placing the honour of God first, we may live without offence to mankind. GREEK Ex. They next assign the cause of their sadness, the ut sup. betrayal and passion of Christ; and add in the voice of despair, *But we hoped it had been he who should have redeemed Israel.* We hoped, (he says,) not we hope; as if the death of the Lord were like to the deaths of other men. THEOPHYL. For they expected that Christ would redeem Israel from the evils that were rising up among them and the Roman slavery. They trusted also that He was an earthly king, whom they thought would be able to escape the

sentence of death passed upon Him. BEDE; Reason had they then for sorrow, because in some sort they blamed themselves for having hoped redemption in Him whom now they saw dead, and believed not that He would rise again, and most of all they bewailed Him put to death without a cause, whom they knew to be innocent. THEOPHYL. And yet those men seem not to have been altogether without faith, by what follows, *And besides all this, to day is the third day since these things were done.* Whereby they seem to have a recollection of what the Lord had told them that He would rise again on the third day. GREEK EX. The disciples also mention the report of the resurrection which was brought by the women; adding, *Yea, and certain women also of our company made us astonished, &c.* They say this indeed as if they did not believe it; wherefore they speak of themselves as frightened or astonished. For they did consider as established what was told them, or that there had been an angelic revelation, but derived from it reason for astonishment and alarm. The testimony of Peter also they did not regard as certain, since he did not say that he had seen our Lord, but conjectured His resurrection from the fact that His body was not lying in the sepulchre. Hence it follows, *And certain of them that were with us went, &c.*

Aug.
ut sup.

AUG. But since Luke has said that Peter ran to the sepulchre, and has himself related the words of Cleophas, that some of them went to the sepulchre, he is understood to confirm the testimony of John, that two went to the sepulchre. He first mentioned Peter only, because to him first Mary had related the news.

25. Then he said unto them, O fools, and slow of heart to believe all that the prophets have spoken :

26. Ought not Christ to have suffered these things, and to enter into his glory?

27. And beginning at Moses and all the prophets, he expounded unto them in all the Scriptures the things concerning himself.

28. And they drew nigh unto the village, whither

they went : and he made as though he would have
gone further.

29. But they constrained him, saying, Abide with
us : for it is toward evening, and the day is far
spent. And he went in to tarry with them.

30. And it came to pass, as he sat at meat with
them, he took bread, and blessed it, and brake, and
gave to them.

31. And their eyes were opened, and they knew
him ; and he vanished out of their sight.

32. And they said one to another, Did not our
heart burn within us, while he talked with us by the
way, and while he opened to us the Scriptures ?

33. And they rose up the same hour, and returned
to Jerusalem, and found the eleven gathered together,
and them that were with them,

34. Saying, The Lord is risen indeed, and hath
appeared to Simon.

35. And they told what things were done in the
way, and how he was known of them in breaking of
bread.

THEOPHYL. Because the above-mentioned disciples were
troubled with too much doubt, the Lord reproves them, saying, *O fools*, (for they almost used the same words as those
who stood by the cross, *He saved others, himself he cannot
save.*) And He proceeds, *and slow of heart to believe all
that the prophets have spoken.* For it is possible to believe
some of these things and not all; as if a man should believe
what the Prophets say of the cross of Christ, as in the
Psalms, *They pierced my hands and my feet;* but should not Ps. 22,
believe what they say of the resurrection, as, *Thou shalt not* 16.
suffer thy Holy One to see corruption. But it becomes us Ps. 16,
in all things to give faith to the Prophets, as well in the 10.
glorious things which they predicted of Christ, as the
inglorious, since through the suffering of evil things is the

entrance into glory.　Hence it follows, *Ought not Christ to have suffered these things, and so to enter into his glory?* that is, as respects His humanity.

Isid. lib. iii. Ep. 98. ISID. PEL.. But although it behoved Christ to suffer, yet they who crucified Him are guilty of inflicting the punishment. For they were not concerned to accomplish what God purposed.　Therefore their execution of it was impious, but God's purpose most wise, who converted their iniquity into a blessing upon mankind, using as it were the viper's flesh for the working of a health-giving antidote.　CHRYS. And therefore our Lord goes on to shew that all these things did not happen in a common way, but from the predestined purpose of God.　Hence it follows, *And beginning at Moses and all the Prophets, he expounded to them in all the Scriptures the things concerning himself.*　As if He said, Since ye are slow I will render you quick, by explaining to you the mysteries of the Scriptures.　For the sacrifice of Abraham, when releasing Isaac he sacrificed the ram, prefigured Christ's sacrifice.　But in the other writings of the Prophets also there are scattered about mysteries of Christ's cross and the resurrection.　BEDE; But if Moses and the Prophets spoke of Christ, and prophesied that through His Passion He would enter into glory, how does that man boast that he is a Christian, who neither searches how these Scriptures relate to Christ, nor desires to attain by suffering to that glory which he hopes to have with Christ.

GREEK EX. But since the Evangelist said before, *Their eyes were holden that they should not know him,* until the words of the Lord should move their minds to faith, He fitly affords in addition to their hearing a favourable object to their sight. As it follows, *And they drew nigh to the fortress whither they were going, and he feigned as if he was going further.* Aug. de Qu. Ev. lib. ii. c. 51. AUG. Now this relates not to falsehood.　For not every thing we feign is a falsehood, but only when we feign that which means nothing.　But when our feigning has reference to a certain meaning it is not a falsehood, but a kind of figure of the truth.　Otherwise all the things figuratively spoken by wise and holy men, or even by our Lord Himself, must be accounted falsehoods.　For to the experienced understanding truth consists not in certain words, but as words so also deeds are feigned without falsehood to signify a particular thing.

GREG. Because then He was still a stranger to faith in their hearts, *He feigned as if he would go further.* By the word " fingere" we mean to put together or form, and hence formers or preparers of mud we call " figuli." He who was the Truth itself did nothing then by deceit, but exhibited Himself in the body such as He came before them in their minds. But because they could not be strangers to charity, with whom charity was walking, they invite Him as if a stranger to partake of their hospitality. Hence it follows, *And they compelled him.* From which example it is gathered that strangers are not only to be invited to hospitality, but even to be taken by force. GLOSS. They not only compel Him by their actions, but induce Him by their words; for it follows, *saying, Abide with us, for it is towards evening, and the day is far gone,* (that is, towards its close.) Greg. Hom. 22 in Ev.

GREG. Now behold Christ since He is received through His members, so He seeks His receivers through Himself; for it follows, *And he went in with them.* They lay out a table, they bring food. And God whom they had not known in the expounding of Scriptures, they knew in the breaking of bread; for it follows, *And it came to pass, as he sat at meat with them, he took bread, and blessed it, and brake, and gave it to them. And their eyes were opened, and they knew him.* CHRYS. This was said not of their bodily eyes, but of their mental sight. AUG. For they walked not with their eyes shut, but there was something within them which did not permit them to know that which they saw, which a mist, darkness, or some kind of moisture, frequently occasions. Not that the Lord was not able to transform His flesh that it should be really a different form from that which they were accustomed to behold; since in truth also before His passion, He was transfigured in the mount, so that His face was bright as the sun. But it was not so now. For we do not unfitly take this obstacle in the sight to have been caused by Satan, that Jesus might not be known. But still it was so permitted by Christ up to the sacrament of the bread, that by partaking of the unity of His body, the obstacle of the enemy might be understood to be removed, so that Christ might be Greg. ut sup. Aug. de Con. Ev. lib. iii.c. 25.

known. THEOPHYL. But He also implies another thing, that the eyes of those who receive the sacred bread are opened that they should know Christ. For the Lord's flesh has in it a great and ineffable power.

Aug. ut sup. AUG. Or because the Lord feigned as if He would go farther, when He was accompanying the disciples, expounding to them the sacred Scriptures, who knew not whether it was He, what does He mean to imply but that through the duty of hospitality men may arrive at a knowledge of Him; that when He has departed from mankind far above the heavens, He is still with those who perform this duty to His servants. He therefore holds to Christ, that He should not go far from him, whoever being taught in the word communicates in all good Gal. 6, 6. things to him who teaches. For they were taught in the word when He expounded to them the Scriptures. And because they followed hospitality, Him whom they knew not in the expounding of the Scriptures, they know in the breaking Rom. 2, 13. of bread. For not the hearers of the law are just before God, but the doers of the law shall be justified.

Greg. ut sup. GREG. Whoever then wishes to understand what he has heard, let him hasten to fulfil in work what he can now understand. Behold the Lord was not known when He was speaking, and He vouchsafed to be known when He is eating. It follows, *And he vanished out of their sight.* THEOPHYL. For He had not such a body as that He was able to abide longer with them, that thereby likewise He might increase their affections. *And they said one to another, Did not our hearts burn within us while he talked with us by the way, and while he opened to us the scriptures?* ORIGEN; By which is implied, that the words uttered by the Saviour inflamed the hearts of the hearers to the love of Greg. Hom. 10. in Ev. God. GREG. By the word which is heard the spirit is kindled, the chill of dulness departs, the mind becomes awakened with heavenly desire. It rejoices to hear heavenly precepts, and every command in which it is instructed, is as it were adding a faggot to the fire. THEOPHYL. Their hearts then were turned either by the fire of our Lord's words, to which they listened as the truth, or because as He expounded the Scriptures, their hearts were greatly struck within them, that He who was speaking was the Lord. Therefore were they

so rejoiced, that without delay they returned to Jerusalem.
And hence what follows, *And they rose up the same hour,
and returned to Jerusalem.* They rose up indeed the same
hour, but they arrived after many hours, as they had to travel
sixty stades.

AUG. It had been already reported that Jesus had risen Aug.
by the women, and by Simon Peter, to whom He had de Con.
Ev.l.iii.
appeared. For these two disciples found them talking of c. 25.
these things when they came to Jerusalem; as it follows,
*And they found the eleven gathered together, and them that
were with them, saying, The Lord is risen indeed, and hath
appeared to Simon.* BEDE; It seems that our Lord appeared to Peter first of all those whom the four Evangelists
and the Apostle mention. CHRYS. For He did not shew
Himself to all at the same time, in order that He might sow
the seeds of faith. For he who had first seen and was sure,
told it to the rest. Afterwards the word going forth prepared the mind of the hearer for the sight, and therefore He
appeared first to him who was of all the most worthy and
faithful. For He had need of the most faithful soul to first
receive this sight, that it might be least disturbed by the
unexpected appearance. And therefore He is first seen by
Peter, that he who first confessed Christ should first deserve
to see His resurrection, and also because he had denied Him
He wished to see him first, to console him, lest he should
despair. But after Peter, He appeared to the rest, at one
time fewer in number, at another more, which the two
disciples attest; for it follows, *And they told what things
were done by the way, and how he was known of them in
breaking of bread.* AUG. But with respect to what Mark Aug.
says, that they told the rest, and they did not believe them, ut sup.
whereas Luke says, that they had already begun to say, *The
Lord is risen indeed,* what must we understand, except that
there were some even then who refused to believe this?

36. And as they thus spake, Jesus himself stood
in the midst of them, and saith unto them, Peace be
unto you.

37. But they were terrified and affrighted, and
supposed they had seen a spirit.

38. And he said unto them, Why are ye troubled? and why do thoughts arise in your hearts?

39. Behold my hands and my feet, that it is I myself: handle me, and see; for a spirit hath not flesh and bones, as ye see me have.

40. And when he had thus spoken, he shewed them his hands and feet.

CHRYS. The report of Christ's resurrection being published every where by the Apostles, and while the anxiety of the disciples was easily awakened to see Christ, He that was so much desired comes, and is revealed to them that were seeking and expecting Him. Nor in a doubtful manner, but with the clearest evidence, He presents Himself, as it is said, *And as they thus spake, Jesus himself stood in the midst of them.*

Aug.
de Con.
Ev.l.iii.
c. 25.
AUG. This manifestation of our Lord after His resurrection, John also relates. But when John says that the Apostle Thomas was not with the rest, while according to Luke, the two disciples on their return to Jerusalem found the eleven gathered together, we must understand undoubtedly that Thomas departed from them, before our Lord appeared to them as they spoke these things. For Luke gives occasion in his narrative, that it may be understood that Thomas first went out from them when the rest were saying these things, and that our Lord entered afterwards. Unless some one should say that the eleven were not those who were then called Apostles, but that these were eleven disciples out of the large number of disciples. But since Luke has added, *And those that were with them,* he has surely made it sufficiently evident that those called the eleven were the same as those who were called Apostles, with whom the rest were.

But let us see what mystery it was for the sake of which, according to Matthew and Mark, our Lord when He rose again gave the following command, *I will go before you into Galilee, there shall ye see me.* Which although it was accomplished, yet it was not till after many other things had happened, whereas it was so commanded, that it might be expected that it would have taken place alone, or at

least before other things. AMBROSE; Therefore I think it
most natural that our Lord indeed instructed His disciples,
that they should see Him in Galilee, but that He first presents
Himself as they remained still in the assembly through fear.
GREEK EX. Nor was it a violation of His promise, but rather
a mercifully hastened fulfilment on account of the cowardice
of the disciples. AMBROSE; But afterwards when their hearts
were strengthened, the eleven set out for Galilee. Or there is
no difficulty in supposing that they should be reported to have
been fewer in the assembly, and a larger number on the
mountain. EUSEB. For the two Evangelists, that is, Luke
and John, write that He appeared to the eleven alone in
Jerusalem, but those two disciples told not only the eleven,
but all the disciples and brethren, that both the angel and the
Saviour had commanded them to hasten to Galilee; of whom
also Paul made mention, saying, *Afterwards he appeared to* 1 Cor.
more than five hundred brethren at once. But the truer 15, 6.
explanation is, that at first indeed while they remained in
secret at Jerusalem, He appeared once or twice for their
comfort, but that in Galilee not in the assembly, or once or
twice, but with great power, He made a manifestation of Acts 1,
Himself, shewing Himself living to them after His Passion 3.
with many signs, as Luke testifies in the Acts. AUG. But Aug.
that which was said by the Angel, that is the Lord, must be ut sup.
taken prophetically, for by the word Galilee according to its
meaning of transmigration, it is to be understood that they
were about to pass over from the people of Israel to the
Gentiles, to whom the Apostles preaching would not entrust
the Gospel, unless the Lord Himself should prepare His way
in the hearts of men. And this is what is meant by, *He shall
go before you into Galilee, there shall ye see him.* But
according to the interpretation of Galilee, by which it means
" manifestation," we must understand that He will be revealed no more in the form of a servant, but in that form
in which He is equal to the Father, which He has promised
to His elect. That manifestation will be as it were the true
Galilee, when we shall see Him as He is. This will also be
that far more blessed transmigration from the world to eternity,
from whence though coming to us He did not depart, and to
which going before us He has not deserted us.

THEOPHYL. The Lord then standing in the midst of the disciples, first with His accustomed salutation of " peace," allays their restlessness, shewing that He is the same Master who delighted in the word wherewith He also fortified them, when He sent them to preach. Hence it follows, *And he* said to them, Peace be unto you; I am he, fear not. GREG. NAZ. Let us then reverence the gift of peace, which Christ when He departed hence left to us. Peace both in name and reality is sweet, which also we have heard to be of God, as it is said, *The peace of God;* and that God is of it, as *He is our peace.* Peace is a blessing commended by all, but observed by few. What then is the cause? Perhaps the desire of dominion or riches, or the envy or hatred of our neighbour, or some one of those vices into which we see men fall who know not God. For peace is peculiarly of God, who binds all things together in one, to whom nothing so much belongs as the unity of nature, and a peaceful condition. It is borrowed indeed by angels and divine powers, which are peacefully disposed towards God and one another. It is diffused through the whole creation, whose glory is tranquillity. But in us it abides in our souls indeed by the following and imparting of the virtues, in our bodies by the harmony of our members and organs, of which the one is called beauty, the other health.

BEDE; The disciples had known Christ to be really man, having been so long a time with Him; but after that He was dead, they do not believe that the real flesh could rise again from the grave on the third day. They think then that they see the spirit which He gave up at His passion. Therefore it follows, *But they were terrified and affrighted, and supposed that they had seen a spirit.* This mistake of the Apostles was the heresy of the Manichæans. AMBROSE; But persuaded by the example of their virtues, we can not believe that Peter and John could have doubted. Why then does Luke relate them to have been affrighted. First of all because the declaration of the greater part includes the opinion of the few. Secondly, because although Peter believed in the resurrection, yet he might be amazed when the doors being closed Jesus suddenly presents Himself with His body. THEOPHYL. Because by the word of peace the

Marginal references:
Greg. Orat.22.
Phil. 4, 7.
Eph. 2, 14.

agitation in the minds of the Apostles was not allayed, He
shews by another token that He is the Son of God, in that
He knew the secrets of their hearts; for it follows, *And he
said to them, Why are ye troubled, and why do thoughts
arise in your hearts?* BEDE; What thoughts indeed but
such as were false and dangerous. For Christ had lost the
fruit of His passion, had He not been the Truth of the resurrection; just as if a good husbandman should say, What I
have planted there, I shall find, that is, the faith which
descends into the heart, because it is from above. But those
thoughts did not descend from above, but ascended from
below into the heart like worthless plants. CYRIL; Here
then was a most evident sign that He whom they now see
was none other but the same whom they had seen dead on
the cross, and lain in the sepulchre, who knew every thing
that was in man.

AMBROSE; Let us then consider how it happens that the
Apostles according to John believed and rejoiced, according
to Luke are reproved as unbelieving. John indeed seems to
me, as being an Apostle, to have treated of greater and
higher things; Luke of those which relate and are close akin
to human. The one follows an historic course, the other is
content with an abridgment, because it could not be doubted
of him, who gives his testimony concerning those things at
which he was himself present. And therefore we deem
both true. For although at first Luke says that they did
not believe, yet he explains that they afterwards did believe.
CYRIL; Now our Lord testifying that death was overcome,
and human nature had now in Christ put on incorruption,
first shews them His hands and His feet, and the print of the
nails; as it follows, *Behold my hands and my feet, that it is I
myself.* THEOPHYL. But He adds also another proof, namely,
the handling of His hands and feet, when He says, *Handle
me and see, for a spirit hath not flesh and bones as ye see
me have.* As if to say, Ye think me a spirit, that is to say,
a ghost, as many of the dead are wont to be seen about their
graves. But know ye that a spirit hath neither flesh nor
bones, but I have flesh and bones.

AMBROSE; Our Lord said this in order to afford us an
image of our resurrection. For that which is handled is the

body. But in our bodies we shall rise again. But the former
is more subtle, the latter more carnal, as being still mixed
up with the qualities of earthly corruption. Not then by
His incorporeal nature, but by the quality of His bodily
resurrection, Christ passed through the shut doors. GREG.
For in that glory of the resurrection our body will not be
incapable of handling, and more subtle than the winds and
the air, (as Eutychius said,) but while it is subtle indeed
through the effect of spiritual power, it will be also capable
of handling through the power of nature. It follows, *And
when he had thus spoken, he shewed them his hands and his
feet*, on which indeed were clearly marked the prints of the
nails. But according to John, He also shewed them His
side which had been pierced with the spear, that by manifesting the scar of His wounds He might heal the wound of
their doubtfulness. But from this place the Gentiles are
fond of raising up a calumny, as if He was not able to cure
the wound inflicted on Him. To whom we must answer,
that it is not probable that He who is proved to have done
the greater should be unable to do the less. But for the
sake of His sure purpose, He who destroyed death would not
blot out the signs of death. First indeed, that He might
thereby build up His disciples in the faith of His resurrection. Secondly, that supplicating the Father for us, He
might always shew forth what kind of death He endured for
many. Thirdly, that He might point out to those redeemed
by His death, by setting before them the signs of that death,
how mercifully they have been succoured. Lastly, that He
might declare in the judgment how justly the wicked are
condemned.

41. And while they yet believed not for joy, and
wondered, he said unto them, Have ye here any
meat?

42. And they gave him a piece of a broiled fish,
and of an honeycomb.

43. And he took it, and did eat before them.

44. And he said unto them, These are the words
which I spake unto you, while I was yet with you,

*Greg.
Mor. 14.
c. 55.*

that all things must be fulfilled, which were written in the Law of Moses, and in the Prophets, and in the Psalms, concerning me.

CYRIL; The Lord had shewn His disciples His hands and His feet, that He might certify to them that the same body which had suffered rose again. But to confirm them still more, He asked for something to eat. GREG. NYSS. By the *Greg. Orat. 1. de Res.* command of the law indeed the Passover was eaten with bitter herbs, because the bitterness of bondage still remained, but after the resurrection the food is sweetened with a honeycomb; as it follows, *And they gave him a piece of a broiled fish, and a honeycomb.* BEDE; To convey therefore the truth of His resurrection, He condescends not only to be touched by His disciples, but to eat with them, that they might not suspect that His appearance was not actual, but only imaginary. Hence it follows, *And when he had eaten before them, he took the remnant, and gave to them.* He ate indeed by His power, not from necessity. The thirsty earth absorbs water in one way, the burning sun in another way, the one from want, the other from power. GREEK EX. But some one will say, If we allow that our Lord ate after His resurrection, let us also grant that all men will after the resurrection take the nourishment of food. But these things which for a certain purpose are done by our Saviour, are not the rule and measure of nature, since in other things He has purposed differently. For He will raise our bodies, not defective but perfect and incorrupt, who yet left on His own body the prints which the nails had made, and the wound in His side, in order to shew that the nature of His body remained the same after the resurrection, and that He was not changed into another substance. BEDE; He ate therefore after the resurrection, not as needing food, nor as signifying that the resurrection which we are expecting will need food; but that He might thereby build up the nature of a rising body. But mystically, the broiled fish of which Christ ate signifies the sufferings of Christ. For He having condescended to lie in the waters of the human race, was willing to be taken by the hook of our death, and was as it were burnt up by anguish at the time of His Passion. But the honeycomb was present to us at the resurrection. By the honeycomb He wished to represent to us the two natures of His person. For the honeycomb is of wax, but the honey in the wax is the Divine nature in the human. THEOPHYL. The things eaten seem also to contain another mystery. For in that He ate part of a broiled fish, He signifies that having burnt by the fire of His own divinity our nature swimming in the sea of this life, and dried up the moisture which it had contracted from the waves, He made it divine food; and that which was before abominable He prepared to be a sweet offering to God, which the honeycomb signifies. Or by the broiled fish He signifies the active life, drying up the moisture with the coals of labour, but by the honeycomb, the contemplative life on account of the sweetness of the oracles of God.

BEDE; But after that He was seen, touched, and had eaten, lest He should seem to have mocked the human senses in any one respect, He had recourse to the Scriptures. *And he said unto them, These are the words which I spake unto you, when I was yet with you,* that is, when I was yet in the mortal flesh, in which ye also are. He indeed was then raised again in the same flesh, but was not in the same mortality with them. And He adds, *That all things must be fulfilled which were written in the Law of Moses, and in the Pro-* Aug. de *phets, and in the Psalms, concerning me.* AUG. Let those Con.Ev. lib. i. then who dream that Christ could have done such things by c. 11. magical arts, and by the same art have consecrated His name to the nations to be converted to Him, consider whether He could by magical arts fill the Prophets with the Divine Spirit before He was born. For neither supposing that He caused Himself to be worshipped when dead, was He a magician before He was born, to whom one nation was assigned to prophesy His coming.

45. Then opened he their understanding, that they might understand the Scriptures,

46. And said unto them, Thus it is written, and thus it behoved Christ to suffer, and to rise from the dead the third day:

47. And that repentance and remission of sins should be preached in his name among all nations, beginning at Jerusalem.

48. And ye are witnesses of these things.

49. And, behold, I send the promise of my Father upon you: but tarry ye in the city of Jerusalem, until ye be endued with power from on high.

BEDE; After having presented Himself to be seen with the eye, and handled with hands, and having brought to their minds the Scriptures of the law, He next opened their understanding that they should understand what was read. THEOPHYL. Otherwise, how would their agitated and perplexed minds have learnt the mystery of Christ. But He taught them by His words; for it follows, *And said unto them, Thus it is written, and thus it behoved Christ to suffer,* that is, by the wood of the Cross. BEDE; But Christ would have lost the fruit of His Passion had He not been the Truth of the resurrection, therefore it is said, *And to rise from the dead.* He then after having commended to them the truth of the body, commends the unity of the Church, adding, *And that repentance and remission of sins should be preached in his name among all nations.* EUSEB. For it was said, *Ask of me, and I will give thee the heathen for thine in-* Ps. 2, 8. *heritance.* But it was necessary that those who were converted from the Gentiles should be purged from a certain stain and defilement through His virtue, being as it were corrupted by the evil of the worship of devils, and as lately converted from an abominable and unchaste life. And therefore He says that it behoves that first repentance should be preached, but next, remission of sins, to all nations. For to those who first shewed repentance for their sins, by His saving grace He granted pardon of their transgression, for whom also He endured death.

THEOPHYL. But herein that He says, *Repentance and remission of sins,* He also makes mention of baptism, in which by the putting off of our past sins there follows pardon of iniquity. But how must we understand baptism to be performed in the name of Christ alone, whereas in another place He commands it to be in the name of the Father, and the Son, and the Holy Ghost. First indeed we say that it is not meant that baptism is administered in Christ's name alone, but that a person is baptized with the baptism of Christ, that is, spiritually, not Judaically, nor with the baptism, wherewith John baptized unto repentance only, but unto the participation of the blessed Spirit; as Christ also when baptized in Jordan manifested the Holy Spirit in the form of a dove. Moreover you must understand baptism in Christ's name to be in His death. For as He after death rose again on the third day, so we also are three times dipped in the water, and fitly brought out again, receiving thereby an earnest of the immortality of the Spirit. This name of Christ also contains in itself both the Father as the Anointer, and the Spirit as the Anointing, and the Son as the Anointed, that is, in His human nature. But it was fitting that the race of man should no longer be divided into Jews and Gentiles, and therefore that He might unite all in one, He commanded that their preaching should begin at Jerusalem, but be finished with the Gentiles. Hence it follows, *Beginning at Jerusalem.* BEDE; Not only because to them were entrusted the oracles of God, and theirs is the adoption and the glory, but also that the Gentiles entangled in various errors might by this sign of Divine mercy be chiefly invited to come to hope, seeing that to them even who crucified the Son of God pardon is granted.

Rom. 3, 2. Rom. 9, 4.

CHRYS. Further, lest any should say that abandoning their acquaintances they went to shew themselves, (or as it were to vaunt themselves with a kind of pomp,) to strangers, therefore first among the very murderers themselves are the signs of the resurrection displayed, in that very city wherein the frantic outrage burst forth. For where the crucifiers themselves are seen to believe, there the resurrection is most of all demonstrated.

Chrys. Hom. i. in Act.

EUSEB. But if those things which Christ foretold are already receiving their accomplishment, and His word is perceived by a seeing faith to be living and effectual throughout the whole world; it is time for men not to be unbelieving towards Him who uttered that word. For it is necessary that He should live a divine life, whose living works are shewn to be agreeable to His words; and these indeed have been fulfilled by the ministry of the Apostles. Hence He adds, *But ye are witnesses of these things, &c.* that is, of My death and resurrection. THEOPHYL. Afterwards, lest they should be troubled at the thought, How shall we private individuals give our testimony to the Jews and Gentiles who have killed Thee? He subjoins, *And, behold, I send the promise of my Father upon you, &c.* which indeed He had promised by the mouth of the prophet Joel, *I will pour my Spirit* Joel 2, 18. *upon all flesh.*

CHRYS. But as a general does not permit his soldiers who Chrys. Hom. i. in Act. are about to meet a large number, to go out until they are armed, so also the Lord does not permit His disciples to go forth to the conflict before the descent of the Spirit. And hence He adds, *But tarry ye in the city of Jerusalem, until ye be endued with power from on high.* THEOPHYL. That is, not with human but heavenly power. He said not, until ye receive, but be endued with, shewing the entire protection of the spiritual armour. BEDE; But concerning the power, that is, the Holy Spirit, the Angel also says to Mary, *And the power of the Highest shall overshadow thee.* And the Luke 1, 35. Lord Himself says elsewhere, *For I know that virtue is* Luke 8, 45. *gone out of me.*

CHRYS. But why did not the Spirit come while Christ was Chrys. ut sup. present, or immediately on His departure? Because it was fitting that they should become desirous of grace, and then at length receive it. For we are then most awakened towards God, when difficulties press upon us. It was necessary in the mean time that our nature should appear in Heaven, and the covenants be completed, and that then the Spirit should come, and pure joys be experienced. Mark also what a necessity He imposed upon them of being at Jerusalem, in that He promised that the Spirit should there be given them. For lest they should again flee away after His resurrection, by this expectation, as it were a chain, He kept them all there together. But He says, *until ye be endued from on high.* He did not express the time when, in order that they may be constantly watchful. But why then marvel that He does not reveal to us our last day, when He would not even make known this day which was close at hand.

Greg.
de Past.
3. c. 25. GREG. They then are to be warned, whom age or imperfection hinders from the office of preaching, and yet rashness impels, lest while they hastily arrogate to themselves so responsible an office, they should cut themselves off from the way of future amendment. For the Truth Itself which could suddenly strengthen those whom it wished, in order to give an example to those that follow, that imperfect men should not presume to preach, after having fully instructed the disciples concerning the virtue of preaching, commanded them to abide in the city, until they were endued with power from on high. For we abide in a city, when we keep ourselves close within the gates of our minds, lest by speaking we wander beyond them; that when we are perfectly endued with divine power, we may then as it were go out beyond ourselves to instruct others.

AMBROSE; But let us consider how according to John they received the Holy Spirit, while here they are ordered to stay in the city until they should be endued with power from on high. Either He breathed the Holy Spirit into the eleven, as being more perfect, and promised to give it to the rest afterwards; or to the same persons He breathed in the one place, He promised in the other. Nor does there seem to be any contradiction, since there are diversities of graces. Therefore one operation He breathed into them there, another He promised here. For there the grace of remitting sins was given, which seems to be more confined, and therefore is breathed into them by Christ, that you may believe the Holy Spirit to be of Christ, to be from God. For God alone forgiveth sins. But Luke describes the pouring forth of the grace of speaking with tongues. CHRYS. Or He said, *Receive ye the Holy Spirit*, that He might make them fit to receive it, or Aug. de
Trin.15.
c. 26. indicated as present that which was to come. AUG. Or the Lord after His resurrection gave the Holy Spirit twice, once on earth, because of the love of our neighbour, and again from heaven, because of the love of God.

50. And he led them out as far as to Bethany, and he lifted up his hands, and blessed them.

51. And it came to pass, while he blessed them, he was parted from them, and carried up into heaven.

52. And they worshipped him, and returned to Jerusalem with great joy:

53. And were continually in the temple, praising and blessing God.   Amen.

BEDE; Having omitted all those things which may have taken place during forty-three days between our Lord and His disciples, St. Luke silently joins to the first day of the resurrection, the last day when He ascended into heaven, saying, *And he led them out as far as to Bethany.* First, indeed, because of the name of the place, which signifies " the house of obedience." For He who descended because of the disobedience of the wicked, ascended because of the obedience of the converted.   Next, because of the situation of the same village, which is said to be placed on the side of the mount of Olives; because He has placed the foundations, as it were, of the house of the obedient Church, of faith, hope, and love, in the side of that highest mountain, namely, Christ. But He blessed them to whom He had delivered the precepts of His teaching; hence it follows, *And he lifted up his hands, and blessed them.* THEOPHYL. Perhaps pouring into them a power of preservation, until the coming of the Spirit; and perhaps instructing them, that as often as we go away, we should commend to God by our blessing those who are placed under us. ORIGEN; But that He blessed them with uplifted hands, signifies that it becomes him who blesses any one to be furnished with various works and labours in behalf of others.   For in this way are the hands raised up on high.

CHRYS. But observe, that the Lord submits to our sight the promised rewards.   He had promised the resurrection of the body; He rose from the dead, and conferred with His disciples for forty days.   It is also promised that we shall be caught up in the clouds through the air; this also He made manifest by His works.   For it follows, *And it came to pass, while he blessed them, he was parted, &c.* THEOPHYL. And Elias indeed was seen, as it were, to be taken up into heaven, but the Saviour, the forerunner of all, Himself ascended into heaven to appear in the Divine sight in His sacred body; and already is our nature honoured in Christ by a certain Angelic power.

CHRYS. But you will say, How does this concern me? Because thou also shalt be taken up in like manner into the clouds. For thy body is of like nature to His body, therefore shall thy body be so light, that it can pass through the air. For as is the head, so also is the body; as the beginning, so also the end. See then how thou art honoured by this beginning. Man was the lowest part of the rational creation, but the feet have been made the head, being lifted up aloft into the royal throne in their head.

BEDE; When the Lord ascended into heaven, the disciples adoring Him where His feet lately stood, immediately return to Jerusalem, where they were commanded to wait for the promise of the Father; for it follows, *And they worshipped him, and returned, &c.* Great indeed was their joy, for they rejoice that their God and Lord after the triumph of His resurrection had also passed into the heavens. GREEK Ex. And they were watching, praying, and fasting, because indeed they were not living in their own homes, but were abiding in the temple, expecting the grace from on high; among other things also learning from the very place piety and honesty. Hence it is said, *And were continually in the temple.* THEO-PHYL. The Spirit had not yet come, and yet their conversation is spiritual. Before they were shut up; now they stand in the midst of the chief priests; distracted by no worldly object, but despising all things, they praise God continually; as it follows,

Ezek. 1, *Praising and blessing God.* BEDE; And observe that among
10.
Rev. 4, the four beasts in heaven, Luke is said to be represented by
7.
Exod. the calf, for by the sacrifice of a calf, they were ordered to be
29, 1. initiated who were chosen to the priesthood; and Luke has undertaken to explain more fully than the rest the priesthood of Christ; and his Gospel, which he commenced with the ministry of the temple in the priesthood of Zacharias, he has finished with the devotion in the temple. And he has placed the Apostles there, about to be the ministers of a new priesthood, not in the blood of sacrifices, but in the praises of God and in blessing, that in the place of prayer and amidst the praises of their devotion, they might wait with prepared hearts

for the promise of the Spirit.   THEOPHYL. Whom imitating, may we ever dwell in a holy life, praising and blessing God; to Whom be glory and blessing and power, for ever and ever. Amen.

BAXTER, PRINTER, OXFORD.

ERRATA, PART II.

Page 392. l. 14. *for* he *read* He
394. l. 1. *for* dealt *read* dealing
 l. 4. *after* those *insert* children
395. l. 13. *for* tries by temptation him who has nothing to set before him,
  who *read* proves by temptation who has—Him, and who
411. l. 16. *for* Here *read* Hic
437. l. 31. *for* the body *read* our Lord's body
477. l. 23. *for* he *read* He
491. l. 22. *for* he *read* He
498. l. 27. *for* out of all wisdom *read* full of &c.
504. l. 16. *after* this *read* seeking
527. l. 32. *for* to One He ordains *read* to one He assigns
531. l. 13. *for* nor had *read* nor had had
551. l. 1. *for* attendant *read* abundant
552. l. 7. *for* He does not make wisdom *read* He makes wisdom not
649. l. 6. *for* understood *read* so interpreted
710. l. 38. *for* edify *read* advance
723. l. ult. *after* be *read* ;